For Good

ALSO BY KARELIA STETZ-WATERS

Something True

For Good

KARELIA STETZ-WATERS

FOREVER
YOURS

New York Boston

Forever Yours
Hachette Book Group
1290 Avenue of the Americas
New York, NY 10104
forever-romance.com
twitter.com/foreverromance

First published as an ebook and as a print on demand: July 2016

Forever Yours is an imprint of Grand Central Publishing.
The Forever Yours name and logo are trademarks of Hachette Book Group, Inc.

The publisher is not responsible for websites (or their content) that are not owned by the publisher.

The Hachette Speakers Bureau provides a wide range of authors for speaking events. To find out more, go to www.hachettespeakersbureau.com or call (866) 376-6591

ISBNs: 978-1-4555-3784-6 (print on demand); 978-1-4555-3783-9 (ebook)

For my parents, in celebration of their fiftieth anniversary.
You taught me to believe in happily ever after,
and you showed me how to live it.
And, always, for Fay

Acknowledgments

Writing this book has led me on many adventures, from having lunch with a paroled murderer to enjoying an inmate-organized poetry reading inside a maximum-security prison. Many things surprised me. My image of prisoners doing push-ups in their cells was shattered when I stepped inside one of the cells and realized there wasn't enough room to do a push-up. At the same time, the prisons I visited weren't dungeons. They were brightly lit and exceedingly clean. The maximum-security Oregon State Penitentiary was peculiarly windy inside, while the medium-security Oregon State Correctional Facility smelled like dryer sheets and contained a room full of cubicles in which inmates answered the DMV call line. It looked a lot like the offices I worked in when I was in college.

What surprised me most in the end was the cost. To re-mand a parolee back to prison costs an average of fifty thousand dollars, money that can be levied at the behest of a single parole officer for infractions as minor as crossing a state line or failing to report. As an educator, I can't help but wonder what the country would be like if teachers had that kind of money to spend on troubled and vulnerable students before those students landed in prisons, jails, or juvenile detention facilities.

I'd like to thank the parolees, inmates, and correctional staff who shared their experiences with me. A big thank-you also goes to my wife, Fay Stetz-Waters, for answering my never-ending stream of legal questions. More importantly, thank you, Fay, for making my life a true happily-ever-after story. Thanks also to my wife and my friend Scott McAleer for taking me to eastern Oregon to get a look at the real-life Tristess County. Thank you to Chris Riseley for helping me work out plot points by the river and showing me that the answer is "whiskey and welding."

Thank you to all my friends and colleagues at Linn-Benton Community College and to all the friends, near and far, who make my life rich.Thank you to Jane Dystel and Miriam Goderich for opening the doors of the publishing world for me. Thank you to Madeleine Colavita and the staff at Forever Yours for making this book the best it could possibly be. Finally, thank you to my parents, Elin and Albert Stetz, for providing a beautiful model for marriage and for life. Happy fiftieth anniversary, Mom and Dad!

For Good

Prologue

Marydale Rae had never been in this part of the Holten Penitentiary, with its high windows and bars painted the same dull yellow as the walls. A uniformed guard sat behind a desk, reading. Marydale waited for a long time, watching the top of the guard's head as he studied his paperwork or ignored her. She couldn't tell which. There had been a time when she had known how to lean on a desk or a lamppost or a rangeland gate. She would have said, *Whatcha doing, cowboy?* and the man would have coughed and stuttered. Now Marydale said nothing. Finally the guard looked up.

"Damn parole board." His lips pulled into a tight grimace. "After what you did. Six years with good behavior." He glared at the paper before him. "Ridiculous! Some people don't know right from wrong."

"I was told to report," Marydale said, keeping her gaze on the ID badge pinned to the guard's shirt.

"Well, what are you waiting for?" he barked. "A written

invitation?" He took a clear plastic bag from beneath the desk and pushed it across the table. "Bathroom's back there. Make it quick."

In the bathroom, Marydale opened the bag. She pulled out her jean jacket, the one with the pattern of hearts embellished in rhinestones, the one that had belonged to her mother. There was her Tristess High seniors T-shirt, too, and a skirt of some light material with tiny pink flowers printed on it. There was a name for that fabric. Six years ago she had known it and every word in her SAT flash card deck. She pressed the T-shirt to her face, but everything in the bag smelled of mildew. She changed quickly.

When she came out again, the guard tapped his desktop with an accusing look, as though Marydale might try to steal her orange jumpsuit and he had cleverly caught her in the act. Marydale dropped the folded prison-issued uniform on the desk, and the guard glared. Marydale lifted her eyes to his chin. He slid a piece of paper across the desk.

"You have forty-eight hours to report to your parole officer. He'll go over the conditions of your supervision, but it's pretty simple. No drugs. No guns. No fighting. No dating. No burner phones. Don't leave the county. Don't change your address. Don't fraternize with felons or other deviants—" He picked at his tooth, staring directly at her. "Sign here."

She signed.

The guard pressed a button beneath his desk, and behind Marydale, a set of metal gates rattled to life and drew back slowly. She turned without speaking and moved toward the exit. Her sandals felt like a foreign country.

At end of a long outdoor walkway, she arrived at a tiny kiosk. Inside, she heard a radio crackle. Another guard eyed her, or at least he directed his mirrored sunglasses at her. Marydale presented her release papers.

"I know you," the guard said.

She felt his eyes on her. The guards were always looking, but her orange jumpsuit had hidden her body. Now she wished she had gone into Holten Penitentiary wearing jeans, but six years ago she wasn't thinking about release. Six years ago she had just turned seventeen.

"If I had my way…pretty girl like you. A waste," the guard said.

The last gate rolled open, its wheels grinding on loose gravel. Beyond the gate, a two-lane highway stretched into the vast rangeland of eastern Oregon. Marydale could almost hear her friends inside yelling, *Just go, girl, before they change their minds!*

She turned to the guard. "I wasn't expecting to get out until Monday." She tried to pitch her voice low and soft. It didn't help to demand. "May I call my friend Aldean to come pick me up?"

"I don't have a phone," the guard said, although Marydale could see one on the desk in front of him.

"But how do I get to Tristess?" she asked.

The penitentiary was at least twenty miles from town. Around her the land was motionless. Only the heat rippled. The guard's sunglasses traveled the length of the empty horizon.

"Guess you'll be waiting a long time if you hitchhike."

Part One

1

Kristen Brock was quickly realizing that her glamorous move from adjunct professor of legal writing to deputy district attorney of Tristess County was only glamorous as long as no one in Portland actually knew anything about Tristess, Oregon. She poked at the pile of iceberg lettuce and steak strips in front of her, the Ro-Day-O Diner's take on *market-fresh salad*. The leaves were almost white. The steak had thought about visiting a frypan. If *fresh* meant *raw*, she had gotten what she ordered.

"You like the salad?" the waitress asked, gliding by, a pot of not-so-fresh coffee dangling from her long fingers. "I think the meat's from Dan Otto's ranch out by the quarry. Slaughtered a week ago Thursday."

Kristen approved of locally sourced food, but something about knowing the animal's date of death made her feel like a cannibal. Before she could reply, her phone buzzed on the table.

Kristen's friend Donna Li greeted her in her usual clipped tone. "How's Tristess? How's living in the outback?"

"It's all right," Kristen said.

"You're practicing real law," Donna said. "Do you know what I'm doing? Rutger Falcon's mother's *friend's* divorce! She's decided she's a lesbian. The husband's run off with some thirty-year-old. They're both in their seventies. And they're fighting over a time-share in Lubbock, Texas. I mean, is there anyone who wants to go to Lubbock, Texas, on vacation?"

Kristen frowned. Four weeks living in a town the size of her graduating class, stuck at the far southeastern corner of Oregon, was making Lubbock, Texas, sound pretty good. The waitress passed by and shot Kristen a smile, as if to say, *That's life.*

Donna must have been driving because she added, "Is this your first day on the planet, Prius?" To Kristen she said, "The Falcon Law Group. What was I thinking taking this job? You're actually doing something. You're practicing law!" To an unnamed traveler on the road, Donna added, "Stop maximizing your gas mileage and drive!"

Kristen heard Donna's turn signal. If there was one thing she could say about Tristess—and there really was only one thing—it was that she got great cell phone reception. Some entrepreneurial spirit had wrecked the view of the Firesteed Summit by leasing space to every cell phone provider in Oregon, Idaho, and Nevada. Now the Summit bristled with towers.

"I guess," Kristen said modestly. After almost two decades

of intensely courteous competition, at which Kristen almost always failed, she had finally earned a hint of resentment in Donna's voice. That was something. "How's Elliot?" she asked.

"Elliot!" Donna said. "Gorgeous. Horrid. Wedded to the army. What am I doing with him?"

"Your mother would set you up with a nice accountant."

"God! Yes, she would. How's your sister?"

"She started community college." Kristen rested her chin on her upturned palm. "On her first day she made friends with some guy named Frog. Apparently he's a pansexual or polyamorous or something. She's decided she's a vegan, and she's already dropped her math class. I told her I'd tutor her on Skype, but she's mad I left Portland."

"She'll be fine." Donna's other line beeped through. "That'll be Lubbock again. Gotta go."

Kristen set the phone down and spread out a battered copy of the *Tristess Tribune*. The newspaper wasn't even online. The whole place made her lonely.

Kristen felt someone at her elbow.

"Refill, hon?"

The waitress hovered her pot of stale coffee over Kristen's cup. Kristen glanced up. Way up. The woman's head barely cleared the little chains that dangled from the ceiling fans.

"You looking for a used gun?" the woman asked, peering at the FOR RENT/FOR SALE page.

"Do I look like I need a used gun?"

The woman—who was probably Kristen's age, although it was hard to tell with women in Tristess—stepped back and looked Kristen up and down.

"No. You look like you can handle your own." The waitress's long blond curls hung almost to her waist. A silver cross dangled in the low-cut V of her blouse. And she was missing a front tooth. "I'm just playing with you."

"I know. The girl from the city." Kristen pushed her glasses up on her nose.

Almost everyone she'd met in Tristess had said it…in so many words. Kristen was from the city. She didn't understand their good, old-fashioned country ways, but she sure was lucky to have escaped Portland, not that she'd have the good sense to stay in Tristess. She might as well have had a bumper sticker reading: HELLO FROM SODOM. But the waitress's smile was kinder than most, and while Kristen expected a sneer, she just looked rueful. "Deputy DA Kristen Brock," the waitress said, confirming what Kristen had already guessed: everyone knew everything in Tristess. She probably knew Kristen had killed the potted palm from the Chamber of Commerce. "You're looking for an apartment."

"Yeah."

"You're actually going to stay?"

"That's the plan." Kristen touched the ads with the tip of her pen. "But this one had a bucket full of cat litter in the heating grate. This one smelled like a dirty diaper. This one had a hole in the bathroom wall. And this one had a live squirrel."

"That's good eatin'," the waitress said, with a smile that said, *Believe that, and I'll tell you another.*

She set her coffeepot down on the table and leaned over to look at the newspaper, her long curls almost brushing

Kristen's hand. Kristen caught a whiff of perfume. She tried to lean away without looking like she was leaning away. The waitress—whom Kristen had seen every day at breakfast and dinner for the past month—was the friendliest person she'd met in town, even if it was just her job to be nice to abhorrent out-of-towners.

"Try this one?" The waitress tapped an ad on the page.

"Rented," Kristen said.

"There aren't a lot of nice places. Not the kind of places you're used to in the city."

"There're some rough places in the city, too."

"But you must make a bundle."

"Hardly," Kristen said.

"Not like on TV?"

Across the street, Kristen's current residence, the Almost Home Motel, looked like a postcard from the apocalypse, the faded sign flashing VACANCY on and off in the hot September sun.

"Nothing in my life is like TV," Kristen said.

"I know that story. I live off Gulch Creek Road. It's not much, but if you're looking for a place and you don't mind something a little rustic…"

Kristen leaned back so she could take in all of the woman's corn-fed tallness. In Portland, the waitress would have been a hipster, an ironic version of the person this woman actually was, a Roller Derby girl with some cowgirl pseudonym who bowled over smaller women on the track. The waitress was big, Kristen thought, but all that blond hair and those large breasts just made her size more of a good thing. The thirty pounds Kristen had put on during law school made her more of a humanoid pear. She felt a little twinge of jealousy, but the missing tooth and the woman's wry smile made her hard to dislike.

"The rent's cheap. Really. A couple hundred dollars and you chip in for utilities and a cord of wood in the winter, and we could call it even. My name's Marydale."

A few tables over, Kristen saw one of the other waitresses watching them, her cherubic face registering both awe and disapproval.

"That's nice of you," Kristen said. "But I'm looking forward to living alone. I've had my sister with me for years."

"Of course," Marydale said, and ducked her head as if remembering the missing tooth.

"I mean, it's not…" Kristen didn't finish the sentence. Something about the way the waitress looked away made the refusal feel personal, and Kristen wanted to say, *It's not you.* But of course it wasn't her. Kristen was the one from Sodom and Gomorrah.

In the back of the diner, the chef hit the order-up bell.

"Marydale!" he called out. "If you wait long enough, this burger will get up and walk itself over to table four, but I don't think anyone wants to wait."

"Sorry, hon. That's me." Marydale picked up her coffeepot.

Kristen watched Marydale stride toward the kitchen until her phone vibrated on the table. Her sister, Sierra, had texted her a photograph. For a sickening second, Kristen thought it was a crime-scene photo: Sierra's pretty blond hair snarled around a blunt force trauma to the head. Only there was no blood, just a rat's nest of hair. The text below read, *I'm growing dreadlocks. I am the Lion of Judah.*

Kristen typed the words, *You're white! How are you going to get a job?* Then she paused, deleted, and texted, *How are classes going, sweetie?*

Marydale glided by her table on the way to another customer. Kristen waited for her to turn around and give her that smile that seemed to say, *Life! What are you going to do?* But she didn't, and Kristen tucked her phone into her briefcase and headed to work, stopping at the Arco Station to buy a Snickers bar to make up for the fleshy salad.

2

Just after sunset, Marydale Rae pulled to a stop in the gravel lot in front of the Pull-n-Pay junkyard where her childhood friend Aldean Dean lived with his grandfather, Pops. Aldean had lit a fire in the fire pit, illuminating the sea of wrecked cars. Marydale's dog, Lilith, bounded from the cab of her truck and slipped through the narrow opening in the fence. Marydale followed, ducking under the locked chain.

"Aldean?" she called. "You out here?"

Marydale picked her way through the labyrinth of fenders and windshields. In the center of the yard, a shipping container stood rusted shut, its origins and its contents—if any—a mystery that Aldean and Marydale had spun into a thousand imaginary treasures when they were growing up.

"In here," Aldean called from a shack tucked between the container and an old VW bus with the words *not for sale, don't ask* spray-painted on its side. Inside, a single bulb illuminated several small barrels propped on their sides on a worktable.

"You're off early," Aldean said as she entered. "Try this." He held out a red Solo cup.

Marydale held it to her nose and inhaled deeply.

"A bit of leather. Juniper reclamation fires." She swirled and took a sip. Her mouth filled with smoky lighter fluid. "Oh God! Aldean, you've made it worse!"

Marydale eyed the wooden barrels lined up on the workbench, each marked in Sharpie on a piece of scrap wood: THREE MONTHS (MARYDALE), NINE MONTHS (MARYDALE), TWELVE MONTHS (ALDEAN), TWENTY-FOUR MONTHS (ALDEAN).

"No. That's a good whiskey." Aldean touched the brim of his battered Stetson. "You're only jealous because it's not yours."

She was jealous. Twenty-four months ago Aldean was pouring Poisonwood whiskey into a barrel he had bought at the Burnville Flea Market, hoping that somehow aging Poisonwood in questionably cured wood would improve the flavor. Twenty-four months ago Marydale was in solitary—protective segregation, they called it—because a woman named Dixie-Lynn had tried to stab her with a shank fashioned out of a melted toothbrush.

She poured the dregs of the Solo cup onto the dirt floor and tried her own three-month infusion.

"Smooth. Slightly floral," Marydale said. "High desert up front with a kind of sweet lost-youth aftertaste."

Aldean took her cup from her, sipped, and handed it back.

"That's a girl's whiskey." He clucked his tongue. "And I do like a girl who drinks whiskey."

Aldean gestured for Marydale to follow him, and they headed out to the fire. He picked up a metal grate and set it over the pit. From a cooler nearby, he produced a package wrapped in white paper. Soon two steaks were sizzling on the fire. Marydale settled down in a lawn chair. Lilith circled around the fire, sniffing for the meat. Aldean pulled a cigarette from behind his ear, lit it, and inhaled. In the firelight, his face was all cheekbone and rugged stubble.

"So. What about the new girl?" he asked.

"There's a girl in Tristess you don't already know?"

"New to me. New to you." He kicked his boots out in front of him. "She's from the city. You know how they are."

"No, I don't, and neither do you."

"I know how to rope a calf. Don't matter where she comes from." Aldean talked around his cigarette the way his Pops did, but he managed to make it look sexy. "You like her?"

"No."

"She's got that repressed-librarian thing going. Just makes you want to squeeze her."

"No!" Marydale laughed. "It doesn't."

But the lawyer did have that *repressed-librarian thing*…No, it wasn't repressed. It was focused. Marydale could see her with her tortoiseshell glasses, her brownish-blond hair that wasn't any color and that she clearly didn't care about dying. She always wore gray: gray suits, gray pumps, silky blue-gray blouses the color of winter skies. She was pretty the way the high desert was pretty: in muted shades. Marydale liked the way the lawyer concentrated on her phone or her papers, the way she hadn't noticed the trio of rangeland firefighters who had admired her from their perch at the counter. She must have felt their gaze like a hand on her back, but she hadn't looked up until Marydale had come by with a carafe of coffee. Then she had smiled shyly, a little embarrassed, like a good apostolic girl opening up her Bible on her lap. *Well, Marydale, I'm so glad you asked about our Savior.*

"So you gonna hit it and quit it?" Aldean asked.

"I asked her to move in with me."

"No!"

"She can't find a place to rent."

"That's not how you hit it and quit it."

"I wouldn't," Marydale protested.

Aldean stood up again and retrieved a set of tin plates from somewhere in the darkness behind the fire. Lilith followed him, her muscular, white body glowing in the firelight. He handed a plate, fork, and knife to Marydale, then sat down with his own dinner. Lilith sat beside him while he cut up his steak. When he had reduced the meat to the same pea-sized bites he cut for Pops, he scraped a quarter of the meat onto the ground for Lilith.

"You spoil her," Marydale said.

"What did she say?" Aldean asked. "She gonna come look at your place?"

"No." Marydale stabbed the meat on her plate. "Of course she's not going to rent from me. She's the DA."

"You gonna do anything about it?"

"No."

"I know," he said. "This fucking town."

Marydale glanced over. Aldean nodded slowly, his eyes hidden in the shadow of his hat. Behind him the Firesteed Mountains stood in black relief against a navy sky.

"Back in the day, you would've," he said.

"Back in the day," Marydale said, "was a long time ago."

3

Kristen stood in front of her boss's desk, her pen poised over a notepad. District Attorney Boyd Relington hadn't asked her to sit down, and the moment to sit anyway—because they were colleagues and she shouldn't need an invitation—had passed. Now sitting felt like a statement.

"These are your case files for next week," Relington said.

"Are these all the cases that came in?" Kristen asked.

"We got a stack of cases from the police. The new chief sends everything our way."

Kristen was fairly sure she'd heard someone say that the "new" chief had been in his position for more than ten years.

"Back in the day," Relington went on, "some people knew when to leave well enough alone, but I went through the paperwork from the police. I'll be prosecuting the O'Rourke case. You'll be doing Alioto, Esso, Scappa, De La Pedraja." He rattled off a few more names.

"Can I see the rest of the files that came in from the police?" Kristen asked.

"Not every arrest warrants a prosecution."

Everything Relington said was a counterargument. He was like all law students she had gone to school with and then taught in first-year legal writing, only older and untempered by the constant influx of more brilliant, young legal minds.

"I mean is there a selection process?" Kristen had rehearsed her speech. *I trust your judgment, but I'd like to select my own cases.*

"Do you really want to discuss this now?"

Relington checked his watch. It was Friday, four thirty. The afternoon sun cut through the sagging venetian blinds, illuminating the Tristess memorabilia that filled Relington's office: football jersey behind glass, a set of old stirrups. It was like the Western-themed Silver Rush Bar in Portland...only not ironic.

"Yes," Kristen said. "Now is fine."

"Okay. What's this about, really? Sit."

"I'd like to select the cases I try." Kristen lowered herself into a chair.

"These are good cases." Relington leaned forward and tapped the stack of files on his desk. "I selected them."

"I'm sure they're good cases."

"How long have you been here?"

"About a month."

"And how long are you planning to stay?"

Kristen had lain awake for the past week, working on the

equation. Leaving in less than a year would negate the benefit of having deputy DA on her résumé, but two years would be more than plenty.

"I don't have any plans to leave," she said.

Relington snorted. "Do you know why I hired you?"

Kristen could feel the insult coming.

"It doesn't matter," she said. "What matters is that I'm here, and I want to do my job. I want to serve this community, and I want to help you."

"This community." Relington rose and walked over to one of the framed photographs on the wall. "That's my father, my grandfather, and my great-grandfather. This man here—" He pointed. "That's Ronald Holten." He spoke the name reverently. The municipal building that housed the court, the elementary school, and the nearby penitentiary all bore the name *Holten*.

"Tristess is my family," Relington went on. "Every case we try, I know them. I know what happened to them as children. I know their parents, their grandparents. Let me ask you, Ms. Brock, if you got in trouble and you had to go to court, would you want someone who'd been in town for a whole month deciding your fate, or would you want someone who knew your story? Some of these guys, if they go to jail for a week, they don't get their herd in for the first round of auction. Their hay goes sour. They're not there to call the vet for a breech. People don't have money here, like they do in the city. Honestly, tell me what you'd want?"

Kristen felt her face flush. "I'd want the law to decide."

"We *are* the law," Relington said in a tone that said *I* not *we.* He pushed a slip of paper across the desk. "Speaking of Mr. Holten. He heard you were having trouble finding a place to rent. Meet him here at twelve thirty tomorrow."

"Ronald Holten?" Kristen asked, but Relington's expression told her the conversation was over.

4

Saturday noontime found Kristen gazing up at a three-story Victorian sandwiched between a nail salon and a used tire dealer. If she narrowed her field of vision, it looked exactly like what she had optimistically hoped all of Tristess would be: elegant and windswept, with just a touch of Wild West brothel. Kristen took out her phone, cropped out Sandy's Nails and the tire shop, and texted the picture to Donna. Donna loved architecture. She'd gone through a whole mansard-roof period.

Kristen heard an engine come to a stop behind her. She turned. A man had just pulled up in the largest, shiniest pickup truck she had ever seen. He stepped out of the enormous vehicle.

"She is a beauty, isn't she?" he called out, nodding toward the house. "It is so good to finally meet you. I'm Ronald Holten." Holten came toward her, hand extended. "Please call me Ronnie. Everyone calls me Ronnie." His wide, sunburned face opened in a smile, but his teeth were perfect and shadowless, like dentures or the carefully filed teeth of actors.

No one calls you Ronnie, Kristen thought.

"I know a girl like yourself is perfectly capable of finding her own apartment, but I hated to think that you'd found Tristess unfriendly. Come."

They climbed the front stairs. At the door, Holten reached into his pocket, feigning surprise at the discovery of a key. Kristen offered him a smile, but it felt like a grimace.

"See what you think," he said.

He unlocked the door and stepped aside so she could precede him into the house. Inside, a stained-glass skylight bathed the foyer in amber light, and a curving staircase wound its way up to the next floor.

"It's amazing," Kristen said with real awe.

"My great-grandfather had this place built." He ushered her into a large, furnished parlor. "Now, I know you may be looking for something a little more modern." The room had chair railings—Donna had taught her that term—and armchairs with dragons carved into the legs.

"My wife would love to move into town, but we've got grandsons. They need a place to run." He touched his thumb to the corner of his eye. When he spoke again, there was a manly roughness to his voice. "And family comes first for us. Always has, always will. Of course, we wouldn't expect you to pay rent while you're serving the county. Just take good care of the place and pay the utilities. You'd be doing us a favor."

The tour of the house was an hour and a half of Tristess history, which was also Holten family history. When they finished, Holten led her back to the kitchen, where a bottle of Poisonwood whiskey rested on a silver tray with two snifters.

"Looks like someone got you a housewarming present," Holten said with a look of contrived surprise, as though the bottle were a mysterious apparition.

Kristen wondered if he had stopped by the house earlier to drop it off or if he had staff or a wife in a lacy apron to run his errands for him.

He pulled the foil from the cap, poured two shots, and handed one to her.

"What do you think of the Poisonwood?"

Kristen took a sip. The liquor seared her tongue like some medicinal poison pioneers used to cut the pain of childbirth or dentistry. Kristen remembered her last year in college: she had briefly dated a philosophy major who'd claimed that microbrews and art films were bourgeois traps. He had taken to drinking Mad Dog and watching kung fu movies on VHS. He would have liked the Poisonwood, Kristen thought.

"It's nice." She choked down another sip.

"This town's seen some good times and some bad times," Holten said. "I guess that's true everywhere, but here you can feel it. It's a community, and that's worth protecting."

"I am here to do my best," Kristen said.

Holten held his glass up to the light coming through the kitchen window.

"There's a lot you can learn from a man like Boyd Relington, and I'm not just talking about the law. I've seen young DAs like yourself come in here and think they can change things," Holten went on. "They think they should change things, without understanding the town. But I have a good feeling about you. I think you know what I'm saying."

I think you know what I'm saying. It was the kind of thing her mother's boyfriends said right before she dodged out from under their boozy embrace, but her mother had a type, and it wasn't the type who owned Victorian houses. Her mother liked strip-club bouncers and ex-felons. Holten had power.

"Tristess is a real special place." Holten said it the same way he'd said the house was a beauty. He owned it, and he was proud.

"This is a lovely house," Kristen said. "May I have just a day or two to think about your offer? I…" She searched for a lie. "I should have mentioned this." Kristen fumbled for words. "I promised my friend I'd move into her place, and this is so much nicer, but I need to make sure I'm not leaving her in the lurch with the rent and all."

"A woman who fulfills her obligations," Holten said. "I like that." But his sunburned smile had lost its sunshine. "Let me know." He held out the bottle of Poisonwood. "Welcome to Tristess."

5

The lawyer did not come by the next day or the day after. Marydale tried not to notice. She'd told herself it was fine to have a crush. A crush was fun. She imagined a shiver of electricity passing between them when she refilled the lawyer's coffee. Just thinking about it made the twelve-hour shifts go faster. But when the lawyer didn't come in after Marydale offered her a room to rent, the disappointment Marydale felt made her chest ache.

She paused in her round of coffee top-offs and extra napkins to lean on the counter where Aldean was eating a piece of Frank's lemon chiffon pie. Across the street, the Almost Home Motel sat motionless.

"So. That lawyer," Aldean said between bites.

Marydale felt her cheeks flush like a teenage girl caught fawning over a photo of the high school quarterback. The lawyer would never look up at her and whisper *I've been waiting for you, Marydale,* the way she did in Marydale's daydreams. The lawyer probably didn't remember her name, and even if she did…a girl couldn't have those dreams in Tristess. Marydale had learned that lesson the hard way.

"You gonna tap that?" Aldean asked.

Marydale tried for an easy smile. "Aldean!" She slapped his wrist.

He set his fork down. "I'm giving you first dibs."

"You said she looked like a repressed librarian."

"Yeah, but that's not a bad thing, and she's from the city. She can't be that repressed. We're not going to have to do it with the lights out and her mother's doll collection up on the dresser."

"Jaylen from the Burnville Walmart?"

"She was hot, but then she told me all their names, and they were just looking at me. I *had* to turn the lights out."

"You're such a dog." Marydale slouched lower on the counter.

"Excuse me!" It was sixteen-year-old Tippany in her hand-embroidered apron. "If you have time to lean, you have time to clean." It was probably some sort of resolve Tippany had made with her friends at the Tristess High Values Club. She was going to stand up to wrongdoers. "A job is a privilege, not a right."

"Sorry," Marydale said slowly. "I was just looking for the Moguls. It's a biker gang."

Tippany hadn't role-played this part of the conversation. "The Woodrows want a new bottle of ketchup," she said, talking loudly, as though volume could return the conversation to its proper track.

"They're supposed to be coming through town before sunset," Marydale added casually. "They're looking for virgins. I wish I wasn't closing tonight. Although technically, I don't count, even though I gave up my, ah, virgin chalice to a girl." She blew a little kiss toward Tippany. "But you're just their type. Isn't that right, Aldean?"

Aldean looked up at Tippany, and the girl fidgeted with the flounce of her apron. She might have sewn abstinence pledge bracelets for all her friends, but there were few straight women whose wombs didn't flutter at the sight of Aldean Dean.

"God's own truth," Aldean said.

Tippany hurried way.

"You're terrible," Aldean said.

Marydale leaned her elbows on the counter. "Ronald Holten offered her a place to rent."

"The lawyer. I know. At the Holten House," Aldean concurred. Of course he had heard. "I'm sorry," he said. "Your place is nicer."

"No. It's not. I know she wasn't going to rent a room from me, but she doesn't know Ronald Holten. She's going to think he's just a nice guy with country hospitality or some shit."

"Don't do that." Aldean pointed a warning fork at her.

"Do what?"

"Get all protective. Get attached."

"You're ridiculous." Marydale picked up a cloth from behind the counter and started polishing. "I don't even know her."

Still, she watched the glowing windows of the Almost Home Motel as she put the last of the chairs up on the tables. She wasn't attached. She wasn't even optimistic. According to the conditions of her parole, she wasn't allowed to date. Hell, she wasn't allowed to drive across the county line to Burnville. But as she went to put the locking pin in the door, she stopped. A figure emerged from the side of the Almost Home, and Marydale recognized the lawyer's stride, confident and purposeful, her head bowed slightly, like a businesswoman walking though rain. And Marydale knew Kristen wasn't coming to see her. She was coming for an order of pie or chicken fries or one of the stale candy bars they kept under the glass counter by the register, and yet Marydale's heart beat faster. She tried to fix her hair, but she could feel her unruly curls exploding in the humid air. She stepped outside, still trying to tuck strands back into their alligator clip.

"I'm so sorry. We were just closing up," she said when the lawyer reached her. "But I could get you a piece of pie to go."

"No. I…wanted to talk to you about that room for rent." The lawyer's brow creased over the frames of her glasses.

Marydale swallowed and shoved her hands in her jeans pockets, pretending she didn't know what was coming next. The lawyer would say it had been an inappropriate offer. *I'm the DA…I talked to your PO…*

"It's got a great view of the mountains," Marydale offered. "And if you got a burro or two, we could put them up in the barn." Marydale waited for the lawyer to tell her it was no joking matter. Marydale ought to know she wasn't a free woman. Just because she was out of prison didn't mean she could make decisions like everybody else; she'd given up that right.

"What the hell is a burro?" the lawyer asked.

"A small donkey…for packing."

"Packing my used gun?"

It took Marydale a moment to make sense of the comment, and then she felt a warm glow light her chest. The lawyer had remembered their banter in the diner. She had noticed.

From down the street a man's voice called out, "We don't need you 'round here. You need to go back where you came from."

For a second, adrenaline seized Marydale's body. She remembered a woman from the penitentiary, Grace-Louise her name was, but everyone called her Gulu. She saw her striding down the block, her prison-issue jeans slung low around her hips, the sharpened end of a ballpoint pen pinging against the bars. *She'll cut a new boot like you just 'cause you're scared,* Marydale's cellmate had whispered, stepping back against the far wall of their cell. *You better learn to fight.* Now Marydale took a deep breath. *You're out,* she told herself. *You're out. You're out.*

Anyway, it was just a pair of young ranch hands stumbling home from the Lariat Lounge, probably drinking with fake IDs.

"He doesn't mean you," Marydale said quietly. In a louder, more cheerful voice, she added, "You boys get on home."

"But I could fuck you," the other man yelled.

"That's no way to talk to a lady," Marydale said.

"She's not gonna fuck *you*, if that's what you're thinking."

The pair staggered in their direction.

Marydale whistled. From the bed of her pickup in the parking lot, Lilith appeared like a flash of motion in headlights. A second later, she had skidded to a stop at Marydale's feet.

"What the…" the men exclaimed.

"Walk away," Marydale said. "We're having a conversation here."

"Cops'll shoot your dog," the first man yelled.

"You ain't supposed to have a dog like that!" his friend added.

Lilith revealed a row of sharp white teeth wedged into pink gums.

"That won't mean much when your face is in her belly."

The men staggered back.

When they were a safe distance away, the lawyer laughed nervously. "I'd like to have you on my side in a bar fight."

"You call me anytime," Marydale said.

They both hesitated for a moment.

"Are you off work?" the lawyer asked.

"Basically."

She adjusted her glasses. "I'm Kristen." She held out her hand. "I don't think we've been officially introduced."

"You don't have to be introduced in Tristess. Especially you. You're the most interesting woman in town."

"I've never been the most interesting anything," Kristen said dryly.

Marydale twirled a length of hair around her finger and tucked it behind her ear. Aldean would say, *Girls want a little chase. Make 'em think you're not interested.* But the girls in Tristess weren't interested. That was the problem.

The men had paused at the end of the block to pee or to argue.

"You want to walk?" Kristen asked, gesturing in the other direction.

Marydale said "yes" too quickly.

"About the room," Kristen began as they set off.

"I'm sorry about that," Marydale said. "I know I shouldn't have mentioned it."

"Ah, shit," Kristen said. "Did I just do that that thing where someone makes an offer like 'come by anytime,' but you're not actually supposed to come by, and you do, and it's awkward?"

"No. I meant it!" Marydale said. "I'm just surprised. You're the DA and all. Come by anytime."

Kristen laughed. Marydale recited the address, and Kristen typed it into her phone. Marydale expected Kristen to turn back toward the motel, but she didn't, and the cool breeze at their back seemed to carry them forward.

"What's it like living in a town where everyone knows everyone?" Kristen asked.

And before Marydale knew, they were talking, and Kristen's casual questions reminded her of Aldean. There was no hidden meaning behind her small talk.

"Do you like working at the diner?" Kristen asked, not *Frank's a good man to give you this chance, ain't he?*

"It's all right," Marydale said. "I hear a lot of gossip."

"What's the best thing you've heard?" Kristen asked.

Marydale paused. People in town didn't talk about the *best* gossip. Only one really interesting thing had ever happened in Tristess, and Marydale knew that story too well, even if people in town didn't tell it out of deference to her *poor, dear mother.*

"You've heard of a Landrace?" Marydale asked.

"You mean like a 5K, like a run?"

Marydale smiled. "It's a kind of swine. I heard Mrs. Woodrow say"—she added a little twang to her voice—"that she heard from Ella at the bank that last year at the county fair when Lu-Anne Stewart's boy, Kent, showed his Landrace and won the blue ribbon for heaviest year-old, it wasn't a true Landrace." She paused, lowing her voice with mock seriousness. "The National Swine Registry won't record a Landrace with less than six functional teats on each side of the underline, and Mrs. Woodrow said Ella saw an inverted teat on the back left side."

Kristen stopped, her smile cocked at an incredulous angle. "That's a thing?"

"Ella thinks Lu-Anne paid off the judge."

"With what?"

Marydale imitated Mrs. Woodrow's shocked whisper. "I can't say, but she has the harlot's mark on her."

Kristen chuckled. "Sounds like Portland law: who slept with whose paralegal, which big firm is stealing which clients. No one tells me anything here." She shook her head.

"You're new," Marydale said. "They'll warm up to you."

The sidewalk narrowed, and Marydale fell into step be-hind Kristen. Kristen did look like a librarian with her tor-toiseshell glasses and her gray suit fitted a bit too tightly around her ass. She probably hated the way her jacket flared up in back and strained a little at the seams, but Marydale didn't mind.

Marydale wanted to take her hand. No, it was more than a want. It was that familiar feeling that there was another life, another world where another Marydale was walking hand in hand with a woman like Kristen. If she could just close her eyes or run fast enough or sprinkle gold dust…but that was what Aldean was always warning her about.

"This guy Ronald Holten offered me a house to rent for free," Kristen said. "Do you know anything about him? I just got this feeling…I'm not used to taking anything for free."

Kristen stared up at a streetlight. In profile, she looked like one of the Greek statues in Holten State Penitentiary's *Encyclopedia of Western Culture*, plain but in a way that made other women look cheap.

"The Holtens always want something," Marydale said. "There are people in town who won't like you for turning down Ronald Holten. Things would be easier for you if you said yes, but…I'd say no."

They had arrived at the little grass octagon that served as the town "square." In the center, a wooden gazebo housed the Pioneer Poison Well.

"Easier how?" Kristen asked.

"Just easier."

"That's cryptic."

"He owns everything. He likes it that way."

They stepped into the darkness of the gazebo. The well was a concrete barrel with metal bars across the top and a plaque documenting the forty-seven pioneers poisoned by the water. Marydale leaned over, feeling, as she always did, that if she had anything precious, it would slip off her like a necklace and plunge into the blackness.

"That's a depressing fucking monument," Kristen said.

Marydale laughed in surprise. "No shit. Everybody loves the Poison Well. Tristess has a *day*. People dress up. I say it was just bad, fucking luck. A bunch of pioneers got this far, probably killed how many Indians, and then died from drinking the water."

Kristen leaned over, too, the crowns of their heads almost touching.

"What do you get if you throw a coin in? Bad karma?"

"Must be," Marydale said. "I've thrown a lot of coins in."

6

After work the following day, Kristen put Marydale's address in her phone's GPS, but no directions were necessary. She scanned the map. It might as well have said, *Go north until you pass the end of nowhere.*

When Gulch Creek Road turned to gravel with no sign of reverting back to pavement, Kristen called Donna.

"Hey, listen. I'm going to give you an address," Kristen said. "On the off chance that you never hear from me again, this is where my body's at."

"What? Where are you?"

The only sign of human habitation—besides the road itself—was a collection of buildings at the end of a long driveway. They looked like litter swept up by a giant broom and deposited at the foot of the Firesteed Mountains.

"I'm looking at a room to rent. I met this waitress at the local diner."

"Do you really think she's dangerous?"

"I'm kidding," Kristen said.

Gravel rumbled under the car as Kristen neared the end of the drive. Marydale's house looked like a child's drawing, too narrow to be real, with a peaked roof and four identical windows. A porch circled the house, and Marydale sat on the porch swing, her dog at her feet, a book in her hands. The whole scene looked like the soft-focus shot at the end of a pharmaceutical commercial, the one that played while a compassionate voice-over listed the side effects, like dry mouth and instant death. Only this was the real thing and actually beautiful.

"I've got nothing to worry about," Kristen said in a tone she kind of hoped conveyed *I've got a lot to worry about, being such an important public figure, but, naturally, I have everything under control.*

"Kristen. You came!" Marydale called as Kristen got out of her car.

She smiled, and Kristen could see the dark space where her tooth should have been.

"I'll show you around. It's not much, but it's nicer than the Almost Home." Marydale pushed the front door open. "How was your day?"

"The public defender keeps referring to me as a *female* attorney; a *female* should understand these things."

"Breeding stock. It's good for the gene pool," Marydale said so seriously, it took Kristen a moment to realize she was joking.

"I thought people hated out-of-towners."

"Love-hate," Marydale said, looking coquettishly over her shoulder.

Inside, a faded portrait hung by the front door, featuring a girl of about ten and two older women dressed in so many sequins they looked like drag queens.

"Three generations of rodeo queens," Marydale said, following Kristen's gaze.

Kristen looked at the child.

"That's you."

The girl's smile was wide and practiced. The mother and grandmother looked like they were separated by no more than fifteen years.

"Three years running," Marydale said. "My mother always said you could be pretty or you could be lucky." She touched her fingers to the woman in the center of the photograph. She clicked her tongue. "We were pretty. Come on."

The tour of the house took five minutes. Downstairs there was a living room, dining room, kitchen, bathroom, and a pantry Marydale called the *canning cellar*. Upstairs there was a bathroom and two bedrooms, both of them furnished but impersonal, one with stacks of library books on the dresser.

"I've been using this one, but we can trade if you like." Marydale tucked a length of hair behind her ear. "I know you're probably used to something nicer. I mean, before the Almost Home."

"I don't have to share a room with my sister. It's a step up," Kristen said.

Marydale led her back downstairs and onto the porch.

"Try this." Marydale retrieved a growler from beneath

the porch swing and produced two small canning jars. She poured an inch of cedar-colored liquid into each jar.

Kristen took a sip and coughed. It was awful, but there was a hint of something sweet behind the burn of bottom-shelf alcohol, a kind of smoky-floral taste the philosophy major might just have done the honor of deeming *bourgeois*.

"It's not bad. If you know what to expect," Kristen said.

Marydale laughed. "I'll take it."

They discussed the details of the rental. Month to month. Shared utilities. The cord of wood. Marydale said she was happy to have a roommate, and Kristen promised to draw up a contract on paper. They finished their whiskey, and Kristen knew it was time to go, but the idea of one last night reading legal briefs in a stuffy room at the Almost Home wasn't particularly appealing.

"Do your parents still live around here?" Kristen asked.

"They passed." Marydale walked to the porch railing and looked out.

"I'm sorry."

The land around the house was dry and brown, except for a patch of sunflowers. Squash vines and tomatoes tangled around their feet, and their heads turned toward the sun setting behind the house. Kristen watched Marydale's profile in the golden light.

"I miss my mom." Marydale pursed her lips in an apologetic smile. "It's all been such a mess. If I had a dollar for everyone who told me I should feel lucky my folks aren't around to see what I've done with my life…"

"You'd be rich a woman?"

"I'd be something."

"People are assholes. What's wrong with being a wait-ress?"

If Marydale had teared up and started a long-winded ren-dition of her life story, Kristen would have mumbled some-thing about needing to study the next day's docket, but Marydale just shook her head.

"You miss her. That's something," Kristen added. "I haven't talked to my mother in more than a year, and I don't miss her. A year isn't long enough."

"But she's your mom." It wasn't an accusation.

"She's living in Vancouver with some guy she met on an app call Cream Meet."

"Ooh. Grade A," Marydale said. "I bet he's fabulous."

If Donna had said it, Kristen would have told her to fuck off, but if Donna had said it, it would have been a jibe. *My parents might not speak English, but at least they're not pick-ing up drunks at the Tik Toc Bar.* Marydale smiled slightly and looked down, just missing Kristen's eyes. And Kristen felt like Marydale was holding open a door. *Come on in,* she seemed to be saying. *We're friends now.*

"The last time I talked to her, she wanted me to buy her a whole set of recording equipment from Craigslist," Kristen said. "She'd been to some seminar that told her she had to *manifest the dream in real life.*"

"And her dream is to own a recording studio?"

"She thinks she's a singer. She wants to be a star, but all she does is karaoke bars and guys at karaoke bars. And she sends videos to those reality TV shows. She got called in for an audition once, and they aired it for two seconds along with a bunch of other train wrecks. She thought she was going to be discovered."

"Did you buy it for her?" Marydale asked, but her face said she knew Kristen wouldn't do that.

"No."

"What did you tell her?"

"I was so mad about that fucking equipment." It felt good to say it out loud. She remembered her mother wheedling on the phone. *You always were my girl, Kristi.*

"She shouldn't have asked," Marydale said.

"When I said no, she tried to get my sister, Sierra, to drop out of high school and *manifest the dream* with her. They were going to be a duo." Kristen remembered the tiny apartment she had shared with Sierra, their cramped bedroom with their two twin beds. They were like orphans or spinsters, except that Sierra wanted to go clubbing in Old Town. "I told her Sierra needed to manifest high school. She needed to manifest college. Sierra's smart. If she'd just focus, she could do anything. I wasn't going to let my mother ruin that for her. My mom said I was stifling Sierra's inner light or something ridiculous."

"You're a good sister."

"I wish. We don't have anything in common. We don't do anything together."

"That means a lot." Marydale shrugged. "If you were best friends, it'd be easy. My mother always said, 'You don't get points for easy.'" Marydale looked up at the evening sky. "Hey, can I show you something? It's behind the house."

On their way past the little garden, Marydale reached up to one of the sunflowers. It was a foot taller than she was. She pulled it toward her and pressed her face into its dark center.

"They don't really smell," she said. "My mother used to say they just give you a kiss."

She beckoned to Kristen. "Can I give you a kiss?"

Kristen stepped back, startled, but Marydale only wanted to guide the flower to her face.

"I think you can smell the whole earth in a sunflower," Marydale said, then laughed. "That's the kind of corny thing people say out here, isn't it? You don't go around smelling things in Portland, do you?"

"Oh, sure we do. Patchouli. Essential oil. Weed. Beer. Wine. My friend Donna's always going on about the afternotes of citrus in Oregon pinots."

Kristen raised her face to the flower and breathed in a nutty smell like the scent of dry earth and oak. Then they proceeded around the house. The ground was cracked, the fissures so wide, they caught the heel of Kristen's pumps. She stumbled, and Marydale held out her hand.

"We city folks need a lot of help, don't we?" Kristen said.

"Nah," Marydale said.

They stopped a little way beyond the house, facing the mountain. Marydale stood close to Kristen despite the expanse of land around them.

"It's pretty," Kristen said.

"Wait."

Marydale touched her back so lightly, Kristen thought she might have imagined it. Somewhere in the eaves a bird let out a cry, like the first two notes of a wood-flute solo. Then the sun dipped behind the mountain, burning its way down until only a crescent remained visible. Even the dog stood at attention. Then the sun dropped a little lower, and Kristen saw a ravine that cut through the Summit, glowing as the light poured through it like molten lava. She looked at Marydale, her face illuminated like the sunflowers.

"That's the Firesteed Summit," Marydale said. "If you get up to the top and look out on the other side, you can see the whole world."

After court the next day, the public defender, Douglas Grady, ambled over to Kristen's side of the aisle. His bowed legs suggested that part of him still thought he was on a horse. His cream-colored suit suggested otherwise.

"Bet you did good in law school," he said. "Remembered every rule, didn't you?" He returned his enormous white cowboy hat to his bald head. "Want a little advice?"

The last members of the six-person jury hurried past them.

"The jury doesn't like you. It's not your fault." He pulled a handkerchief out of his pocket and wiped his forehead. "You're from the city. You can't help it. But I hear you made yourself a new friend. You thinking about moving in with Marydale Rae?"

Kristen had spent her last night at the Almost Home imagining a kind of Lifetime Television movie friendship with Marydale. Of course, that meant one of them would eventually have to get cancer, but in the meantime they would sit at the kitchen table taking shots of whiskey and telling stories. Eventually, they'd end up at a bar in Burnville, hooking up with cowboys. Kristen didn't really think it would happen that way, but it was better than the alternative: she was moving even farther into the middle of nowhere with a waitress who was Kristen's best friend in Tristess by virtue of the fact she didn't hate Kristen for coming from *the city*. Kristen folded her arms across her chest.

"Yes," she said. "Not that it's really any of your business."

"I know. I know," Grady said. "Small towns."

He set his briefcase on the edge of Kristen's table, fingering the handle. He glanced around the empty courtroom.

"So it's purely social?" he asked.

"I'm renting a room in her house."

"Marydale's a nice girl. I don't know if I should give you this advice or not."

"Probably not."

Grady nodded grudgingly.

"Probably not," he echoed. "But you've noticed it's a small town. What I don't know is if you've noticed is that not everyone in town likes Miss Marydale Rae. Some folks…I'd say they downright dislike her."

"And?" Kristen glared at Grady.

"Look, I think Marydale could use a friend, even one like you."

"If you're trying to insult me, Mr. Grady…"

"Okay. Especially a friend like you," he amended. "But before you go down that road carrying water, make sure you're not looking to join the City Council. People 'round here like a little law and order. They trust Boyd. They'll warm up to you, but there's ways to make that easier and there's ways to make it harder. And Marydale is a rocky road to travel."

"I'm here to do my job. I don't care what people think about my roommate."

Grady chuckled deep in his throat. "Come on, Law School. Everybody cares what everybody thinks."

"Well, I don't," Kristen said.

"All right, then. Move in with Marydale." Grady rose, headed toward the exit, then turned back. "Like I said, she could use a friend. And that big trial in two weeks. The Hersal case." He waved a hand at her pantsuit. "You might want to soften this up a bit."

7

"You're living with a roommate?" Sierra asked.

"I told you I was," Kristen said.

"But you're living with her! You should be living with me."

Kristen sat in Marydale's dining room, her work spread out in front of her, her phone to her ear. A breeze from an open window brought in the smell of cooling earth and twilight. It stirred her papers.

"Isn't it nice to have your own place?" Kristen wanted to be kind. She wanted to say, *You know I miss you*, but she was afraid one word of encouragement would have Sierra on a bus to Tristess, or worse, in the backseat of some pansexual's Buick LeSabre.

"I want to live with you!" Sierra complained. "I don't want to live in Beaverton. I want to be with you. I could be your assistant, and we could solve cases together! Like Charlie's Angels. I don't have any friends at college."

"What happened to the vegan hippie guy?"

"He's not you."

"Hey, I don't solve cases. It's not that interesting. Mostly I file paperwork," Kristen said, shuffling her files.

"How is she?" Sierra asked petulantly. "Your roommate."

"I am not cheating on you," Kristen said. "I can have a roommate. And she's great. Hardworking. Neat."

As far as she could tell, Marydale owned nothing, had only one friend, and spent most of her time at work. But when they were both home, they had fun together. Marydale cooked, singing and sipping whiskey as she moved around the kitchen. Kristen told Marydale about Sierra and Frog and about her court cases. Marydale told her about the diner and how all the women in Tristess had a crush on her friend Aldean. Kristen told her about the law professor she had briefly dated. Marydale told her about being a kid and playing pirates and aliens in the junkyard where Aldean lived with his grandfather.

"I wish she was around more."

Just then, a movement caught in the corner of her eye. She jumped, startled to see Marydale leaning in the doorway…and happy, too. She'd been disappointed when she'd come home to find the driveway empty. Now, even as she blushed a little, she hoped that Marydale had overheard her. It wasn't wrong to want a friend.

"You just get home?" Kristen asked.

"I got off early," Marydale said.

"What?" Sierra asked.

"I was talking to Marydale."

"Fine," Sierra huffed.

Kristen said goodbye to Sierra. To Marydale she said, "I ordered a desk. I'll get out of your dining room soon."

"It's *our* dining room." Marydale wandered in and sat on the edge of the heavy wood table. "And I don't mind. But it's Friday night."

"Are you going out?" Kristen asked.

"In Tristess?" Marydale twisted her hair up behind her head, then let it fall. "I guess I could go shoot cans or get drunk at the Lariat Lounge. You want to go get drunk at the Lariat Lounge?"

"The district attorney's not supposed to visit bars."

"Probably a wise choice."

"What do you do for fun?" Kristen noted the book in Marydale's hand. "Besides read?"

Marydale shrugged. "Aldean and I cook a couple of steaks on his fire pit," she said. "We want to build a still."

She stretched her arms over her head, exposing an inch of skin below the knotted tail of her shirt. It seemed to Kristen that Marydale had gotten taller since she'd first met her. Taller. Prettier.

Kristen set her pen down.

"I never get Friday off," Marydale said. "Come outside with me. Have a drink. You can't work all night."

On the porch a little while later, Marydale poured two small glasses of vanilla whiskey, then shut off the porch light.

"Bugs'll get you if you leave it on," she said, balancing herself on the porch railing. "So what would you be doing in Portland right now?"

Kristen sat on the swing, nudging it back and forth with her foot. "Working. Studying. Trying to explain to Sierra why I can't celebrate the solstice by swimming naked on Sauvie Island."

"You swim naked?"

"With *my* body?" Kristen leaned her head back and stared up at the roof above the porch. "Sierra can't stand that we're apart. I don't get it. It wasn't like we had this great life."

"She got to live with you," Marydale said. "Do you wish you'd stayed in Portland?"

"I wish I could have stayed."

Marydale looked away, and Kristen wanted to take the words back.

"You know why I really moved out here? I failed the bar twice."

Marydale's face did not register shock.

"Failing is a big deal. I'd gotten a job at a big firm right after I graduated, but they don't keep you on after something like that."

"Well, they're assholes, then," Marydale said. "They should have waited for you."

Somewhere an owl issued its muffled cry.

Kristen took a sip of the vanilla whiskey. "They fired me the day after the results came in. No. My position had been *reprioritized due to a changing fiscal climate.*"

"The day after your results?"

"Yep. I told people I didn't want to spend my career guessing what kind of lattes the partners wanted. I said I wanted to practice real law. But the only job I could get was teaching part-time at the law school. I think they hired me because they were embarrassed."

"Embarrassed. Why?"

"I'd been on all sorts of scholarships. It looked bad to the alums. They'd given all this money to help 'nontraditional students' succeed, and then there I was. But working at the college was like living in the dorms after you graduate. It wasn't a big honor."

"Nontraditional?" Marydale asked.

"My mom didn't just want to be a singer. She was pretty fucked up." Kristen hesitated. "I was emancipated when I was seventeen, and I got custody of Sierra. I was supposed to be this big success. Child of drug addict makes good. Goes to law school. Changes the world." Kristen exhaled heavily. "It's all a long, sad story. You don't want to hear it."

"Of course I do," Marydale urged.

Kristen thought back. "My mom didn't beat us, but she never paid for stuff either. Food. School stuff. Pads when I got my period. We never stayed in an apartment more than a month or two. I got a work permit when I was fifteen. I was just sick of it. But my mom thought it meant she'd be able to buy *outfits* for her *performances*. She told the manager at the taco place where I worked that she had to collect my money because I'd spend it on drugs. She was the one using."

"That's awful."

"Finally my manager called my high school, and my guidance counselor helped me find a lawyer who would take my case pro bono. I think that's when I decided I wanted to be a lawyer. I remember going into the courthouse. My mom was there, and she kept talking about how she was just about to get her big break, and I couldn't do this to her because I was *her girl*. And I almost said no. I almost said I wanted to stay with her, but Sierra was ten, and I saw what was going to happen to her if she stayed with our mom. I think my mom was on meth at that point. Then it was all over, and Sierra and I were on our own."

"That must have been hard."

"It was easier without my mom."

"You're tough."

"I just did what I had to do."

"I know that story," Marydale said.

Kristen waited for her to say more, but when Marydale spoke again, she asked, "Did you leave anyone else in Portland besides Sierra?"

"My friend Donna. We grew up a mile or two away from each other on Eighty-Second Avenue. Her parents are dishwashers at this dim sum place called Golden Lucky Fortune. They used to save food for me and Sierra. Donna and I used to see each other every day, but I don't think she misses me much. She's dating this career military guy. Special ops. They'll make a movie out of him. He's a jerk, but somehow she likes it. He's got an amazing jawline. And before that, there was the opera singer, the police chief, and I think there were at least two CrossFit teachers. Poor Donna."

"And you? Did you have a boyfriend in Portland?" Marydale leaned back, perfectly balanced on the railing. "Someone you miss?"

"In college, I think I was still looking for 'the One,'" Kristen said slowly. She had cried when the bottom-shelf philosopher dumped her, but after that her dates had faded into the landscape of adult responsibility: specific prearranged meetings at restaurants both parties had researched independently. Sex after an appropriate period of time and using all the modern precautions. "After college I dated, but I never really had the time to…care."

"Were they all nice guys?"

"You mean were they abusive? No."

Marydale looked away, and Kristen had the impression that she had misunderstood Marydale's question.

"It's not like guys notice me much," Kristen added.

Marydale slid off the railing and sat next to her. "I find that hard to believe."

Kristen took in the sweep of Marydale's body, from the scuffed turquois boots to her rhinestone belt buckle to her hair.

"You don't have that problem," Kristen said.

Marydale tilted her head to one side, revealing a faux-diamond earring.

"I think you've got that sexy-librarian thing." Marydale draped one arm over the back of the porch swing. "Any girl can blow out her hair and put on some false eyelashes and a pair of Peel-n-Stick Push-Ups—"

"Do I even want to know?"

Marydale cupped her own breast with one hand.

"In case the Good Lord didn't provide, but you don't need all that."

Judging by the swell of her breast rising from the low-cut V of her shirt, Marydale didn't need them either.

"But you...you're different." Marydale rubbed the tips of her fingers into Kristen's shoulder. "You remind me of the range."

"The range?" she asked.

Marydale ran her fingers beneath the coil of Kristen's French twist, into her hair, along her scalp, sending a shiver of pleasure down her spine. Kristen remembered that Sierra had always had a flock of girlfriends who cuddled one another. Kristen had suspected they would soon trade those affections for teen pregnancy, but maybe she was wrong and this was just something women did when they were friends and not as prickly as Donna Li. Kristen tried to form some polite refusal. *No thank you. I don't...*

"It's always beautiful, but it doesn't come at you. You know? And you don't need to put a bunch of fake diamonds on it. I bet men notice you," Marydale said. "I think they're probably just afraid to mess it up."

Kristen felt the glow of the compliment touch her cheeks. "I work all the time," she said. "I'm not really...fun."

"I think you're fun."

Marydale continued to massage her neck. Kristen didn't move. She knew she should pull away, but it had been a long time since anyone had touched her, and Marydale's fingertips felt deliciously good against her skin. It wasn't so odd for two lonely women to do this—whatever this was. Wasn't that the plot of every soft-core porn movie? Two horny cowgirls start making out in a field and are joined by some well-hung men in chaps? But of course they weren't going to do that, and that wasn't going to happen, even if Marydale did have the hair of a porn star.

"I should probably just date one of the accountants Donna's mother is always finding for her," Kristen murmured. "They're boring as hell, but they're very respectable...men."

Marydale drew back, her hand still resting on Kristen's back, her blue eyes dark in the shadow of the porch.

"Not that it matters," Kristen added. Marydale had not moved, but it seemed like they were sitting very close, and "horny" didn't capture the star-speckled electricity that suddenly ran through Kristen's body.

"I think you want more than a respectable accountant," Marydale purred, her tone seductive and self-effacing at the same time, as though she was quietly mocking her own flirtation.

"How about you? Do you have a respectable accountant?" Kristen's voice came out rough and hushed.

"No," Marydale said. "People 'round here don't really approve of...me."

"Approve?"

Marydale leaned in.

"Approve of what?" Kristen whispered.

Then Marydale's lips were on hers, her fingers in Kristen's hair. Marydale's breath tasted of clean water and a hint of berry-flavored ChapStick. Kristen waited for Marydale's tongue to touch hers, but it didn't. In the back of her mind, warnings flashed in concepts more than words. *Roommate. Small town. Bisexual.* But she wanted to feel Marydale's tongue with a desire that was curious and eager and shy all at the same time. She leaned in closer and touched the tip of her tongue to Marydale's, feeling its slight roughness and the heat of Marydale's breath. Then they were kissing the kind of deep kiss that had always left Kristen feeling vaguely strangled; it didn't now. She clutched Marydale's back. Marydale moaned so quietly it was barely an exhale, but the sound was all lonely, sensuous yearning, and it sent a jolt of desire through Kristen's body so intense she pulled away as though something had stung her.

"Oh." Kristen pushed her glasses back on her nose. The bobby pins that held up her French twist had come undone and hung in the tangle of her hair.

Marydale's eyes were wide. "I shouldn't have done that, should I?"

"I…" Kristen could still feel Marydale's lips on hers, like a flash of light imprinted on the retina. "Um." She laughed. "I'm not…We're roommates. I didn't…"

But she had. She had felt the air tighten around them like static before a storm.

She touched her lips. "I'm not gay or anything like that. I don't want you to get the wrong impression."

Marydale hung her head. "I'm sorry. I didn't mean to."

"You didn't *mean to*?" Kristen didn't know if she wanted Marydale to say that she meant the kiss or that of course she didn't mean it; she was straight. They were friends. That was all.

Marydale stood up and walked to the porch railing, staring out at the dark yard.

"I won't tell anyone. I know I get it wrong," Marydale said.

Kristen thought she saw Marydale's shoulders tighten.

"You're a lesbian," Kristen said.

It was obvious now. She heard the man outside the diner yelling, *She's not gonna to fuck you, if that's what you're thinking.* She saw Grady tipping the brim of his enormous hat. *Some people downright dislike her.*

It was easy to forget there were places like Tristess. In Portland, everyone was gay. Even the straight men were gay, with their shoulder bags and their hair pulled up in man-buns. In Tristess, women were still *females,* and there seemed to be a rhinestone quotient that every woman was required to meet.

Marydale shook her head, but she wasn't saying no.

"Hey." Kristen stood up and put her hand on Marydale's shoulder. "It's okay. I'm straight." It came out sounding like a question. "But it's not a big deal. I know it probably is here, but it's not in the rest of the world. Forget about it. I'm flattered, really."

Kristen wanted to pull Marydale back into a kiss, not for sex but because Marydale looked so sad. Kristen wanted to say, *Do you know how beautiful you are?*

Instead she said, "I'm sure there's someone out there for you." She thought of the teenage waitress at the diner with her sweet, mean smile, and of the grim, heavy women who pumped gas at the Arco, and she thought of the books

Marydale had tucked around the house. And she thought, *Probably not.* "I know it's hard in Tristess. You could always move."

Marydale ran her hands through her hair. Kristen could almost see her slipping into her persona, like the girl in the family portrait putting on her glittery, red smile.

"I can't," Marydale said. "But I understand…I understand if you need to."

It took Kristen a moment to realize what she was saying.

"We're roommates. It would be weird if we…you know. But I don't have to move because you're gay. If you knew how little stuff like that matters in Portland. Really," Kristen said. "I'd be more upset if you started bringing some creepy boyfriend home. A lot of my friends…" She was going to say *are lesbian,* but in truth, the lesbians she knew at the law school had been an intimidating bunch, with their faux-hawks and their bracelets made out of old bike tires. "I like you as a friend," she finished. "It doesn't matter what you are."

Back in her bedroom, Kristen stood in front of the dresser mirror. She took off her glasses and leaned in. Her shoulder-length hair looked professional, but it also looked matronly. When she was eighteen, people had told her she looked like a young Jodie Foster, but she had not grown up to be a twenty-seven-year-old Jodie Foster. She had grown up to be the kind of woman who left parties early to finish her laundry. But Marydale Rae had kissed her. Beautiful Marydale. *She's just lonely*, Kristen thought. *We're just lonely.* But still she replayed the moment again and again in her imagination. When she lay down, she slipped her hand under the hem of her nightgown and touched herself slowly, trying to remember every detail of their kiss.

8

Marydale sat in a plastic chair in front of her parole officer's desk, a Bookmobile library book clasped in her hands. Behind her, the door was open to *prevent false allegations of misconduct between parolee and parole officer.* The office hummed with the sound of copiers and muffled voices.

"What do you think you're up to?" Cody Densen folded his arms across his chest, obscuring the word *parole* stamped there in white block letters.

Marydale looked at the book in her hands and then back at Cody. They had gone to the same high school although he had graduated the year before she started. She had been in Future Farmers of America with his sister.

"Is there something you want to tell me?" Cody asked.

"I report on Tuesdays," Marydale said. "I'm reporting."

The office was stuffy. A high, narrow window behind Cody's head let in the sun but no view. Cody leaned back in his chair and twiddled a pencil between two fingers. His thinning hair was slicked with gel.

"I heard you were talking to that new DA."

"I talk to all my customers," Marydale said. "I've been demonstrating pro-social behaviors by maintaining regular employment and staying within the county lines unless in possession of written permission to travel."

The last time she had left the county—by accident, because she'd forgotten that State Road 7 dipped into Harney County for two miles—Cody had sanctioned her to fifteen days in jail.

"Are you telling me how to do my job?" Cody demanded.

He had small, close-set eyes that made him look piggy, like an underfed American Landrace.

"No, sir," Marydale drawled.

"Don't you get fresh with me. I will sanction you," Cody said. "Do you want thirty days? I'll give you thirty days."

"Cody." Marydale sighed. "Sir. Mr. Densen. I'm reporting. What do you want?"

Cody's lips tightened into a thinner line. "Don't think she's going to find some loophole and get you off supervision. You are on supervision. Period. You can't bribe your way out of this."

"Bribe?"

"You offered her a room."

"I *rented* her a room."

Cody pressed his palms to the top of his desk. "Ronald Holten found out that she turned down his rental to live with you. Does she know about you?"

Marydale tried for her best competition smile. "I thought you'd be happy. I'm not supposed to associate with criminals. If I get out of line, she can have me tried and convicted without leaving the house."

"Does she know?"

"I don't know," Marydale said. "I don't have to tell her. That's not a condition of my parole."

Did she know? The question was like bad news in an unopened letter. She knew it was there; she just hadn't looked. When truckers came through the diner for a coffee and a shortcake, they'd glance at her, then lean in to the waitresses and whisper, *Heard she was the rodeo queen for three years running. Youngest queen west of the Rockies, and she did six years out at Holten Penitentiary. That a true story?* Then Glenda or Janice or Frank would fold their arms and say, *Her mother was a good woman, bless her.* It was a way of saying *yes* and *we don't talk about it* all in the same breath. And Marydale was always meant to overhear.

"She wouldn't be looking at renting a room from you if she knew, unless she's looking…" False realization dawned on Cody's piggy face.

"It's not like that," Marydale said quickly. "She's not."

She thought of Kristen's kind refusal. *I'm flattered, really.* Her body ached.

"She better not be. You know the conditions of your parole."

Marydale clutched the book in her hands. "I'm not allowed to enter into a relationship without your permission."

Somewhere in the building a phone rang and rang. In the

hall outside, two women laughed, and one said, "I swear I'll go crazy if I don't get to Disney soon."

"You are not allowed to enter a *female* relationship without my permission," Cody said.

"I know," Marydale said. "But you can't stop me from renting a room to a respectable citizen. Even if Ronald Holten doesn't like it."

"You may be out, but you are not a free woman."

"*I know*!" Marydale said.

"You better. And she better know about you and not some whitewashed version you want to tell her, because I might come by and pay you both a visit. Remember, I can come in your house any day, anytime, and I will tell her the truth."

"I'm sure she knows! Everybody fucking knows!"

"Watch your language."

Marydale's heart raced in her chest.

"She's the DA. They've got Aaron Holten's name on the courtroom and on every bench on the square."

"There are two benches on the square."

"Yeah. The Aaron Holten Memorial Bench and the Other Aaron Holten Memorial Bench. I can't believe they haven't made a bronze cast of him doing the Heisman."

"You shouldn't talk about him that way. He was a good man."

"I'm not talking about him. I'm talking about my life. She knows!"

* * *

Marydale's truck skidded to a stop in the gravel outside the Pull-n-Pay. She leaped out of the cab and banged through the gate and into Aldean's shed.

"She doesn't know!" Marydale cried.

Aldean was kneeling on the concrete floor, an acetylene torch in one hand and a piece of scrap metal held in a pair of tongs in the other. He thumbed the gas, and the torch fizzled out. He pushed the welder's hood away from his face.

"What?"

"Kristen Brock. She doesn't know about Aaron Holten. She doesn't know about me."

Outside the autumn sun was right overhead, and the little shed held the heat and the smell of paint thinners and gas.

"You asked her to live with you, and you didn't tell her?" Aldean stood up and set his torch down on the workbench. "She's the DA. Mary, what were you thinking?"

Marydale sat down on an empty metal drum. It tipped precariously. "I thought somebody'd probably told her."

"And you didn't check?"

"No. I didn't," Marydale said glumly. It had just felt so nice to be Marydale-the-waitress, not Marydale-the-felon, Marydale-the-pervert. "But they didn't tell her, did they? Because of my mother, *bless her* damn *heart*." Marydale leaned her head back against the wall. "I'm such a fucking idiot. I knew she didn't know. How could I not know? She would never live with me if she knew. She would never talk to me if she knew."

Aldean ambled over and stood beside her. "Aaron was an asshole. If she knew that…"

"It doesn't make it okay."

"Only it kind of does."

Marydale kicked the heels of her boots against the metal drum.

"Careful of those." Aldean pointed toward the metal pieces on the floor near her feet. "They're hot. I'm working on the reflux for the still."

"It looks like a muffler fucking a drainpipe," Marydale grumbled.

Aldean lit a cigarette, insensitive to the faded warnings on the acetylene tank.

"So she doesn't know. You served your time. You paid your debt to society, right?"

Marydale hesitated. "I kissed her."

Aldean took the cigarette out of his mouth. "I knew I'd lose this one!" He slapped her shoulder.

"She said no."

"Don't they all say no to you?" Aldean affected a soprano. *"Oh, Marydale, I can't. What would Jesus do? Well, okay, maybe just this once."* He blew out a stream of cigarette smoke. "Damn, girl, I lost a lot of tail to that we're-just-girlfriends-who-really-love-each-other routine back in the day."

Marydale couldn't bring herself to laugh.

"Hey, I'm sorry," Aldean said.

"She said no, but she was cool about it. If she finds out…"

"You got to just get in there before she does, do what you girls do, and get out. Then you can tell her. Maybe she likes it a little rough," Aldean suggested. "Maybe she watched that

Netflix show, and now she wants to feel what it's like to do it with a criminal."

Usually Marydale would give Aldean a friendly punch. Now she just stared at the ground. A few shards of shattered windshield glass had made their way into the shed, and now they reflected the light from the door. She slid off the drum, picked one, and held it up to her eye so the shed fractured into a dozen visions of itself.

"I want more than that."

"I know," Aldean said quietly.

Marydale thought about how many hours she'd spent in the junkyard with Aldean, playing as children, sneaking beers as teenagers, crying in his arms the night before she had to report to court.

"I think she liked it," Marydale said finally.

"That's right." Aldean put his arm around her, enveloping her in the smell of cigarette smoke and burnt acetylene. "You know why I'm not a happily married man?"

"Because you're a slut." Marydale leaned against him.

"It's because the only woman who's really worth having won't play for my team."

"That's bullshit, and you know it."

Aldean laughed. "Well, if she doesn't fall madly in love with you, she's an asshole and a damn fool." He squeezed her a little closer. "Just don't get your hopes up too high. Okay, princess?"

9

The next week passed uneventfully, the hot weather breaking and then getting hot again. Marydale left for work early and came home late, and the house on Gulch Creek Road felt empty. When she and Kristen did cross paths, Marydale would offer her a little wink and a "hey, gorgeous," but then she'd disappear into her bedroom or whistle to Lilith and vault up into the cab of her truck.

On Monday Kristen went back to work feeling, as she often had in Portland, that there was something she wished she could have done, someplace she wished she could have been. But instead of a vague yearning for something *out there*, it was Marydale. Marydale singing as she cooked. Marydale reading in an easy chair while Kristen watched TV. Marydale sitting on the porch railing, a little jam jar of whiskey dangling from her fingers.

In the courtroom, Kristen barely heard Douglas Grady, "You still here, Law School?"

"Yeah," she said, staring at the clock above the judge's bench.

"What's it been, a month and a half?" Grady added. He made it sound both too long and not long enough to be proud of. "I don't know why you brought this case."

Kristen didn't know either, especially when Relington had passed over two domestic-violence cases that had landed the victims in the Burnville walk-in clinic.

"Ask your friend Boyd," she said.

"Boyd Relington's no friend of mine." Grady glanced at his client, a dark-haired man in a plaid shirt. He looked like a boy compared to Grady, in yet another pearlescent, off-white suit. Grady looked back to Kristen. "This is a bullshit case, and you know it."

She cared, but she was thinking about Marydale.

The arrival of Judge Kip Spencer interrupted their talk. Grady stood, resting his hand on the enormous white hat on his table. Kristen rose also.

The case was a simple bicycle theft. She hadn't wanted to prosecute. The price of the trial could pay for a hundred ten-speeds. But Relington had called it a gateway crime and had demanded that she prosecute.

Kristen called her first witness. The woman confirmed the details in the police report. She had seen a Latino man riding the bicycle at dusk on the night it was stolen. She later identified the defendant in a photo lineup.

Grady crossed and shuffled a stack of photographs in front of the woman. She picked one with confidence.

"Mrs. Peterson," he said with overdone courtesy. "Thank

you for taking time out of your day to be with us here. Can you tell us a little bit about what it's like to live out on Old State Post Highway 10?"

"Objection, irrelevant," Kristen said.

Judge Spencer glanced at her over the expanse of his handlebar mustache. "Really, Miss Brock? Been watching *Law and Order*? I'll allow it."

The woman described life on a small ranch where her family had lived for three generations.

"Off the main road, aren't you?" Grady asked.

"About half a mile."

"Hard to know if you're looking at Mr. Juan here." He shuffled the photos in front of her. "Or Mr. Jose."

"Objection. This isn't a shell game," Kristen protested.

"Withdrawn," Grady said, and ambled back to his seat. "Your turn, Law School."

Kristen called a man named Old John who had found the bicycle behind his transmission repair shop.

"Would you say that Mr. Ortega is a frequent visitor to your shop?" she asked.

"Yep," Old John said, managing to look and sound exactly like a man smoking a cigarette, without actually having one in his mouth. "But he didn't do it."

"How do you know that?"

"Because I know who did."

"Okay. Who did it?" Kristen asked.

"The Holten boys. Adam and Jackson. Ronald Holten's grandsons."

"Why do you say that?"

"Because that's what they do. They stole Mrs. Ellington's grill. The plates off Mr. Fisher's scooter. We didn't used to have kids like that in Tristess, but kids'll do anything if they can get away with it." He chewed his invisible cigarette.

"Did you mention your suspicions to the police?"

"I did," Old John said, folding his arms.

"A compelling legal argument." Grady clapped his hands slowly. "Old John is right and, by the way, Mrs. Peterson, Mr. Ortega's photo is not in the stack." He held up the photos. "I got these off something called Flickr. Judge, I move to dismiss this case."

"You can't just dismiss in the middle of a trial," Kristen protested.

She was waiting for Judge Spencer to invite them to the bench, but he called out across the floor.

"Ms. Brock, are you going to pursue the Holten boys if I dismiss?"

"If the evidence suggests they're involved."

"We'll proceed with the trial," Judge Spencer said.

An hour later, the jury came back with a guilty verdict.

"I hope you're happy, Law School," Grady said as he swept past her, the brim of his hat almost hitting her as he exited.

Kristen was glad to see Marydale's truck in the driveway when she got home, but inside, the house was quiet. Marydale's bedroom door was closed. Kristen dropped her briefcase in the hall and searched the kitchen for the ever-present bottle of whiskey. She only realized she was slamming cupboards when Marydale appeared in the doorway wearing a red camisole and matching silk shorts and rubbing her eyes.

"Are you asleep already?" Kristen asked.

Marydale yawned. "I got up at four to help with prep."

It was a cheap negligee set, the kind sold at the Burnville Walmart. From where Kristen stood, she could see the lace edging unraveling and the fabric straining around Marydale's breasts. The fabric was so thin she could see the slight texture of Marydale's areola. And then she realized she was staring. She tried to look away, but not looking at Marydale in lingerie—cheap or otherwise—was like not looking at the Firesteed Mountains at sunset. Even staring at the floor, Kristen could feel Marydale's beauty lighting up the room.

"Is everything okay?" Marydale asked, and Kristen didn't know if Marydale was asking about the banging cupboards or the flush that Kristen could feel spreading down her neck.

Kristen raised her eyes, following the curve of Marydale's hip, her breast, and her shoulder half hidden by her hair.

"I…I had a weird day in court," she mumbled.

Marydale blinked a couple of times. "I'm sorry. You want to talk about it?"

An hour later, they were sitting at the kitchen table. Kristen hadn't forgotten Marydale's nightwear, but she had acclimated to it, and she had also recounted the details of the Ortega case. Marydale had asked a dozen questions about court procedure and terminology and listened to the answers, nodding.

When Kristen finished, Marydale said, "It's not your

fault." She sounded as defeated as Kristen had felt leaving court that afternoon.

"I didn't want to win," Kristen said. "I wanted the court process to arrive at the right decision. Mrs. Peterson couldn't pick Mr. Ortega out of a lineup, and he was sitting right in front of her, and she claimed to have seen him from half a mile away, at twilight, while he was riding a bike. It could have been anyone. Are people still that racist? He's Mexican so he must be a thief?"

"It could be that," Marydale said. "Or it could be the Holten boys."

"They weren't even part of the case."

"But everyone knows who's on the jury. Was it Judge Spencer?"

"Yeah."

"He's not going to let the Holten boys go down." Marydale stared at the tabletop, tracing flecks of metallic gold in the old Formica. "The law's always going to side with the Holtens. Always."

"But this isn't the Wild West. The Holtens don't own people. They don't lynch people."

"They got here first," Marydale said. "After the Indians. There was a big fight between the farmers and the ranchers, and eventually the ranchers won. The Holtens have a big family, and they stick together. That's the thing. They don't all have money, but if something happens to one of them..."

"Then what?"

"Ronald Holten owns land that surrounds a lot of the

BLM range. If he doesn't grant an easement, people can't graze their herd. And he's loaned people money. Some people even say he's got connections in the military. Someone's son enlists, Ronald can make sure he stays safe or gets sent out to the middle of nowhere in Afghanistan. I don't believe that part, but other people do. That's all that matters. Everyone owes the Holtens something."

"Do you?"

"My mom sold him a lot of our land when she got sick. He paid a fair price. He didn't have to. And I owe them other things, too, but not the kind of things you can pay back."

Marydale sounded sad.

"That doesn't mean Mr. Ortega should be convicted of a crime he didn't commit."

"What are you going to do?"

"I'll tell Douglas Grady to appeal. He already knows that. Maybe move to have the appeal heard in a different county. Mr. Ortega won't get more than probation, but it's still on his record."

They sat in silence for a moment, the evening light filling the windows like amber.

"There's a place I like to go when I want to think," Marydale said. "Would you like me to show you? It's a little drive from here."

Kristen nodded. "Sure."

"I'll change," Marydale said. "Get a sweater. It'll be colder than you think."

* * *

When Kristen came back downstairs, Marydale was wearing jeans and a sheepskin coat. She had produced two old blankets, striped red, green, and orange.

"Knockoff Pendleton wool," she said as she tucked them under one arm.

A few minutes later, they were bumping along a gravel road that seemed to go up forever. Lilith rode between them, her tongue lolling cheerfully.

"People say it's God's country," Marydale said, draping her arm over Lilith's back. "You believe it out here."

It was growing dark by the time they neared what Kristen guessed to be the top of the Firesteed Mountains. Kristen could tell they were high up, but all she could see was a field of small boulders and the cell phone towers silhouetted against the sky.

"Okay," Marydale said. "We're almost here. Close your eyes. Keep them closed. Promise?"

Kristen closed her eyes.

The truck bumped over a few more potholes. Kristen could feel Marydale turn it in a full circle until they were pointing back in the direction they came.

"Keep your eyes closed," Marydale said.

Kristen heard the truck door open and Marydale get out, followed by Lilith, who let out an enthusiastic bark. A moment later, Marydale opened Kristen's door and touched her arm, guiding Kristen's hand to the side of the truck. Kristen felt rust on the paint. The air outside the truck was cold and absolutely scentless. But Kristen could smell Marydale's vanilla perfume—not the sweet vanilla reinvented by the

Bath & Body Works, but the rich, sharp scent of real vanilla beans.

"Okay," Marydale said when Kristen was touching the edge of the truck's gate. "Open your eyes."

Kristen opened her eyes and took a step back. Before them, a rocky gorge plunged downward, so wide and so deep, it made nonsense of the nearby rocks. Beyond the gorge, the land stretched out in the fading light, flat and squared like a quilt or the view from an airplane. Marydale touched Kristen's arm tentatively and then withdrew her hand. Kristen shifted her weight so their hips were touching. She looked up at Marydale, wanting to say, *It's okay*, but saying nothing instead.

"That's Nevada," Marydale said, gazing out at the land beneath them. "I like to come up here. Whatever I'm worried about, it seems small. Out there, there's a billion people living their lives. You know?"

Lilith circled their feet. Kristen shivered.

"Yeah."

Marydale had parked a safe distance from the edge, but the gorge was so deep, Kristen felt it tugging at her, and she gripped the side of the truck.

"I got a blanket for you," Marydale said. "Come on."

Marydale let down the tailgate and stepped into the bed of the truck in one graceful move. She held out her hand, and Kristen clambered up, noting the warm strength of Marydale's hand and the slight roughness of her palm. In one corner of the truck, Marydale had secured an insulated dog house, like a giant cooler. Beside this, she unstrapped two low-slung stadium chairs. Kristen sat, and Marydale draped both blankets around Kristen's shoulders. Then she sat next to her.

"Tell me about being a rodeo queen," Kristen asked.

"I never liked the events. Roping. Bronc riding. Most of the rodeos are all right. People care. But the animals still get cut up pretty bad. The Holtens were all calf ropers." Marydale stopped. When she spoke again, her voice was oddly hollow. "You go through a lot of calves that way."

"Go through?"

"It's not the ones in the rodeo that get hurt as much as the ones they use to practice. But I did love being a rodeo queen. I grew up with it. My mother was only seventeen when she had me, so she was still doing rodeos when I was seven or eight." Her voice grew dreamy. "She had this beautiful Andalusian named Trumpet. I remember one year, she was the rodeo queen, and I came in fourth at the Pint Sized. We rode into the ring together on Trumpet."

Lilith made a sweep of the area, then leaped into the back of the truck and disappeared into her kennel.

"How old were you when you lost your parents?" Kristen asked quietly.

"My dad was my freshman year in high school. Heart attack. My mom just found him out by the north acreage."

"Were you close?"

"He taught me a lot. The judges liked that. A rodeo queen who really knows the ranch. My mom died two years later. Cancer. My dad was older than my mom. People said it was a shame she got married so young and he was so much older. But then everyone says she died of grief, too."

In the far distance, Kristen saw a speck of headlights traveling across Nevada, then realized it was an airplane.

"That must have been hard," Kristen said.

Other people's heartbreaks had always made her uncomfortable. In law school she had briefly dated an associate attorney who cried after sex, and his phlegmy confessions left her feeling both coldhearted and deeply in need of a shower. But she wanted to touch Marydale, to hold her. And it felt natural and strange at the same time.

"You can be pretty or you can be lucky." Marydale blew into her hands.

"How did you survive?" Kristen asked.

"I don't know. Maybe I didn't." Marydale shook her head. "I miss them every day, but when you grow up ranching you know. You see things die. Animals. You hear about accidents. You know what's coming...in a way."

Kristen reached out and covered Marydale's hands with hers. Marydale's skin was cold.

"You're freezing," Kristen said.

"I'm fine."

Kristen hesitated. The moment felt like a flame lit on a slender match, burning quickly away. They would get back in the truck. They would go home and take a few sips of whiskey and go back to their respective beds. Or...Kristen hesitated. Then she pulled the blankets off her shoulders and spread them out so they covered her and Marydale together. Kristen glanced at Marydale. She looked even more beautiful in the new moonlight, and her beauty suddenly made her seem vulnerable. Kristen wondered how many people had looked at Marydale and seen only her extravagant hair.

"You're amazing," Kristen said, and leaned in and touched her lips to Marydale's for just a second, then pulled back. "Sorry."

Marydale drew in a breath. In the back of Kristen's mind, a voice cautioned, *You can't do this to her. This is her real life.* Some part of her pretended to listen. Driving back home, Kristen told Marydale about the philosophy student with his VHS movies. She meant it as a warning. *I'm not going to fall for a woman, not for real, not for good.* But the story came out all wrong. She couldn't make her case. The facts didn't support the findings.

Back at the house, they bumped into each other in the hall-way. Kristen thought Marydale would kiss her, but she didn't. They climbed the stairs to their matching bedrooms.

Kristen said, "I guess I should get some sleep."

Marydale nodded.

In bed, the sheets tangled around Kristen's legs. The sense of anticipation that had felt sweet and intimate under the blanket in the back of Marydale's truck felt empty. The match had burned away, and neither of them had made a move, and that was the right choice, Kristen thought. They were roommates, and Marydale was a lesbian and Kristen hadn't even *thought* about women until now, and maybe that was just because all the men in Tristess chewed tobacco and were missing teeth (and so was Marydale, but she wore it well, like the stylish rip in her rhinestone jeans).

Finally, Kristen saw light appear around the edge of her doorframe as Marydale turned on the bathroom light. Kristen heard the toilet, then the faucet and the *clink* of a toothbrush in a cup. She listened, and she did not move. She thought of the undergraduate theater professor who had sometimes taught in the auditorium next to the room where Kristen had taught legal writing. She had often heard him beseeching his students to *be the tiger. Be. The. Tiger!* She had never been the tiger. She wasn't going to stay in Tristess and marry a cowgirl. She wasn't going to grow a fauxhawk or go vegan or buy a motorcycle or whatever incarnation lesbianism took out here. To open the bedroom door now wouldn't be right, and it wouldn't be fair, and it wouldn't be the kind of thing diligent, responsible Kristen Brock did, and she rose as if in a dream.

Marydale stood in the hallway.

"I can't sleep," Kristen said.

"I can get you a whiskey."

Marydale wore only a long T-shirt, and her thighs were thick and muscular, like the legs of some beautiful creature used for portage but meant to run.

"No," Kristen said. "That's not what I want." Marydale hesitated for a moment, looking back and forth between their two bedroom doors. Kristen nodded. Marydale took her hand.

Marydale's bedroom rested in moonlight. The bed lay in disarray, the covers almost on the floor.

"Kristen," Marydale whispered.

Then Marydale bent down and kissed her, her hair falling around Kristen's face. Kristen caressed Marydale's back, not quite daring to slip beneath the fabric of her T-shirt. Questions jumbled among the sensations in Kristen's body, disjointed and urgent. What would happen next? Should they stop? Would they kiss and fall asleep like chaste schoolgirls? What if Marydale touched her and Kristen felt nothing? Even as Kristen formed the question, the thought that the night might end without some kind of release made her clutch Marydale's back and pull away from her kiss at the same time.

"What is it?" Marydale asked.

"I've never done this with a woman."

Kristen kept her arms around Marydale's waist and examined her in the dim light. It didn't make any sense. The world was full of women, and Kristen had felt as much attraction to them as she would to a patch of crocuses or a shapely tree, but Marydale was different.

"We don't have to do anything you don't want to do." Marydale touched Kristen's cheek, and while her expression didn't change, Kristen though she saw a veil of sadness lower over Marydale's eyes. "I really want to do this with you. But if you're not ready…"

"It's not that," Kristen said quickly. "You're just…" *You don't know how lovely you are,* Kristen thought. She pulled Marydale's hips closer to her own, feeling Marydale's warmth and a deeper, more urgent warmth in her own body. "I don't know how to do this with a woman."

Before she could glimpse the sadness in Marydale's eyes again, Kristen leaned forward and kissed the skin at the base of Marydale's neck, tasting a light salt of sweat. Then she bit down very gently, just grazing the edge of her teeth along Marydale's shoulder. Marydale moaned, and the sound sent a frisson of desire through Kristen's body. "I want to," Kristen whispered.

Marydale kissed her again, then guided her to the bed, sweeping away the tangle of sheets.

"Lie down," she said.

Kristen lay down, looking up at Marydale, who lifted her shirt over her head, revealing the full, naked length of her body, her large breasts tipped with tiny nipples, the apex of her thighs covered in curls of blond hair.

"You don't have to do anything," Marydale said.

Kristen was still in her long-sleeved cotton nightgown with the little tulips printed on it. Marydale slid into bed beside her, kissing her, first tentatively, then with more force. Kristen felt her body squirm to meet Marydale's, their breasts pressed together through the thin fabric of her gown.

"Can I take this off you?" Marydale asked.

Kristen nodded, and Marydale tried to lift the fabric over Kristen's head, but Kristen was lying down and the nightgown tangled beneath her, and she had to squirm awkwardly out of the garment. And it didn't matter.

A moment later, Kristen felt the silken strength of Marydale's body as Marydale straddled her. Then Marydale slid down until their bodies were pressed together, readjusting her position so her thigh rested between Kristen's legs. Kristen felt Marydale's skin against her whole body. Then Marydale kissed her, her tongue matching the circular movement of her hips.

In the back of her mind, Kristen thought, *This is what men feel.* This awe. This softness. The generosity of Marydale's body, her breasts, her belly, the smoothness of her skin. Their legs intertwined, the skin of Marydale's thigh pressing into her.

Marydale groaned. Kristen rocked upward and Marydale pressed down, grinding her thigh into Kristen's sex, soft and hard at the same time. In the back of her mind Kristen wondered how it could be sex with no penis to secure the transaction. What made it more than adolescent humping? But even as the thought flitted across her consciousness, Marydale's body touched all the places the philosophy major and the crying attorney had only inadvertently grazed. Instead of the little glimpses of pleasure caught at the upswing of a man's thrust, Kristen felt her whole sex massaged by Marydale's thigh, the pleasure growing fuller and fuller, Marydale's skin never leaving hers. Everything felt luscious. Suddenly Kristen felt a strange, foolish urgency overtake her. She never talked during sex, never cried out her needs or her intentions, but the sensation was so complete and so surprising.

"I'm going to come," she gasped.

Marydale circled her hips. Kristen felt her own hips drive up against Marydale, her muscles contracting, her clit aching for just a little bit more contact, a deeper pressure, a faster…She cried out as the orgasm seized her.

"Oh my God. I'm coming." And a deeper voice inside her whispered, *You did that to me, Marydale. Marydale!* When Kristen had relaxed again, Marydale rolled off her, her smile all pride and accomplishment.

"Wow." Kristen stared up at the ceiling until her breath returned to its normal rhythm. "I never…"

Kristen rolled onto her side. She stroked the length of Marydale's body, across her breasts, flattened now by gravity, and across her hip and her belly. Then she trailed her fingers through the hair above Marydale's sex.

"May I?" Kristen asked.

The smile faded from Marydale's eyes. "You don't have to."

"I want to."

Something about the tension in Marydale's jaw made her look like someone steeling herself for a blow. Kristen touched her very, very gently.

"I've got to pay attention," she said, searching Marydale's face. "Is there anything I should know? What you like? Don't like?"

"I don't know," Marydale whispered.

Kristen stroked Marydale's thighs, feeling the cords of muscle.

"You don't know?" Very gently Kristen touched the curls above Marydale's sex.

"I mean…not really."

Slowly Kristen moved her hand between Marydale's open thighs and slipped the tip of her finger between Marydale's legs, closing her eyes for a second to better feel the structure of her body. *This is the first time*, Kristen thought. Marydale's body felt so delicate, her skin so soft, the moisture of her sex so shy and intimate. Kristen was almost afraid to touch her, afraid to hurt her.

"Oh," Marydale whispered, but although her hips lifted toward Kristen's touch, her eyes remained focused on the ceiling.

"What if I don't find your clit?" Kristen rubbed Marydale's mons, moving the soft flesh around again and again until Marydale's eyes finally met hers again. "I've heard it's very hard to find. Is it here?"

Marydale gasped. She pressed her hips against Kristen's hand, as if trying to guide her, but Kristen moved her touch to the side of Marydale's sex and massaged her outer labia.

"Or here?"

Now Marydale smiled. "You're teasing me."

"I don't know what I'm doing," Kristen said. "Women are very complicated."

"Please," Marydale breathed.

"Tell me if I get it wrong," Kristen said. She found Marydale's clit shielded in a mantle of swollen flesh and circled the tip with her finger so lightly only molecules of their bodies touched. All the while Marydale's breath came in little gasps like white-capped waves on the ocean. Kristen traced the circle again and again.

"There," Marydale gasped.

"Can you feel this?" Kristen slowed her breathing. "This?"

She was surprised how easy it was to ask. Questions like

that had always made her self-conscious, and the corre-
sponding requests had always made her feel vaguely put
upon—*rub harder, pinch it there*—as though she were in
some naughty ceramics class. But she wanted to talk to
Marydale, to hold her close with her touch and her kiss and
her words.

Kristen slid two fingers into Marydale's body, surprised by
how complex she was inside, not just a smooth sheath like
the inside of a condom, but ridged in some places and thick
and swollen in others.

"Is this okay?" Kristen breathed, easing her fingers in and
out and over Marydale's clit and back inside her.

"I think you know what you're doing." Marydale's voice
was rough.

And Kristen felt like she did.

"I'm glad I'm your first girl," Marydale said, pressing her
hips up to meet Kristen's hand.

Kristen leaned down and kissed her, a deep kiss matched
by the movement of her fingers. Kristen wished she could
touch Marydale everywhere all at once. They kissed until
Marydale's back arched and her fingers dug into the sheets.
Kristen released her from the kiss and continued to stroke
her.

"You're killing me." Marydale groaned, but she was smiling, and Kristen thought that nothing had ever flattered her
more.

"What should I do now?" Kristen asked.

"Harder," Marydale begged.

Kristen pressed down, rubbing faster as Marydale's breath

raced. Then Marydale lifted her head off the pillow, her mouth open, her legs closed around Kristen's hand.

"Oh God!" she cried.

When she fell back against the pillows, Kristen could see she was laughing.

Early in the morning, before dawn had brightened the windows, Kristen felt Marydale rise.

"I've got to work," she whispered, pressing her lips to Kristen's forehead. "Will you be here when I get back?"

"I don't know." Sleep held Kristen down. "I might be at work. When do you get off?"

Marydale knelt down on the floor beside the bed, her face close to Kristen's. "I mean, will you be *here*? Will you stay?"

Kristen blinked and rose on her elbow. She cupped Marydale's face. "You mean forever? I don't know," she said gently. "I can't promise you that."

"But tomorrow?"

"Of course I'll be here tomorrow."

10

Everything about the diner was familiar, from the watered-down ketchup to Mr. Fisher's complaint that the meat loaf used to be better. But today it glowed. Even the dust on the faded plastic flowers in the window ledges caught the sunlight and cast shadows. And Marydale had the feeling the world had gotten larger because everything had come closer: the smooth polish on the plates, the origami of newsprint crumpled on an empty table. Every detail was beautiful, and she tried not to think about the past or the future.

"Marydale, I need you to take table twelve," Frank called out from the kitchen. "I know it's Tippany's section."

"Sure," she answered without question.

Four men sat at the table. She didn't recognize them from town. The youngest must have been nineteen or twenty and the oldest seventy, but they all wore the same pale, starched shirts. The older men wore large wire-frame glasses with lenses that extended down their cheeks, as though they might grow a second set of eyes under the ones they had now.

"Wicked are the ways of the world," one said as she approached.

"And they let her work here?" The youngest man still had the decency to whisper.

"We are bathed in sin." His older companion nodded seriously. "But the harlot always wears a tin crown."

Marydale had met men like this before: voyeurs from little towns like Spent, Hayrail, and Deten. They thought a feeble attempt at proselytizing and some talk about sin pitched so she could hear it excused their curiosity. She didn't care. If they knew, Kristen knew.

She whipped their plates onto the table with practiced efficiency, noticing that Frank had undercooked their hash browns and left off their bacon.

"You okay?" he asked after they left.

She had almost forgotten about the men. She had barely noticed them. But she said, "It's slow. Could I take the rest of the day off?"

Frank looked around grudgingly. "Yeah. Go."

The Firesteed Summit looked almost as beautiful in the daylight as it did at night, although in the daylight she could see the smoke from the California wildfires blurring the distance. Marydale sat in the back of her truck, one arm wrapped around Lilith. She rubbed her knuckles against the dog's wide, flat head. Lilith looked up at her with beady eyes.

"It's not going to last, is it, girl?" she said.

Lilith just turned her head to the vista. Marydale did, too, trying to focus on the last detail she could see before the landscape disappeared into the smoke. Was it a barn? The outline of an irrigation circle? A road she wasn't allowed to drive on because the conditions of her parole bound her to Tristess County the way blood and marriage bound everyone else. She had been ready to leave when Aaron Holten had reared up behind her, his thick arms bowing out at his sides like a cartoon strongman. *I'm going to show you what a real man does.*

Back at home, Marydale decided not to cook dinner until she had talked to Kristen, but by four in the afternoon, she had been waiting so intensely, her anticipation hung in the air like the high-pitched buzz of long-distance power lines. She went out into her garden and picked greens for a salad, then thawed a breast of chicken. Then she was putting a pot-pie in the oven. It seemed like time in the kitchen expanded while the clock's count of seconds slowed to a crawl. Finally, at six thirty, Kristen's car pulled into the driveway. Marydale froze, a towel in her hands.

"What a fucking day!" Kristen called out as she entered the house. "I am so glad to be home."

Home.

Kristen slowed down as she entered the kitchen. "Hey," she said, her voice softening.

Marydale wanted to fall into her arms. "Hey."

Kristen crossed the kitchen floor, leaned up on tiptoes, and kissed Marydale on the lips, in the kitchen, with the lights on and her briefcase in her hand. Marydale wrapped her arms around Kristen and held her close, trying to breathe in every detail.

Marydale spoke into Kristen's hair. "We have to talk."

Kristen stepped back. "That doesn't sound good."

"Not like that," Marydale said quickly. "I just...I want to...We have to talk about my story...my past. I mean maybe we don't have to, but we *haven't*."

Kristen put her bag down and took Marydale's hand. "About your parents?"

It was all so obvious. Even the old men from Spent knew. Only the memory of *her poor mother, bless her*, kept it from the lips of the town gossips. Now, with Kristen watching her, touching her, Marydale didn't know how to begin.

"I've never had a boyfriend or wanted one, not even when I was a kid," she said. "And I've been with women. A lot, I guess. But never like last night."

"What do you mean?" Kristen asked gently.

"A lot of the girls around here think it's a sin. We'd kiss, but that's all. And when I was in, no one was ever gentle with me. There wasn't time."

"Someone forced you?" Kristen asked.

"No." Marydale hesitated.

Kristen's forehead was smooth, but her face was full of worry. Marydale touched the silky sweep of her hair.

"You know I was in the Holten Penitentiary, right?"

Kristen stepped back. "What?" Shock and confusion spread across her face.

"Oh God," Marydale said. "They didn't tell you."

"Who told me?" Kristen turned like a boxer anticipating a blow.

"Everyone knows." Marydale was surprised by her own voice because there was no air in her lungs.

Kristen picked up her briefcase. "Tell me what?" Her voice was cold.

"I was in prison." Marydale couldn't look up.

"Convicted?"

"Yes."

"Of what?"

Marydale sank into a chair. The smell of burning potpie filled the kitchen.

"No one talks about it, but they talk about it all the time. They talk about it *without* talking about it. But they didn't tell you."

"What were you in prison for?" Kristen demanded.

"When you came into the restaurant the first time, I liked you so much. And then you came back and you moved in. I thought maybe they'd told you. Maybe it didn't matter."

"What were you in prison for?" The question pressed against Marydale's chest, crushing her breath. "What *the hell* were you in for?"

"Murder."

Kristen stumbled back, tripping on a peeling seam in the linoleum.

"Was it a DUI? Were you drinking that shitty whiskey and driving?"

"I would never do that."

"Then what?"

"I killed a boy named Aaron Holten. He is…He was Ronald Holten's nephew." There it was. The newspaper had told a hundred versions of the story, but they all led to that night. "I was young."

"You're fucking *young* now!" Kristen said in a tone Marydale had never heard before. "I am the *prosecutor* in your town! You asked me to live with you. You fucked me. I'm not even supposed to go into *bars*. I could lose my job. I could lose my license, everything I've worked for! And you didn't *once* think that you should mention that you were a felon? A murderer."

Kristen clutched her briefcase to her chest. "I'm going to go to my room. I want you to leave the house, give me two hours. I won't be here when you get back, and don't come after me. Don't talk to me. I don't know you. You had no right…" She took another step back. "You don't have the right to look at me."

With that she left.

Slowly Marydale undid her apron, crumpling the soft cotton in her hands. She looked around the room at the faded wallpaper and painted cupboards, just old paper and old paint, all of it laid down by her father.

And she remembered Gulu pulling her aside, an arm around her neck, half embrace, half throttle. *You're on the new, so I'm gonna give you some advice*, Gulu had said. *You cry too much.* With that, she had punched Marydale in the stomach, knocking her breath out. While she was struggling to inhale, Gulu had pulled her close and whispered into her hair, *Crying works sometimes. Even some of these bitches'll soften up for a little fluff like you, and the bulls, too. But you're in it for a dime, and sometimes, in here, the only thing you got at the end of the day is you* not *crying.*

11

The VACANCY sign was on at the Almost Home Motel. Of course it was, Kristen thought. Tristess wasn't a place to visit. These guests weren't tourists. This was where failed ranchers went to die and men named Bubba went to pass sexually transmitted diseases to teenagers named Brandissa or Starr. And there weren't even enough of those to fill the building.

Behind the front desk, a young man greeted her with a monotone, "Welcome to the Almost Home. You're almost home at the Almost Home."

"God, I hope not," Kristen said.

"Pardon?" the boy asked.

"I'd like a room for the night."

Kristen couldn't remember her license plate, and when the boy asked for her credit card, it took her a moment to understand the request. When she opened the door to her room, she was startled to see that it looked exactly like her earlier stay, although what she had expected she didn't know.

She didn't bother bringing in her suitcases. She set her laptop on the table and typed *Marydale Rae Tristess Oregon murder*. The headlines were almost eight years old, but the search engine brought them instantly back to life. LESBIAN LOVE TRIANGLE ENDS IN MURDER. RODEO KILLER TO BE TRIED AS ADULT. The articles all featured the same photograph. A younger Marydale, sitting on top of a pyramid of hay bales surrounded by five other girls. The five wore tiaras; Marydale wore a crown. They were all pretty and blond, but Marydale looked like the original after which the other girls had been imperfectly modeled.

The article said she had been seventeen at the time, a volunteer for the American Veterans Support Network, treasurer for the local chapter of Future Farmers of America, and the Tristess rodeo queen three years running. Most of the articles mentioned that she had been orphaned. A few mentioned that she had been researching colleges and wanted to study psychology and eventually get her master's in counseling. *I want to serve other people,* the young Marydale was quoted. *Whether it's tutoring someone at school or helping one of our servicemen find community back home, helping others is the most rewarding thing you can do.*

Nonetheless, on the night of the rodeo coronation, Marydale lured champion calf roper, honor student, and rancher Aaron Holten to her barn and killed him. She waited for him in the hayloft, and when he was halfway up the two-story ladder, she threw three hay bales at him in quick succession. The third bale knocked him off the ladder and to his death. *They can weigh up to a hundred pounds, maybe more if they're spoiled*, a local rancher was quoted as saying. The DA told reporters that Marydale had lured Aaron over with offers of sex. Judge Kip Spencer had presided over the case.

After the murder, the story unfolded to the town's horror and fascination. Everyone who had contact with Marydale had something to say, and the *Tristess Tribune* interviewed them all. Apparently, it was common knowledge that Aaron had courted Marydale for years and that she had rebuffed him. What the town hadn't known was that Marydale had seduced her friend Aubrey Thomsich. *She was wild*, Aubrey told the local paper. *I knew it was wrong what we did, but life was always exciting with Marydale.* The local preacher suggested that the grief over her parents' deaths had *turned her from the right path*. One of Marydale's classmates said that Marydale had always looked at her with the *eyes of lechery*.

The accompanying picture showed Marydale putting her arms around a dog with a cast on its front leg. Kristen stopped at the photograph, touching the screen with her fingertip. It didn't take a trial attorney to see that the town had turned on her. The accounts of her deviance were stacked up against her honors and accolades, as though somehow being a beautiful orphan and a junior soroptimist made the murder of Aaron Holten worse.

Kristen picked up her phone to call…someone. Her hands shook. Who could she call? The last thing Sierra needed was one more person in her life making bad decisions that would appear, to Sierra, as romantic adventures. Donna would love the whole thing. She might be stuck with

the Lubbock, Texas, divorce, but Kristen had fucked a convicted murderer two months into her first job as DA.

No, not *fucked*. Kristen stared at Marydale's picture on
her screen. She had fucked the Mad-Dog-drinking philosophy major and a half dozen other men who had felt, momentarily, like answers to some question her body kept posing.

She lay down on the bed.

"Marydale," she whispered, and tears came so suddenly to
her eyes, they felt like they belonged to someone else. "How
could you do this to me?" She pressed her face into the orange coverlet, not even thinking about how many times it
had *not* been washed. "How could you not tell me?"

12

Marydale woke in the cab of her truck where she had parked at the Firesteed Summit. It took her a moment to realize her phone was ringing, wedged somewhere beneath her hip. She startled more fully awake. It was Kristen. It had to be. She fumbled for the phone and answered it a second before she registered the name on the screen: Aldean.

"Hey, princess," he said.

She rubbed her eyes. The gorge wasn't beautiful without Kristen. The wildfire smoke had washed the color out of the already muted landscape. The squares of brown farmland looked like failure. There was no water. No one won.

"I need you to come over to the Pull-n-Pay," Aldean said.

She didn't want to go. She didn't want to talk about the still. She didn't want to sit around drinking warm Coke and whiskey while Aldean smoked and welded, oblivious to the fact that he was one bad valve away from blowing up the place. She didn't want to report to Cody or go to work or listen to Mr. Fisher complain that the meat loaf tasted meatier in 1960. Weariness settled in the very viscera of her body.

"Can I come tomorrow?" she asked.

"Pops is dead," Aldean said.

Marydale arrived at the Pull-n-Pay an hour later. The sun was up, streaming over the junkyard. Aldean was waiting for her at the gate. He took her hand, which he hadn't done since they were ten. Together they walked through the piles of scrap metal and gutted cars.

Inside, the mobile home smelled of cigarettes and motor oil. Across the small, cluttered living room, Pops lay in his recliner, his mouth partially open, his eyes closed, an ancient man in a flat-brimmed John Deere cap. He didn't really look much deader than usual. Nonetheless, Marydale didn't need to look for the rise of breath to know that he was gone. The stillness in the room was absolute. She and Aldean stood in the doorway for a long time.

Finally Aldean said, "Let's have a toast."

Marydale didn't mention that it was eight in the morning. It wasn't eight in the morning for Pops.

Aldean retrieved a half-empty bottle of Poisonwood and two glasses from the kitchen cupboard, and they went outside.

"Aren't you going to give him some of your good stuff?" Marydale asked.

"Pops always loved Poisonwood."

He poured two small glasses. They stood together, the rising sun making giants of their shadows.

"To Pops," Marydale said.

"To Pops." Aldean uncorked the bottle again and poured a thin, slow stream of whiskey on the ground.

When it was gone, Marydale asked, "Did you just find him?"

"I think I knew last night, but I didn't want them to come take him away in the middle of the night. It just seemed right that he wake up at home." His voice broke. "Or wherever he is now."

Marydale took his hand again, feeling the calluses and smelling the cigarette smoke on his clothes.

"I'm sorry," she said.

"He was a good man. I don't know what I would have done if he hadn't taken me in," Aldean said. "My fucking tweaker dad and tweaker mom…If it wasn't for him, I don't know. Sometimes I thought he was just staying alive until I was old enough to take care of myself. You know? Like he was hanging on for me. And sometimes I wanted to say, 'You can go now.'" Aldean was crying. "He used to make me beans for breakfast. He'd just open the can and put it right on the stove, and he was there *every* morning."

He squeezed Marydale's hand. "Marydale, I can go now. I can leave. I can sell the Pull-n-Pay and go to Portland." He looked at her. "Don't worry. I'll get everything ready. I'll start the distillery, and when your PO agrees to a transfer, you can come live with me, and we'll run it together."

The sun stung Marydale's eyes. The Poisonwood burned her stomach. She saw Kristen's stricken face. She imagined

Aldean's old Dodge pulling out of the Pull-n-Pay for the last time. And she wished that her tears were for Pops, who deserved them, but she couldn't even remember his real name—Floyd or Myron—and she clung to Aldean and cried for herself.

13

Kristen woke early after a night of disjointed dreams: Marydale on the side of a desert road. Marydale in her kitchen serving Thanksgiving dinner to an empty table. Marydale lecturing in a hall at Cascadia Law School. She showered quickly but stared into the bathroom mirror for a long time. Her hair hung in limp wet strands around her face. She looked pale. She kept thinking about the gap in Marydale's smile. Had the tooth been pulled? Had someone punched her? Had anyone cared? She wanted to drive back to the house on Gulch Creek Road, fling her arms around Marydale, and yell, *What were you thinking?*

Instead she dressed in the suit Grady had told her to *soften up*. She was at his office before he arrived, waiting in the parking lot of the low, squat office park. She didn't let him get through the door.

"I need to talk to you," Kristen said.

"Don't tell me you've agreed to that postponement Hersal

and I asked for," Grady said with the confidence of a man used to angry, early-morning visitors. "Because we're ready now. We're going to court."

Behind him, the windows were painted silver, the words DOUGLAS E. GRADY, ATTORNEY AT LAW stenciled on the scratched surface.

"I don't give a shit about the postponement."

"Hersal will be glad to hear that." Grady jingled something in his pocket. "Will that be all, Ms. Brock?"

The two scrawny trees in the parking lot had lost their leaves, and the air held the chill of an early winter.

"You didn't tell me about Marydale Rae," Kristen said. "Was it some kind of a power play? Did you think it was funny?"

Grady bowed his enormous white hat.

"I know you don't like me," Kristen went on. "You *tolerate* me. You don't want city people coming into your town and your court, but what happened to professionalism? We're *colleagues*." She spit the last word at him.

"You'd better come in," Grady said.

He jiggled the key in the lock for a long time. Inside, the space was devoid of decorations. Grady motioned for Kristen to follow him into the back office. He took a seat behind a heavy metal desk.

"I think you've got me figured wrong," Grady said. He pointed to a chair in front of the desk. "Sit."

Kristen stood.

"Despite your personality," Grady said with a leisureliness that made her want to sweep the files off his desk onto the floor. "And your general youth, I like you. You're not as stupid as most people."

"You said Marydale Rae was a 'rocky road to travel,'" Kristen said. "What was that? Driving directions? She's been convicted of *murder*. I'm the deputy DA. I was living with her. You knew that, and you didn't think you should tell me as a professional courtesy?"

"I said Marydale needed a friend."

"Me?"

"Aldean Dean is her only friend. He's a good man, but that's no role model for a girl like Marydale. She's not going to marry him and live in the Pull-n-Pay." When Kristen said nothing, he added, "Her parents are dead. She's an only child. She's a pariah. Sure, Frank at the diner will give her a job if she works under the table. He likes felons that way."

"She killed a man."

Grady looked up at her with bland concern. "You just learned that?" He set his hat on the desk beside him. "You just learned that." This time it was a statement. He sighed. "People don't tell that story as much you'd expect. The Rae women...they're special. Marydale's mom, she was—" He rubbed the back of his neck. "People around here would say she was a good Christian woman, but it was more than that. She made old men feel young again. Children loved her. Drunks stood up taller when she walked into a room."

"What about...?"

Kristen couldn't bring herself to say Marydale's name. It was Ms. Rae, the defendant, the inmate, the felon. Not Marydale with her white dog and her sunflowers and her feet hooked around the rails of the porch, leaning back so she could see the stars.

Grady chuckled. Kristen wanted to slap him or leave or cry.

"Marydale always was her own woman," he said. "She was special, too."

"And so you let me jeopardize my career, maybe my safety? Because she was special? Do you want everyone in jail right now to wait another six months while they recruit another deputy prosecutor because Boyd Relington's busy drinking whiskey with Ronald Holten or whatever he does all day? I don't see a big brain trust around here."

Grady held up his hand. "Kristen."

She glared at him.

"Do you know why I came out of retirement?"

Grady motioned to the chair. Kristen remained standing.

"I had a nice trailer out at Coos Bay. Fishing every day. I could see the elk in the parcel behind my place. Then I heard about what happened to Marydale, not the stuff up at the barn with that boy, not what she did, but what happened right here."

"What?"

"Marydale didn't have any money."

Grady rubbed his hands over his knees, as though easing an old pain. It occurred to Kristen that he was old. She hadn't seen it before. She hadn't really noticed anything but his enormous hat.

"Her father had died. Her mom had died. She'd sold off most of their herd to pay for her mother's cancer. Marydale ended up with some public defender fresh out of law school.

I think he wanted a murder on his résumé because he refused to plead down to manslaughter. He didn't even suggest self-defense, which is what it was."

Kristen saw Marydale standing in the kitchen, her beautiful face wrecked by grief.

She sat down.

"Her attorney should've been able to walk in there and say, 'For God's sake, look at her,' and walk away with a not-guilty verdict."

"There must have been a jury."

"People around here don't like the gays. There's no one here talking about marriage equality." Grady put the words in quotation marks. "But Marydale Rae…" His gazed passed Kristen toward the door. "My grandfather was a sharecropper in Iowa. Corn mostly. Before they had all these insecticides. He said sometimes there'd be a plague of locusts, and they'd eat up everything. And there'd often be one farm or one valley where the wind would blow or the rain would fall just right, and the bugs wouldn't touch it. They'd just pass right over. Marydale was like that…for a while.

"Everyone knew she was a queer. She didn't hide it. I mean she did, but you can't hide anything from anyone, especially when there wasn't a girl in town who hadn't at least thought about kissing Marydale Rae. But she got brash about it after her father died. She was running that ranch, ran it as good as any man could've. She was born to that land, and she was a good Christian. She'd help anyone in a second, took care of her mother till she passed.

"Mrs. Rae died in her arms. Preacher found them there

together, Marydale just sitting up against that headboard with her mother in her arms. And they asked why she hadn't called anyone, and Marydale just said, there wasn't any hurry, "'cause God had already come and taken care of everything that mattered.' People just couldn't hate her for being gay."

"What about Aaron Holten?" Kristen asked.

"The thing about those locusts…you didn't want to be the farm they left alone, the only one to make it." He shook his head slowly. "First they'd say God spared you; then, just as quick, they'd say you'd made a pact with the devil. I've seen the Holten women in court, swearing up and down they ran into a wall. It runs in families. There's a lot of mothers in this town who've seen their girls go off with a Holten boy and cried over it.

"When Marydale killed him, I think…some people hated her because she did it, and some people hated her because they hadn't done it themselves. Some of them just hated her because they owed the Holtens so much money; they couldn't not."

"Didn't she appeal?" Kristen felt the sweat beneath her arms and between her legs.

"Don't know why not," Grady said. "She was too shook up, I guess. I heard about it too late. But that's why I came back, so no one ever had to take a shit-shoveling public defender again, because I can tell you one thing: if I'd been her lawyer, she'd be free."

* * *

The next days passed in slow procession. Kristen thought about Marydale constantly, but she entered the Almost Home from the back so she wouldn't risk seeing her coming out of the Ro-Day-O Diner.

Donna called one evening while Kristen lay on her motel bed, letting the blue glare of the television wash over her and drinking Poisonwood from a plastic cup.

Two of the new hires at the Falcon Law Group had been let go. A third was on her way out.

"You're going to hate me," Donna said, "but I gave Mr. Falcon your name. I know you don't want to do big firm, but I'm lead on this energy-drink patent case."

"And somebody needs to take over the Lubbock divorce," Kristen finished.

She took another sip of the whiskey. Neither the taste nor the alcohol seemed to affect her, or perhaps there was already something numbingly intoxicating about the monotony of the motel, the television commercials, and her thoughts.

"It'd just be for a little while. I told them I'd help find a replacement for the family-law side. It's a big part of our business."

Our business. Donna had edged ahead in whatever race they were running to whatever golden future they'd respectively imagined on the other side of attorney general or Falcon law partner.

"Our clients need to know they can come to the Falcon Law Group for anything, big or small," Donna went on. "I think it'd be an amazing opportunity for you, Kristen."

"I can't just leave my work here." Kristen felt like someone else was speaking for her. "I'm shaping the lives of this community. They count on me and what I can do for them."

"Shit. I know," Donna said. "It was worth a try though."

But in court, Kristen could barely keep the addicts straight. It didn't matter. Every case was the same. Someone got drunk. Someone got high. Someone borrowed a car without permission, which counted as auto theft, but Kristen felt no satisfaction in the guilty verdicts.

"It just gets worse with the rodeo," Grady said, as they exited the courtroom Friday afternoon. "You talk to Marydale yet?"

Kristen glanced around. The hall was empty, but nothing was private in Tristess.

"You know I can't do that," she said. "I could lose my job."

"Your job." Grady waved vaguely in the direction of the courtroom. "My job."

At the end of the week, the rodeo came to town or the town became the rodeo. Kristen couldn't tell which. Tristess was busy and vacant at turns. Main Street was empty. The parking lot of the Almost Home was packed. From the walkway outside her motel room, she could see the sparkle of the Ferris wheel and hear the jingle of carnival music.

Every single person she saw asked if she'd been to the rodeo. The answer was no. She didn't even bother to lie and say she was going soon. She couldn't shake the feeling that she should be going with Marydale. She should be walking under the Ferris wheel with Marydale. She should be listening to Marydale's stories and passing an ice-cream cone back and forth with the intimacy of a kiss.

And every night and sometimes during the day, even in court while Grady was droning on about sight lines and radar calibration, she argued with Marydale in her mind. *You had an obligation to tell me.* It was like briefing a difficult case. She just had to get the words right, and it would be true. *I have to uphold the law. My job requires that I uphold the law.* She tried again and again, but her imagined Marydale never answered back, and her silence became its own castigation.

14

Marlen "Pops" Dean died a good death. Marydale could tell the thought was on everyone's mind as the people of Tristess filed into the Fellowship Hall of the Victory Waters Pentecostal Church. Aldean stood at the door, shaking hands, looking handsome in the same black suit he had worn to Marydale's mother's funeral and to the prom. And although he had choked up as he delivered his eulogy from the pulpit, he grinned at her from over the shoulder of buxom Lucy-Anne Beeker. Grieving Aldean Dean in a pressed suit was every straight girl's dream. Aldean pretended to squeeze Lucy-Anne's tight, black-clad ass.

You dog, Marydale mouthed, but she felt indignant for Pops. *Really?* she added.

Once the last of the receiving line had filed in, Aldean hurried to her side.

"I can't believe this is happening," he said. He wasn't talking about Pops. "Old John said he'll buy it. Cash."

"I know. I heard."

"Old John says he's been wanting to buy the Pull-n-Pay for years, said he thought I'd want to sell, but out of respect for Pops and all…" He looked like the boy she remembered from the sod forts of their childhood. "And I found this industrial park north of Portland, right on the water. They'll even rent me a little houseboat. It's only five hundred square feet, but I swear, with all Pop's junk, that's about all the space we had in the trailer. You'll love it. It's by this bridge that's built to look like one of those big French churches Mr. O'Rourke was always going on about in humanities."

She felt herself tearing up.

"Hey." Aldean wrapped his arms around her. He didn't smell of cigarettes. "How long do you have to keep your nose clean? Three years? It's been at least one. That's two more, and your PO will let you transfer your parole. You're missing out on all the hard work. By the time you get there, we're going to be making the best whiskey in Oregon, and all you have to do is show up."

She hadn't told him about Kristen. It didn't seem fair to mix her tragedy with Pop's death and Aldean's excitement about Portland. She knew he would stay if she asked. If she said, *Don't leave me. I can't live here without you, without her, without anyone*, Aldean would stay, but that was a kind of prison, and she knew too much about prison to wrap a cage around him.

"It's going to be amazing," she said. "Aldean, you're going to do it."

The preacher's wife hurried up to them with an apron in hand.

"We've got the Lord's bounty of food in the kitchen," she said, waving a hand in front of her flushed face. "And not nearly enough hands. I thought since you worked at the diner…Aldean, can we steal her?"

In the kitchen, the women talked about what a good boy Aldean was, waiting until his Pops died before moving to the city. A few of the women even patted Marydale on the back and said it was a shame about her mom dying so pretty and so young, bless her, and Marydale's father, too, although you kind of expected it with a man like that who lived rough for his age.

"They're with the angels now," they all concluded with satisfied smiles. "But it'd sure have been nice to have your mother guiding you up, wouldn't it, Miss Marydale? How many times did you win that rodeo contest?"

They all knew, but she said, "I'm sorry, ma'am, I can't remember."

And in some ways it felt like she really couldn't remember, because it couldn't really have been her. Instead she remembered the day Gulu had pulled her behind a utility box on the far corner of the grounds. They sat, huddled between the gray metal and the inner fence.

You know what day it is? Gulu had asked, lighting a hand-rolled cigarette with the last match in a battered matchbook.

Marydale had said, *No. What day is it?* all the while looking around for the guards who would surely catch them.

Last day for you to file an appeal on that case of yours.

What?

Don't you know about the statute of limitations? It's run out now. But you don't mind, do you? 'Cause you didn't ask for one.

My attorney said I couldn't get one.

You can't now.

Gulu had drawn in a deep drag of smoke, the tiny cigarette burning down to an ember. Then she had taken Marydale's hand, turned it over to expose her wrist, and pressed the ember into her skin.

You're one of us now, Scholar.

When the reception was finally over, the women urged Marydale to take a restaurant-sized pan of leftover tuna casserole.

"Because you don't have nobody to look after you out on that farm," the preacher's wife said, which prompted another round of how beautiful Marydale's mother had been and how sad it was that she died so young, leaving Marydale without anyone to take care of her. "But don't keep the pan. Bring it back," the preacher's wife added, as though stealing baking pans was her particular MO.

"I will make that my number one priority," Marydale said.

The women didn't seem to hear the bitterness in her voice, and Marydale pretended it wasn't there as she hugged them, leaning down until she was bent almost in half.

It was after dark when Marydale returned to her house. She bumped the truck door closed with her hip, the enormous casserole in her hands. It wasn't any heavier than a tray at the Ro-Day-O, but her arms shook. She was tired. The pan smelled of hot mayonnaise and fish. And she smelled like hot mayonnaise and fish. And she had Jell-O on her sleeve. And Aldean was leaving. And the sweet, exquisite moments she had shared with Kristen were as meaningless as a shooting star, just a brief glitter that no one else saw because it existed for only the split second it took to disappear.

She looked up. Someone stood in the shadow of the porch. Marydale whistled for Lilith, who bounded out of her kennel on the side of the house, but Lilith wasn't growling, and a moment later she was circling the porch, wagging her tail. Kristen stepped out of the shadows into the moonlight. Her dark-framed glasses stood out against her pale skin. She was wearing a suit, and her white blouse glowed. Standing at the edge of the steps with her hands clasped before her, she looked like a woman at a train station, both waiting and departing.

The pan grew heavier in Marydale's hands. She wished she had come home with someone, maybe Lucy-Anne Beeker with her enormous breasts heaving their grief for Pops in a low-cut dress. As it was, she had a pan of flaccid bow ties. She ran her tongue over the space where her tooth had been knocked out, feeling the sharp edge. In the back of her mind, her mother said, *There's no excuse to let your looks slide.*

She set the casserole on the hood of the truck, straightened, and placed one hand on her hip.

"You forget something?" Marydale called out.

Kristen hesitated. "You should have told me."

"You should be more careful who you sleep with." Marydale strolled toward her. It was all she could do to keep the tears out of her voice. "You just don't know, even in these small towns."

"I'm serious," Kristen said. "I could have lost my job."

Standing on the stairs, Kristen was taller than Marydale, and Marydale felt like Kristen had always been taller, although of course that wasn't true. It just seemed like Kristen had always been farther away than she realized.

"You didn't do anything wrong," Marydale said, "unless being a lesbian is wrong, but you said that stuff doesn't matter in Portland."

"I'm not a lesbian. I don't know what I am. And it matters that you're a felon. It matters what people think. If you cared about me, you would have thought about that."

Kristen's voice was strained. She kept pushing at her glasses.

"I should have told you." Marydale took a step closer so that she was standing on the step right below Kristen. They were so close she could see the fine weave of Kristen's shirt. "Maybe I didn't want you to know. Maybe I didn't care if you knew. Maybe I wanted to fuck you before you found out, because I knew you'd be gone as soon as you did."

She wanted to fall into Kristen's arms, to tell her about Aldean leaving and the ladies in the kitchen and how tomorrow none of them would look at her. Even when they ordered, they would stare at the menu with their hands clasped in little arthritic fists.

"You want me to say you were never here? Is that what want? Okay, I'll say it. I don't know you. I don't know what people said about us, but it's all lies." Marydale tipped her chin up.

Kristen stepped back, tripping a little on the step behind her.

"You've never been alone," Marydale added.

"Of course I've been alone."

"Not like I have."

She reached up to touch Kristen's cheek, but Kristen turned away and stepped down off the stairs. She didn't stop until she was standing in the drive a few feet away.

"I don't know what to do," Kristen said. Her voice trembled, but Marydale pretended not to hear.

"Go back to court. Go back to Portland and find a lawyer boyfriend."

Marydale didn't look back as she let the door close behind her. She didn't turn on any lights. In the kitchen, she stood at the sink, her hands braced against the cool enamel, staring at the dark silhouette of the oak tree outside. She heard Gulu's voice in her head, *You cry too much, Scholar,* and her mother's voice, *You can be pretty or you can be lucky.*

Behind her, another, gentler voice said, "Are you okay?"

"Go away." She felt Kristen's hand on her shoulder. She shrugged it off. "You're right. I should have told you, but you were never going to stay."

"I talked to Douglas Grady about your case," Kristen said.

"Douglas Grady?" Marydale tried to place the name.

"He's the public defender."

"Not mine."

"No. Not yours. He said your lawyer didn't do his job."

"Everybody hates their public defender."

"Douglas thinks you were innocent."

Marydale felt very tired. "No one is innocent."

"Do you want to tell me now?" Kristen asked.

Marydale traced the edge of the cracked enamel sink with one finger.

"What part?"

"Any of it. All of it."

The house creaked around them. Lilith snuffled in her bed beneath the kitchen table.

"I was happy," Marydale said finally, her back still to Kristen. "My parents were part of a cooperative that sold free-range beef to all the big grocery stores out in Portland." She turned, but she couldn't look at Kristen.

"And you were gay?" Kristen asked.

"My friend Aubrey, she was, too, I thought. She came out to me after my mother died. We were always talking about the future, how we were going to go to college together. I was going to be a counselor, and she was going to be a nurse. We'd work in the same hospital. But then she started talking about who we were going to marry, like it was this choice we were going to make together. I could have Aaron, and she'd take his cousin Pete. Or we could wait a year and marry the Grossman twins when they graduated. I said I wanted to marry her.

"She went along with it for a while. Then one night she got really serious. She told me she'd started seeing Aaron Holten. He was Ronald Holten's nephew. They're the biggest Holtens, the ones with all the land. She said I needed to ask out his cousin Amos or his stepbrother Marcus. I thought she was dumping me, but she thought that we'd always be together, except we'd have husbands. I said I didn't want to sneak around behind some boy's back. Aaron was a jerk, but Marcus was a nice guy. I didn't want to do that to him, and I wanted *her*. I tried to explain that it'd be different in college. People wouldn't care. She just said Aaron wouldn't care. She said what we did didn't *count*." Marydale crossed her arms over her chest, hugging herself tightly. "She said she'd even tell him just to prove it to me."

"Did he care?" Kristen asked.

"He started following me."

"Did he threaten you?"

"He said no one could find out about me and Aubrey. He said if I got close to her again, he'd kill me and he'd kill her."

"Oh God, Marydale."

"I begged Aubrey to leave him, but she wouldn't, and I stayed away from them both after that. But that year at the rodeo"—Marydale stared at the wall—"he won everything, and everyone kept calling us the king and queen. They said he should dump Aubrey and go out with me. We had to ride on the float together, and I remember sitting there, waving to everyone, and I just wanted to cry. That night there was a big thunderstorm." She could smell the lightning, the first drops of rain hitting the dust. Her heart beat faster, and an old fear rose up in her throat. "I had to get back to milk the cows. I still had two cows. I was out in the barn. I heard a truck. I got scared, and I climbed up into the loft."

She saw Aaron: his sharp jaw, his freckles, all sandy-blond

and handsome. They had sat together at the sixth-grade lunch table. The other kids had chanted *Mary and Aaron sitting in a tree...*

"When we were kids, Aaron said he was going to marry me." She knew she was losing the chronology of the story. "I don't know why I was so scared that night. I didn't really think he'd do anything, but I hid behind the bales. I knew it was Aaron before I even saw him. He was looking for me, real systematic, like mucking a stall, getting something done just by doing it. Then he started yelling that I was a dyke and he was going to show me what a real man was. I yelled at him to stop, for someone to help, but there was no one out here. And he started climbing up the ladder to the loft, and I picked up this bale, and I threw it down near him, just to show him that I could."

Marydale thought Kristen touched her arm, but she couldn't feel it.

"He came up that ladder, and I was yelling at him to leave me alone, and I threw another bale at him. And I thought, 'He's going to kill me,' but he wasn't." It was a question. It was *the* question. "He was just angry. I knew him when he was a kid. He wasn't going to kill me."

"It's not your fault," Kristen said quietly.

Marydale closed her eyes and saw the cinder-block walls of the penitentiary, the paint cracking with water and rust, the fence wrapped with razor coils and electrified so that it sparked on humid nights.

"I grew up ranching. You know when a calf's breeched. You know how to tap a jar to hear if the seal is good or how hard you got to hit a log to split it. I think I knew how high he had to climb before the fall would kill him."

Kristen tucked a lock of hair behind Marydale's ear. "That doesn't mean it wasn't self-defense," she said gently. "He cornered you in a barn in the middle of nowhere. He told you he was going to kill you."

Marydale finally met Kristen's gaze. She was surprised by how calm her voice sounded. "But I killed him, and when I picked up that bale I knew I was going to."

"I know."

"I can't take that back."

"I know." Kristen wrapped her arms around her, and Marydale sank into her embrace.

"His parents split up after the trial," Marydale said. "They sold everything to Ronald Holten. I think his mother is living with some guy in Ohio. Someone said his father started drinking. I did that to them."

"Shh." Kristen stroked Marydale's hair. They stood together. Finally Kristen said, "I'd like to park my car around back. I shouldn't be here, but I want to stay with you tonight if you'll let me."

Marydale woke slowly. Her face felt greasy, and her hair still smelled of church hall dinner. She rubbed her eyes. Kristen lay beside her. As if sensing her attention, Kristen stirred and blinked.

"Hello," Kristen said. "Did you sleep?"

"Yes," Marydale said, although her sleep had been complicated by dreams of trains and wildfires. She snuggled closer to Kristen, rolling onto her side with her back pressed against Kristen's belly. Kristen put an arm around her.

"I wish we could stay like this forever," Marydale said.

But the morning light came through the window, blue and cold.

Kristen didn't say anything for a long time, but she held Marydale tightly. Finally she asked, "What was it like in prison?"

Marydale saw the high-ceilinged breezeways, the tiers of cells going up and up. Once again, she felt the strange wind that blew through the blocks despite the fact that there were no doors to the outside.

She had never told anyone about prison except Aldean. No one else had asked. Now, with Kristen's warm body wrapped around her and Kristen stroking her arm as she held her, Marydale felt as if she could unroll the whole story like a faded carpet, and it would be okay because Kristen would understand how it was part of her and how it wasn't. It was her entire life story, and it was just a brief interlude between Trumpet's elegant canter and the smell of sunflowers in the garden.

"It was lighter than you'd think," Marydale began. "There were a lot of windows. You couldn't look out them. They were too high up, but it wasn't a dungeon."

"Was it hard?" Kristen asked.

Marydale tongued the gap where her tooth had been knocked out by an errant elbow. "It was hard." She hesitated. "Especially when I first went in. There was a woman, Grace-Louise, but everyone called her Gulu. She was my daddy for a while."

"Your daddy?"

"It made sense inside. She was straight, but she was in for a long time."

"She was your girlfriend?"

"It wasn't quite like that but kind of."

Kristen hugged her closer.

"Gulu called me 'scholar' because I liked to read. I used to help the girls with their GEDs and their paperwork. We used to work in the laundry together, and she protected me for a while."

Marydale rolled over so she could look at Kristen. She looked unfinished without her glasses, the skin under her eyes thin and veined with blue. And she was beautiful. *You'll break my heart,* Marydale thought.

"It just is what it is," she said.

Kristen smoothed her hand over Marydale's hip.

"After I got out, I tried to get my parole transferred to Portland. There were too many memories here, too many people I knew, but you have to do your parole in the county where you did your crime. I can't even cross the county line without permission. But you know that. You went to law school."

"We didn't study parole," Kristen said.

"If I don't get a sanction for three years, my PO has to consider transferring my parole, but there's always a way to block it. He can say he didn't find anyone in Portland to supervise me. He can say he thinks I'll abscond. He didn't want me to rent you a room."

"He knew?" Kristen looked startled.

Marydale stroked Kristen's hair, messy from sleep. "Everyone knows," she said. "I'm not allowed to date women. I can date men, but being a lesbian…they say it was an exacerbating factor. If I hadn't been gay, I wouldn't have killed Aaron."

"That's bullshit."

"I know, but it still might be true."

Marydale moved closer, pressing her lips to Kristen's so that Kristen would not ask any more questions. She was afraid Kristen would resist, but Kristen eased Marydale onto her back, kissing the hollow of her throat and running her hands over Marydale's breasts, pinching her nipples and sending sparks of pleasure, like bursts of Morse code, through her body. Then quickly, as though it was something she had been wanting for a long time, Kristen slid down the bed, parted Marydale's legs, and kissed her.

Marydale remembered the first time Gulu had touched her. Gulu had pulled her into a supply room and knocked into an oversized bag of broom heads. *Damn it, Scholar. Pick these up.* Even then, a new fish, a baby two months in, Marydale could tell Gulu was an actor projecting her lines toward the guard beyond the half-open door.

A second later, Gulu had shoved Marydale up against the shelves. She pushed her hand past the waistband of Marydale's prison-issue jeans, into the dull-gray underwear that held the smell of cheap detergent and other women's bodies. Gulu's fingers dug into her while Marydale stared, unable to speak. Contact with another inmate was an infraction. Masturbation was an infraction. Gulu jerked her hand a few times, her thumb grinding at Marydale's flesh.

A second later, an inmate in another part of the supply room called out, *Six-five. The floor's wet.* Gulu stepped back, righted the bag of mops. *Why?* Marydale whispered. *So you'll have something that's yours*, Gulu said. All that day, Marydale had felt Gulu's touch like a thumbprint in paste. She felt it as she threw laundry into the washer, as she lined up in the chow hall, as she stood for count. At night the guards walked up and down the metal grates, looking into each cell, the main lights glaring in the atrium. And Marydale felt a reluctant drop of moisture leave her body, not lubrication, just a memory, the last drop of rain ground out of a desert tuber. And she understood.

Now she felt Kristen drawing open the folds of her body. Marydale gasped as Kristen made a wide sweep with her tongue, touching every part of Marydale's sex. It felt like Kristen erased Gulu's touch. Pleasure smoothed away that sticky imprint, and the dry ache that had lingered beneath her skin dissipated with a sigh. Kristen slowed her kisses, exploring Marydale's body with small, hot strokes, her lips trailing across the sensitive skin. The whole time, Kristen murmured her approval.

"You're beautiful. I want to make you happy."

And Marydale tried to tell Kristen that she didn't deserve to be, but she couldn't find the words, and she felt her clit expanding back into her body, turning her very tendons into extensions of pleasure. Then Kristen placed her thumbs on either side of Marydale's clit and rubbed while she tongued the opening of her body, in and up and around Marydale's clit and back in, until Marydale's whole body tensed in pure

anticipation. Behind her closed eyes, Marydale saw a kalei-
doscope of wings, as though a thousand frantic sparrows had
suddenly been released from an attic window, and in that
moment, she had never been imprisoned, and she sobbed as
the orgasm raced through her body.

14

Kristen stepped out of the shower, toweled off, and put on a robe. In the kitchen, the coffeepot was percolating. Marydale stood with her back to the door, tossing something in a skillet. The kitchen window framed her hair in sky blue, and the sunlight caught in the steam from the pan. Kristen thought, *Maybe there's a way.* She walked over and put her arms around Marydale, resting her cheek on Marydale's back, breathing in her vanilla perfume. In the back of Kristen's mind, she remembered how strange her attraction to Marydale had first felt. She had never noticed women before. Her desire for Marydale was like a single electrical circuit left active when the rest of the grid was dark. But it didn't seem strange now. There simply weren't any other women like her. *I love you*, she thought, just to try on the words to see if they fit.

"Hungry?" Marydale asked.

Kristen released Marydale slowly and poured herself a

cup of coffee. It tasted like Portland coffee, not the thin acid they served at the Ro-Day-O. She pictured Marydale working at a bistro in the city, someplace like the Veritable Quandary, where the waitresses wore long black aprons over their black slacks. Or maybe Marydale could start her own café, a ranch-to-table steakhouse or an organic sandwich shop that gave jobs to troubled teens.

Marydale moved with the efficiency of a short-order cook, so Kristen wandered onto the front porch to stay out of her way and to breathe. The rough boards felt cold beneath her feet and the air was clean.

She let out a long sigh. *Happy.* She had no reason to be. She was a deputy DA sleeping with a felon in a town the size of a family reunion. At that moment, her mother was probably waking up with her own felon-lover. Sierra was probably dropping out of college with the pansexual named Frog. And it didn't matter that Frog was dating a man named Moss; Sierra would manage to get pregnant by one of them, and the whole cycle would start over again.

Yet she could not bring herself to worry, because Marydale was in the kitchen cooking. It was Sunday. They had the whole day to lie in bed or walk out into the range, to drink whiskey and stare at the sky. Nothing seemed to matter beyond this day and maybe another and maybe one more. *Maybe there's a way.*

Kristen glanced down the long drive, out to Gulch Creek Road. Two cars appeared in the distance, so far away they seemed to be barely moving. She watched for a long time as they drew nearer. Apprehension flooded her body.

"What's at the end of Gulch Creek Road?" Kristen called back toward the kitchen.

"Nothing," Marydale said. "It just loops around."

It occurred to Kristen she had never seen another car on the road, and now the cars were slowing down as they approached the drive. Her mouth felt dry. She felt sick. The cars turned.

"Someone's here," she said.

It was a proselytizer, she told herself, or meter readers working in a pair, lest they get a flat or run into an unfriendly hermit. Her heart beat high in her chest. Marydale appeared at her side.

"Oh, fuck," Marydale said.

"What is it?"

"You should go to your bedroom," she said. "Hide."

"Who is it?"

"It's Cody. My PO…"

Now that the cars were almost in front of the house, Kristen could make out a man in each car.

"Go," Marydale said.

It felt wrong to leave Marydale standing in the doorway in her long T-shirt and fuzzy, slumped-over slippers, but Kristen hurried up the stairs and closed the door behind her.

She heard Marydale hurry into the other bedroom. A moment later she heard the front door open without a knock.

A man's voice echoed up the staircase, indistinct but stern. "Marydale Rae!"

Kristen cracked the door a fraction of an inch, then

slipped out onto the landing and angled herself so she could glimpse the foyer at the foot of the stairs.

A man stood in front of Marydale, his body accented by a black vest, like an apocalyptic life vest, with the word PA-ROLE printed across the front.

"I'll let you get your shoes and a sweatshirt." The man was chewing gum. It made his words juicy.

Marydale had put on jeans and now stood in the front hall, her back to the wall. "I haven't done anything," she said.

The man grabbed Marydale by the shoulder and peered into her eyes. "I told you not to room with that woman."

"I'm not!" Marydale lowered her voice, and Kristen couldn't hear what she said next.

The man glanced back at the open door. "You disregarded an explicit order from your PO."

"You can't tell me who I can live with. Did Ronald Holten put you up to this? Is this all because he can't admit Kristen didn't want to take his bribe?"

"That's ninety days!"

Kristen held her breath. The other driver appeared in the open doorway, his thumbs hooked into his wide brown belt. Even backlit in the doorway, Kristen recognized Ronald Holten's swagger.

"Trouble, Cody?" he asked.

Marydale squared her shoulders. She was taller than both of them and bigger, too, but there was something heart-breaking about her posture, like the mountain lion that had been seen stalking the neighborhoods of northwest Portland until it got barreled over by a Smart car. Kristen didn't need a law degree to know Marydale was losing.

"Would you like to tell Mr. Holten about your little arrangement?" the parole officer said, striding up to Marydale until they were only a few inches apart. "You want to tell him about Kristen Brock?"

Kristen felt her face flush a hot, sick red like a heart attack about to happen.

"Okay, Cody, I'll go," Marydale said quickly. "You're right. I disobeyed an order. Give me a sanction. I'll go with you."

"All of a sudden you're ready to go," the parole officer drawled, all mean courtesy.

Holten stood in the hall, smiling.

"What's upstairs?" the parole officer asked. Then he lunged for the stairs. Marydale stepped in front of him. He pushed her aside. Marydale stumbled back. He bounded up the stairs. Kristen didn't even bother to hide.

"Well, *fuck* me," he said, grinning. "District Attorney Kristen Brock." Then to Marydale he called out, "You're going down. Guess you already did."

"We weren't." Marydale stood at the bottom of the stairs, looking up. "She lives here. She rents a room."

"You said you weren't rooming with her. Boyd Relington is going to love this!"

"Leave her out of it. She didn't do anything," Marydale yelled. "Cody, this has nothing to do with her!"

"You can't just come in here." Kristen walked past the parole officer and down the stairs. She stopped in front of Holten.

"Are you fucking her?" Cody was right behind her.

"It's none of your business," Kristen said. She turned to Holten. "He doesn't have probable cause to come in here, and as far as I can tell, you're trespassing."

The PO glanced back and forth between Kristen and Holten. Kristen said nothing.

Holten said, "Guess you didn't study parole at that school of yours. Cody doesn't need probable cause. He's Marydale's PO. He just brought me for protection, since we hear Marydale's been getting up to her old ways." Holten looked Kristen up and down. "It's just this kind of behavior that got my nephew killed."

"What kind of behavior?" Kristen spat, but she knew the answer.

Marydale was already holding out her hands to the parole officer. He unsnapped a pair of handcuffs from his belt and clicked the cuffs in place. Then they were gone, and the house was empty. When Kristen returned to the Almost Home and called the jail, they said Marydale was still being *processed*.

On Monday morning, Grady stopped Kristen on her way into the municipal building. A cold wind swirled the dust around their feet.

"Kristen," he said. He seemed about to say something more, then reconsidered, then said, "I'm sorry."

"For what?"

The wind blew her words away, but it didn't matter. Everything was sorry, from the gray sky overhead to the cracked asphalt beneath their feet. Even Grady's cream-white suit and ten-gallon hat—immaculate as they were—looked like a costume from a theater production long since packed up and forgotten.

"This whole damn town," he said. "I'm sorry about the whole goddamn thing."

I'm getting fired, Kristen thought. It wasn't a surprise.

"I talked to Marydale before she got arrested," she said. "She told me what happened."

"Have you gone to the jail to see her?"

"No."

"Go see her before you leave." Grady looked down the street toward the pawnshop and the vacant storefronts. "I don't imagine there's much to stay for now."

Some sad, romantic teenage girl inside Kristen cried out, *I'm staying for her!* Sierra would stay. Maybe that was why she couldn't.

Relington was at her office before she'd had a chance to check her voice mail. He stood in front of her desk without an invitation.

"I got a call from Ronald Holten last night," he said.

"I'm sure you did."

"You have a lot of freedom outside this office, outside your position." Relington's voice was a judge's gavel. "But the district attorney has an obligation to uphold the law and the moral fiber of this community. The people of this county need to know that you will not be swayed by a criminal element to use your power to benefit some while unjustly prosecuting others."

"That's bullshit." Kristen slapped her hand on her desk. "And you know it."

There would be no last-chance agreement, no work plan. She read it in Relington's eyes.

"I know who you prosecute and who you don't, Boyd. How many domestic-violence cases have you passed over? But a Mexican on a bicycle? Can't have that kind of element coming into our town. Can't risk that someone would finger the Holtens, can we?"

"That has nothing to do with your situation." Relington spoke through his teeth.

"I think it has everything to do with everything in this town."

"I will give you twenty-four hours to resign with a neutral reference. Dates of employment only," Relington said. "If you stay one minute longer—and I mean stay in this town—I will file a complaint with the bar."

After he left, Kristen looked around the room. There was almost nothing to collect. The Chamber of Commerce's potted palm had long since died. The photo of Sierra on her desk was the only personal item she had brought to work. She picked it up and stared at Sierra's optimistic smile. On her desk, her phone buzzed. A new text from Donna read, *I know you'll say no, but Falcon's still looking for a family lawyer.*

The Tristess County Jail stood on top of a bluff overlooking a stretch of desert. From a distance, it looked like the building had been carved from stone, but up close it was clearly concrete, the windows barred with heavy black bands of metal.

At the visitors gate, Kristen was greeted by a series of signs bearing paragraphs of fine print. Kristen had gotten to item four—*no weapons, including firearms, etc.*—when a woman's voice blared from a microphone on a pole.

"Purpose?"

"I'm here to see Marydale Rae," Kristen said.

Inside the building, she felt the staff watching her as she presented her ID. Their silence told her they knew. It occurred to Kristen that her mother had probably visited rooms like this, waiting for men named Hooch or Spike to emerge, dressed in their jailhouse uniforms. Her mother would be happy to know Kristen was standing in this line. She wouldn't mind that Kristen was waiting for a girl. She'd just be happy they were finally manifesting the same dream.

A guard in a tan uniform led her into a small room, much like the waiting area of a DMV office. The only decorations were faded drug campaign posters. Chairs were set up in widely spaced rows, some back to back, others facing each other. Half a dozen women were already waiting.

"You sit here," the man said. "Other visitors sit here." He indicated the same row. "The inmate sits there." He pointed to a chair about four feet away. "There's no touching, no exchange of gifts. If either you or the inmate becomes agitated, we will remove you for your own safety. Is that clear?"

Kristen waited for a long time. *This is the right choice, the only choice*, she thought, but the angry calm she had felt in front of Boyd Relington had deserted her. Marydale had to stay. Marydale had to live in Tristess with her PO and Ronald Holten and a whole town of people whispering behind their hands because it was Marydale—not Kristen—who was the most interesting person in Tristess. It seemed so brutally unfair, and yet Kristen couldn't stay. She couldn't.

A door opened. Five women in loose orange shorts and navy T-shirts filed in, followed by a female guard. Marydale straightened when she saw Kristen, and Kristen could tell she was trying to pose, to flip her hair, to put on the parade-float smile. But her eyes looked flat and gray, and Kristen saw a bruise spreading down Marydale's jaw. Another darkened her wrist.

"What happened?" she asked when Marydale sat down.

"Things got a little busy." Marydale shrugged.

"Are you okay?"

"Of course." Marydale glanced at the guard in the corner.

Kristen wanted to wrap her arms around her, to pull her close, to press kisses into Marydale's hair. *I have to make the right choice*, Kristen thought. She opened her mouth, but no sound came out.

"I'm sorry that you had to see this. It's not exactly..." Marydale trailed off.

Kristen felt Marydale scanning her face.

"What is it?" Marydale asked.

"I..."

They were so far apart. Kristen couldn't even touch the tip of her shoe to Marydale's sneaker.

"You're leaving," Marydale said, her voice suddenly hollow. She sank her head into her hands.

"Marydale? Honey?" Kristen wanted to say, *No.* She wanted to say, *I'll stay. We'll make it work.* She knew how

Marydale's smile would open up like the sun rising. "I got fired." Kristen knew if she didn't speak now, she would never be able to force the words out of her mouth. "I'm so sorry."

"No." Marydale didn't look up.

"I'd never get work here. There aren't any firms, and if I open my own practice, I'll be the lawyer who got fired from the DA's office. I wish there was a way you could come with me, but I've got to go back to Portland."

"My parole officer will never let me leave."

"Marydale," Kristen said quietly. "We both knew this couldn't last. Isn't that why you didn't tell me? We had something really beautiful together, and it's still beautiful even though it didn't last forever." It felt like a loophole, the kind of cheap, slimy exemption that made people hate lawyers. "I will miss you so much, Marydale. But you want to get out of here, out of Tristess. They're not going to leave you alone if I'm here. You told me you have to go three years without a sanction. What happens if we've been together for two and a half years and then we get caught? All that time wasted? You have to be perfect, and their version of perfect...doesn't include me."

"I don't care about my parole." Marydale looked up.

"You got beat up in jail," Kristen pleaded.

"It's worth it."

"I can't let that happen to you." Kristen felt tears well up in her eyes, and she felt the guard's gaze on her, and from the great distance of imagination, she felt her mother smile. *You always were my girl, Kristi.*

"If it means I can be with you..." Marydale began.

"Marydale, what if you got really hurt?"

Marydale pulled up the hem of her shirt. "See this?" She pointed at a faint scar on her side.

From the corner of the room, the guard warned, "Inmate!"

Marydale lowered her shirt. "I got pushed off a staircase at Holten. I hit the railing below. And here." She touched her top lip above the missing tooth. "I can barely remember this. I think there was a fight. It had nothing to do with me. You know how I stopped the bleeding? Salt. You mix it with deodorant or toothpaste. It stings like hell, but it doesn't matter." She leaned forward, her breasts heaving with her breath. "It's just a body. You know what it's like to be a rodeo queen? It puts you on the other side. Everyone thinks if they were beautiful enough, somehow everything would be different. But you get up on that float with everyone looking, and you know how much it's really worth."

"I'm sorry," Kristen whispered.

Marydale's skin looked pale against her uniform, but she was still so incredibly beautiful. Kristen thought, *You're wrong. It matters. It makes a difference.*

"I'll get another PO," Marydale said. "Cody will quit eventually. Ronald will forget about me."

"I can't get a job here," Kristen said. "I worked hard to go to law school."

Marydale leaned back, running her hands through her hair, staring up at the ceiling. "I know. I know. I know."

"And I have to set an example for Sierra," Kristen said. "I can't tell Sierra that I gave up on my career, that I'm with a felon. She's got no one in her life except me, and if I make a bad choice—"

"A bad choice?"

"Marydale, you're different…what happened to you… but Sierra won't understand that…and this isn't a life. We're not a couple." Kristen heard her words bounce off the cement walls. She looked around, surprised that no one was staring at them. "We can't *be* together." She lowered her voice. "We can't cook a dinner or see a movie or get a drink or buy groceries or wake up in the same bed. We can't even go to the next county together. Your parole officer can come into your house at any time without a warrant. They could come in when we were…together. They could drag you away. They could beat you. And it would be my fault for staying. That's not a relationship."

"We could run." Marydale laughed, but there was no joy in her voice. "I know where there's a trailer and an old well on BLM land."

Tears stung Kristen's eyes.

"Will you call me?" Marydale asked.

Kristen took a deep breath. She felt like she was standing on the edge of the Firesteed Mountains, looking out at the future. She would move back to Portland and go out for flights of pinot noir with Donna and talk about firm politics. Marydale would call, and it would get harder and harder to find anything to say. And there would be a man eventually, an associate attorney with thinning hair and a good eye for personal finance, and Marydale would still be waiting, longing, dreaming, because Kristen wasn't the one sparkling exception in Marydale's life. Marydale was gay. She always would be. She wanted a girlfriend. She probably wanted to pick out a cat together. If she lived in Portland, she'd have a Prius covered in rainbow flag stickers.

"I don't think I should call you." Kristen laid the words out carefully one by one. "I think that would be too hard for you…and for me. And I don't want you to hope for something that won't happen. I can't be what you need."

"You are, Kristen." Marydale dropped her face into her hands again.

"Maybe we'll see each other sometime," Kristen said. "Maybe in Portland. Maybe we'll be walking down a little cobblestone street in Old Town, and there we'll be. Who knows? You never know. We can't know. But right now I have to go, and I think a clean break…"

She couldn't bear to finish the sentence. She couldn't touch Marydale under the guards' watchful gaze. And as she left the jail, she felt like someone fleeing a burning building because there were only two choices: to save herself or to burn together.

Part Two

Five Years Later

1

Kristen Brock stood in the Falcon Law Group's conference room beside the floor-to-ceiling windows. On the street below, the first snow in five years blanketed the Pearl District. In her hand, she held the obligatory piece of Black Forest cake from the Windsor Bakery. Rutger Falcon had even asked his paralegal to open a couple bottles of champagne, from which the firm was drinking with sober discretion.

"I'd like to take this moment to thank all of you for being an essential part of the Falcon Law Group," Falcon began.

The senior partners continued their conversation in the corner of the room. At the far end of the conference table, the paralegals nodded in inverse proportion to how essential they actually were. The youngest, Willow—whom Kristen guessed they had hired either for her father's political connections or for her amazingly buoyant breasts—beamed and bobbed her head up and down.

"I know we get busy during the year," Falcon went on. "I don't always take the time to appreciate each one of you the way I should, so I'd like to say it today."

When he was done, Willow bounced up and down, her breasts levitating in front of her.

"Guess what time it is?" She didn't wait for an answer. "It's eleven fifty-eight." It was almost noon. "Let's have a count-down!"

Donna Li sidled over to Kristen. "Stick a pin in her," she said. "See if she pops."

The girl pulled out her cell phone, waited a moment, and then counted. "Ten, nine, eight…Happy New Year!" She giggled. "Happy new afternoon."

A moment later, Falcon joined Kristen and Donna by the window. "So, Ms. Brock. Are you celebrating the New Year with anything better than sheet cake?" he asked.

The Windsor cake probably cost upward of four hundred dollars.

"Strippers and cocaine," Kristen said with a shrug that said *I'm kidding, but I don't care if you get it*. She'd earned the right to joke with Rutger Falcon a year earlier, when she won the Mesterland case and netted the firm almost half a million dollars.

"You're going to spend all night working on DataBlast, aren't you?" Falcon clamped his hand on her shoulder the way he did with men in the firm.

"You got me," Kristen said.

"Says the woman who's going to make partner," Falcon added.

Before Mesterland it was *the girl who* wants *to make partner.*

Kristen nodded. "It's an important case."

Falcon squeezed her shoulder and moved on to honor the next employee with half a minute of small talk.

"So what are you really doing?" Donna asked.

"Working on the DataBlast case."

"How's it going?"

"Still looking for the unicorn."

"Someone who's willing to talk?"

"And who knows what they're talking about. They all know the company was up to something, but some guy at the call center isn't going to know how and when."

"You think you'll get someone on New Year's Eve?"

"Somebody's day drinking and wondering what they're doing with their life," Kristen said. "I'm here to provide an opportunity for them to unburden themselves."

Donna skewered her fork in the middle of her cake and set it down. "Smart," she said. "So, what I was thinking was this. Once we find your so-called unicorn…"

Kristen gazed down at the street a story below. A toddler slipped in the snow, and his father scooped him up. The doors to the Market of Choice opened and half a dozen girls spilled out, their scarves flapping in a parade of pinks and yellows. And for a moment Kristen saw a familiar flash of blond hair, a girl turning her face to the sky.

Marydale!

But of course it wasn't. It was just the sudden, unexpected miracle of snow—so rare, the city didn't have enough plows to clear the bridges, let alone the streets—that made Kristen see Marydale in the face of passing strangers. When she had first returned to Portland five years earlier, she had imagined Marydale everywhere. Now she went whole weeks without thinking of her.

"I'm going to get back to it," Kristen said, setting her uneaten cake on the table next to Donna's. "I've got to get to my day drinkers before they forget exactly how DataBlast cheated a quarter million suckers out of their money."

Two hours later, Kristen had placed almost thirty calls, mostly to voice mails. Around her, the office was quiet except for the occasional whir of the fax machine. Even Donna had headed across the river for dinner at the Golden Lucky Fortune with her parents and then off to a party at which she would, almost certainly, break her record of twelve months without a dysfunctional romance.

Kristen's phone rang. She picked it up quickly. "Falcon Law Group. Kristen Brock speaking."

"Happy New Year!" It was Sierra. In the background, cheers and whistles told Kristen she had found day drinkers, just not the day drinkers she was looking for.

"Kristi!" Sierra said. "We're heading out in about an hour. Do you want a ride?"

"A ride?"

"To the Deerfield Hotel for the whiskey festival. Do you want us to pick you up? We've got four-wheel drive, and don't say you've got too much work to do."

"I... The Deerfield Hotel is all the way out in Troutdale. The roads are a mess."

Someone turned up the music on Sierra's end.

"You forgot." Sierra's voice was still cheerful. "How can you be a lawyer and you can't even remember New Year's Eve? You have to come! We have to catch up!"

Just that morning, Kristen had vowed to be a better sister. It wasn't just a New Year's resolution. It was a holiday-season resolution, a birthday resolution, a solstice resolution. The thought had probably crossed her mind on Arbor Day.

"I am so sorry," Kristen said.

"We talked about this," Sierra whined. "We did!"

Kristen tried to remember the conversation. Sierra had mentioned something about New Year's Eve... about an open bar at the historic hotel. Kristen had thought it sounded like a tort waiting to happen. Had she also said yes?

"I... look... I don't have anyone to watch Meatball. That's my fault. I forgot. We'll get together later. I promise. We'll have tea at the Heathman."

The light for the second line flashed on Kristen's phone. She scrawled the incoming number on the back of a file.

"You missed the Halloween party." Sierra's voice had lost a bit of its cheer. "You missed vegan Thanksgiving. And I saw you for, like, two seconds on Kwanzaa. Tonight's going to be great. They're going to have tastings and three different local bands. Fishbowl Pocket Moon is playing! They never play small shows! This is once in a lifetime. This is bucket list. And you said you'd come. And it's snowing!"

On the street below, a pair of young businessmen picked

up handfuls of snow and threw it at each other. The snow made Portland happy. Stores closed and restaurants served pancakes. Even the partners had been calling other firms, checking on their fax lines and their copiers. *If you need anything, just give us a call.* It made Kristen sad. In a few days it would all melt, and the partners would go back to yelling at each other's receptionists. And no one's life would have been transformed, not that Kristen wanted her life to change, she reminded herself. A woman in her midthirties about to make partner at the Falcon Law Group was exactly where she was supposed to be.

"I wouldn't be any fun," Kristen said. "I've got so much work to do."

"It's a whole whiskey-tasting thing. I picked it because you love whiskey," Sierra said. "This is for you."

"I don't love whiskey."

"You always have a bottle of that awful Poisonwood stuff."

"Yes. Right. I know."

There had been a moment, five years earlier, when she could have told her sister everything. Instead she had told Sierra that she left Tristess because big-firm work offered more growth potential. *You have to think about a career, not just a job,* she had said. A moment later, Kristen had realized it was the wrong lie. She could just as well have said, *I came back to Portland to be closer to you.* Now they were the kind of sisters who didn't see each other for months on end even though they lived in the same city.

"It's really nice of you to think of me," Kristen said.

She was ready to interject over Sierra's protests, but Sierra said nothing for several seconds. Then she said, "Okay," with a finality that Kristen had never heard before. "I don't want to force you to spend time with me."

In the background, Kristen heard a man ask, "Is everything okay? She's coming, right?"

"Wait." Kristen exhaled heavily. "Does this place you're going...? Do they take dogs?"

Sierra's voice brightened again. "Of course they take dogs!"

"I have to make a few more phone calls," Kristen said reluctantly.

"We'll pick up Meatball, and I'll pack you a bag. You can work right up until we leave. We'll honk the horn when we get there. I know your window."

"We?" Kristen asked, but Sierra was already hanging up, saying, "You'd better be there when we get there."

Two hours later, Sierra arrived in her company car, a retrofitted, first-generation Range Rover with BIODIESEL emblazoned across the top, like a warning to low-flying drones. Reluctantly, Kristen headed downstairs. Sierra was already standing on the snowy sidewalk.

"We're going to have so much fun. I promise!" Sierra said. She glanced at Kristen's Burberry coat open over her gray suit. "Look at you. See? You *are* ready for a party."

Kristen did not point out that Burberry and Max Mara weren't whiskey-festival attire. It didn't matter. The moment to avoid the trip had passed, and now she was committed.

In the backseat of the SUV sat two men, their hair pulled

up in matching buns on top of their heads. One wore a sweater with snowflakes embroidered on it. The other wore a heavy canvas skirt with pockets and loops for as-yet-unidentified tools. It was Frog and Moss. Kristen recognized them from half a dozen house parties she had stayed at just long enough to pound a vodka-spiked kombucha and invent a crisis in the office to call her away.

Meatball sat on Frog's lap, his pointed ears twitching back and forth. The men motioned for her to take the front seat, smiling encouragingly. Sierra had probably regaled them with stories of Kristen, her sad, workaholic sister who preferred a normal office job to pressing apple cider by hand or drawing mandalas of her vagina or whatever the latest edition of Sierra's online magazine, the *HumAnarchist*, suggested the readers try.

Sierra hopped back into the driver's seat, offering a high five to both of the men. "And we're off!" she said.

Frog leaned forward and grinned at Kristen. He had a remarkable array of milk-chocolate-colored freckles.

"You want a joint?" he asked.

"No!"

"It's legal," Sierra said, pulling a lighter out of her shirt pocket.

"It's not legal to smoke in a moving car," Kristen said.

Moss produced a plastic bag and pulled out something that looked like Silly Putty or human skin. Meatball whirled around with surprising agility and goggled at him, his bat ears trembling slightly.

"Don't worry," the man said. "It's soy curl." He popped

the substance into Meatball's wide mouth. "Something for everyone, right?" He took the joint from Frog, and the smell of marijuana filled the Range Rover.

"Don't worry. I'm not smoking," Sierra said. "I'm driving."

"You'll get a contact high," Kristen said.

"That was just propaganda DuPont used to stop the production of hemp-based fiber products," Moss declared, shoveling another soy curl into Meatball's mouth.

"I'm so glad we're doing this," Sierra said, making more eye contact than Kristen thought appropriate for someone driving sixty-five miles an hour through what newscasters were dubbing *Snowpocalypse*. "I'm so psyched you could come, Kristen. We are going to have the time of our lives."

Kristen stared at the blur of highway, contemplating her own death at the hands of her sister's weed-addled driving.

"Please, watch the road," she pleaded. "I have things to live for. I'm going to make partner."

Sierra shot her a long, pointed look.

"Drive!" Kristen protested.

But a voice in the back of her mind said, *Partner, really? Another case? Another half marathon? Another corporate banquet? Would it make her happy?* A glimpse of Marydale's face flickered across her memory like the last frames of a black-and-white movie, but it was just the snow. It made the city look like Christmas and the end of the world all at once, and it made it easy to revisit old memories, Kristen told herself. For the rest of the drive, she forced herself to think through the details of the DataBlast case, making a mental list of all the people she had called and all the calls she had yet to make.

By the time they reached the historic Deerfield complex, the sun had set and the parking lot was blanketed with white. The early cars were already snowed under. More recent arrivals were parked at odd angles, wedged around mounds of snow. Kristen's foot had cramped from pressing an imaginary brake pedal as Sierra flew, albeit without mishap, along the icy highway. Now Kristen climbed out, accompanied by a wave of marijuana smoke. She teetered a little bit as her heels slipped on the packed snow.

"Kristen." Sierra placed her hand on Kristen's laptop bag. "You don't need this. It's New Year's Eve."

"I'll just put it in my room," Kristen said.

"But you're carrying the psychic weight."

Reluctantly, Kristen handed it over. "Lock it up, okay?" she said.

Sierra snatched the briefcase, calling out to her friend, "Frog, do you have Meatball's jacket? Moss, grab my bag, would you?"

Frog and Moss were a couple, but the whole trio moved like one organism, handing bags back and forth and steadying each other on the ice. Sierra had known the men since her first days at Portland Community College, which seemed strange to Kristen since the only friend she had carried over from childhood, college, or law school was Donna Li, and sometimes she wondered if that even counted as a friendship.

Frog came around the side of the Range Rover with Meatball in his arms like a large, plush bowling ball. Someone had put a green vest on the dog. There was a plastic tag clipped to the vest with a bar code and Kristen's name written in black Sharpie with a date.

Realization dawned on Kristen as she read the word SER-VICE on Meatball's vest.

"They don't take dogs," she said.

She wondered how long it would take to get a cab home.

"Of course they do," Sierra said. "They have to. It's the law. Moss made the vest today out of a recycled army duffel bag. Reduce. Reuse. Recycle. Re-peace! It fits perfectly."

"No," Kristen said. "No. You can't do that."

Frog placed Meatball in Kristen's arms and attached an official-looking green lead in place of Meatball's usual blue rhinestone leash.

"All you have to do is walk him into the hotel and put him in your room," Sierra said. "He might as well be a service dog."

"He eats underwear, and he has a brain the size of a walnut. He would walk off a cliff if there were Cheetos at the bottom. What is he protecting me from?" Kristen checked the tag. "What does this even say?"

"He's for anxiety."

"I don't have anxiety. Do you know what will happen if I get cited for forging a service-dog license? For bringing an unauthorized pet into an eating establishment?"

"His mouth is cleaner that yours," Sierra said.

"It's fraud," Kristen protested.

Frog draped his arm around Sierra's shoulder and leaned his head against her blond dreadlocks. "Namaste. It's all good. We're all in service to each other."

"This is supposed to be fun," Sierra said quietly. "Come on, Kristi. Please. Don't make me feel like I dragged you here."

Kristen sighed inwardly, remembering her resolve to be nicer to Sierra. She was going to invite her to coffee and have sister-to-sister chats about men or face cream or, God help her, the latest issue of the *HumAnarchist*. She was going to say things like, *I'm so proud of how you've accomplished the goals you set for yourself,* but when it came down to the end of a busy week, Kristen just wanted to sit on her sofa and watch the sunset reflecting off the mirrored surface of the U.S. Bancorp building.

She glanced back toward the highway, just visible on the horizon. A single semitruck crawled across the ice.

"Okay," Kristen managed.

Despite everything, the Deerfield complex was beautiful. The main hotel glittered from behind a screen of trees. Behind it, outbuildings, now converted to tiny bars, added their pinpricks of light. Inside, the halls were hung with eerie American-primitive paintings: ghostly women in pillbox hats, carnivals of skeletons dancing on barroom tables. In the hallways, the red carpet swerved back and forth across the floor like a vision in a fun house mirror.

Sierra handed out keycards. She held Kristen's for a moment.

"Half an hour," Sierra said. "If you're not at the bar, I'm coming to get you."

In her room, Kristen sat down on the bed, staring at a mural of cavorting watermelons with little fangs and human eyes. Meatball planted himself on the bed. She tossed him one of the soy curls as she left.

An hour later, Kristen was crowded into a subterranean bar, feeling overdressed in her suit. She pulled up the last vacant seat by a teetering bistro table.

"I'll just sit here," she told Sierra and her friends.

Moss handed her a foldout map with several business logos printed on it.

"They're doing a whiskey tasting," Moss said. "If you try all twelve, you get a free T-shirt."

It seemed like a bad idea. Why invite guests to have one drink in one bar, when they could stumble around fifty acres of hipster-inspired landscaping, in the dark, collecting booze stamps?

"This one is Sadfire whiskey." Sierra read, "'Portland's newest distillery, Sadfire, has been selling commercially for only two years, but in that time has won several distinguished prizes, including the Multnomah Whiskey Exposition's Best Whiskey Under Ten Years and the Portland Better Business Bureau's Community-Engaged Small-Business Award.' Look. They employ felons to give them *a second chance through productive employment*."

"Because that's a good idea," Kristen said. "Put felons in a factory with a thousand gallons of whiskey."

She was thinking about Marydale.

"It's important to give people a chance to rehabilitate," Moss said.

"I know," Kristen said quietly.

But Marydale hadn't rehabilitated. Maybe she hadn't had the chance. After Kristen left Tristess, she had looked Marydale up on the statewide database that tracked parolees. Marydale had been released a month after Kristen left Tristess, then arrested again a month after that. She had been jailed, released, and jailed again and again.

Kristen told herself she was lucky to have left when she did, to have put enough time and distance between their affair and her office at the Falcon Law Group. But every time she had seen Marydale's name next to a new parole sanction, she had felt a cold ache in her stomach, until one day she exited the database and promised never to look again.

Sierra threw her arm around Kristen, snapped a selfie, and then shoved the camera at Kristen so she could see the picture. A diet of protein bars and a five-day schedule of running had defined Kristen's cheekbones like a sculptor's chisel. *Pretty or lucky?* she wondered.

A trio of musicians in the corner struck up a little accompaniment.

Sierra eased up to the back of the crowd, rising on tiptoes. "She's eating fire!" she said. "Come on. Get over here and check this out."

Kristen couldn't see much more than polar fleece and the occasional Portland Timbers sweatshirt. The crowd hushed.

Kristen heard a man at the front of the crowd say, "Now

I'm going to let my colleague tell you about what you're going to taste." A few people clapped.

A melodic woman's voice chimed in. "Thank you. We both come from a farming-ranching background, so we understand the importance of raw ingredients. We have our own twelve-acre farm north of St. John's."

The room was hot.

Sierra said, "It's really crowded. Do you want to try the next one?"

"We put our heart and soul into this production." The woman's voice floated over the crowd.

Kristen couldn't see her, but the cadence was familiar. It was the same slight twang that had infused Marydale's voice when she told stories about Tristess.

The man interrupted. "My friend here actually waters the ground with her tears."

The crowd chuckled.

"No, I'm serious," the man said. "The first night after planting she goes out to the fields—"

"And you're going to taste all of that," the woman cut in, "when I pour the first round."

Kristen edged forward, listening.

"What is it?" Sierra asked.

The couple in front of Kristen stepped to the side, and Kristen stepped into the space they had vacated. Behind a folding table covered in a black cloth, a banner read SADFIRE DISTILLERS. On either side of the table, a bronze contraption, like some steampunk creation from the Alberta Arts Walk, released a blaze of flame. But Kristen wasn't admiring the craftsmanship or thinking about the liability of open flames in a low-ceilinged room almost certainly over the 148-person capacity listed by the door. She wasn't thinking about anything now, because she wasn't breathing, because it *was* Marydale behind the table, like a vision in a dream. Her blond hair was pulled up in an aggressive bouffant ponytail, and her arms were tattooed in a swirl of oxblood and black, the bodies of women intertwining in the ink. She looked older and tougher and gorgeous.

"So what are we going to taste, Mary?" It was Aldean beside her.

Marydale took a skewer from the table, wrapped a piece of cotton around the end and dipped it into a snifter.

"We're going to start with the Consummation Rye," Marydale said. She flicked the end of the skewer through the flame at her side, tilted her head back, opened her mouth, and, accompanied by the "ooh" of the crowd, she lowered the torch into her mouth. The flame disappeared. She set the skewer down and lifted the snifter to her lips and, in flagrant violation of Oregon Liquor Control Commission server regulations, took a long sip.

"Well played," her friend said. "What do you taste, Mary?"

Marydale turned to Aldean. "You're going to find this surprisingly smooth for such a young whiskey, although it does still have a bite, and I think that's part of its charm. It's going to mellow, but you're going to miss its youth."

Kristen felt the stiff, gray fabric of her suit holding her

in place. Marydale was there, only feet away, real, breathing, her hair glistening. Kristen had practiced this moment in her imagination a thousand times, this exact moment when their eyes met and Marydale recognized her.

For just a second, Marydale seemed to lose her train of thought. Then she resumed. "Large commercial distilleries produce consistent quality, but they sacrifice character."

Kristen had dreamed about this reunion. She had seen Marydale in the crowds around Pioneer Square and in the quick flash of a TriMet window, her face forever disappearing into another person's image. A rational voice in the back of her mind told Kristen she was overreacting. The strange longing that filled her when she thought of Marydale was just the first pangs of middle age creeping into her thirties. It was the kind of nostalgia Sierra and Donna would never feel because Sierra lived in a semi-platonic, semi-polyamorous partnership with Frog and Moss, and Donna dated a never-ending roster of assholes.

Marydale held the glass up to the flame. Someone lowered the lights, making dark shadows of Marydale's eyes.

"First," she said, "you'll smell the earth. Now, don't let those wine connoisseurs get away with telling you it smells *earthy*, like that's a thing. Earth is specific. Farmers know that. This is our parcel." She smelled the whiskey. "If you're very careful—and please don't drink to excess because you'll miss everything—you can smell the roots of our heritage oak. Yes. Aldean is right. They're there, too." She put the glass to her lips and took another sip. "It's frost on a really clear day in December when you're lonely despite all the

Christmas going on around you. You can also taste summer's wildfires. This batch was aged in barrels made out of ten percent reclaimed wood from the Firesteed burn. And if you haven't seen one of those fires up close, you haven't looked into the eye of God."

The crowd hushed.

"Now, here I've got a little bit of water," Marydale went on. "It's from Multnomah Falls, and, friends, even if you don't take your whiskey with water, you need to at least *taste* it with water. Water opens the whiskey up." She poured a little bit of water from a silver pitcher and smelled it again. "There it is." She paused and looked directly at Kristen. "Your old lover's perfume woken from the leather seat of your pickup the day you take it to the scrap yard. The body. Lovemaking. Loan. Madrone bark in sunlight. The pencil you once used to write love letters." Her voice grew louder. She raised the glass to the crowd. "A woman's hair slick with sweat. That first taste, so strange and so familiar." She took a sip of the whiskey, set it down, and beamed at the crowd. Her teeth were perfect.

The crowd applauded.

"That, friends, is how you taste a whiskey," Aldean said.

The lights brightened. The crowd moved toward the table or away, depending on their desire to taste oak tree and Marydale's tears. Kristen stood frozen, staring at Marydale, because the reasonable voice in the back of her head had gone silent. All she heard was the beat of blood in her ears.

"Are you going to taste?" Sierra asked.

Frog and Moss appeared beside them, smelling of marijuana. Frog draped his long arms around Sierra's shoulders. She took his hands.

"Fishbowl Pocket Moon is playing in the Tiny Barn Bar," he said.

"I can't," Kristen hissed to Sierra.

"You are not going to go back to your room to work," Sierra said.

"Just go," Kristen said.

Kristen glanced at Marydale and looked away.

"What is it?" Sierra touched Kristen's arm.

"Nothing."

When Sierra had left and the crowd had thinned, Kristen made her way to the front of the room. Behind the table, Marydale and Aldean moved in perfect coordination, pouring samples, opening bottles, and clearing away the little plastic tasting cups without ever bumping into each other.

Marydale smiled as Kristen approached the table, but it was the same smile she had just offered a trio of college girls ahead of Kristen.

"What can I pour for you? Tonight we're tasting the Wildfire Barrel Aged, the Consummation Rye, and the Solstice Vanilla Infusion."

Her gaze barely touched the surface of Kristen's face

"Marydale, it's me. Kristen."

"Kristen Brock. I know."

Aldean tossed a bottle in Marydale's direction, and she caught it behind her back.

"Thanks, man." To Kristen she added, "What'll it be? Are

you doing the whiskey passport? Can I stamp your card?"

The whiskey passport? Kristen held the flyer in her hand, crumpled and damp.

"I…" She stopped, stricken by Marydale's easy smile.

"How about I make you a sidecar," Marydale said. She pulled a few bottles out of a cooler behind her. "On the house." She poured a few ingredients in a shaker and then handed a plastic cup to Kristen. "Nice to see you, Kristen."

A group of men in kilts moved in behind Kristen, and Marydale turned her smile in their direction. Unconsciously, Kristen touched her own lip. It was strange to see Marydale's smile unmarred. It was strange to see her older, but Kristen was older, too. Everyone who saw old pictures of her said she'd changed. And she had an irrational urge to run up to Marydale and plead, *It's me, Kristen*, as though Marydale had turned away because she didn't recognize her.

Instead Kristen made her way out of the bar and into the snow. Dazed, she stood for a long time, not drinking, not moving, just clutching the cup in her hand. The door to the bar opened. A few hotel guests passed her, nodding a greeting.

Someone said, "Can't believe this snow."

Kristen heard someone else speaking in her own voice, saying, "They say we haven't gotten a snow like this since 2006," as though she cared about the weather, as though she had ever looked up comparative snowfalls in Portland, as though she didn't want to lie down in the snow and cry at Marydale's casual *nice to see you, Kristen.*

With that thought, Kristen dumped her drink in the

snow. If work at the Falcon Law Group had taught her nothing else, it had taught her to confront. She marched back into the bar. Marydale was describing the complexities of the Solstice Vanilla to a pair of middle-aged women.

"I need to talk to you," Kristen said. It sounded like she was hounding opposing counsel.

Marydale and Aldean exchanged a look. Then he leaned over and whispered something in Marydale's ear. Her face said *no*, but she nodded.

"Okay."

Outside, Marydale said, "Yes? What?"

"I'm surprised to see you here," Kristen said. She could feel the snow seeping in around her pumps, dampening her nylons.

A group of people poured out of the bar, blowing paper horns.

"It's almost midnight," someone called out.

"You thought I'd be in jail?" Marydale asked.

"No. I…" She was still holding the empty cup. "This was good."

Around them, the snow had transformed the bushes into a menagerie of mythical beasts all shrouded in white. Above them, an old water tower stood sentinel over the grounds, an orange light at its base illuminating it in a sepia glow.

"So?" Marydale said. "I'm working. What can I do for you?"

Snowflakes dissolved on Kristen's glasses, blurring her vision.

"How have you been?" Kristen asked. The question felt small.

Marydale gave a little laugh but said nothing.

"So you work at a distillery?" It was small talk, like all the legal banquets she had attended on behalf of Falcon Law Group. *So I hear you're with a new firm. Yes. Patents. How interesting.*

"I own a distillery," Marydale said. "Me and Aldean do."

"And you're in Portland." *You're here.* "Are you living on the east side?"

Marydale raised an eyebrow, a calculated expression as deliberate as a handshake. "Are we really going to do this?" she asked.

"I haven't seen you for years." It sounded like an accusation.

"Five years," Marydale said. "It's a small city. We were bound to run into each other eventually." She turned her palm up to the sky and caught a snowflake that melted immediately.

"I'd like to give you my number." Kristen was shivering, and her words came out in choppy bursts like Morse code. "We could do tapas at Nel Centro or tea at the Heathman. Is your distillery in the city? I could meet you there."

Marydale looked at her. "Why?"

Kristen felt her heart tighten in her chest. Marydale looked so beautiful, like a new incarnation of the girl Kristen remembered. Older. Brighter. Sharper. Her sleeves rolled up. Her tattoos a splash of color against the white snow. The cold didn't seem to touch her.

"We knew each other." Kristen wanted to grab Marydale by the shoulders, to grip the fabric of her shirt and hang on. "I don't think it's unreasonable to get coffee."

"Unreasonable." Marydale's lips curled in a wry frown. "It's been a long time. I'm not exactly hard to find."

"I…I looked you up."

"Ah," Marydale said, her face registering a rebuff. *I could have found you, but I didn't.*

"I mean, I didn't want you to get in trouble with your parole officer…We said…" *I said.* Kristen never fumbled in court, never said one word or made one gesture that wasn't calculated to accomplish her ends. Now she felt the conversation slipping out of her control. *I missed you*, she thought, while she heard herself say, "My firm has an excellent Web presence. If you don't want to take my number, you can just look me up."

Marydale turned away, and Kristen gazed at her profile outlined in snow. Her lips were full and glistened with a touch of gloss. There were a few fine lines beside her eyes, a faint shadow beneath them, the kind of imperfections Kristen hid behind her glasses, but they didn't look like imperfections on Marydale.

"In my experience, these things are always better if you're just honest," Marydale said.

"These things?"

Marydale shrugged. "We don't even know each other. Let's skip the brunches and just chalk it up to life experience. If you'd wanted to find me, you would have." With that, Marydale turned and headed back into the bar.

"Wait," Kristen said.

"This is a coincidence," Marydale called out behind her. "This is New Year's Eve. It's snowing. It doesn't change anything."

Kristen took a few steps and stopped. She steadied herself against a mound of snow, the icy crust burning her fingers.

"Marydale," she whispered.

And there was the truth, realized, as if in dream, impossible and absolute: she had loved Marydale, and when she had left Tristess, the trajectory of her life had stopped, and she had done *nothing*.

2

Kristen made her way back toward the hotel complex like a patient in receipt of bad news. She wasn't even sure how she found the bar where Sierra and her friends were listening to the band. Inside the humid room, Frog moved from guest to guest, anointing them with glitter gel from a little pot. As Kristen entered, he approached her with a finger full of goop. Before Kristen could protest, he had smeared it on Kristen's cheek. It smelled like patchouli.

"Happy New Year," he said.

Kristen wiped at the cold gel.

The bar was crowded, the guests in everything from cocktail dresses to cargoes. Reluctantly, she took a seat with Sierra and Moss.

Moss adjusted his man-skirt and leaned in to listen to Sierra.

"Sometimes I think we've gotten too big," she said, projecting her voice over the music. "You know? What happened to running everything out of a van and a laptop?"

Ordinarily, Kristen would have pointed out that running an online magazine from a dilapidated bungalow, with a sagging green roof, in which one or two (or six or more) people lived at any given time, was hardly selling out to corporate America. As it was, she just stared past Sierra at the crowd of revelers.

"We were following our heart path back then," Moss said.

"That's what I'm talking about," Sierra said. "Are we doing what we set out to?" Her eyes were bright, and Kristen guessed she had gotten there via a fully stamped whiskey passport.

The trio continued their conversation. Sierra thought maybe they should demonetize the *HumAnarchist* blog. Moss had been researching his great-grandfather's logging camp. He wanted to write a story on the birth of the lumbersexual. He was thinking about getting the periodic table tattooed on his arm, to help him *remember the fundamentals.*

Kristen checked her phone. She wished there were a way to hurry the clock to midnight so they could toast. Sierra could kiss her entourage. Kristen could retreat to her room. She was so lost in thought that it took her a moment to realize Sierra was talking to her.

"Hey, it's that bartender," Sierra said. "Did you know her?"

Kristen turned quickly, gracelessly, her eyes meeting Marydale's instantly. She stared. Marydale had traced her lips in a dark red lipstick and traded the Sadfire T-shirt for a black blouse with a Western-style yoke, her sleeves rolled up to reveal her tattoos. Everyone in Portland had tattoos, and everyone wanted to be a cowgirl hipster, but somehow it was clear Marydale wasn't being ironic. She hadn't fashioned an image of herself after her logger grandfather, and she hadn't gotten the tattoos to reject the corporatizing of her profitable anarchist blog. She just *was*: motionless and beautiful and stern. And Kristen thought of all the attractive attorneys she'd argued against or chaired cases with—so many pretty women—yet not one of them could touch Marydale's beauty.

"Who is she?" Frog asked, descending on the table in a wave of patchouli.

They were all looking at Marydale.

"Marydale Rae," Kristen said.

Sierra glanced at Kristen.

Marydale leaned against the bar, one foot kicked up behind her, her glass held loosely between her fingers. Still there was something tense about her posture.

"Excuse me," Kristen said, and rose.

It took a long time to make her way through the crowded room, and she lost sight of Marydale twice. *If she leaves*, Kristen thought. *If she says no*... Part of her wanted to flee, to face whatever catastrophe the roads had become. Run back to her room, grab Meatball, drive south until she escaped the snow and the rain and the city with its blue-gray high-rises, to drive until she reached some sunburned street named *Jacinto* or *Reina del Valle* and became someone she had never met before.

Marydale set her drink down on the bar as Kristen approached.

"You came back," Kristen said.

Marydale regarded her. "I didn't leave."

There was something there. Kristen felt it. "I'm glad."

Marydale's eyes were a sharp, clear blue like the world before smog. She cocked her head to one side and brushed her own cheek, looking significantly at Kristen.

"What happened there?" she asked.

Kristen rubbed at her face and looked at the glitter on her fingers.

"My sister's friend."

Kristen could feel Sierra watching them.

"It doesn't suit you," Marydale said.

Kristen gazed at the color on Marydale's arms. A woman blended into a dragon that blended into a wave, not the familiar coloring-book lines of tattoo-parlor samples, but a sweep of real brushwork as though an artist had painted the scene on her body.

"An ex did them for me."

Marydale extended her arm with her wrist up so that Kristen could examine the work. Kristen reached out to touch her, then stopped.

"An ex?"

"You didn't think I'd just been pining for you," Marydale said, her tone both bitter and flirtatious.

Kristen swallowed, trying to think of what to say besides *yes*, because that was exactly what Marydale had been doing in every dream she'd had about her: pining. Now, looking up at Marydale's sardonic smile, Kristen wondered what cool Portland whiskey drinker *wouldn't* want Marydale. She could have her pick of any man or woman in the bar.

The band played a final chord.

The lead singer called out, "Everyone! It's time. Ten, nine…"

The room counted with him.

"Three, two, one." The room cheered. The band struck up the melancholy notes of "Auld Lang Syne."

"I…" Kristen stopped.

"You?" Marydale said, and when Kristen said nothing, Marydale stepped forward so quickly Kristen stepped back. Marydale did not let her retreat. She gripped the back of Kristen's head and pressed her lips to Kristen's. A second later, she drew away. Her lipstick had smeared. Kristen touched her own lips and transferred the color to her fingers. She looked around, startled to find that no one was looking. It seemed like the whole room should be staring because everything in the entire world had changed.

"Would you like to go back to the hotel?" Marydale asked, her voice a soft drawl.

Kristen nodded.

"I'm not inviting you to have tea," Marydale added.

"I don't want tea."

Marydale produced a jacket of some heavy, canvas material and draped it over Kristen's shoulders.

When they were outside, Marydale said, "We'll have to go to your room. I was supposed to go home tonight."

She took Kristen's hand, her palm rough with calluses.

Kristen did not know if she led Marydale to the main hotel building or if Marydale led her. Their clasped hands felt more like a contract than a gesture of affection.

Inside, the hotel was quiet. The carpet swerved beneath their feet. The eerie paintings gazed down at them from both sides, little doll girls with large eyes and Cheshire-style cats with grinning fangs.

"Everybody wants to be a hipster," Kristen said.

Marydale looked pointedly at Kristen's suit. "Not you."

Kristen glanced up at her. *Not you*, she thought.

Kristen's room was on the second floor, with a window onto the snowy grounds. Marydale pulled the sheer curtains closed, letting in a filter of moonlight. Then very slowly, very deliberately, she removed Kristen's glasses, set them on an end table, and kissed her. They said nothing. Kristen's whole body felt like a tightly strung instrument, and she could not remember the last time she had felt this way, if she ever had—even with Marydale. Their first kisses in Tristess had been gentle and searching. Now desire seized Kristen's body. She tried to part her legs, to feel the welcome pressure of Marydale's thigh intertwining with hers, but her narrow skirt thwarted contact. Marydale seemed to sense her distress, although Kristen could not tell if she shared it.

Marydale guided her back until she was leaning against the wall. Kristen grabbed Marydale's ass through her pants. Kristen could hear her own breath in her ears.

"I missed you," she said, although what she felt was darker and more dazzling.

"Really?" Marydale murmured. "I think you're just trying to get me into bed."

They were standing very close, their breath mingling. A moment later, Marydale's hands were in her hair. The calluses on her palms scratched the back of Kristen's neck, and it seemed to Kristen that nothing had ever felt so erotic or so intimate. She needed to feel the same touch on the most delicate parts of her body.

With one hand, Marydale braced herself against the wall. The other hand she slid down Kristen's side, cupping her breast. Then she drew two fingers across the waist of Kristen's skirt to the place where the fabric pulled tight over Kristen's sex. Kristen tried to spread her legs, but the skirt held them tight. On this taut drum of fabric, Marydale stroked a slow circle.

Kristen couldn't stand the faint touch exactly where she needed more, and she pulled the hem of her skirt up to her waist so Marydale could reach her. In the back of her mind, she wondered why she hadn't been having sex with everyone all the time because the blend of torment and indulgence felt so good.

At the same time, she knew; she had been with men. She could have been with women if she'd wanted. And the men she had dated recently were good lovers, better than thoughtful, passionate even. And she always came away from sex feeling embarrassed both by her reticence and her own attempts to hide it behind half-feigned cries of pleasure.

Now she whispered, "Fuck me," and she meant it.

Marydale pressed her fingers into the seam of her nylons.

The fabric muffled the touch. Kristen pressed her forehead against Marydale's neck.

"Now. Please. Marydale, I can't wait." She bit down hard on Marydale's shoulder.

Marydale's lips brushed Kristen's ear. "I'm going to rip these, okay?"

Kristen nodded. "Do it."

Marydale made a quick, deft motion with both hands, and Kristen heard the fabric rend. Marydale slid a finger between the nylon and Kristen's underwear, stroking the damp cloth, the pressure of the pantyhose holding her touch close. Then gently, Marydale squeezed her thumb and her fingers together, capturing Kristen's labia through her underwear, massaging slowly. Inside the cloak of flesh and fabric, pleasure seared Kristen's clitoris, acute and insufficient. She closed her eyes. Marydale massaged her until Kristen was aware of only this one point of contact.

She only realized that the muscles behind her knees were giving way when Marydale caught her and wrapped an arm around her and guided her to the bed. Marydale leaned over her, increasing the pressure and speed of her ministrations. The orgasm built beneath Marydale's touch, inevitable and impossible at the same time.

"Oh." Kristen scratched the covers beneath her. "That's so…That's so…"

Marydale slipped her fingers beneath edge of Kristen's underwear, finding her clitoris. The sensation was exquisite. Kristen felt herself lifting closer and closer to an orgasm that rose just beyond her reach. She closed her eyes. Fragments of memory kaleidoscoped behind her eyelids. Marydale's farm-house. A long, straight highway. A bare tree against a snowy sky.

"Marydale," she whispered, her eyes closed, her head thrown back. *I love you.*

Kristen felt herself grow smaller and smaller until she was nothing more than the tiny point of pleasure at the fulcrum of her body and Marydale's touch. Kristen tensed. Time stopped. Kristen poised on the edge of orgasm. Then she was coming, her body dissolving into Marydale's hand like sugar.

"You're amazing," Kristen said when she had caught her breath.

Marydale kissed her forehead. "A girl learns a few things in prison," she said, and her voice was light, but later, when Kristen tried to touch her, Marydale mounted her instead, pressing her damp body against Kristen's thigh. It felt good to feel Marydale's weight and watch her face strain, but at the same time, Marydale seemed far, far away.

When she rolled off Kristen, Kristen could not tell if Marydale had come, so she asked, "What can I do to make you happy?"

"Happy," Marydale said, as though it was a question she had pondered and forgotten. "This isn't supposed to make us happy."

3

Marydale rose and dressed quietly. Dawn was turning the hotel window into a square of deep blue. In the bed before her, Kristen slept, looking vulnerable, her glasses on the bed-side table, a length of blanket clutched in her arms. But even the women at Holten Penitentiary had looked vulnerable when they slept, and when Kristen woke, she wouldn't be the girl Marydale had kissed in the old farmhouse in Trist-ess. Gone was the girlish lawyer in her cheap, unlined suits. Gone was the baby fat. Gone was Kristen's hesitation, her uncertainty. *I've never done this with a girl before.* She was all sinew now, her body an accomplishment. It was a sign to other women: I've won.

Marydale felt a pang of sadness at the fact that she would never know which sport had turned Kristen's calves into hard muscle, would never watch Kristen cross a finish line, but she *wouldn't*. She had promised herself that as she waved goodbye to Aldean. *Be careful*, he had called after her. *I'm just curious.* She had saluted Aldean casually. *Hey, it's New Year's Eve.*

But it was more than New Year's Eve, and she wished she had something to leave Kristen, a little poem scrawled on one of the Deerfield postcards, something to say, *I remember.* She had a case of the Solstice Vanilla still left in her truck, but this new incarnation of Kristen Brock was no poet and no drinker. Even if it was true that the Solstice chilled with a large cube of ice had an aftertaste of tears, Kristen wouldn't know how many Marydale had shed for her. Even if she did, it didn't matter. Kristen had left, and she had not looked back, and maybe she had been right to leave all along.

Marydale's mournful thoughts were interrupted by the unnervingly unexpected presence of a bulldog sitting on an easy chair by the window, looking like an imperial toad or like one of the bizarre Deerfield Hotel paintings come to life. *I watched you*, it seemed to say. She couldn't imagine that she had entered the room, made love to Kristen, and slept through the night and not noticed the dog, but the thought that someone had snuck it into the room while they were sleeping, like some weird hipster room service, was equally implausible.

Tentatively she ran her hand over the dog's stony skull. It displayed a wide, pink smile. Marydale shook her head. She knew dogs, and it was certainly harmless. *Take care of her*, she mouthed, glancing at Kristen one last time. Then she slipped out the door, blinking back tears as she strode down the hall toward the snow and the blue dawn.

Outside, the early light was thin as skim milk and the

roads were packed with ice. Stranded cars littered the high-way, and it was almost ten by the time Marydale reached her houseboat, the *Tristess*, on the river beneath the St. John's Bridge. Next door, on the deck of the *Beautiful Wreck*, Aldean stood smoking a cigarette, shirtless in jeans and an old hunting jacket. With a shade of stubble on his cheeks, he looked like something out of an L.L.Bean catalog, what *country* was supposed to look like—minus the cigarette, of course.

Marydale made her way down the metal gangplank that led to their shared pier. "Happy New Year," she called out, trying for a cheer she did not feel.

"You're home early," Aldean said. "No breakfast after?"

"I'm going to make eggs," Marydale said. "That's break-fast." She threw one leg over the side of her boat. "You com-ing?"

A moment later, Aldean let himself into her kitchen, a cigarette still lit in one hand.

"Did you at least leave a note?" he asked.

Marydale handed Aldean a mug for the ashes. "Aren't you worried you'll get hooked again?" she asked. "It took you forever to quit."

Aldean sat down at the small counter that doubled as a dining table. Marydale cleared away a stack of sketches she'd done of a new still.

"That's why I only smoke on New Year's Day, and that's the point. People think the goal is to eliminate temptation, sin, vice, pleasure." Aldean inhaled. "Where would we be then? We run a distillery." He tapped his cigarette against the rim of the mug. "Temptation is where the human and the animal meet. Give up the craving for salt, and you give up the craving for blood."

"You're a fucking philosopher." Marydale reached into the micro-fridge for a carton of eggs. "How are Marlboro Lights part of our animal nature?"

"They are." He stubbed out his cigarette and lit another with a lighter from his pocket.

Marydale cracked four eggs into a skillet on the one-burner stove.

"So, Kristen Brock." Aldean crossed his ankle over his knee and leaned his chair back until the front legs lifted off the floor. "I'm guessing you didn't just talk about old times."

Marydale watched the eggs solidify. "No."

"And?"

"Portland's a small city. We were bound to meet."

"Women that age have a certain something," Aldean said, nodding to himself. "Not as…" He squeezed the air. "But they're into it. You know? They've gotten over that thing where they don't want you to look at their ass. Cougars. It's not a bad word."

"Kristen is not a cougar."

"Hmm. You'd have to be younger to make her a cougar."

"I'm the same age as you."

"Women age faster."

"You're a dirty old man."

Marydale flipped the eggs one by one and slid all four onto a plate. She handed Aldean a fork.

"The legs are still nice at that age." Aldean dropped his

cigarette into the mug and took a bite of egg. "It's the last thing to go."

"She's probably thirty-five! You're such a sexist."

Marydale sat down, digging her fork into the eggs on the other side of the plate.

"Are you going to see her again?" Aldean asked.

"I left."

"Ninja-like?"

"Stealth."

"You dog," Aldean said appreciatively. "No note? No *call me later*?"

Marydale stared out the window at the river. The Willamette was dishwater gray, the surface deceptively slow. She didn't know which felt worse, the thought that Kristen might have searched for her, hoping she had just stepped out for a coffee, or the thought that Kristen had rolled over and silently thanked her for saving them both the awkward morning light.

"I feel like shit," Marydale said.

"You and everyone else who went out last night."

"Not like that."

"So find her." Aldean skewered another slice of egg.

"I know where she works," Marydale said.

"Call her."

"I don't want to see her."

Aldean leaned back again.

"She could have found me," Marydale said. "Hell, she could have just stopped in for a bottle of whiskey and said hi."

"She stopped *in* last night."

Marydale ignored the insinuation in Aldean's voice.

"What am I doing, Aldean?"

"You had a couple drinks and fucked your ex. I'd say you're doing what the holiday requires. That's pretty much like getting a tree for Christmas."

"I didn't mean to fuck her," Marydale said.

"You just tripped on the carpet and bam?"

Marydale gave a little laugh.

"I didn't…"

She had meant for it be tender, a benediction, a way to give Kristen up for good. But as soon as the hotel door had closed behind them, Kristen had clutched her, moaning with each exhale, and Marydale had found herself rushing to relieve Kristen and to increase her torment. Then, when Kristen came, Marydale didn't know what to do with the longing in her own body, and she had fallen asleep frustrated and sad.

"I can't do this again," she said.

Aldean pushed the plate aside and took Marydale's hands in his. "What *are* you doing?" he asked.

"Nothing. I'm not going to see her. I'm not going to call her. I'm not going to put myself through that again."

"I've never had a Kristen Brock," Aldean said.

"What do you mean?"

"Whatever this is." He squeezed her hands. "Whatever you two have. Unrequited love. Tragedy."

"Men are too smart for that."

Aldean shook his head. "Some people just have the *capacity* for it. Others don't."

"Don't tell me it's a gift and everything happens for a reason."

"That's not it. You and Kristen Brock, it's epic." He shook his head. "You love her in your blood."

"I haven't thought about her in years."

"You haven't *talked* about her in years."

Wasn't that what the last five years had been all about: *not* Kristen Brock? Not looking for her. Not thinking about her. Not remembering. A half a dozen lovers who were not her. What had she expected? That Kristen would run into her arms crying, *I love you, Marydale?* Even if she did, it didn't erase five years of silence, five years of knowing that Kristen could have found her and didn't.

"If she'd been kidnapped and held in a basement with no phone…" Marydale said.

"Then you'd forgive her?" Aldean asked.

Outside a cormorant swooped down from the white sky, dove under the water, and resurfaced.

"She's changed."

"You've changed."

"She could have found me."

"So you said. And you could've found her. She may be an asshole, but she's still hot"—Aldean released her hands, cocked his thumb and forefinger in the shape of a pistol, and pointed it at Marydale's chest—"for an old woman. And you're going to go for it eventually, so skip the angst and just call her. But wait a few days. Girls like that. It makes them think you don't care."

Marydale shook her head. "You don't get it, Aldean. She doesn't care. That's the whole point."

4

Kristen sat at the end of the table with Rutger, Donna, and some of the other partners.

"Tell us about DataBlast," Donna said.

Kristen had found the unicorn. One of the people she had called on New Year's Eve called back two days later. His name was Jason. A hardworking accounting student, the company had given him just a little too much responsibility, and he'd been smart enough to understand what he saw in their records. Kristen had met him at a coffee shop on the Park Blocks. He had a pleasant face and a neatly trimmed beard that made him look older than his twenty-two years. *How do you feel about your former employer?* she had asked. He said they were a bunch of corporate scumbags. *In that case...* Kristen had placed her recorder on the table between them.

She had also left a message on the Sadfire Distillery voice

mail. She had called after hours, like a shy teenager. Marydale had not called her back.

"Our key witness, Jason Miter, was an accountant for DataBlast between…" Kristen rattled off a list of dates and responsibilities. "He also has a background in computer programming, so he had a basic understanding of the code they were using to cheat thousands of customers out of the pay-per-click advertising they were purchasing."

No one had really suffered. Thousands of individuals and companies had paid DataBlast to advertise their products—mostly self-published books and weight-loss creams—on the flashing sides of cheap websites and in off-brand search engines. For every ten advertisements they paid for, one or two were actually posted, while a well-designed cookie, downloaded without the customers' knowledge, projected their own advertisements wherever they looked. When the customer searched the Web, their product was omnipresent. When their customers searched, there was nothing.

"Hundreds of thousands of advertising dollars were lost," Kristen said, clicking to the next slide in her PowerPoint. A pie chart showed a swath of blue, representing dollars spent without service in return. "Moreover, if we can show that DataBlast customers forwent other advertising opportunities, believing their message was reaching targeted buyers, we can argue that they lost millions in potential revenue." She adjusted her glasses and regarded the partners.

"The Falcon Law Group hasn't attempted a class action of this kind for a long time," Donna added.

"It's no secret that we're considering you for partner," Falcon said. "Usually we'd have several people on a case this size, but Donna suggested you could handle it alone, with her standing in as cocounsel, purely for our clients' peace of mind."

"Right," Kristen said, but she was thinking about Marydale. The morning of New Year's Day, she had felt Marydale rise and assumed she was going to the bathroom. She had drifted off, but when she woke, the bed was cold.

"We want to try this case by May," Falcon added.

Outside, the rain had resumed, turning the magical snow into a gray slurry.

"But that is going to require your complete dedication. There is no time for distractions, Ms. Brock. Do you understand what I'm saying?"

"Yes."

"Are you prepared for that?"

"Yes."

One of the younger partners, an attorney from the East Coast who handled their contracts division, added, "Are you excited?"

He was handsome. Donna had always thought so, and occasionally they talked about him over drinks. Kristen couldn't see it now, and she couldn't formulate the right answer. Was she excited for a chance at partner? To invest in the Falcon Law Group and, in return, earn a percentage of their sizable profits? To buy a larger condo? A better car?

"It's my job," she said.

Falcon laughed. "That's the spirit. Cool as a cucumber."

The men left the room, talking over each other and checking their phones. Donna came by her office later and closed the door behind her.

"Rutger is salivating over this settlement."

"It's not going to be that much after we settle between all the claimants."

Kristen tried to focus on Donna and not the streams of rain sliding down the window.

"You're so cute," Donna said. "He doesn't want the settlement. He wants Tri-State Global Advertising."

Kristen shook her head.

"DataBlast's competitor!" Donna exclaimed. "Kristen, where are you? He's wanted them for years. You know that. If the court hits DataBlast with a couple millions dollars, DataBlast is out of business, and Tri-State Global signs on with the Falcon Law Group. *That account* will make millions."

5

Marydale stood in the back of the Sadfire Distillery, trying to show the latest interns from the First House, a halfway house and felon rehabilitation center, how to affix the sepia-toned stickers to the tops of a new batch of Consummation Rye. She put a sticker on a bottle, perfectly centered with the label. The interns, Mike and Ax, regarded her with bored expressions.

"Now, we'll pay you minimum wage while you're here," she said, repeating the stickering process again. "I remember what it was like to be out of prison and have everyone think they can cheat you because you're so damn grateful to have a job."

"Do we get a bottle?" Ax asked. He was about twenty-five, with a blurry tattoo of a date and the words *RIP Jayden* on his neck.

"Yeah, dog!" Mike bumped fists with Ax, although Mike could easily have been Ax's grandfather.

"Do you really think bringing a bottle of alcohol back to a transition house where a lot of people are recovering from addiction is a good idea?" Marydale asked.

"We could drink it on the way back," Ax suggested. "On the TriMet."

Marydale shot him a look. She usually liked working with the parolees from the First House. She liked their banter and their bravado and the boyish humility that lived just below the surface of their prison tattoos and gold-plated jewelry. But today she had no patience.

"If you think this is about drinking whiskey out of a Coke bottle on the train—"

Ax and Mike laughed.

"It's not!" Marydale picked up a bottle. "Whiskey is about a story. It's about a place and time and a moment you share with your friends, your God, your land. If you want to pound shots, you might as well just hit your head against that wall there. Because that's not what we do here."

She shoved a strip of labels into Mike's hand.

"Sheesh," Mike said.

Ax said, "Sorry, ma'am."

He tried sticking a label across the top of a bottle. It went on crooked, and he tried to peel it off.

"It's fine," Marydale said. "Just put one goddamn sticker on every bottle. That's not hard."

Aldean hurried in from the front office, where he had been checking purchase orders. He looked worried.

"What?" Marydale asked. "We're just getting started here."

Aldean touched her arm. He turned away from Ax and Mike. "Kristen's here," he said.

"Tell her to go away."

Aldean shook his head. "She's called six or ten times."

"And you've never dodged a girl's calls."

"That's different." Aldean dropped his voice to a whisper. "You're miserable, Mary. Just go talk to her. If you don't, I'm going to send her back here."

Mike and Ax looked interested.

Marydale hurried to the back bathroom and checked her face in the cloudy mirror. She was wearing an enormous Sadfire sweatshirt, a misorder from an overseas screen printer. She could hear her mother: *bone structure, good posture, and bright eyes.* She straightened her shoulders and walked into the tasting room, where Kristen was standing by the counter.

"Hello," she said as Marydale approached.

Marydale leaned on the counter.

"I wanted to see you," Kristen said.

Aldean appeared in the doorway.

"It's freezing in here, Mary. You should take her down to the *Tristess.*"

Marydale didn't want Kristen sitting in her tiny houseboat with its cheap wood veneer and its peeling Formica counters, but she didn't want to talk to her in front of Aldean or in the range of Mike's and Ax's curious glances.

"I live around the corner," she said reluctantly.

She didn't look at Kristen as she exited the building. Together they picked their way down the metal gangplank to the *Tristess.* Marydale threw her leg over the side of the boat and climbed onto the deck. She didn't offer Kristen a hand. When they were inside, she gestured for Kristen to sit on one of the benches that lined the living room. She sat across from her, as far away as the tiny space allowed.

"You didn't call," Kristen said.

"You've never had a one-night stand?" Marydale stretched her arms along the back of the bench.

"Not with you," Kristen said.

Marydale said nothing.

Kristen sat very upright. Beneath the open front of her overcoat, her suit fit her body perfectly, or perhaps her body fit the suit, like a mannequin designed to wear the smallest size behind glass. Still there was something raw in her voice. Marydale looked away.

"I know sex doesn't have to mean something," Kristen added. "People sleep together and don't get married, but I'd like to see you, just to have coffee or a happy hour drink after work. I want to get to know you again."

"I run Sadfire. There. You know me."

"When I saw you at the hotel…" Kristen clamped her hands together with a decisive gesture. Marydale could imagine her negotiating with a lawyer on the other side of a case. She'd never raise her voice, and she'd never lose. *I have all day to wait for you to be reasonable*, her face seemed to say. "I'm not asking for a commitment, just a possibility."

Marydale remembered Kristen sitting across from her in the jail five years earlier. *I worked hard to go to law school.* The five years that had intervened felt like a breath. Kristen had come back. Kristen had found her. But five years had changed everything, and Marydale had rehearsed this moment in her mind. She had practiced, so she would get it right now.

"You look great," Marydale said, "and if it was just sex, I'd give it one more go, but I don't think that's a good idea, and I don't want to get drinks. New Year's Eve was fun. Let's make it a clean break."

"I—" Kristen began.

"All the reasons why you left…nothing's changed."

"I've changed," Kristen said.

"I didn't think you'd stay in Tristess. I didn't think we'd get married and run a ranch," Marydale said. "But I thought you'd at least write. I thought you'd at least be my friend. Maybe it was easy for you to forget—"

"It's wasn't easy!" Kristen stood and crossed the room in one stride. She sat next to Marydale. "I never forgot you."

"And now you want to do happy hour. I had to live in Tristess for two years after you left. I had no one. Aldean was in Portland. They sanctioned me so many times. I was so *fucking* unhappy, and all I wanted was to know that you remembered me."

As soon as she uttered the words, she knew her practice was for nothing. She had meant to be cool, a bit flirtatious, and absolutely certain. *I'm afraid you missed your chance, Ms. Brock.* She hadn't meant to be honest. Marydale looked down at her hands. Her nails were dirty, and there was a burn on the back of her hand from when she'd been soldering a clamp onto one of the tanks.

"You didn't look for me either," Kristen said.

"I couldn't leave the county. And what would you have done if I'd shown up at your firm? A felon on parole on abscond?" Suddenly Marydale wanted to cry. "How could I feel like I had the right when you left because just rooming with me put your whole life at risk? You had all those dreams."

"I wasn't just *rooming* with you."

"New Year's Eve was a mistake." Marydale pushed up her sleeves, revealing her tattoos. "I'm a con. I'm a felon. I'm never going to get away from that."

Kristen reached for Marydale's wrist, running the fingers of her other hand up Marydale's arm, stroking the delicate skin at the apex of her elbow. Marydale tried to pull away…but not really…and Kristen held her with a gentle grasp.

"You've lived through so much," Kristen said.

"Or not enough."

Kristen touched Marydale's cheek and then her ear, rubbing the swirl of Marydale's ear with her thumb, around and around, until Marydale lowered her head toward Kristen's caress.

"I don't think we're just two people who slept together on accident," Kristen said.

"It happens all the time," Marydale said. "It's what single people do on New Year's Eve."

In the back of her mind, Marydale thought of the women she had been with since Kristen left her in the Tristess jail. How many times had she hurried through a kiss or ended an embrace so she could grab her lover's hand and press it to her crotch. *Like this. A little harder. Faster.* Getting off: that's all she'd wanted. Now Marydale longed to sink into Kristen's arms like a lover, like a child, like a sinner in a country church. But between them was a wealth of cashmere and tailored linen. Kristen was a lawyer from Portland's most conservative law firm, or so the *Willamette Weekly* had labeled the Falcon Law Group. A professional. A winner.

"I live in a houseboat," she said. "It's like a trailer on the water. It's poor white trash with a view."

Kristen ran her hand down the front of Marydale's sweatshirt, and Marydale felt her nipples harden.

"You're lonely. You're bored," Marydale said. "I've dated other women who thought it'd be fun to fuck a con for a while."

She didn't tell Kristen that she had broken off most of those affairs. The ones she hadn't ended deliberately had ended in the silence of her unreturned phone calls.

"You're not going to take me to the company party," Marydale added.

"If you knew how awful those parties are, you wouldn't ask."

"Have you even been with other women?"

"It's just you." Kristen whispered. She unbuttoned her blazer and dropped it on the floor. "You're the only woman."

"That doesn't change anything." Marydale said, but she felt like her blood was changing.

Kristen unbuttoned her blouse, her gaze fixed on Marydale. Then Kristen rose, unzipped her skirt, and let it fall.

Behind her, the wraparound windows looked out on the river and the neighboring houseboats.

"Tell me to stop," Kristen said.

Marydale could almost feel Kristen's lean thigh between her legs. She felt as though the delicate muscles of her core had awakened and were pulling tight, yearning, the fibers of her body sending out chemical distress signals. Release: her body already knew how good it would be with Kristen, how much better it would be than the quick, blunt orgasms she had had with other women. Her body longed for it. Her legs felt weak. Her stomach filled with stars. *Don't*, a voice in the back of her mind said. *You'll regret it.*

Slowly Marydale knelt down by one of the benches and undid the latch that secured the hold. She lifted up the seat of the bench to reveal a tiny staircase. Kristen looked momentarily surprised; then she stepped out of her heels. Marydale lowered herself into the small bedroom in one practiced move. She held her hand out to Kristen, who climbed awkwardly down. The bed took up the entire room, and there was barely enough space to stand upright. Marydale turned on the pink salt-rock lamp by the head of the bed.

Kristen set her glasses on the bedside table. A second later, they were in bed, Kristen wrapping her nylon-clad legs around Marydale's heavy work pants. Her weight felt divine, and Marydale moaned. She pulled at Kristen's bra, and Kristen dragged Marydale's sweatshirt over her head. Then they were all arms and legs, fumbling as they tried to undress each other without ceasing the luxurious pressure of their intertwined bodies.

"Wait, wait," Kristen breathed.

She stood up just long enough to pull off her nylons and her underwear. Marydale admired her body, as lean as a model, but real, not airbrushed to preadolescent perfection. She had a faint stubble of blond hair on her legs, a small surgical scar above her belly button, and red marks at her waist and around her chest, where her undergarments had pressed into the skin. Marydale thought she was even more beautiful for these slight imperfections, and then she couldn't think of anything, because Kristen pushed her back onto the bed. After a brief struggle, Kristen released the button of Marydale's fly and pulled her pants off, casting them on the floor as though their presence offended her.

Marydale had worn red lace panties because she had been almost out of clean laundry. Now Kristen stroked the rough lace, her movements quickening to a frantic pace that matched the urgency Marydale felt.

"I'm going to tear these," Kristen said breathlessly.

Marydale gasped. Kristen gave her a sly smile and pulled. The elastic lace stretched and snapped back in place, stinging the delicate skin of Marydale's sex and sending a surge of desire through her body. She raised her hips, longing for Kristen to ease the sensation or to amplify it. Kristen pulled again, but the lace only stretched.

"What is this stuff?" Kristen laughed, and in her laugher Marydale heard an echo of the life they could have had. If they were lovers, girlfriends, wife and wife, if they were friends, it would be like this. Sex would be a funny, delicious game, and the pleasure they felt would be deeper than their skin, deeper than Kristen's fingers inside her…now…moving in and out, the damp fabric of her panties pushed aside.

"Fuck me," Marydale cried out. She felt her body mounting toward orgasm.

Kristen pull Marydale's panties off and mounted her, sliding her leg between Marydale's thighs, tilting her hips so their bodies touched at their hottest, most intimate center. Marydale gasped. Kristen settled deeper into her. Marydale pressed upward, reaching for that heat. Perfect. Excruciating. She wanted to cry out for more and she wanted to hover there forever, their sexes touching but the architecture of their bodies preventing the deep rubbing that would relieve her longing. She wanted to tell Kristen how good it felt, better than any other woman she had ever been with. She wanted to beg her, *Don't leave me.*

Then, before Marydale knew what was happening, Kristen shifted her position so she was riding Marydale's thigh. Marydale felt the moisture from Kristen's body, as Kristen dragged the folds of her own sex up and down Marydale's leg, crying out with each pass.

"I want you. Oh God, I want you!" Kristen grabbed Marydale's shoulders. "It's so fucking good. Yes. Yes!"

With a final thrust, Kristen collapsed on Marydale's chest. Her hair was damp and tousled. Marydale stroked it while Kristen caught her breath.

A moment later, Kristen rolled off her.

"Now you," Kristen said. A red flush had spread across Kristen's chest and up her neck, and yet…she looked like a barrister.

Marydale fell back against the pillows and stared up at the water-stained ceiling. Her body throbbed. She knew she would come with one thrust of Kristen's thigh, a few seconds of Kristen's fingers on her clit. If Kristen placed her delicate lips against Marydale's sex, rolled her tongue against her clit…Just the thought made Marydale's body contract.

"You'll have to give me some pointers. I'm a little out of practice," Kristen added.

Marydale thought Kristen meant to be flirtatious, but she sounded efficient, a woman used to getting complicated tasks done quickly. Kristen glanced at the delicate gold watch on her wrist. Somehow it had survived the hurricane of their disrobing. Marydale could almost see the buttons of Kristen's prim, ruffled blouse buttoning themselves back up again, her suit reasserting itself, like a time-lapse flower blooming in reverse.

Kristen sat up a little, leaning on one elbow. "Well, my dear?" she asked.

Marydale glanced at Kristen's athletic legs next to her own fleshy thighs. Compared to Kristen's breasts, her breasts felt huge, heavy and obvious, like her desire. She felt the long nights in the Tristess jail stretching out behind her. *We both knew this couldn't last…the right choice.*

"Fuck." Marydale rolled away from Kristen.

"What is it?"

Marydale groaned. Her unmet desire felt like a physical pain, but as surely as she knew she would come at Kristen's slightest touch, she knew she would cry as soon as the orgasm released her. She could feel the tears welling up from deep inside her throat.

"This isn't going to work," she said.

"What isn't?" Kristen asked innocently.

Kristen had gotten what she came for, Marydale thought, just like she herself had taken her pleasure with the women she picked up at the Mirage.

"I know how this goes," Marydale said.

"What?"

"This." Marydale motioned to the rumpled bed and their clothing on the floor. "I've done this, too, and"—she hesitated—"I want more than this."

"I do, too." Kristen sounded earnest.

Marydale's body sang out, *Believe her, believe her*, but she knew better.

"You've never been with another woman," Marydale said. "Even if I wasn't a felon, even if I was a lawyer or a doctor…you left me in Tristess for a reason. You're straight or straight enough. You've got that option. You want something simple."

"I want you."

"For today, but what happens when your law firm finds out? What happens when you get labeled the *lesbian* partner?"

"I haven't made partner yet."

Marydale picked up her sweatshirt. "And would you? If you were with a woman? Would you fit in?"

"This is Portland," Kristen protested. "It's the twenty-first century. Nobody cares about that stuff. This isn't Tristess."

"I think you care more than you know," Marydale said.

"That's not fair." Kristen's gray eyes were very dark. "Give me a chance." She sounded like an attorney negotiating a plea deal.

"I did," Marydale said, "back in Tristess."

She turned from Kristen and pulled her sweatshirt back over her head, the Sadfire motto circling her chest: *SPERO. AMANT. DOLERE.* Hope. Love. Grieve.

5

Like many places purported by some to be sinful dens of lechery, Portland's only lesbian bar, the Mirage, was not as fraught with tantalizing mystery as Kristen had expected. At four o'clock, it looked like any other neighborhood dive bar. The walls were dark. The lights were low. The seats were empty. The walls were covered with large mirrors etched with BUDWEISER and pictures of horses charging through snowy forests because that...had absolutely nothing to do with being a lesbian in Portland.

The bartender emerged from the back just as Kristen was about to turn around and leave. Dressed in a leopard-print bodysuit, she fulfilled Kristen's half-realized expectations more than the mirrors and the inflatable Corona bottles hanging from the ceiling.

"We're open," the bartender said. "What can I get you?"

Kristen scanned the rows of flavored vodka. "You don't have Sadfire whiskey, do you?" she asked.

"Of course!" the bartender said, as though Kristen had just guessed a secret password. "We love Sadfire. They sponsor all our Pride Week events. Neat? On the rocks?"

"Neat."

The bartender poured a shot and slid it across the counter. "Have you met the owners, Marydale and Aldean?"

Kristen choked on the familiar names, coughing as the whiskey hit the back of her throat.

"The Consummation Rye is no joke," the bartender said sympathetically. She filled a glass of water for Kristen. "Marydale is amazing. She does all this work with paroled felons, real social consciousness. My best dishwasher came through her program. Only stayed with us six months, but that's okay. She got a job bartending at some fancy whiskey bar downtown. That's the point of working with felons, right? Reintegration? Anyway, make yourself at home. Special today is popcorn shrimp and fries. Let me know if you want some food."

The only other customer was a woman with short, dark hair who sat at the other end of the bar, glaring at her laptop. Kristen stared at the mirror behind the bar, wishing she had brought her laptop or a book. She had left her phone in the car. It felt like the moment to take up video poker, just so she'd have something to do. She had imagined herself dancing with some faceless woman on a crowded dance floor—although why she thought that would happen at four o'clock in the afternoon she could no longer fathom. In her fantasy, Marydale appeared, watching jealously. *I thought you were straight*, Marydale said. *How could you have thought that?* Kristen asked, leaving the woman and falling into Marydale's kiss. But in her fantasy, the Mirage was also crowded, suffused with red light and redolent with the smell of rich perfume, not stale beer. She nursed her whiskey for a long time.

Five o'clock brought a few more customers, including a trio of male construction workers who seemed to be regulars despite the fact that it was a lesbian bar. The bartender disappeared for a long time and reappeared wearing fake eyelashes.

"Can I get you another?" she asked.

"I don't know," Kristen said. "I should probably be going."

"I'm Vita," the bartender said.

Ignoring Kristen's refusal, she poured another shot of Consummation Rye into Kristen's glass and set a bowl of peanuts in front of her.

"I went to a therapist once to figure out why I was attracted to women with personality disorders," Vita said as though they had been having a conversation from which this comment flowed naturally. "He said, if you can't talk to the people you know, just pick a stranger, a random stranger. Tell them everything. You're never going to see them again. If they think you're a Freudian mess two days away from being committed, so what? You don't know them. And you get practice."

"Practice doing what?" Kristen asked, wondering if she should just leave a twenty on the counter and walk out.

"Talking," Vita said. "I'm a bartender. I'm a professional. I can tell." She set her elbows on the bar and leaned in, examining Kristen closely. Her eyelashes looked like caterpillars. "You're depressed."

"I'm not," Kristen protested.

The woman at the end of the bar spoke without looking up from her computer.

"Don't pay any attention to her. Vita talks shit *all* the time."

The woman looked like a lesbian, with baggy tuxedo pants and suspenders over her crisp white shirt. Kristen wondered for a foolish second if she should buy a pair of suspenders or cut her hair. Maybe if she shaved her head and got a rainbow flag tattooed on her biceps Marydale would forgive her, would take her back, would…love her. She sipped her drink and sighed. She hadn't been that silly when she was eighteen. Even her visit to the Mirage suddenly felt pathetic. What was she supposed to do? Go back to Marydale's houseboat and say, *I went to a gay bar; will you go out with me now?*

"I'm not depressed," Kristen said quietly.

The woman with the laptop looked up and gave her a half smile.

"Vita's good, though. She can read people, even if they hate it. This your first time here?"

"No. Yes. I was just in the area."

Kristen had never *just* been in the area. The mossy Eastside neighborhood held nothing of interest except the green-roofed bungalow that housed the *HumAnarchist,* and that was not the kind of interest Kristen wanted to visit regularly.

"It's a nice bar," the woman said. "I met my wife right here." She tapped the bar.

Vita said, "Let me tell you! They were crazy for each other from the minute they saw each other. It was like pythons mating."

"No," the woman with the laptop said with a wave of her hand. "It was not *anything* like pythons mating. Vita makes stuff up." She held out her hand, and they shook over the expanse of empty barstools. "I'm Tate."

"How did you meet your wife?" Kristen asked. "I mean, you were here, but how did it happen?"

The story that followed was sweet and romantic with lurid interludes from Vita. Apparently Tate had fallen in love with the woman who was trying to buy the coffee shop where Tate worked. Tate's future wife, Laura, had been a real estate developer and, at the time, deep in the closet. Laura's father was a conservative politician. Tate had been out, proud, broke, and lost.

"And somehow it just all worked out," Tate said. "That was almost ten years ago. Laura started a development business here in Portland. I went back to college."

"They're sickening," Vita said. "You'd think they met yesterday. They can't keep their hands off each other."

Tate shook her head. "No, Vita. That part is your imagination."

Vita laughed. "But I do tell a good story." She turned to Kristen. "You got someone special?"

"No." It came out sounding mournful.

"And that's your story, isn't it?" Vita said. "Did she dump you? Cheat on you with an oboist?"

"An oboist?" Kristen asked.

Tate said to Vita, "You know, a woman is allowed to come in and have a drink by herself without you prying into her personal life."

"You should tell *her*." Vita nodded toward Tate.

"Tell her what?" Kristen asked.

"All your dark Freudian secrets. If you're going to pick a stranger to talk to, Tate's the one. She's good people. I mean it. I've known her since I tried to burn her house down back in high school."

"Since before then," Tate agreed.

"See?" Vita said, and with that she disappeared into the back.

"Sorry," Tate said. "That's just Vita. There's a line between her business and other people's business, and it means nothing to her."

They were quiet for a moment. Tate glanced at her laptop but not with any real interest. Kristen took a deep breath.

"Did you…?" Kristen began tentatively. "…always know you liked women?"

"Absolutely," Tate said. "Since I was little."

"Before puberty?"

"Yeah."

"And your wife?"

"She was married to a man for a while, but she says she knew before that."

"Damn." Kristen took a sip of her whiskey.

"Are you…?"

"There's this woman." Kristen rotated the shot glass around in a circle.

Maybe Vita was right. Maybe there were stories one couldn't tell friends, Kristen thought, or maybe she just didn't have any real friends.

"She thinks I'm straight, and she thinks I'll leave her."

And she's a felon, and I did leave.

"Are you straight?" Tate asked.

"I don't know. She's the only woman I've ever dated. She's the only woman I've ever been attracted to. But sometimes I think there's only ever been her, man or woman. She doesn't believe me though."

"It's hard."

"Portland is so liberal. I don't get what she's worried about."

She was thinking of Marydale standing in the kitchen of her farmhouse confessing. *I thought he was going to kill me.*

"I don't think it's hard to be gay in Portland," Tate said slowly. "But if she's lived someplace where it was a lot easier to be with a man, she might just be afraid that she's not good enough for you to, you know, take that risk. At least another lesbian doesn't have the choice. Another lesbian can't choose to be with a man if things get rough. Or maybe she's been burned before."

"She's been burned before," Kristen said, staring at the bar top before her.

"You just have to show her that you're not the kind of person who runs away," Tate said with a friendly shrug. "It'll work out. I know that sounds like such a cliché, but if you're meant to be together, it'll work out."

6

"Where are we going again?" Marydale asked as Aldean opened the passenger door of his pickup and offered her a hand up, despite the fact that her Ford F-150 was actually higher off the ground.

"*Your* lesbian bartender's birthday party," Aldean said.

"Right, right," Marydale said. "Vita Galliano."

"If you say so. You put it on our calendar," Aldean said. "You sponsored her bar at PrideFest. I was going to set up a booth at the Rose City Adult Entertainment Expo that weekend, but no."

"You were not going to sell top-shelf whiskey to Casa Diablo's Vegan Strip Club," she said.

Aldean settled into the driver's seat and pushed the truck into second gear.

"Nothing says *drink more whiskey* like a naked girl and some tempeh," he said.

Marydale wasn't in the mood. She didn't want to go to

Vita Galliano's birthday party. She didn't want to listen to the latest gossip from the Mirage. She didn't even want to talk about the new pinot noir barrels they'd bought from the Alderglen Winery and whether or not they would lend the same cinnamon character as the French oak they had used before. She wanted to lie on the floor of the *Tristess*, turn out the lights, and feel the river flowing beneath her.

"You could just call her," Aldean said, as they turned onto Highway 30.

"I can't cancel on her. I said we were coming."

"Not Vita. Kristen."

"I'm not calling her."

It was only half true. She *hadn't* called Kristen, but she had looked up Kristen's firm and written the phone number on a slip of paper that had drifted around the kitchen of her houseboat for days. Every time she looked at it, she reminded herself of all the reasons an affair with Kristen would never work out. She knew in her mind, but her dumb, optimistic heart beat, *Maybe. Maybe. Maybe.*

"Well, you'll have to cheer up if you're going to sell some whiskey at this party," Aldean said.

"We're not selling anything. We're going to celebrate one of our local purchaser's birthdays."

The directions Vita had provided led them into the northwest hills. The roads were narrow and clung to the forested hillside. On the other side, the houses were built on stilts with long driveways like drawbridges over the abyss.

"So this is how the other side lives," Aldean said. "Didn't know owning a lesbian bar made so much money."

"I don't know how you could live up here and not get vertigo," Marydale grumbled. "I think it's Vita's friends' house. Tate and Laura. Laura's big in the green-construction industry. She probably built the place."

Vertigo or not, the house they arrived at was gorgeous. Inside everything was blond wood and pale furniture. Marydale could see clear through the living room and out the windows on the other side. Far below, the city sparkled with lights. In the living room, a dinner table with a dozen leaves had been decorated with candles and festoons of green garlands.

"Come in, come in!" Vita effused, hugging both of them.

"This place is amazing," Aldean said.

"Make yourselves at home," Vita said. "It's not my place, but that makes it even better. You can spill on the carpet."

The only carpet Marydale saw was a delicately woven rug hung on the wall above the fireplace.

Marydale handed Vita a bottle of First Anniversary, the first good whiskey Sadfire had produced after Aldean arrived in Portland. Vita invited them into the open kitchen and started mixing an elaborate drink with the whiskey they had just brought.

A moment later, Vita pushed a drink into Marydale's hand.

"It's called the Lightning Rod. I invented it for the party. You can put anything in it. Whiskey. Vodka. Gin. Tequila. All of the above."

Marydale took the drink and managed a friendly smile.

Around them, the other guests looked like a backstage

party for an eclectic fashion show. A man in a ball gown talked with animated gestures to a stone-faced woman in coveralls. Two women in schoolgirl jumpers skewered bits of cheese on toothpicks, while a man with a chest-length beard shoveled them into his mouth. Nearby, an old woman in a fountain of lace hugged an Asian boy in a Portland Blazers jersey. On a deck overlooking the city, two women who Marydale guessed to be Tate and Laura, talked to a trio of men in tuxedos.

Marydale wondered if Kristen had a house like this, perhaps in this neighborhood. Her friends would be a different set, all in gray suits, trousers for the men and skirts for the women. They might be having a party right now, drinking sidecars and talking about their respective court cases.

On the deck, the trio of tuxedoed men dispersed. One of them laughed and called out, "Round two. To the Lightning Rod!" And Marydale saw a third woman standing with Tate and Laura, her hair pulled up in a twist, her trim gray suit an elegant contrast to the carnival of outfits around her.

Kristen.

Vita appeared at Marydale's elbow. Marydale jumped

"I'm a bartender," Vita whispered. "I know *everyone*."

Vita shuttled off to the next cluster of guests. Marydale looked around for Aldean, but he was leaning against the counter, chatting with the women in schoolgirl jumpers.

Aldean, she mouthed.

He shot her a look that said, *I'm busy*.

To the women he said, "Whiskey's very sensual. You have to be in your body when you drink whiskey."

Then Marydale's eyes met Kristen's, and although the room was large and crowded with voices, Marydale felt everything go silent and still, as though the mist that sometimes covered the Willamette River at dawn had drifted up the hills and blanketed the party. Only Kristen was visible. Kristen raised one hand, tentatively, not quite a wave. Tate and Laura glanced back at Marydale, spoke something to Kristen, and then disappeared.

And Marydale knew what she should do: make small talk, feel awkward, sit at the opposite end of the table from Kristen at dinner, and go home. The thought made her feel so tired, she knew if she sat down she would fall asleep, like a drunk in the corner of a bar. At the same time, beneath that fatigue, she felt a tense, queer giddiness, like the excitement she had felt when she had broken the conditions of her parole and driven out of the county—just to do it—the feeling that there was no future price that outweighed the exquisite now.

She walked through the crowd and onto the deck. The air outside was cool. Kristen watched her.

"I'm surprised," Marydale said when she reached Kristen.

Kristen looked down. "I met Vita at the Mirage."

Marydale took a step closer. She touched Kristen's arm, and Kristen's eyes flew upward. And Marydale knew that she could kiss her, that she *would* kiss her, and maybe heartbreak would follow, but tonight the city lights were sparkling and, despite the orange glow they cast in the sky, there were still so many stars.

"Did you like the Mirage?" Marydale asked.

"Yes."

"Did you go dancing?"

Kristen offered her a rueful smile. "I'm not a dancer."

"I don't know about that," Marydale said.

Their words felt weightier than small talk.

"I'd be so stiff. I don't think I even danced in college. I think once I was walking across the quad and some drunk people bumped into me. That's as close as I got to dancing," Kristen said. "Do you dance?"

"Not anymore. I did a little Western dancing back home. You can't be a rodeo queen and not take a turn, but I was pretty bad at it. I always wanted to lead."

"I bet you were lovely. Did you have a big skirt with ruffles?"

"And four hundred pounds of sequins."

"Ah," Kristen said. "Armor." She glanced at the party inside. "I'm sorry about the other day."

"You're sorry that you came to the distillery?"

Kristen pursed her lips in a pensive expression that did not look like an attorney planning her strategy. "You said no," she said quietly. "And I didn't listen to you."

"I don't think anyone could accuse you of forcing me." Marydale stepped a little closer. "I'll run it by my lawyer, but I don't think it'll hold up in court."

"But I came by to talk, to see you." Kristen reached out as if to touch her hand, then stopped. "I didn't come there to make you uncomfortable. And I pushed you into something you didn't want."

"Well," Marydale drawled, "I wouldn't say I didn't want

it. The trick is just to only want those things that are good for us. But Aldean says we're in the business of temptation. It's only fair that we be tempted. What did you want to talk about?"

"I—"

Vita poked her head out the porch door. "Come on, you guys. We're eating."

"Sit with me," Kristen said.

Inside, Tate lit the candles and raised a toast to Vita. Vita thanked Tate and Laura for hosting. Toasts were made. Glasses clinked. White china tureens were passed up and down the long table. Aldean kept up a friendly banter about the rain and the *estery* profile of their latest release. Tate asked about gin distilling. Kristen and Laura talked about zoning laws with impenetrable specificity. And Marydale nodded and laughed and looked up and down the table as the conversation bounced back and forth. But she wasn't really listening. She was feeling the air between her shoulder and Kristen's, the distance be-tween her hand on the stem of her wineglass and Kristen's hand on the tablecloth beside her plate. She was so fo-cused on the millimeters that separated them and on the way Kristen's knee brushed hers beneath the table that she did not hear Vita calling the guests to order, declaring, "You won't believe this." Vita added, "Marydale Rae! Are you listening?"

"What?" Marydale asked.

Vita waved her arms over her plate like a referee. "I have a terribly sad story to tell," she said enthusiastically.

"Vita, don't," Tate said. To Marydale and Kristen she added, "She meddles. Don't listen to her."

"Heartbreaking," Vita said.

"Vita!" Tate scolded, but the table had already fallen silent, all eyes focused on Vita.

"I was at the bar," Vita began melodramatically. "This woman came in. She talked to Tate for, like, an hour."

"Hardly," Tate said.

Vita laughed. "She was there for *hours*. This poor girl was weeping in her Sadfire whiskey. She was *in love*." Vita beamed, managing to look both loving and predatory at the same time. "Oh, she was so in love, but she was bi, or maybe she was straight, but she'd fallen for this one girl, and the heartless lesbian dumped her. Do you know why?" She didn't wait for an answer. "Because she had the *stain of man* on her."

One of the men at the table chuckled.

"I don't mind the stain of man on me," he said.

"And do you know who this terrible lesbian was?" Vita went on. "This cruel woman who wouldn't accept her bisexual lover? Who would say no to a girl just because she'd never been with another woman? And she was very pretty, by the way. This girl was very professional, very polished. I wanted to bed her just to mess up her hair."

Under the table, Kristen touched Marydale's leg. When Marydale glanced over, Kristen was blushing a red so deep it matched Vita's lipstick.

Vita leaned over, nearly dragging the sleeve of her velveteen leopard-print blazer in the hollandaise sauce.

"Marydale Rae, you'll never get your toaster like that!" she declared.

The whole table laughed.

When they quieted down, Aldean asked, "What does a toaster have to do with it?"

There was another round of laughter.

"For flipping a straight girl." Vita grinned. "We get one every time we get a girl to play for our team. Signing bonus from the Lesbian Nation."

Kristen leaned over and pressed her forehead to Marydale's shoulder, hiding her face from the guests at the table.

"Where are you going to put your toaster?" she whispered.

Marydale could hear that she was smiling. She kissed the top of Kristen's head.

Someone said, "Aw!"

Someone else said, "Oh, it's her!"

Kristen looked up at Marydale, and Marydale gently placed a kiss on her lips.

"That's more like it," Vita exclaimed, and the talk at the table broke into half a dozen smaller conversations, some of the guests discussing toasters and the chance that Marydale might upgrade to a Vitamix, while farther down the table someone described an enormous dildo they had seen at Spartacus Leathers, and another trio of talkers burst into a rendition of "I Kissed a Girl."

Kristen squeezed Marydale's hand under the table, and they looked at each other. Then they were both laughing at their own embarrassment and at the ridiculous conversations and at the ease that flowered between them and at the sudden certainty that the air around them had changed. Somewhere the first pale crocus had broken through gas-station bark dust. Somewhere, in the darkness, a leafless cherry tree had turned, miraculously, pink with spring.

7

The party drew to a close around midnight. The first guests left with hugs and prolonged goodbyes. Aldean caught Marydale's eye from across the table, a question in his cocked eyebrow. Marydale didn't know what to answer, but Kristen leaned close to her.

"Come home with me," she whispered.

Marydale couldn't contain the smile that spread across her face. She nodded to Aldean and then to the door. Aldean rose, tipping an invisible hat to Marydale and Kristen. A half hour later, Marydale was sitting in the leather seat of Kristen's car as they glided down the wooded hills toward the city. Soon Kristen pulled up in front of the Sentinel Building. The massive apartment complex rose like a monument to 1920, its windows reflecting the city, much closer now than when they stood on the deck of Laura's house.

"I love this building," Marydale said.

"You've been in?" Kristen asked.

"No. I've just seen it from outside."

"Come on." Kristen took her hand. "It's beautiful inside, too."

Kristen held Marydale's hand as they rode the bronze-plated elevator in silence. When they neared the top of the building, the elevator chimed. Kristen led Marydale down a carpeted hall warmed by the light of vintage chandeliers. She unlocked the last door, and Marydale looked around the condo. The city lights greeted them again, but Marydale wasn't looking at the high-rises. A huge photo mural dominated the back wall of the living area, lit by a discreet row of track lights. The photo was the Firesteed Summit at dawn.

Marydale walked over to the mural and touched the surface.

"It's like a giant sticker," Kristen said. "You send the photograph to the company, and they print it."

Up close, the pixilation turned the scene into a pointillist painting.

"The Firesteed Summit," Marydale said. "Why?"

She looked around at the distressed leather sofa, the red, green, and orange Pendleton throw, and the wooden end table resting on a base of antlers. She touched the blanket and frowned.

"For you." Kristen's voice was raw. "I fucked up, Marydale. I left Tristess, and I wanted to die. I missed you so much. And I don't know why I didn't do anything." Kristen stood in the center of the room, like a single player on a stage. She looked around as though the room was as new to her as it was to Marydale. "I should have told Sierra. She would have told me to follow my heart chakra or something ridiculous like that, but she would have told me to go back for you. I just stayed and missed you, and I looked you up a hundred times, and I didn't go, and it doesn't make sense. I hate all those Portland hipsters with their fake glasses and their lumberjack beards, and look at all this." She waved her hand vaguely in the direction of the antler table. "I got all this stuff because it made me think of you. Even the dog."

Marydale noticed the dog from the Deerfield Hotel sleeping on a cushion beneath the table, wrapped in a blue and yellow sweater, its round chest rising and falling peacefully.

"I don't have time for pets," Kristen said, as though the thought had just occurred to her. "I don't know what to do with a dog. I had to pawn Meatball off on Sierra for six months to housebreak him."

"You got a dog because of me?"

"You had Lilith."

As if sensing his role in the conversation, Meatball raised his head and smacked his wide mouth.

"I had a *ninety*-pound pit bull," Marydale said. "You got a French bulldog named Meatball. It's wearing a sweater."

She meant it as a joke, but Kristen's next breath was a tremulous sob. She turned away, rubbing her eyes with the heels of her hands.

"Is it too late?" Kristen asked.

Marydale hurried to her side and put her arms around Kristen, surprised by how small Kristen felt.

Kristen pressed her face to Marydale's chest. "How can you trust me?" she asked, her voice muffled. "Why would you take me back after the way I left? I can't ask that. I don't have the right to ask that. It doesn't make sense. I knew. I knew! And I didn't do anything. What kind of person does that?"

"Knew what?" Marydale asked.

Kristen drew back a little and looked up at her. "That I love you."

Kristen's face was all angles and shadows cast by her glasses. And they were strangers, more so now than the day Marydale had offered Kristen a room, yet as she watched Kristen, she thought, *I've always known you.*

"When I saw you at New Year's Eve…" Marydale couldn't finish the sentence. The sentiment was too huge. Instead she leaned down and kissed Kristen. Her lips were cool, and Marydale's whole body ached to warm her.

"Please be with me," Kristen said, and took Marydale's hand and led her to the bedroom.

Like the living room, the bedroom offered a view of the skyline. In the back of her mind, it occurred to Marydale that the bedroom was probably bigger than her entire boat. Then she lost track of everything but Kristen's kiss.

Soon they were tumbled together, their feet hanging off the edge of the bed. Kristen's movements were gentle but certain as she divested Marydale of her shirt and bra. And Marydale briefly thought of how many times she had unhooked a woman's bra like this and how, suddenly, now, beneath Kristen's hands, she felt the magnitude of the act.

Then Kristen straddled her, so light, yet the pressure of

her hips sent a hot surge of longing through Marydale's body. It was more than sex, more than just the swelling of her clit or the moisture between her legs. Her hips moved of their own accord. Marydale tried to kick off her boots, but they remained stubbornly in place.

Kristen caressed Marydale's chest. She could barely cup Marydale's large breasts in her hands.

"You're perfect," she said, her face serious. "You didn't want me to touch you in the hotel or in your boat." It was a question.

"I've been with other women," Marydale said. "A lot, I guess. But with you…" *I'm scared.* She couldn't say it.

Kristen rolled off Marydale and lay beside her, gently stroking Marydale's naked chest, trailing her fingers along her collarbones, down her sternum, and along the sides of her breasts.

"I don't want to pressure you," Kristen said. "We don't have to hurry."

Marydale's body said otherwise.

"Aldean says I learned how to pick up women from him, which is bullshit, because I was picking up straight girls at church camp when we were fifteen. And Portland's a good place to meet women. But those girls haven't meant anything to me. It was just physical, and I probably should have thought about that. I just didn't really think there was going to be…more. I'm a felon. What can I expect? Damaged goods, you know?"

"Oh, Marydale." Kristen pulled her closer.

"At Deerfield and at my place…" Sheltered in Kristen's

embrace, Marydale could say it. "...I was afraid. I wanted it too much. I don't know where this is going, where we're going, but I want to know it means something to you."

"It does. It means everything."

"I guess it's karma." Marydale tried to laugh. "These past few years, I couldn't get out of a girl's room fast enough. As soon as we were done, as soon as I came...I was thinking about how to leave."

"Are you going to leave if I make you come?" Kristen asked, her voice both serious and flirtatious.

"No," Marydale said.

Kristen leaned down and drew Marydale's nipple into her mouth and sucked gently for a long time. Marydale felt an answering pull deep inside. She pushed her breast up toward Kristen's kiss, and Kristen grazed the engorged flesh with her teeth, sending a shiver down Marydale's spine.

"Mmm." Kristen sighed. When she finally released Marydale, she asked, "So how did these girls...these other girls you loved and left...how did they make you come?"

"The usual ways."

Kristen nodded with mock solemnity. "Ah, the *usual* ways."

Marydale smiled. Kristen touched her cheek.

Very quietly Kristen asked, "May I kiss you in the usual ways?"

Marydale laughed and nodded, and Kristen slipped her fingers under the waistband of Marydale's jeans. She felt Kristen's fingers drifting over her cotton underwear, not touching any particular spot or repeating any particular motion, just stroking like one might stroke a cat or finger a piece of velvet.

"I missed you," Marydale said, closing her eyes to focus on the sensation.

Kristen continued to touch her, and Marydale squirmed.

"Are you sure this is okay?" Kristen asked. "If something happened to you and you're not ready, I can wait."

"No," Marydale said. And part of her knew that a week earlier, a day earlier, the moment before she walked into the party, she would have said, *You happened to me.* Now Marydale whispered, "I want you."

Kristen rose and pulled Marydale's boots off and then her pants and then her underwear. Then she stripped her own clothes, and they were both naked. Kristen kissed Marydale on the lips, then moved her kisses down Marydale's body until she lay between Marydale's legs. Kristen parted the soft skin of Marydale's labia and pressed her tongue into Marydale's body. The heat of Kristen's tongue startled her, and the sensation stole all her words away. Kristen massaged Marydale's thighs while she moved her kiss from the opening of Marydale's body to her clit and back again. Marydale felt like she was rushing toward orgasm and then falling away. She clutched the sheets as her body arched.

"Oh, yes!" Marydale gasped, as she lifted her body to Kristen's kiss. She tensed. She couldn't breathe, and she couldn't bear the pleasure, and she couldn't bear for Kristen to stop. She felt like a trapeze artist flung to the farthest reach of her swing and then frozen, motionless, at that utmost height.

As if sensing her distress, Kristen slowed her movements and pulled away.

"No!" Marydale cried.

"No, stop?" Kristen murmured, her breath touching Marydale's sex. "Or no, don't stop."

Marydale's hips strained upward.

"Don't stop. Just…go gently."

Kristen chuckled softly, and her laugh was full of love. She blew on Marydale's sex, then opened her mouth and exhaled a warm breath against Marydale's skin.

"Yes," Kristen whispered.

She circled Marydale's clit with a light touch. Then she slipped a finger inside Marydale's body, still teasing Marydale's clit with her tongue while she moved her finger in and out. She stayed like this for a long time, and Marydale relaxed. Then Kristen touched the inside of Marydale's body, right behind her clitoris, and she drew Marydale into her mouth—her clit, her labia, her hair, her salt, her center—and sucked very gently, all the while moving her tongue slowly and pulling with her lips and pressing on Marydale from inside. Marydale felt a bright, wild joy mount inside her. Then suddenly she was tumbling over the edge of a waterfall, exploding into stardust.

"I'm coming!" Marydale cried.

Kristen held Marydale in her mouth until the last spasms of orgasm subsided. Then she draped her arm over Marydale's hip and pressed her cheek against Marydale's belly. Marydale stroked her hair, staring up at the enormous window and the city lights.

"Don't leave," Kristen whispered.

Marydale wrapped her arms around her shoulders. "No," she said. "I won't leave."

A moment later, Kristen stirred. "May I?" she asked.

She straddled Marydale's thigh, rubbing her sex into Marydale's leg with hard, confident determination. Part of Marydale felt she should do something. She should make Kristen come. But watching Kristen move against her, her eyes closed, her head thrown back, was so beautiful and so arousing, she simply held Kristen's hip bones, awed by her lean strength.

"That day on the *Tristess*," Kristen said, her voice strained with pleasure, "I'm sorry. I was so embarrassed."

"Why?" Marydale said quietly, not wanting to interrupt Kristen's rhythm.

"I…" Kristen drew in a fast breath. "I…came like some teenage boy. I wanted to seduce you."

She looked like she was close to coming now.

"You're lovely," Marydale said.

"I've wanted you so much." Kristen gasped. "You're the only one…the only one…"

Marydale urged her on, rocking her hips to meet Kristen's.

"Yes," Kristen cried out. "Nobody…It's never been like this…Oh God! Now! Yes. Yes. Yes!"

Kristen arched her back, her mouth open in a silent cry. Then she collapsed against Marydale's chest.

As they lay together, Marydale wanted to tell Kristen how vividly she remembered Kristen's first shy touch and how much she enjoyed the confident pressure of her body now, and that whatever time or distance stretched between those two points, it didn't matter because they were here now. But it was too much to explain, and a few minutes later Kristen rolled over and said apologetically, "I have to walk Meatball. Will you come with me? I don't want to leave you even for a minute."

They dressed, and Kristen wrapped an extra scarf around Marydale's neck. They rode the elevator down in tender silence. Outside, the rain had stopped and the sky had cleared. On Twenty-Third Street, the bars were still open. Christmas lights were still hung from every lamppost. The smell of chocolate wafted out of the late-night coffee shops. Meatball moved down the street like a heavy canister vacuum cleaner, snuffling up the city's crumbs. Somewhere Aldean was probably flirting with a woman whose heart he would invariably break, all the while checking his phone to make sure Marydale was okay. She pulled out her phone and texted him, *I won't be home tonight.*

"I'm so happy," Kristen said, putting her arm through Marydale's and leaning against her.

Marydale leaned down and kissed her, in the bright light of a streetlamp, in front of the wide window of a wine bar, full on the lips for everyone to see.

"I love you, Kristen."

8

Kristen woke before Marydale and tiptoed into the kitchen. It was seven thirty. The high-rises in her window were turning from gray to blue. She called work.

"I'm not going to be in today."

The law school intern assigned to the receptionist's desk sounded worried. "Mr. Falcon's here. He wants to talk to you about DataBlast."

"I'm sure he does," Kristen said.

"And Donna wants to know if you've invited the partners from Steward-Gore to the corporate law banquet. Last year they didn't go, and Donna wants to make sure they get a personal invitation from the Falcon Law Group. She said to catch you as soon as you came in."

The banquet. The class action against DataBlast. The partnership that Donna was negotiating for her, perhaps because they were friends, perhaps because Donna needed another ally in the firm.

Above the city, the sun had broken through the clouds, illuminating a single golden shaft of rain. Kristen had bought the condo for the view—the green city, the glass high-rises, the pink Bancorp tower rising up and up above it all—but she had never noticed how beautiful it was or how the photographs of the Firesteed Summit reflected on the glass, as though she were living in a valley that was both the city and the mountains.

"Good morning," Marydale said behind her.

To the receptionist Kristen said, "I've got to go."

Kristen turned. Marydale was naked. Kristen's whole body sang, *She's here.* She wrapped her arms around Marydale's waist.

"I called out from work today," Kristen said. "I know you've probably got stuff to do, but…"

"I'll text Aldean again," Marydale said.

Later, walking Meatball on the street below, it seemed to Kristen that the sidewalks felt new. The air was sweet. The bare branches of the trees were a miracle. She returned with coffees and pastries from a little bakery she had never visited although it was only blocks from her building. And they ate and talked and made love again.

Afterward, as they relaxed in bed, their hands drifting over each other's bodies, Kristen said, "I want to know everything about you."

Marydale stretched her arms over her head, lifting her large breasts, flexing the muscles in her shoulders.

"Like what?" she asked, with a smile that said she knew just how beautiful she was.

"Anything. What happened to Lilith? What's it like living on a houseboat. Tell me about all these awful women you've dated. How did you get to Portland?"

"Lilith died," Marydale said wistfully. "She was old, so it was okay. And the women I dated…they aren't even worth mentioning."

Kristen snuggled closer, and Marydale rested her cheek on top of Kristen's head.

"I'm still on parole," Marydale said. "You need to know that. I can't live the same way you do."

"How long are you on supervision?" Kristen asked.

"Right around the time I…of my conviction…some legislators wanted to get tough on crime, so they passed a lifetime provision."

"You're on parole for life? No matter what? That doesn't make sense."

"They changed the law a few years later. It was too expensive, and it didn't really make a difference, but they don't change your sentence when the law changes. You get stuck with whatever was on the books when you offended, but you know that."

"How did you get to Portland?"

"Aldean moved out to Portland about the same time you left Tristess."

Kristen wished she could see Marydale's face. She took Marydale's hand and held it to her chest instead.

"It was hard," Marydale went on. "My parole officer at the time wouldn't let me date women or associate with gays or lesbians. I couldn't leave Tristess County. I started violating my conditions, crossing over the county line just to do it. I made it all the way down to Nevada once. I don't know if I was going to run away, or if I just wanted to prove they couldn't control who I was. I got sanctioned so many times. I lost my house. I couldn't pay the taxes. I had to put most of my stuff in storage in Tristess. I think they sold it all at auction one time when I got locked up. Finally my parole officer, Cody, quit his job. My new PO...she's good. She cares about people. There was no way I could move to Portland with that many sanctions on my record, but eventually she just let me go anyway."

"And when you got here?" Kristen asked.

"Aldean was waiting for me. Good thing, too. He's great at running a business, but he makes shitty whiskey. He gets all manly about it, and it comes out tasting like somebody's leather shoe." Marydale grew serious again. "I can't give you the kind of life someone else could. I can't take you to Ireland. I can't leave the state. I can't even go across the river to Vancouver for dinner."

Kristen stroked Marydale's arm, examining the swirls of her tattoo.

"I think it was malpractice." Kristen sat up so she could look at Marydale. "You should never have been convicted. We could look into it." It had been years since she practiced criminal law. "I wonder if we could get your parole changed to probation. We might be able to void the original sentence."

"Post-conviction relief?"

"I'll have to check the statute of limitations, but if we won a post-conviction relief hearing, you wouldn't just be off parole; they'd erase your record. It would be like getting an innocent verdict. It's a long shot, but you deserve it."

"I can't," Marydale said. "My PO bent the rules for me. If someone finds out where I am, they could send me back to prison. At the very least, they'd send me back to Tristess, and I'd have to stay." She rolled over onto her back. "I know you don't have to live like that."

Kristen put her arms around Marydale, pulling her close, burying her face in the vanilla scent of Marydale's hair.

"Baby," Kristen whispered. "It doesn't matter to me. I don't care if we don't go to Ireland or Vancouver." She drew back so that she could look into Marydale's eyes. "My life stopped when I left Tristess."

She remembered a commercial that she had seen shortly after she returned to Portland. She had been staying up until three or four every morning, staring at the television. Every few commercial breaks, a genderless cartoon character trudged across the screen while a voice-over asked, *Have you lost interest in things that previously made you happy?*

"I ran three marathons and I don't know how many half marathons," Kristen said. "For a while I was running every road race I could find. I bought the condo. I went out in the evening like it mattered, but it didn't matter. I wasn't happy."

That night Marydale invited Kristen back to the *Tristess* and lifted the trapdoor in the sofa-bench. Kristen eased her way down the short ladder. The room glowed in the light of the pink salt lamp.

"You can't really convince a girl you brought her down here to play board games," Marydale said, draping herself across the bed.

Kristen remembered a fantasy she'd had as a teenager, going to school in the day and working the night shift to pay the bills her mother left unopened on the kitchen table.

"When I was a teenager," Kristen began. "I used to pretend I had this imaginary place I could go. It was a hidden park or a secret room in our apartment, someplace only I knew about. When I went in, time stopped for everyone but me, and I could just…be. That's silly, isn't it?"

She lay down next to Marydale and looked up at the low ceiling.

"What did you want to do in your secret room?" Marydale asked.

"Sleep mostly or do my homework or read. I didn't have time for anything. I was always working or looking after Sierra."

Marydale rolled over onto her side and looked at her. "That's a shame. Every kid should have time."

"Your boat reminds me of that room," Kristen said. "It's like a secret world down here. I didn't even know people lived on the river." Marydale traced the curve of Kristen's jaw.

"You can come here whenever you like."

Kristen nestled closer. "You can come to my place whenever you like, too. I'd like to give you a key, if that wouldn't feel weird to you."

Kristen had been afraid Marydale would demure. It was too soon. She wasn't ready. But Marydale said only, "I'd like that."

When they made love, Kristen felt her body shrink to a single point of pleasure and concentration, like a first star. And even as she felt herself distilled into that intensity, the room expanded, spreading out over the water, over the city, above the rain into the night sky.

When they were sated, Kristen and Marydale resumed their conversation and talked until the dawn light turned the tiny porthole window gray. At work the next morning, at the ubiquitous partners' meeting, Donna Li's voice washed over Kristen like so much traffic noise. Donna had to ask her three times whether Kristen had invited the Steward-Gore partners to the corporate law banquet.

"That's the Saturday before DataBlast," Falcon interjected. "You can't bother her with that."

"It's one phone call. Kristen, did you call them or not?" Donna asked.

"What?" Kristen said dreamily. "No. I didn't call them."

Meanwhile, north of town, in the distillery, Marydale pulled a ladleful of mash from the fermentation tank, swirled it in her mouth, and spit it into one of the drains in the concrete floor. She couldn't tell if it was ready. Everything tasted good. The stale Little Debbie Snack Cake she had bought at the mini-mart south of Diablo's tasted as fine as any organic raisin brioche from the Pearl Bakery. Even the smells of the city wafting around the little convenience store—diesel and tar and damp cigarette butts—smelled right, because the whole world was right.

Aldean ambled up to Marydale where she stood pondering the fermentation. He clapped a cheerful hand on her shoulder.

"Haven't see you in around…oh…forty-eight hours." He took the ladle from her and tasted the tank. "Not ready yet, is it?"

Marydale looked down to hide her smile.

"Look at you." Aldean chuckled.

"I know you're going to tell me to be careful. Hit it and quit it, right?"

Marydale looked up at the tanks and the industrial halogen lights suspended from bars across the ceiling.

"Fuck careful," Aldean said. "You're in love."

9

On the night of the corporate law party, Marydale dressed in the tiny bathroom on board the *Tristess*. It had been a long time since she'd worn a real dress, and the shimmering red fabric felt strange against her skin. The crepe gripped her belly, and the bra pushed her breasts up and forward. She tugged at the edges of the underwire.

She wondered if the red had been a bad choice. The color accented her tattoos, and in the store she had liked the dyke-prom-queen contrast between the ink and the dress. Now it felt too garish for a lawyers party

When Marydale stopped by the Falcon Law Group to take Kristen out to lunch, every woman she saw wore a slim, gray pencil skirt, and even though spring had blossomed in the Pearl District, they all wore long sleeves and nylons. They were all runners. And Marydale loved that leanness on Kristen. She loved how Kristen's body felt as strong as braided wire and yet vulnerable and small at the same time. Marydale clamped her hands over her own breasts in an attempt to rearrange them into a smaller, more discreet version of themselves. It was too late to buy a different dress now, and she had nothing else in her tiny closet that was appropriate for more than a night at the Doug Fir Lounge.

She stepped out into the kitchen to show Aldean.

"Not bad." Aldean dropped his eyes down to her waist and then back up to her breasts. "They come into a room. That's for sure."

"God! Aldean!"

"You look great. You're the fucking rodeo queen." Aldean lifted a flask to his lips and took a sip. "They're rodeo sized."

Marydale tossed a dish towel at the side of his head.

"Thank you, because that's what *every* girl wants to hear." She eyed her reflection in the windows. "If I could ride in on Trumpet, it'd be great."

"What are you stressing about?" Aldean took another sip. "All those corporate women, they've got nothing on you."

Marydale sat down on the bench next to him.

"You'll do great," Aldean said.

"Kristen says she doesn't care what I tell them, even if I tell them I was in Holten Penitentiary."

Marydale took the flask out of Aldean's hand and took a sip.

"What are you going to say?" Aldean asked.

"That I run a distillery."

"See?" Aldean said, taking back the flask. "They're not going to run your name before they pass the champagne. They're going to think that Kristen Brock got a hot girlfriend, or they're just going to wonder if Kristen is gay, or they're not going to think anything at all, because nobody gives a shit."

"Do you believe in premonitions?" Marydale asked.

"No."

"Come on. Everyone does."

"I don't believe in premonitions about you going to Kristen's company party." Aldean leaned back a little. "You're hot. You're going to be the prettiest woman there, and Kristen's going to love it. You girls may be lesbians or feminists or whatever, but Kristen likes to win, and when you walk into that room, every man there is gonna know she beat the shit out of them in this competition. Do you know why I never hit on you? You know, back in Tristess, before Aaron Holten?"

"Because I'm a lesbian and your best friend and possibly your cousin."

"Yeah, sure. You're a lesbian and everyone in Tristess is probably some sort of cousin." Aldean touched two fingers to the bottom of her chin as though gently readjusting a painting hung ever so slightly off-kilter. "You were out of my league, Mary Rae. That's why. You were always out of my league."

"No woman has ever been out of your league."

"I want to say *yes* to that." He cocked his fingers in the shape of a gun and clicked his tongue. "But a man's gotta know how far he can ride out. Your mom'd be proud of you."

"Because I can still blow out my hair?"

"Because you're still you."

* * *

Marydale felt an old confidence return to her limbs as she lifted herself into the cab of her pickup, careful not to catch her heel on the running board. The pedals felt familiar as she eased onto Highway 30. The roads were slick with rain, but a girl who'd grown up with a 1980 stick-shift Dodge and no power steering could drive an F-150 in the rain. She glanced in the rearview mirror. The smoky black eye shadow and red lipstick that had looked a little tawdry in the *Tristess* worked in the dark.

Traffic paused as Highway 30 neared the edge of the Northwest Industrial District.

"Come on." She tapped the steering wheel. "What are you waiting for?"

Suddenly the darkness behind her lit up with a flash of blue and red. She froze, her foot on the brake, her hands gripping the wheel. She felt as though someone had clamped a towel over her mouth, an iron band around her heart. Everything around her came into sharp focus: the dimples on the rubber steering wheel, the raindrops on the windshield, the police lights reflecting in her rearview mirror.

She scanned the road. It couldn't be for her. The traffic was crawling. She put on her blinker and checked her blind spot twice, easing up against the side of the curb, holding her breath, waiting for the police cruiser to pull ahead, waiting for the other cars to move over. As soon as the police passed, she would get off the highway. She would find another route. In the back of her mind, Gulu whispered, *They know once you've been in. Once you've been in, you got a caul on you. They can smell it.*

The lights remained in her rearview mirror, alternating red and blue. Marydale's foot trembled on the brake. Her legs shook. She couldn't see the police officer in the car, but she thought she saw the cruiser door open.

No, no, no, she whispered to herself.

A second later, someone tapped on her window.

"Roll down."

"I'm sorry," she said, leaning on the window button. "I'm sorry." She tried to arrange her face.

"License and registration."

All she could see was a duty belt and a gun.

The purse in Marydale's hands felt strange. She couldn't undo the clasp. When she finally did, it took her several seconds to pull out her driver's license.

The officer leaned down so he could see in her window.

"Don't worry," he said. "Your brake light's out. That's all. It's just a warning. We're beefing up security down here. People are moving out into the Industrial District, and they're getting nervous 'cause it's not the Pearl District, you know?"

"Yes, sir." She looked down.

Act cool, Gulu whispered, but Marydale couldn't remember what cool felt like. In the back of her mind, she could hear the guards yelling. *Inmates. On the ground. Down!*

"And your insurance?" the officer prompted.

She reached for the glove box.

"Have you been drinking?"

Marydale thought of the sip she had taken from Aldean's flask.

"No."

"Okay. One moment." The officer excused himself.

She saw the cell block, three tiers high, all the cells looking down on the same cold breezeway.

Marydale stared at the window, the raindrops trickling down the glass like tears. She imagined Kristen standing in the ballroom of whatever elegant hall the Falcon Law Group had rented. Marydale could see Kristen scanning the room for her arrival. *I'm sorry I have to be there so early,* Kristen had said. *I wish we could ride together. I can't wait to show you off.*

I love you, Marydale thought.

"Ma'am." The officer's voice broke through her thoughts. "Please get out of the truck."

Her heart seized. She felt the blood in her body stop moving. She was suffocating with the breath still filling her lungs.

"What is it?"

The rain hit her face.

It had been raining the night Aaron had followed her home. She saw him climbing the ladder, his thick hands on the rungs. *I'm going to show you something, you fucking dyke. I'm gonna fucking kill you.* He was grinning. *Help me!* she cried. Then he was falling. She was running for the house, for the phone. *He was trying to kill me. I think I've done something awful.* Two cruisers were moving up the gravel drive in a fierce parade of light.

"You're under arrest."

"That's not how it happened," Marydale whispered. "The

chief didn't want to, not right away. He said it was self-defense."

"There's an outstanding warrant. Parole violation. Ma'am, you need to get out of the vehicle and come with me."

Marydale wanted to run. She wanted to hurl herself back in time to a moment when this had not happened. She stepped out of the truck.

Through the haze of her panic, she heard herself say, "I think there might have been a mistake."

"Your PO put a warrant in the system. Looks like he thinks you've been on abscond for quite some time."

"I haven't done anything. She knows where I am," Marydale said. "I pay my supervision fee. I tell her if I leave the county. You can call her."

The officer shook his head. "I'm sorry. I don't know the details of your case."

The damp air felt frigid against her bare arms.

"I have to call my girlfriend." A new fear swelled in her heart. Kristen knew she was on parole. Kristen said she understood. They couldn't go away on vacation in Ireland. But who could understand this?

"They'll take care of that at the jail," the officer said, unclasping a pair of handcuffs from his belt.

He reminded Marydale of some of the ranchers in Tristess. His face was kind and craggy at the same time. He was sorry; the thought struck her like a blow. He didn't want to arrest her, and she hadn't done anything, and it didn't matter.

8

Kristen stood in front of her desk, a stack of DataBlast files in a neat pile before her. Across the table were strewn her notes from the night before: every hospital, every police station, every sheriff, in Portland, in Salem, in Tristess. Fourteen sleepless hours of searching.

Aldean had called her as soon as he realized what had happened. She had taken his call in the foyer of the University Club, surprised to hear his voice. He always made her a little nervous. Although they had drunk manhattans on the deck of the *Tristess* and chatted when she visited the distillery, he watched her warily. He reminded her of Lilith, circling Marydale, friendly but ready to lunge at anyone who threatened her. And Kristen liked him for the love he so obviously bore for Marydale. But when he called her at the University Club, he had felt like a stranger on the other end of the line. *Marydale's been arrested. You know she's on parole. I can't find her.*

Now she clutched her phone to her ear.

"Holten State Penitentiary," a woman's voice said.

There was no *How may I help you?*

"I'm looking for…someone."

The vocabulary didn't fit: *an inmate, an offender, a parolee.* She was looking for Marydale's cascade of golden hair.

"I'm with the Falcon Law Group in Portland," Kristen said. "I'm looking for a parolee. She was arrested last night, and I can't track her down."

"A client?" the woman growled.

"A client." The lie stuck in her throat, but *client* mattered more.

"Arrested last night?"

"Yes. Probably around seven. Her name is Marydale Rae."

The woman paused. "We don't have her."

"No one has her!"

"Then she's probably in transit."

"Probably? She's a human being. Someone needs to know where she is!"

"If she got arrested in Portland, she wouldn't be coming here."

"She was paroled in Tristess. I've called everyone in Portland. Please check to see if you have a record of her."

"Hold."

Kristen could hear the force with which the woman punched the hold button. There was no friendly elevator music or public service announcements on the line, just silence. Only the green call icon on her phone told her she was still connected.

Eleven and a half minutes later, a man came on the line.

"Looking for Rae, Marydale Marie?" he asked. "She's in transit. Should be here tonight. They got hung up at the Coffee Creek Correctional Facility, waiting for some paperwork to come through. Looks like an abscond. She didn't have permission to leave the county."

"I need to talk to her," Kristen said. "This is a mistake. She had permission to be in Portland. She's a business owner."

"I'd just call on Wednesday or Thursday. We're not as busy then. Her PO will put a sanction into the system within fifteen days, and then there'll be a hearing. Are you representing her?"

"There shouldn't even be a hearing. She didn't do anything wrong!"

The man sighed. "We just got a new director. Turns out some POs have been letting their nonviolent offenders do whatever. Move. Travel. As long as they stay out of trouble. New director's been cracking down on that. Cleaning house."

"Why are they sending her back to prison?" Kristen asked. "Why not a county jail?"

"They closed down the women's jail in Tristess. Everyone's coming here. It's a damn mess, if you ask me. We can't keep a stable population. That's the whole point of prison. It's for people who've got a year or more. Now we got inmates coming in for two-week parole sanctions. But nobody wants to pay for a woman's jail, so what are you gonna do?"

Kristen checked the time on her laptop. She didn't need to call up Google Maps to know the answer to her question.

It was Sunday, and it was nine hours and thirty-two minutes from Portland to Tristess if she didn't catch any traffic. It would be almost seven in the evening by the time she arrived. If she were going to get back to court in the morning for the first day of DataBlast, she'd be able to stay for only an hour or two before turning back around…if Marydale was even there.

"How late do you allow visitors?" she asked.

"Tuesdays and Thursdays," the man said. "Ten to four."

9

The nine-hour drive to Tristess County took twenty. Mary-dale sat in the transport van, dressed in orange scrubs, her hands cuffed in front of her, staring out the window. Eventually she closed her eyes, not to sleep but to see Kristen. Kristen stepping out of the shower, her hair damp against her face. Kristen sitting on a lawn chair on the deck of the *Tristess*, wearing one of Marydale's old sweaters, her glasses fogging in the steam from a mug of coffee. Kristen above her as they made love.

I love you, Marydale thought. She repeated the words over and over in her mind, trying to recapture what she had felt as a teenager kissing girls in the back of her pickup: that it didn't matter if they got married or bought a parcel and raised sheep. They had *kissed*. Against all prohibitions, despite the pundits on the AM talk shows screaming about the *sanctity of marriage* and *sins of lust*, they had claimed a few seconds of life. That had mattered when she had lived in

Tristess. That had comforted her. Now all she felt was a tight, hard pain in her chest.

After being photographed, fingerprinted, and made to sit in a body-cavity scanner the inmates called the Boss, Marydale was escorted to a windowless office off the main prison wing. She stood in front of the desk of the woman identified as her counselor. Around the office, someone had taped black-framed posters. TEAM: TOGETHER EVERYONE ACHIEVES MORE. DREAM AND THE WINDS WILL CARRY YOU. The photograph of an eagle set against a blue sky made the windowless room even bleaker. The woman looked wilted, like a plant that had lived too long under fluorescent lights.

"The prison is like a city within a city," the counselor began. "Everyone in our city has a role to play."

The familiar speech: the city inside. They all had responsibilities and jobs. The guards were like the police, making sure that citizens of the city obeyed the laws. But it wasn't a city. A city had a sky. A city had cherry blossoms. A city had glass high-rises so tall the windmills on their rooftops looked like insects.

"If it were a city"—Marydale stared at the black ink on the pads of her fingers—"I could leave."

"You had a choice about the behavior that put you in here," the woman said. "Even though you're here on a parole violation, you'll be treated like the other inmates. You work. You keep your house clean. You get in trouble, you go to segregation." The woman regarded her over the top of purple reading glasses. "Do you understand?"

"I think I should be in jail, not prison." Marydale was careful to keep her tone level and her eyes down. "I don't know why I got remanded to prison. I haven't had a hearing."

"They closed down the women's jail." The woman looked at a file on her desk. "You've been here before. I'm sorry to see you back."

"I'm sorry," Marydale said reflexively.

"Okay," the counselor called to a guard outside the door. "She's ready."

A female guard appeared and nodded to Marydale to follow her.

"Everything comes off this main corridor," the guard said as they walked.

The floors were shined to a high gloss. The air smelled like cheap detergent, clean but cloying at the same time. High above their heads, fans—painted the same dull yellow as the ceiling—rotated furiously.

"You walk on the right." The guard continued her lecture undeterred. "Hands to yourself. No moving around the prison unless you're on work assignment or have a pass. You probably won't be around long enough to get one of the good jobs." The woman paused at a guard station and took a couple slips of paper off the counter. "Kite forms." She handed them to Marydale. "If you get sick, you need to make a phone call, you want to report bullying, you kite the guard on duty. They'll pass your message on. You can read and write, yes?"

"Yes, ma'am."

"Make it legible. They're not going to send someone back

to ask you what you wanted. Count is at midnight, three a.m., five a.m., seven thirty, noon, four fifteen, and nine p.m. Ten, noon, and nine on the weekends." They had arrived at the block. Three stories of barred cells looked out at the desert.

"A13," the guard called to the guard station.

Someone pressed the button that unlocked cell A13.

"Rae. That's Julie Kelso." The guard pointed to Marydale's new cellmate. "Kelso, get her set up."

Marydale froze in the doorway. The cell felt chillingly familiar: two bunks, one seatless toilet, a plastic mirror, a hand broom tucked against the bars so they could keep their *house* clean. Above the sink were installed shelves, their thin metal edges surprisingly sharp in a world where paper clips were contraband. There wasn't enough room on the floor to do a push-up.

Kelso lay on the bottom bunk. "Stay out of trouble for a couple of weeks, and you can probably get moved to the dormitory," she said, without looking up from the battered *People* magazine she was reading. "If you don't like the cell."

"Wait," Marydale said to the guard. "I need to write a kite."

"What do you need a kite for already?" the guard asked.

"I need to call my lawyer."

From the bottom bunk, the woman said, "You're lucky if they care." Marydale guessed the woman was about twenty, but she looked older. Her bleached-blond hair was growing out, and the roots were dark rings counting the months.

"Write it up and give it to me at count," the guard said. "Kelso, loan her a pencil."

Marydale felt a hand on her back, and she stumbled into the cell. The bars closed behind her. Kelso dropped the magazine she was reading and glared at Marydale.

"You been here before?" she asked.

"Yeah."

Kelso slipped on a pair of flip-flops from beside the bed. Then she knelt down and opened the two drawers beneath her bunk. From one, she pulled a sweatshirt and some menstrual pads. She crammed them in the other drawer. "There. That one's yours."

"Thanks," Marydale said. She touched the two-rung ladder to the top bunk. "May I?"

"Whatever." Kelso flicked a page of her magazine. "I don't got a pencil though."

The dark blue mattress was stained around the seams. The blanket was rough, like the padding movers threw over wood furniture. Marydale lay down and crossed her arms over her chest. *You cry too much, Scholar.*

Marydale woke to the sound of footsteps. She had been dreaming about the distillery. She was late to work, and Aldean was outside, stomping on the deck of the *Tristess* to wake her. She sat up quickly, almost hitting her head on the ceiling above her bunk before she remembered where she was. The women in the cells above hers were calling out insults and invitations to someone coming down the breezeway.

Marydale swung her legs over her bed. She had been cold under her blanket, but the air outside her blanket was freezing.

"What's going on?" she asked.

"Somebody's getting a visit," Kelso said.

"A lawyer?" Marydale asked. She couldn't keep the excitement out of her voice.

"Not a lawyer. They got special rooms for that." Kelso peered out the bars. "It's the new parole boss. He's in here all the time, givin' people shit. He'll be gone before I get out of this shithole though." She flopped back on her bunk. "He's just some dumb—"

"Rae! Visitor!" The young female guard's voice was too deep for her small frame. "Wake up, Rae!"

Reflexively, Marydale came to the bars, wrapping her hands around the peeling metal. A moment later, she saw a familiar figure striding down the breezeway toward the guard. Marydale stepped back.

The guard softened her voice to a conversational tone. "Here she is, Mr. Holten. I can't believe you caught her. I can't believe the bitch who killed Aaron almost got away."

Marydale must have made some sound because Kelso said, "You all right?"

Marydale shook her head. The cell tightened around her. She wanted to press her face into the corner of the wall, to throw her blanket over her, to pull the drawers out from beneath the bunk and break them against the blunt edge of the toilet. She didn't move.

Ronald Holten ambled up to the bars, the guard hovering

at his elbow. He hooked his thumbs through his belt loops. "Marydale Rae," he pronounced slowly.

His hair was still dusty blond, and he was still handsome, his lips smiling without actually radiating any cheer. It reminded Marydale of an African folktale she had read about a village girl who fell in love with a handsome man who lured her into the wilderness. Once in the bush, his head slowly transformed from a man's head into a bare white skull, with teeth that chattered and smirked even when he was sleeping.

"On abscond," he said. Everything was a drawl. "For years."

Marydale stared at his mouth, willing her face to reveal nothing. "I had permission from my PO."

"Did you?"

"I paid my supervision fee every month. I wouldn't have paid it if I was trying to hide. I have phone records. I called in."

"Your PO wanted you to go up to the big city so you could make friends?" Holten continued as if she hadn't spoken. "Couldn't find any of your type out here, could you? Apparently she had a lot of special arrangements with her cons, but she's not working for us anymore."

He touched the plastic badge clipped to his shirt pocket. DIRECTOR OF PAROLE, TRISTESS COUNTY.

"I have a business. I didn't do anything wrong," Marydale protested.

"You didn't get a transfer." He strutted back and forth in front of her cell. "You didn't transfer because you couldn't keep your nose clean."

"I couldn't keep my nose clean because Cody Densen wouldn't leave me alone."

"Oh, we're supposed to leave you alone? Is that how it works? Maybe I should let you set up a meth kitchen, maybe get some kids to sell for you? Finance your lifestyle."

"I didn't sell drugs!"

"What did you do in Portland?"

"I run a distillery."

"Oh, and you don't sell drugs."

"It's fifty dollars a bottle. We sell to restaurants."

The first round of inmates was heading out to breakfast.

The guard yelled, "Stay to your left," as the inmates filed around Holten.

Marydale held Holten's gaze. She knew she shouldn't. Deference was the only defense. Nod. Smile. Agree to everything. Then palm any stray piece of thread or wire, a bolt, the broken plastic handle off a pair of scissors. Watch the cameras. *You gotta learn the dance, Scholar.* But Marydale couldn't push her rage down far enough.

"I wasn't allowed to date. I wasn't allowed to be friends with people like me." The blood pounding in her ears erased the sounds of the block. "You can't live like that. That's not the way the rest of the world works, and if you lived two days in a town where people didn't marry their fucking cousins—"

"Rae!" the guard warned, as though Holten needed her protection.

Marydale remembered Kristen pleading with her. *What happens if we've been together for two and a half years and then we get caught?*

Holten stepped closer to the bars. She could smell his minty breath.

"People like you," he said. "Listen to me, Rae." She could see his skull-teeth clacking in his head. "I don't give a shit that you're a fucking dyke. You killed my nephew. You killed a Holten."

"It was self-defense and you know it."

"Maybe I do. I knew Aaron. I knew what he was like, and I say more power to him. I'm just sorry he didn't finish the job."

Marydale stepped back, bumping into the sink.

"As far as you're concerned, I'm your PO now." The cadence of Holten's voice was light. If Marydale had overheard the tone and not the message, she'd have thought he was discussing the Tristess High football team. But his eyes were little slits of black lava rock. "I am judge, jury, and prosecution. I don't care what some hug-a-thug parole board said when they let you out. You're right where you should have been all along, and I'm going to make sure you stay this time."

10

At the seven-thirty count, Marydale held a kite form out to the guard.

"Please," she said quietly. "I need to call my lawyer."

"Don't they all," the man said, folding the paper and putting it in his pocket, but he returned about an hour later. "You're in luck. I got your lawyer on the phone."

Marydale felt the cold light of the block grow a little bit warmer. Kristen had found her. She'd called.

"Cell A13," the guard yelled to the control station at the end of the block.

The latch clicked open. It was so easy—just a press of a button—yet she was not even allowed to push the bars open after the electronic lock had been released. The guard had to open the bars and lead her to one of the telephones mounted on the wall by the guard station. Marydale touched the receiver.

"Well, pick up," the guard said.

Her hands were shaking. "Hello?"

"Marydale." Kristen sounded oddly formal. "This is Kristen Brock from the Falcon Law Group. The prison monitors all calls except confidential communication between attorney and client. Do I have your permission to represent you in your upcoming hearings?"

"Yes."

"What happened?" Kristen asked, her voice gentler.

"My taillight was out. Ronald Holten works in parole. I think he fired my PO."

"That's not okay. I'm going to look into that," Kristen said. "They can't have a relative of the victim supervising a parolee. I'm going to file a complaint today. I just started the DataBlast case," she added. "It'll take a week, maybe two, but I'll be there as soon as I finish. I wish I could be there now."

"You're going to make partner." Marydale could feel someone watching her with more than the guard's paid-by-the-hour attention.

"In the meantime," Kristen said, "I'll need you to write down everything you remember about your case."

"You mean the taillight?"

"No. Start with Aaron, when he first threatened you. You shouldn't have been convicted. I'll think of something. And I'll be there soon. I promise."

Marydale heard someone on the other end of the phone line call to Kristen.

Kristen said, "In a minute."

"What is it?" Marydale asked. "Where are you?"

"I'm at the courthouse."

"You almost done, Rae?" the guard called out.

"Kristen?" Marydale said. It was a plea. It was a prayer. "I love you."

"I will call you tomorrow," Kristen said. "I love you, too."

Slowly, Marydale returned the receiver to its metal hook. It felt like closing a door to air and light.

A few prisoners were lingering by the guard station. Marydale felt someone's eyes on her, as demanding and inescapable as a hand on her shoulder. She looked up.

It was like seeing Kristen at the bar in Deerfield only in reverse; instead of hope suddenly surging through her body, it was fear and a cold, clammy feeling of being fondled from afar. Gulu stood by the wall, pushing a mop slowly back and forth across the shining floor. *Hello, baby*, she mouthed. And Marydale wanted to run back to her cell and close her eyes and close out the walls around her.

Gulu called to the guard on duty. "Sir, I've got to move a pallet of floor wax. My back's killing me. Would you send Scofield or Oberlan out to help?"

The guard's face said, *You really think I'd fall for that?* But he already had.

"Inmate." He pointed to Marydale. "What's your name again?"

"Rae," she said reluctantly.

"Go help Clarocci with her wax."

I got you, Gulu's eyes said.

Marydale followed a pace behind Gulu as Gulu led her down the wide central corridor to a supply pantry. Behind a wire mesh grate, an older woman with a tight helmet of box-dyed curls watched four television screens.

"Name?" the guard asked from behind her mesh window. "What do you need?"

Gulu flashed her custodial pass. The woman pressed a button and the door beside them opened. The guard glanced at Marydale.

"Station said I could bring her to help me lift up a crate," Gulu said.

The woman pushed a sign-in clipboard through a slot beneath her window. Marydale wrote her name and showed the woman her ID badge.

"Five minutes," the guard said, and returned to the gray-and-white screens at her station.

Inside the large supply room, Gulu ducked behind a shelf stacked floor-to-ceiling with bottles of cleaning fluid shrink-wrapped on pallets. She leaned up against one of the shelves.

"Were you talking to your girlfriend?" Gulu asked.

"You said you needed floor wax," Marydale said.

"Chester and Tia saw you at lunch, said you didn't even come over to say hi. You too good for us now?"

"I'm not looking for any trouble." Marydale folded her arms.

Gulu came closer. "You were always trouble, Scholar."

"What do you want?"

"Only thing I've ever wanted." Gulu's face was inches away from hers.

"You say that to all the girls." Marydale knew it was only half true.

"We could pick up where we left off."

"Where was that?"

"Did you miss me, Scholar?"

The answer was *once* and *not anymore*, but that was too complicated to explain in the minutes afforded by a guard's lethargy.

"No," Marydale said.

Gulu grabbed the back of Marydale's hair and yanked her into a grinding kiss. Their teeth collided. Marydale smelled the familiar stink of prison breath and cheap toothpaste. She knew better than to fall back or protest. She did not need to look for the camera to know that Gulu had positioned them in a tiny, perfect blind spot.

"I thought you'd at least have come back around to say hello, put a little something in my commissary," Gulu said when she pulled away.

"I have a girlfriend," Marydale hissed.

"What's going on in there?" the guard yelled.

"We're almost done," Gulu called out.

"Three minutes," the guard said.

"She straight?" Gulu asked.

"You're straight!"

"Not in here, and I'm not getting out anytime soon, so…" Gulu planted her hand on the shelf behind Marydale's head. "Anyways, you always liked the straight girls. So tragic." She laughed. "And that's not what I meant. Is she *straight*."

"She's a lawyer," Marydale said. It felt like holding up a talisman to ward off a loaded gun. She saw Kristen in her gray suit and her tortoiseshell glasses. Kristen cared, but she was so far away, farther than the miles between Tristess and Portland. There was a distance between the prison parking lot and the cells that could not be measured on a map.

"Well, shit, a lawyer!" Gulu said. "She gonna come and save you? I heard you got out of Tristess. This girl gonna come down from Portland and visit you on Thursdays? For how long? You gonna sit around and cry for her? You know Ronnie Holten's in charge now. He's got a hard-on for everyone, but he *loves* you." Her smile tightened. "She's not coming, Scholar. And if she does, she won't stay."

Gulu took a strand of Marydale's hair and twined it around her fingers, then gave a sharp pull. "I've been here long enough. I've seen girls like you come and go, and I know. I can smell her on you. City girl. Big lawyer. Maybe that's why you fucked her, told yourself you loved her. But once you're in here, you can't go back. But we could still be something, Scholar. You were always special."

"I'm not interested."

"You're not getting out, if that's what you're hoping."

"It's a parole violation," Marydale shot back. "They can't hold me forever."

"You think so?" A split second later, Marydale felt Gulu's arms clasp around her. She thought Gulu was going to kiss her again. Then she felt Gulu's fist connect with the bottom of her rib cage. Gulu pushed her backward, hitting again and again…but not hard. The blows weren't the attack; it was Gulu's screams that were dangerous.

"Help me," Gulu yelled. "Guard! She's got a piece. She's going to cut me!"

With the grace of a stage actor, Gulu stumbled backward, clutching Marydale to her as she fell slowly. They barely made a sound when they hit the floor, but Gulu screamed, "It hurts. Get off me. She's going to kill me!"

Marydale felt a cold scrape of metal as Gulu slipped something into the waistband of her pants. She tried to rise, but Gulu squeezed her, even as she thrashed around beneath Marydale. An alarm sounded. The lights in the pantry brightened. Someone hit an emergency lockdown switch. Guards' footsteps pounded the floor.

Gulu whispered in Marydale's ear, "Ronnie Holten says to say hi, Scholar. We missed you."

11

The first days of the DataBlast class action went so smoothly Kristen barely remembered them. No, it wasn't that she didn't remember; she hadn't been there. Some other woman with her face had walked back and forth in front of the jury. *When a corporate giant like USA DataBlast enters into a contract with private citizens...* Her heels had kept time with the beat of her words. *A trust that binds our business community together... The fact that each individual transaction was practically invisible... hundreds of thousands of dollars stolen. A fraud... recognized at the highest levels of the company...* All the while, she had seen Marydale in her mind's eye. Marydale standing in the snow. Marydale naked in the moonlight of her farmhouse bedroom. Marydale bruised in a prison uniform. *This kind of injustice...* Kristen had finished the sentence but only because it was written in her notes.

And she was brilliant. Everyone at the Falcon Law Group agreed. At the end of the fourth day, even Falcon wanted to go out for a drink at Huber's. He and Donna kept up a steady replay of the case. When Kristen said nothing, Falcon exclaimed, "Damn, look at her. She's just cool as a cucumber."

"I told you Kristen's got this," Donna said, and caught Kristen's eye and smiled.

When they had finished their drinks, Kristen headed back toward her rented parking spot in the lot behind the courthouse. She turned onto Burnside as if to head home, but before crossing over I-405, she took a quick turn onto the freeway on-ramp. She wasn't thinking about visiting Sierra. She hadn't planned to, and she was surprised that she remembered the exact location of the *HumAnarchist* headquarters without consulting her GPS. But there she was.

The garden in front of the bungalow was conspicuously weedy. Old cornstalks lay in piles, probably sheltering kale starts or fledgling artichokes. The columns in front of the house were wrapped in moldy knitting. A hand-painted wooden sign rose from the garden's wreckage: THE HUMANARCHIST: SUBVERSIVE SELF-IMPROVEMENT FOR THE NEW REVOLUTIONARY.

Kristen rang the doorbell, which sounded with the lugubrious voice of a didgeridoo. Frog answered the door, his curly black hair fashioned into two pom-poms on either side of his head. He appeared to be wearing a chain-mail shirt made out of bottle caps.

"Is Sierra here?" Kristen asked.

Frog beckoned her in. Inside what had once been the living room, two women tapped away at Mac desktops, one speaking rapidly into a headset. A copier chunked out flyers in the front hall. Somewhere in the back, a fax dialed. Everywhere the walls were covered in paper. Classic punk-rock band posters overlapped with pesticide-usage-by-county charts. An ad for a lecture on healthy BDSM relationships overlapped a calligraphied quote from Emma Goldman.

Frog hurried upstairs, calling Sierra's name. From somewhere above them, Kristen thought she heard Sierra say, "What does she want?" A moment later, Sierra descended the stairs, ducking to miss a Donald Trump piñata with dollar signs for eyes. She held a stack of papers in one arm and a cell phone in the other. Despite her knee-length sweater and striped socks, she looked like a businesswoman interrupted before an important meeting.

To Frog, she said, "We need a high-res logo for the Hemp Association, and tell the folks at Out in Southwest Portland Coffee we'll run their ad for free for three months if they donate the space for the Purple Tie fundraiser. Get that urban goose farmer on the line, too. I want to sell his handbook in featured merch." Sierra made no move to step off the last stair. To Kristen she said, "Yes?"

"I...Can you come out for a drink or coffee?" Kristen asked.

"Our newsletter is going live tonight," Sierra said.

Kristen wanted to protest that it was an *anarchist* website. They had posted a recipe for placenta. What could deadlines mean to the *HumAnarchist*?

Instead she said, "I know. I'm sorry. I need to talk."

"Okay," Sierra said with less enthusiasm than Kristen expected for a woman who had, just six months earlier, suggested they try living in a micro-house together to *reconnect in adult sisterhood.*

"Where?" Sierra asked.

"Anywhere you like," Kristen said.

The last time she let Sierra choose the bar, they'd ended up in a vegan coffeehouse featuring an art exhibit of multimedia sculpture made out of dildos. A few minutes later, they arrived—Kristen by car, Sierra by adult-sized tricycle—at the bar Sierra had selected. The Port Call, it was called, and the interior was decorated with kitschy paintings of shipwrecks and an unnerving quantity of philodendrons.

Sierra sat by the window, her blond dreadlocks piled on top of her head and secured with a purple scarf.

A tendril of philodendron touched Kristen's shoulder. She lifted a snifter to her nose, smelling the familiar burn of Poisonwood.

"I'm sorry I didn't stay for breakfast with your friends on New Year's Day," Kristen said. It suddenly seemed strange—no, inexcusable—that she hadn't talked to Sierra since that morning. So much had happened, and she had thought about Sierra and talked to her in her imagination, but she hadn't called.

"You got a cab," Sierra said. "You didn't even say goodbye."

"I'm sorry."

"I called to see if you were okay, and you *texted* me back. Are you too busy to talk to me now?" Sierra took a large sip of her beer. "I saw you with that woman. You know you could tell me if you're gay or bisexual or trans or something. You know it doesn't matter to me."

"I didn't really think the owner of America's most successful online anarchist magazine would hate me because I was gay."

"So you're gay?" Sierra turned away, tilting her chin up slightly, as though the subject was suddenly beneath her.

"No. I'm not gay," Kristen said.

"Bi?" Sierra offered. "We're all bisexual in some way, especially women. There's a fluidity to our sexuality even if we don't act on it."

She sounded like she was reciting something from the *HumAnarchist* advice column.

"Bisexual." Kristen sounded out the word. "It's not even that. It's not…"

Sierra pulled the lemon off the side of her beer and chewed it.

"It's just her," Kristen said.

Kristen longed for Sierra's cheerful, *We have to catch up!* She wanted her to lean forward, to say *Talk to me*, to say, *What's wrong, Kristi?*

"You didn't just meet her at the bar, did you?" Sierra asked.

"Do you remember my roommate in Tristess?"

"That's her?"

Outside, a spit of rain marked the sunny sidewalk. Somewhere there would be a rainbow, but not here. Kristen took a deep breath. She was suddenly aware of a film on her glasses, like tears blurring her vision.

"We were together in Tristess." She tried to piece her memories together. "Law school was hard for me. Everyone was driving Saabs and working at their father's firm. You remember. We were broke, and you were at the Portland Night High School. Then I got that job at the school, and I felt like I was the kid who never left home. Then all of a sudden I was in Tristess, and I was this big-city lawyer everyone hated. And Marydale got it. She got what it felt like to always be on the outside. I knew she was gay, and I wasn't, but I was attracted to her. I was attracted to who she *was*. I think I was in love with her." She saw beautiful Marydale Rae with her tattoos and her perfect smile. "I'm in love with her now."

"Why didn't you tell me?" Sierra asked.

Kristen continued. "I left Tristess because people found out."

"They found out that you were with a woman?" Sierra's voice softened but only a little bit.

"They found out that I was living with her. That I was sleeping with her. She has a past."

She tried to lay out the story the way she would present a case at the partners meeting, but she kept starting over. Did the story begin with Aaron Holten? Or with Marydale's parents? Or with the first Holten to arrive in Oregon and claim it as his own? All she knew was that all versions of the story ended with the Aldean's voice on the phone as Kristen huddled in a corner of the University Club trying to catch a good cell signal. *Marydale's been arrested.*

"Douglas Grady, this defense lawyer I met in Tristess, he thought it was self-defense," Kristen went on. "He thought she was the real victim. Now she's stuck out there, and I've got this fucking case I'm supposed to try." The words tumbled out. "I remember driving away. I stopped at this little town. It's just a gas station. It was night, and they were closed, and I stayed in the parking lot and cried and cried. I thought she didn't count. I mean, she meant everything to me, but she just wasn't part of…my life. And now I'm doing it again. I should be there with her."

She felt a cold knot tighten in her throat. She blinked quickly.

Sierra's pixie face was set in a look so cold, for a second she was unrecognizable.

"She's not a killer," Kristen pleaded.

"You never told me," Sierra said.

"I know. I'm sorry."

"I'm your sister!" Sierra scooted her chair back.

"I didn't tell anyone. I couldn't."

"Even *me*? You dated a lesbian murderess, and you didn't tell me? After everything we've been through with Mom and all her shit?"

"*We*'ve been through?" Kristen stopped. "I took care of you while Mom was off singing 'Free Bird' at some bar in Gresham. I set a good example. I couldn't tell you about Marydale. I didn't want you to end up like Mom."

"You thought I was like Mom?"

Sierra's lips had straightened into a thin fissure, and Kristen suddenly saw the woman Sierra was in business. Her dreadlocks might actually contain live birds, and she might ride a tricycle when she wasn't driving an SUV powered by French-fry oil, but she had built an empire of *HumAnarchist* merchandise. She employed a staff with benefits. She owned property in one of the best neighborhoods in Portland. And she was—except for this exact moment—happy.

"You didn't. You aren't," Kristen said.

"Mom was an addict," Sierra went on. "She did meth and God knows what else. She didn't love herself enough to say no to all those sleazy guys. You really don't get what I'm doing with the *HumAnarchist*. I mean, that's what it's all about, giving people another option, to be free enough and happy enough and whole enough to come into their own, to love themselves, for *society* to break out of the habits that are killing us."

"By making dream catchers?" Kristen didn't mean it as a dig. It just seemed so sad, and she couldn't help picturing Marydale is some bleak cell, tying feathers to a wicker hoop, waiting for society to change.

"Dream catchers are a sacred Native American tradition," Sierra said. "The *HumAnarchist* would never appropriate another culture like that."

"I'm sorry."

Sierra pulled a pair of fingerless lace gloves out of a pocket in her jacket.

"I think it's a beautiful story, you and this woman. You loved her. You fucked up. Maybe it's karma." Sierra yanked on the gloves and planted her elbows on the table. "Did you not trust me? Or did you just hate it that you didn't get to be the perfect sister who did everything right?"

"Sierra, I don't think that," Kristen pleaded.

She could feel the old men at the bar watching them. She pressed her knuckles against her lips.

Sierra stood up. "I know we don't have a lot in common. I know you think the magazine is stupid, but I followed my dreams, and you followed yours, and we made it. I knew we didn't always understand each other, but we didn't understand each other *at all*, did we?"

A moment later, Kristen was alone with the burn of cheap whiskey in her throat and no one in the world to talk to.

The next morning found Kristen sitting in the courtroom with Donna. Donna was wearing a navy suit with a red pocket square and pearls. Red, white, and blue like a politician's wife. Without any preplanning, Kristen had worn a matching outfit.

"Today's the real deal." Donna leaned over. "Rutger wasn't going to come, but he said you were so good yesterday. You were damn good!" Donna nodded toward the men sitting in the gallery to their left. "And look who's here."

Kristen didn't need to know their faces to recognize the CEOs of Tri-State Global. On the other side of the aisle, the defense had lined up a phalanx of men in suits.

"They're all interns," Donna whispered. "The DataBlast shareholders are selling off as fast as they can. They can't afford this."

Kristen stared at her phone resting on the desk in front of her. The wallpaper screen was a photograph of Marydale leaning against the railing of the *Tristess*. It took her a minute to realize that Rutger Falcon had appeared at her elbow and was speaking to her. Kristen looked up.

"She's focused," Donna said.

"Sorry," Kristen said.

"You ready for today?" Falcon asked.

"Of course she's ready," Donna said.

At the front of the court, the door to the judge's chambers opened and the judge emerged in his black gown. The bailiff began the familiar liturgy of the court. Across the aisle the CFO of DataBlast fidgeted with his pen. In the gallery, Falcon took his seat behind the Tri-State Global contingency.

"Spectator sport, isn't it?" Donna added. Then she shot Kristen a quick smile. "Ream them."

A few minutes later, Kristen called her first witness. She and Donna had gone over the question set a dozen times. The witness knew his answers like an A student. It all sounded perfectly natural.

"Cross?" the judge asked when Kristen was done.

On the desk before Kristen, her phone lit up with a silent plea. She glanced at the number. There were only four area codes in Oregon. Five-four-one could have been anywhere outside of Portland, but the sudden twist in her stomach told her no. Kristen stood up, touching *accept* without putting the phone to her ear.

"Your Honor, may I have a five-minute recess?" she asked.

Donna glared at her. *What?* she mouthed.

"Three minutes," the judge said.

Kristen heard the courtroom murmur behind her as she walked out.

An automated voice on the other end of the line asked her if she would accept a collect call from an inmate at Holten Penitentiary.

"Yes," Kristen said.

A second later, Marydale came on the line.

"I'm in court. I've got three minutes," Kristen said.

Marydale gasped.

"What is it?" Kristen asked.

She hurried down the hallway, past the information desk, and out onto the street. The trees had leafed, and sun dappled the sidewalk, but Kristen couldn't feel its warmth.

Marydale was sobbing.

"Slow down," Kristen said. "I can't understand you."

For a second, Marydale was silent. She seemed to have expended all her breath and could not draw in another one.

"She tried to fight me," Marydale finally managed. "I'm never going to get out. I can't do this."

"Are you hurt? What happened?" Kristen asked.

"She doesn't want to hurt me. She's working with him, or at least she says she is. She thinks she is. She'd do it for commissary. They add time for bad behavior. I'll get charged. She'll tell the guards I hit her. I saw her cut herself with a shiv once, just to put another girl away. The girl got criminal charges. It added years to her sentence."

"Slow down, Mary." Kristen had never used the diminutive Aldean called Marydale, but now it felt like the only word that could calm the torrent of Marydale's speech. "Who are you talking about? Who's doing this? Talk to me, Mary."

Marydale started to cry again. "Gulu always said once you go in, you're always in," she sobbed. "You never get out. She's in for life. This is her whole world. She said Ronald Holten missed me. Gulu's got nothing to lose, Kristen. Whatever they tell you, I didn't do it. She'll plant drugs on me. She'll find a way to make it real. They'll believe her. You'll believe her. Kristen, I can't—"

"Kristen!" Donna had appeared at the end of the block and was hurrying toward her. "What are you doing?" She waved a skinny arm across her chest in angry semaphore. "We're in court!"

Kristen checked her watch. The three minutes were long gone. Inside, the fate of USA DataBlast hung in meaningless balance. If she won, the CEOs would parachute to safety. The plaintiffs would get checks for odd, useless sums of money. Twenty-nine cents. Nine dollars and one penny. The DataBlast staff would be absorbed into Tri-State Global or not. Some would quit. Others would collect unemployment. Only the color of the cubicles would change. And she would be made partner, and the Falcon Law Group would pay for an ad in the bar bulletin, a full-color photograph of Kristen standing in front of the Portland skyline, her hand on the corner of her desk. *Welcoming our newest partner to the Falcon legacy.*

"Mary, listen."

Kristen was going to say, *I'll be there soon, as soon as I finish with DataBlast. I'll rush the case.*

Donna was talking over her. "What are you doing? You have to get back in there. Everyone is waiting for you."

Kristen watched her gesturing. She heard Marydale breathing heavily on the other end of the phone, trying to contain her sobs. She felt the sunlight filtering through the new spring leaves.

"I will be there tonight," Kristen said. "I will see you tonight. They have to let you talk to your lawyer. I will be there."

"Where the hell are you going?" Donna demanded as Kristen pocketed her phone.

"You're a good attorney, Donna," Kristen said. "No, you're a great attorney."

"What are you doing?"

"I have to go."

"You can't do this to me." Donna cut sharp swaths of air as she gestured. "I put you up for partner. That's my reputation on the line."

"You know this case as well as I do."

"Tri-State Global doesn't want the Falcon Law Group. They want you."

"Tri-State Global is a company. They don't want things." It sounded like something Sierra would say. "This doesn't matter."

"If you want to work for Falcon Law, *it matters*!" Donna brushed her bangs out of her eyes.

"I'm sorry." Kristen turned.

"You're making a mistake."

"I already made a mistake," Kristen said, "a long time ago."

12

Marydale returned to her cell while the other prisoners exercised in the yard. She asked the guard for a book, but he just laughed.

"I'll tell room service," he said, and closed the bars behind her.

Marydale climbed up onto her bunk and closed her eyes. There was a trick to prison, a kind of half sleep that made the hours pass. She tried to remember the exact details of the distillery, the copper-batch still, the fermenting tanks, and the bottling station. They were almost ready to bottle the Solstice Vanilla. Aldean would say it tasted too soft, *a girl's whiskey*. She tried to cork the bottles in her mind. Aldean would fill. She would insert the stopper with the Sadfire logo facing the label, pull a strip of sealing tape over the top, polish the bottle, place it in a crate. She went through the process again.

She was almost asleep when she heard Gulu whisper,

Scholar, we missed you. She couldn't tell if it was a real voice
or if Gulu was calling to her from another part of the prison.
She might be only a few feet away in the cell above Marydale's, or she could be at the far end of the block or outside.
Marydale felt like she could hear everything. The guards
laughing. The zip of a folded note being whisked from cell
to cell on a thread. The air-handling system. Sometimes she
thought she could hear cars on the road outside the prison,
but she knew it couldn't be true. She tried to focus on the
imaginary bottles, to blot out everything else, but the harder
she tried, the more she heard Gulu's voice in her head. *She's
not coming, Scholar. You're never getting out of here.*

"Get up, Rae."

The other women were coming back from the yard, but
the guard outside her cell wasn't looking for them.

"I'm guessing you won't mind a field trip." It was one
of the older guards, a skinny man with silver hair. He was
the kind of guard who had to keep order with a calm word
and a look not his bulk or his boom. Marydale liked him
as much as she could like anything in Holten. "You got a
visitor. Hurry up," he said. "It's almost count. Don't keep everyone waiting."

She struggled to her feet. The guard let her out of her cell.
Walking down the central hall, Marydale looked for Gulu
without turning her head. A moment later, she was in a small
conference room with a little table and two chairs.

The guard took a pair of handcuffs out of a pocket in his
uniform. "Sorry," he said.

A window in the door faced the corridor outside, and

Marydale caught her reflection in its glass. The skin beneath her eyes looked bruised. Her hair hung limp. She tried to brush it with her fingers, but the handcuffs hampered her movements. She pinched her cheek to bring a little color into her face and heard her mother's voice. *A girl can always do something.*

The air felt close. She could hear the hands of a clock ticking somewhere in the hallway. Deep inside the building she heard a siren start up, like the angry wail of a business alarm in some rundown strip mall. On and on it blared, until it became a part of the silence itself, and she wondered if it had been sounding since she arrived at Holten.

Finally, the door opened, and Marydale released a breath she didn't realize she'd been holding. It was Kristen, led by the silver-haired guard.

Kristen looked beautiful, her blouse buttoned to the top button, her double-breasted blazer almost military in its precision. Marydale wanted to weep, and she wanted to fall at Kristen's feet and cling to her knees and beg, *Love me.*

"Are the handcuffs really necessary?" Kristen asked the guard, her voice cool and professional.

"It's a precaution."

"Is it a requirement?"

"Not strictly."

"Then I'd like you to remove them, please. We've got a lot of paperwork to go through. It'll be easier."

The guard withdrew a metal lanyard from his pants pocket and unlocked the cuffs. Marydale rubbed her wrists, her eyes following the guard as he closed the door behind them. The lock clicked into place, and they stared at each other.

"I…" Marydale began. "What about DataBlast? Aren't you supposed to be in court?"

"It's taken care of."

Marydale glanced around the tiny room. She drew in a breath to say something, but words escaped her.

"Come on," Kristen went on. "Let's talk about your case."

Marydale recounted her arrest, Holten's arrival, and her fight with Gulu.

"Ronald Holten. The director of parole." Kristen's face was calm, but her hand was clamped in a fist. "I've found an administrative rule against a victim's family member overseeing a parolee, and I've written to the parole board and called them. I'm waiting to hear back. We'll sue if we have to."

"He hates me," Marydale said. "I guess he should."

"No," Kristen said. "He shouldn't. No one should."

"I did it," Marydale said quietly.

"It was self-defense. Why didn't you appeal at the time?"

"Eric, my lawyer, he said I wouldn't win an appeal. I trusted him. Why would he lie? How could all those people on the jury be wrong?" She pressed the heels of her hands against her eyes. "I understand that I had a right to do what I did because Aaron was going to hurt me, but back then…." She drew in a shuddering breath. "I always tried to make the best of everything. I don't know how I can do that now. Gulu's going to hang me." She covered her mouth. She felt the room closing in on her. Gulu would get another inmate to say Marydale had touched her. Gulu would fashion a little packet of baking soda cut with just enough cocaine to test positive…

Kristen leaned forward. "We're going to get through this."

"Everything gets so small in here." Marydale was thinking of the little notes shuttling back and forth between the cells. They said nothing. A few expletives. A curse against the guards. Marydale closed her eyes.

"I walked out of court," Kristen said.

Marydale's eyes flew open. "What?"

She reached across the table and grabbed Kristen's hands.

"I drove straight over," Kristen said. "I had to see you. I told Donna to finish DataBlast."

"But you were going to make partner."

Kristen glanced over her shoulder at the narrow window in the door behind her. She squeezed Marydale's hands and then let go.

"I'm not leaving Tristess until I leave with you. I'll think of something, and if you have to stay here, this time I'll stay, too."

13

The next days passed in a blur, both frantic and interminable. Kristen moved back into the Almost Home. The pool was still empty. Most of the rooms around her were still vacant. But someone had redecorated her room. The orange bedspread had been replaced by a purple comforter, and the cowboy prints had been replaced with Asian mountain scenes. The woman behind the counter was Indian and wore the red bindi between her brows. Kristen wondered briefly what her life was like in Tristess. Was she an outsider like Marydale had been? And if so, why did she stay? But it didn't matter how the hotel room was decorated; Kristen longed to be in her own bed in Portland with Marydale curled against her side.

On her third day in Tristess, Kristen called Doug Grady's office, surprised to find that he was still practicing law, still the only defense attorney in town. He met her for lunch at the

Heavenly Harvest, the new incarnation of the Ro-Day-O.

"So you just walked out in the middle of your case?" Grady asked.

Outside the sky was a thin haze of unshed snow. The spring that had come to Portland had not reached the high desert. Grady twirled a strand of spaghetti around his fork, the delicate movement at odds with his large hands. His cream-colored suit was immaculate.

"My cocounsel was there," Kristen said. "I called my sister, told her to take care of my dog, and left from downtown. I didn't even go home to pack."

Grady put his fork down. "I always knew you had character."

"You thought I was a bratty law student from the city," Kristen said.

"You couldn't help that." Grady dabbed at his lips. "I liked what I heard about you and Marydale. She needed a friend who wasn't part of this place. Is that why she moved to Portland?"

Kristen swirled the last drops of coffee around in her mug. "No. We lost touch...for a while."

Grady nodded.

"I'm not going to let that happen again," Kristen added. "She shouldn't be in Holten. She shouldn't even be on supervision."

"Was she convicted under one of the lifetime supervision laws?"

"Yeah. It's not right. If she were dangerous, if she were violent...but she's not. I got a copy of her parole records.

There was a two-year period where she was jailed at least six months out of twelve, and it was all for stupid stuff. She went to the Walmart in Harney County. She got a post office box without permission. Her *house* had been foreclosed on. She was living in a motel, and she got sanctioned for that, too, because she's not supposed to live with other felons, and some guy with a record was renting a room on the other side of the building. She couldn't win."

"And then she got someone to transfer her to Portland," Grady finished.

"She got a new PO, and she reported and paid her supervision fee. She did everything she was supposed to do, except the PO was supposed to transfer her supervision to an officer in Portland, and she didn't. Marydale didn't have a clean enough record to get a transfer, but she couldn't stay out of trouble in Tristess. I think she was just too unhappy, and the rules were stacked against her. She wasn't even supposed to date."

"Did Marydale know it wasn't legit?"

Kristen pushed the salad around on her plate. "She knew."

"And now Ronald Holten is in charge of parole," Grady said. "Word on the street is his ranch is failing. People are starting to say he never was a rancher, just a moneylender. One of the grass-fed cooperatives even sued him over easements into BLM land. He'd been charging people thousands to run their herd over some pathetic little strip of land he owned all around the big Clear Creek parcel. Court said he could do that, but then they seized three mile-long sections. Condemnation via eminent domain. They said they needed to run some utility lines through those sections. Now all people have to do is divert the herd a half mile this way or that, and they're in for free."

A waitress appeared at their side. Under her apron, she wore a T-shirt with the words LIFE IS GOOD printed across the front.

"For dessert we've got lemongrass gelato and rosemary-apricot pie," she said.

"Gelato," Grady grumbled. "What happened to chocolate, vanilla, and strawberry? Breyers was good enough for my dad. Things are changing around here." He wiped the edge of the table with his napkin, then rested his elbows on the surface. "But it's going to be tough. Ronald Holten's going to say she didn't have permission to be in Portland. She's been on abscond. He'll make her stay, and he'll make her keep her nose clean."

"By not letting her go to the grocery store...or date." Kristen pushed her uneaten lunch aside and pulled out her tablet.

"What are you going to do?" Grady asked.

That was the question. Kristen tapped the surface of her tablet and the parole board website appeared on the screen. "I can help her petition for a transfer to Portland, and there'll be a hearing to determine how long she's in prison for this violation."

"But she doesn't deserve any of it." Grady finished her thought for her.

"I've been looking into post-conviction relief. I know every felon tries for it, and it doesn't work, but this time I think it might. But here's the thing. I haven't talked to my boss yet, but I'm pretty sure I'm getting fired right about now." Kristen could picture the meeting. Donna would speak first. *I recommend dismissal. The liability.* She would talk quickly, as though that would prevent the other partners from remembering that she had championed Kristen's promotion. "I don't have time to set up as a sole practitioner," Kristen went on. "I need to practice under someone else's insurance."

"Mine?"

"Yeah."

"You come rolling in in whatever that is." Grady glanced at Kristen's Audi in the parking lot outside the restaurant. "Big-city lawyer, going up against the Holtens. Do you know what that would do to my practice if people knew you were working out of my office?"

"You said things are changing."

"We got fancy ice cream. It's not a revolution."

"You said you moved back to Tristess so that what happened to Marydale didn't happen to anyone else."

Grady steepled his fingers. "It's about time I pack up into the sunset anyway. You can practice under my insurance. We'll go back to my office and do the paperwork today, but tell me, what kind of law do you practice in Portland?"

"Class actions, mostly cell phone stuff and Web advertising."

"That's what I thought. When's the last time you did criminal?"

"When I was here."

"So maybe you don't know: the statute of limitations ran

out on post-conviction relief. It's too late for Marydale."
There was no *gotcha* in Grady's expression. "I know because
I looked into it when I came out here. It was too late then,
too."

Kristen sat back on her vinyl bench. She looked out the
window. The name of the restaurant had changed, but the
view was still the same: the Almost Home Motel with its
empty swimming pool, its faded sign silhouetted against the
sky. Beyond the motel, a procession of fast-food restaurants
and payday loan shops marked a dozen dead ends.

"I thought life in the country was supposed to be beautiful," Kristen said.

"Used to be. Still is sometimes, if you can get out of
town."

Kristen thought of Marydale in her thin orange uniform.
"What do I do?"

"The only way you can get post-conviction relief now is if
you find evidence that couldn't have been discovered at the
time of the trial."

"A unicorn," Kristen said, not so much to Grady as to
the window and the empty pool and the lane of predatory
lenders.

"A fucking unicorn," he agreed. "A goddamn fucking unicorn."

14

That night Kristen pored over post-conviction relief cases and the court files from Marydale's case, toggling back and forth between screens on her laptop, then standing up and pacing, then willing herself to sit down and focus. She highlighted every name in Marydale's case file, and during the day she called each person.

The calls yielded one of two replies.

Aaron Holten's father answered her from a pier in Atlantic City, the sound of the ocean growling in the background.

"They should have locked her up and thrown away the key," he said. "If I ever met the bastard who let her out on parole! You know Texas brought back the firing squad. That's what I say. Why should they get three hots and a cot? After what she did to my boy!"

The former Tristess police chief said, "Poor kid. With her father dying and her mother dying so young, bless her, and Marydale being, well, different."

"Yes?"

"She was bound to get herself in trouble one way or another."

"Did you think it was self-defense?"

"It might have been a fair fight, but that's the problem, isn't it? A girl's got to be strong to throw a hay bale like that. You don't do that by accident. I feel sorry for her, but she was at the wrong end of that throw."

When Kristen called Marydale's defense attorney, Eric Neiben, all she got was a voice mail in return.

"I lost, okay?" he said. "Lawyers lose cases. She didn't appeal. That's it. That's final." By nightfall on her fourth day in Tristess, the sky had cleared. Kristen stared out her motel window at the parking lot. The room felt cramped and empty at the same time. Kristen put on a coat, scarf, and hat and tucked her laptop under her arm and her phone in her pocket. Outside the air was cold and dry. Kristen walked around to the front of the hotel, stepping over the low, wrought-iron railing that surrounded the patio around the empty pool. She sat at one of the tables. The metal chair felt icy.

She checked her phone for the hundredth time, but the only new messages were from Donna. Donna had been calling, leaving a couple of messages a day. The Falcon Law Group had put Kristen on unpaid administrative leave. She had seventy-two hours to procure a medical diagnosis explaining her sudden change in behavior. Then she had forty-eight hours. Then she had twelve. Kristen had deleted the first half a dozen messages without return-

ing them. Marydale's case was more important. But with
the case stalled and the night stretching out before her
with nothing to do but wait and hope, it felt churlish not
to speak the words: *I quit. I'm sorry.* There was no way
to pretend that that part of her life wasn't over. Kristen
touched *call back*.

Donna greeted her with, "What the hell?"

"I know," Kristen said.

"Kristen!" For once, Donna seemed at a loss for words.

"I'm sorry," Kristen said.

"Everyone has a midlife crisis," Donna hissed. "I don't
see why yours couldn't have waited until after DataBlast.
Are you crazy? Suicidal? Are you being blackmailed? Did
you start doing drugs? Did some parasite get in your blood-
stream and eat a hole through your...your..." Always pre-
cise, Donna searched for the exact neurological structure.
"Your *brain!*" she finished, apparently deciding that fury
outweighed medical specificity.

"I know I'm getting fired," Kristen said. "But you'll do
great with DataBlast. You deserve that case. You did as much
work on it as I did."

"I won DataBlast," Donna said. "DataBlast is over."

"Already?"

"Yes, already. And we didn't get the Tri-State Global contract. And yes, you're getting fired. I had to talk Rutger out
of an involuntary commitment."

"You'd never get a four twenty-six on me. You can't prove
danger to self or others."

"I'm kidding, Kristen, but, seriously, what happened?"

The stars overhead were cold. Kristen's breath steamed before her.

"You want to know what happened?" Kristen had Google open on her laptop. Absently, she typed in the name of Marydale's defense attorney for the hundredth time. "You ever take a lit class in college?"

"I don't know. Probably."

"You ever read one of those stories, like a Greek myth, where someone does one thing wrong? You know, they step on the sacred spring or something, and it ruins their life?"

"They sleep with their mother," Donna suggested. "Kill their father."

"You ever do anything like that?"

"No," Donna said without hesitation. "I have not slept with Ma Hualing, and I'm pretty sure my father is doing just fine."

Donna Li, Kristen thought. The daughter of Hualing and Junjie Li. Donna who wore three-inch heels to pick up milk at the Dairy Mart. Donna who got a score on the bar exam so high they had to readjust the curve. Donna who had grown up in the same squat, narrow-windowed apartments that Kristen had, only for different reasons.

"You've been in love. You know," Kristen said.

"I have not been in love," Donna said with indignation.

"What about the opera singer and the CrossFit guy and that military guy with the great jaw?"

"You thought I was in love with them?"

"Why would you go out with them if you weren't in love?"

"Um, because," Donna said in a way that made the answer obvious. "What's this about?"

"I was in love," Kristen said. "I am in love. Do you remember the job I had in Tristess?"

The story unfolded like her own personal creation myth. Five years earlier, she could have sat in the jailhouse visiting room and promised, *We'll make this work.* Instead, she had left, and now she had to move back into the Almost Home, like some flying Dutchman of small-town law, and recount the whole absurd, tragic, starry-eyed story to practical Donna Li.

On the screen in front of her, she stared at a blurry photograph of Neiben at his wedding many years earlier, a slender man with dark, oily hair. Behind him, the wedding party wore an assortment of sport coats and gunnysack dresses.

"So that's it," Kristen said when she finished. "I came back to work her case. I'm going to practice under Doug Grady's professional liability insurance. He does defense down here."

She looked up. In the distance, headlights cut the darkness.

"You quit over a girl?"

"Yeah."

"You were going to be partner!"

"Marydale's the most important thing to me," Kristen said.

Donna blew out a quiet breath. "Better you than me. You would have been a good partner. We could have taken the firm somewhere." Donna was quiet for a moment. "How is the case?"

"It's a dog." Kristen tried to keep the panic out of her voice.

An SUV pulled into the darkness at the far end of the parking lot, and a small group of people got out and made their way toward the hotel lobby. They were barely visible in the nonexistent security lighting, but Kristen thought they looked happy. They moved with the loose-limbed gait of people on vacation.

"Statute of limitations ran out unless we can find evidence that wasn't available at the time of the trial," Kristen went on.

"You need a Jason Miter," Donna said mildly.

Kristen looked around at the empty pool and the wide main road beyond.

"What if I don't find one?" she asked.

"You lose," Donna said. "That's law."

It took them a long time to say goodbye. Although Donna had been known to end a conversation in midsentence with *That's enough of us talking* or *Okay, I'm sick of this now*, this time she demurred like a true Oregonian.

"Right on…" Donna hedged. "Well, keep me posted… Okay, good luck… We'll talk soon."

The longer Donna dragged out their goodbye, the more certain Kristen was that they would never talk again. Finally she touched *end call*.

The tourists had disappeared into the motel lobby. Now they emerged again, their silhouettes black against the yellow windows: a cowboy hat, two topknots, a woman whose outline suggested she carried a giant basket of twigs on her head.

The woman's voice floated across the empty pool. "I can see the stars."

Kristen knew that voice.

"Sierra?" Kristen said out loud.

The woman raised her hands to the sky. "Hello, stars!" she called out.

"Sierra!"

Kristen stood.

A moment later, Meatball appeared, as if from nowhere, barreling up to the wrought-iron fence, which—at three feet—presented an insurmountable obstacle to his bowling-ball weight and Samsonite girth. He wedged his froggy smile between the fence posts.

"Kristi!" Sierra called, breaking into a run and flying toward Kristen with her arms outstretched, her dreadlocks breaking loose from their scarf and flying around her like the hair of an energetic Medusa.

A second later, Kristen was engulfed in her sister's embrace. Behind Sierra, Frog and Moss ambled over along with Aldean Dean, who touched the brim of his hat, looking slightly embarrassed.

"What are you doing here?" Kristen asked, still hugging Sierra.

"We're here for you and for Marydale," Sierra said. "We all are. And we'll visit her every day in prison. We'll take shifts. We'll stand outside with a petition and signs, and if that doesn't work…" Sierra dropped her voice. "Aldean will show us where to tunnel in, and Moss and Frog will get a drone and fly over the prison so we can get a blueprint of the layout. But first we'll write a story about her. About injustice and homophobia and the prison industrial complex. The *HumAnarchist* is about social change." Sierra pulled back, holding Kristen at arm's length. "If you don't think it would hurt Marydale's case. I mean, maybe there'll be a jury, and we can't taint all the jurors by telling her story, but maybe we *can*! They'll read the story, and then they'll be on the jury, and they'll acquit her."

"There's not going to be a jury," Kristen said. She didn't mention that the chances of a Tristess jury reading the *HumAnarchist* were about as good as the chances of the Heavenly Harvest running out of the sprouted tofu bowl.

Sierra said, "We'll think of something." Behind her, Moss and Frog nodded vigorously. "We're HumAnarchists. We'll think outside the box."

Sierra squeezed her again, enveloping Kristen in the smell of essential oil, stale marijuana, and the failure of natural crystal deodorant.

"Are you mad that I'm here?" Sierra asked.

Kristen pressed her face into her sister's dreads. "Sierra, I'm sorry," she said.

"For what?" Sierra asked, as though she had not stomped out of the Port Call.

Everything, Kristen thought. "The other day at the bar," she said instead, "you said we both followed our dreams. You followed your dreams. I followed mine. We had that in common."

"Yeah."

Above their heads, the stars sparkled in frozen abandon. The motel felt like a tiny enclave on a vast, alien landscape, a tiny trailer beneath a UFO sky.

"I didn't follow my dreams," Kristen said. "You followed your dreams. I ran away."

15

Marydale sat in the chow hall, a tray of peas and hamburger crumbles before her. The halogen lights made everything white. Even the bright orange of her uniform bleached out beneath the glare.

Across the room she felt Gulu watching her.

A woman at the next table called out, "Hey. New girl. Do I know you? I never seen you in the yard."

Marydale said nothing.

"I hear you're Gulu's baby," the woman added.

Another woman at the neighboring table muttered, "More like Gulu's bitch."

Marydale drew in a deep breath and let it out slowly. She tried to picture Kristen's apartment, then the distillery, but the images felt like pictures torn from a magazine, flat and well lit but unreal and unreachable.

The two women rose, moved to her table, and sat down on either side of her. Marydale glanced back and forth.

"Me and Jazz are playing poker," the older women said. She had dark circles around her eyes, and Marydale could not tell if it was eye shadow or diabetes. "We need four to play." She reached into her sleeve and pulled out a stack of paper slips, each adorned with a hand-drawn card.

"You and your cheating cards," Jazz said. "How do I know you don't have them all marked?"

"You want to play or no?" the other woman asked. "We play with whatever. Peas." She pointed her fork at Marydale's tray. "That's like a hundred pennies from your commissary. We'll settle up later."

"She always cheats," Jazz said, wrapping her long dark ponytail around her wrist and then letting it slide off. "And what about you? You cheat at cards?" She nodded to Marydale.

"I don't want to play." Marydale showed her empty hands. "I don't know how."

"I'll teach you."

Marydale jumped at the voice directly behind her ear. The two women laughed. Marydale turned. Gulu stood behind her, her prison-issue jeans hanging off her hips, and her tight gray T-shirt outlining more muscle than breast. Marydale remembered Gulu doing bench presses in the open-air gym in the yard, the rain beating down on her face as she breathed out and pushed up. *One hundred one. One hundred two.*

"She's sneaky, isn't she?" the older woman—Marydale thought her name might be Leena—said.

Gulu swung her leg over the bench across from Marydale.

"This is my girl," she said, pointing her chin in Marydale's direction. "She's been my girl for a long time."

Marydale made a move to rise, but Leena clamped her hand on Marydale's shoulder.

"You talk to your Jane?" Gulu pressed the tip of her tongue to her top lip and sucked it back.

Marydale let her face settle into a stony stare, but her heart was racing. Gulu sat across from her, but that was close enough. The guards wouldn't see, and Gulu would be careful. Leena kept her arm around Marydale's shoulder. Touching was forbidden, but from behind it would look like a friendly gesture. If the guards balked, Leena would apologize. If Marydale tried to rise, Gulu and her friends would catch her ankles under the table.

Leena dealt. Gulu raised Jazz's bet by rolling two peas across the table, her thumb squashing them slightly, leaving a streak of moisture on the plastic surface. "Scholar's got some posh girl, but I don't think it's gonna last, do you, Scholar? Not much you can do for her in here."

Marydale didn't touch the cards in front of her. "I don't have anything to bet."

"You will. I got a feeling you'll be staying for a while," Gulu said. "Scholar put a fork in Aaron Holten when he touched her girl back in the day." Gulu had added a few small prison tattoos to her neck. They looked like liver spots.

"You butched out on the outside, too?" Jazz asked Marydale, then dismissed her own question. "Who even gives a shit, right?"

Leena said, "You did a Holten? You're down for a dime.

I hate that family. Buck Holten down at PD in Burnville called INS on my brother, Brian. Brian was born here. Brian don't even speak Spanish."

"I heard one of the new fish saying she's scared of you," Gulu said to Marydale. "You got snake eyes, she said. All flat like you've done hard time." Gulu's smile was all low, sleek curves like the back of a coyote moving through sheep. "Scholar thinks she's getting out, but I think she fits right in."

Gulu and the young woman folded. Leena won and the deal went to Gulu. Gulu and her friends kept talking, running over old gossip like diners at the Ro-Day-O. Still, there was something in the way they projected their conversation. It was a scrim over other, more subtle communications. Out of the corner of her eye, Marydale saw Gulu slip something from hand to hand. Marydale stood up. "Inmate, where are you going?" a guard yelled.

Marydale felt something touch her hip. She tried to brush it away.

"Guard!" Gulu cried. "She's got contraband!"

The tiny packet lay on the ground by her shoe. Marydale froze. They would charge her with possession, smuggling contraband into a secure facility, maybe dealing. In her mind's eye, Marydale saw Kristen disappearing like a figure on the horizon. Time slowed down, and she was watching Aaron Holten fall again, every dust mote in the barn illuminated by the bulb hanging overhead so that he fell, not through darkness, but through a glowing snow of stars.

Then the guard was at her side.

Leena rose and bumped into her. "Watch it, *guera*!" she said. To the guard, Leena added, "She's trouble. Don't let her get near me!"

But when Marydale looked down, the packet was gone.

The guard gave a cursory pat to Marydale's pockets and the back of her sports bra.

"Clarocci, watch it!" the guard said to Gulu.

Gulu leaned over. "Don't worry. I'll find a way to make you stay."

Marydale said nothing. She heard Gulu inhale deeply.

"You going on the rag soon," Gulu whispered. "I can smell it. Does your girl know how you get before your rag? All pent up?"

A guard called time, and the crowd rose. Some women lined up for the yard. A few lined up to return to their cells. Gulu stepped close, and Marydale felt Gulu's hip bone against her ass.

"It's hard in here. You probably got a whole box of toys up in Portland. Got no relief here. Eh, Scholar? You think your girl's going to do you in the bathroom at visitors? She a little slut like you are?"

"Fuck you," Marydale said without looking at Gulu.

Leena glided by, flashing Marydale and Gulu a quick glimpse of the contraband in her fist.

"What the…!" Gulu hissed.

Leena glanced over her shoulder. "Waste not, want not. Anyway, she cut a Holten. I owe her one."

16

A week after arriving in Tristess, Kristen visited Aubrey Thomsich, Marydale's high school girlfriend. She spoke the address into the dashboard GPS as she pulled out of the Almost Home's parking lot. Forty minutes later, she found the trailer at the end of a dirt road lined with RVs, mobile homes, and houses draped in blue tarps. She knocked on the door. Inside, a TV blared. A moment later, a woman appeared, a baby in one arm and a small boy pulling on the belt loop of her jeans.

"What?" the woman asked.

"I'm looking for Aubrey Thomsich." Kristen glanced into the cluttered room behind the woman.

"If this is about his child support, he's paid it. Okay? And it nearly broke us this month, but it's paid."

Kristen stared at her. She looked younger than Marydale but worn out, too, with stringy brown hair and an odd accumulation of fat around her shoulder blades.

"Are you Aubrey?"

The woman twisted her lips in an expression that said, *Who's asking?*

Kristen realized she'd been expecting a beauty. *You're not worth it*, Kristen thought, although, of course, she knew it shouldn't matter.

"It's not about child support." Kristen put on her courtroom voice, calm and disinterested. "I just want to talk to you for a few minutes."

"About what?"

The baby squalled, and Kristen smelled the sharp rankness of diaper.

"About Aaron Holten and Marydale Rae."

"I don't want my name in the paper."

Aubrey started to close the door, but Kristen stepped into the doorway. "Marydale Rae is in prison for something that wasn't her fault."

Aubrey gave a short, sharp laugh. "Who's innocent anyway?" She switched the baby roughly to her other hip, and it began crying again. "They all say babies are innocent. They're the worst. Little tyrants."

The baby howled.

"Did Aaron Holten ever threaten you or say that he was going to harm Marydale Rae?" Kristen asked.

"Are you on TV?" Aubrey straightened a little. "Like one of those true crime shows."

"I'm an attorney. I'm trying to help Marydale. Did Aaron Holten ever threaten her?"

"Aaron said a lot of shit." Aubrey glanced down the gravel drive.

"Like what?"

"Like nothing that matters. All the Holten boys are assholes. I just married the wrong one, thanks to Marydale."

"You married a Holten?"

"Amos, but he's not good for shit. Aaron would have taken care of us. I told her that."

"What do you mean?"

"I was going to marry Aaron, and she was going to marry his cousin Pete, and we could've been happy. It wasn't going to be like this. Look at this shit." Aubrey kicked a child's toy to the side. "What happened between me and Marydale was a mistake. For all I know, maybe she did trick him back to the barn so she could kill him. She was real pretty back then, and she thought she could do whatever she liked."

It sounded rehearsed.

"Do you really believe that?" Kristen said.

Aubrey held the baby with the casual irritation of a teenager carrying her little brother.

"I think you cared about Marydale," Kristen added, hoping it was true. "I think you still do."

The little boy tugged at his mother's shirt, and Aubrey grabbed the boy by the crown of his head and pushed him back.

"Go play out back," she said.

The child protested.

"Outside!" Aubrey barked.

She stepped away from the door into the house, and Kristen moved into the space she had vacated. Wicker blinds hung over the windows, leaving the house in shadows.

"I told her to handle him." Aubrey sat down in an armchair in the cluttered space that passed for a living room. "It wouldn't have killed her to flirt a little, make nice with Aaron until he forgot about us."

Kristen sat down on a folding chair, facing Aubrey. "Are you a lesbian?"

Aubrey shrugged. "Doesn't matter anymore." She sniffed. "Marydale will get out sooner than I will. Look at this mess. She did fine for herself, right? She got out, went up to Portland."

"She's in Holten Penitentiary right now on a parole violation. If she's lucky, we'll be able to get that down to three months. If she's not, it's half a year. If you know anything about the case…"

"Fuck," Aubrey said. "I thought she got out."

Kristen looked around at the clutter: boxes and children's toys, a fake Christmas tree in one corner, dirty dishes in the tiny kitchen. On the wall, a younger Aubrey and a man—presumably Amos—grinned out of their wedding frame, their smiles strained.

"I want to get her out. I want to get someone to look at her case again, to prove it was self-defense. Can you think of anything, anything at all, that would help Marydale?"

The boy ran up to Aubrey again and clung to her waist. This time she put an arm around him.

"I visited Marydale when she was locked up," Aubrey said. "You're from the city. You wouldn't get it."

"Get what?"

"Get what it's like to be gay out here. Marydale ever take you down to the quarry?"

"No."

"I guess she wouldn't."

Kristen tried to keep her body relaxed, her face neutral. She had interviewed a thousand potential witnesses. From DataBlast. From the "environmentally friendly" chemical company that repackaged generic household cleaners with a hemp label. From a dozen other class actions. Talking had its own momentum, and everyone had an impulse to confess, but the inclination was skittish. The listener could scare it away by holding their pencil too tightly. She watched Aubrey without making eye contact.

"We used to go swimming in the old quarry. It was clean, not like the Poison Well, but somewhere along the line they put a bunch of cement up to keep people out. You drove down this long road, and there were, like, a dozen dead end signs. Then this cement wall. For a while, all the kids thought they could find a way to tear it down. We'd shoot at it, and some of the boys made up a fertilizer bomb, but you couldn't get through."

Kristen nodded, not *yes*, just *I hear you*.

"That's what it was like for Marydale, you know? Being gay around here. There were a couple of us at the high school. Me. Marydale. This kid name Cutty. And some others who never talked about it. She was the last one up against that wall, kicking at it, when you knew it wasn't going to come down."

"I thought people accepted her," Kristen said quietly.

"Sure they did." Aubrey wrapped her arm around the little boy and pulled him awkwardly onto her lap. The baby had fallen asleep, and the little boy touched the baby's hand. "No one said you couldn't go shooting at the wall. No one said you couldn't try. But you weren't ever gonna win."

"Why didn't you leave Tristess?" Kristen asked.

"By the time you're old enough, Tristess has got a little piece of you." Aubrey pressed her lips to the baby's head. "I'm sorry Marydale got sent back. I thought she'd make it."

"Can you think of *anything* that might help her case?" Kristen asked again.

Aubrey looked around with a frown. "Ronald Holten bought us this place. He got Amos a job, not that Amos kept it long. If you think the Holtens got something they shouldn't have, look for the money."

But a week and a half later, Kristen had found nothing. Her visits to the small legal-consult room in the prison felt strained. The more often she visited, the closer the guards watched them. Quietly, she pleaded with Marydale, "You have to help me think of something."

Marydale pleaded back, "I can't dodge Gulu much longer. I don't know who her people are. I'm trying."

"Can you think of *anything* we can use?"

The last time she had visited, Marydale had broken down, sobbing into her folded arms, the last vestiges of the rodeo queen dissolving with her tears. Kristen had promised herself she would not ask again, but now the question came back of its own will.

"Marydale, anything?"

Kristen wanted to hold Marydale. She wanted reach back in time to the seventeen-year-old girl waving from the parade float. She wanted to cradle that girl in her arms, and she wanted to strip Marydale of her orange scrubs and kiss her. But the guard's footsteps marked time like a clock, and Kristen heard herself barrage Marydale with questions.

"I thought you were looking!" Marydale shot back.

"I'm sorry," Kristen said. "I can't find anything." It felt like a diagnosis, a doctor walking slowly into the examining room. *I'm sorry*... Kristen took a deep breath. "The best I've got is that Eric Neiben was a shitty lawyer, and some people around town thought you got a rough deal." Kristen's laptop was open to a waiting screen, but there were no answers to type. "You're going to have a parole hearing next week. That will determine whether you'll be in prison for three months or six. I'll try for three, and then I'll try to get your parole transferred to Portland. You've got a support system and employment, so they may agree. If they don't, we can try to sue for wrongful imprisonment, based on the fact that Ronald Holten knows you. We won't win, but it might scare the county since I can try it for free, and they'll have to pay. But that's losing the war. We can't bank on some small-town politician's fears."

Marydale ran her hands through her hair. "I know. I know."

"Help me," Kristen said. "There's got to be something."

Outside the room, the guard's footsteps receded on the linoleum.

"Kristen." Marydale traced a crack in the surface of the table. "You've never been in prison."

"No."

"I love you so much." Marydale's voice sounded far away. "But you don't get it. We don't win. We can't. I can't. I wasn't mad at you. I want you to know that."

"What do you mean?"

"When you left Tristess. I know why you left. I know what happens when someone goes into the system. If you leave now"—she straightened—"I'll understand. This isn't your life. You didn't do this."

"What?"

"I won't hate you."

"If I leave?"

"Eventually, you will. You have to. It's over for me. This is all my life is going to be. This. Maybe I'll be able to do something in Tristess. Maybe after enough time passes…"

"You can't give up."

Kristen clutched Marydale's hand. Marydale pressed her other hand over Kristen's.

"Sweetie," she said, as though Kristen were a little girl stomping her feet against death. "Sometimes you just lose." Her smile was incalculably sad.

"No," Kristen said.

"Yes. I've spent the last ten years pretending it's not true, but it is. It just is."

Without thinking, Kristen rose, grabbed Marydale's hand, and pulled her to her feet. The small window in the door watched them like an eye, but the hallway outside was momentarily empty. Kristen drew Marydale toward the corner of the room where a passing guard could not see them. Then she spun Marydale around and pushed her against the wall. Marydale's eyes went wide. Kristen pressed her hands to Marydale's cheeks, holding her face and her gaze.

"Marydale, we'll get through this."

Then her tongue was in Marydale's mouth, their kiss fierce and hard. Kristen felt every sense heightened. The guards were only fifty feet away. She could hear them laughing, their muffled footsteps shifting around at the end of the hall.

"I love you," Kristen whispered.

She kissed Marydale again. The material of Marydale's uniform was so thin Kristen could feel her body as if through a sheet. She could feel Marydale's heartbeat. She could hear the blood in her own ears. She felt her body light up with desire and grief and rage at the world. Without thinking, she squeezed Marydale's ass, clinging to her, drawing her closer, tighter.

"You can't give up, Mary."

The wall behind them creaked. They both stopped.

Through the wall, Kristen heard one of the guards say, "Is Rae done in there?"

A woman's voice replied, "Lawyer's got another ten minutes."

Marydale pressed her forehead against Kristen's shoulder. "I don't want this to be your life, too."

Kristen clutched the back of Marydale's head with one hand. With the other, she caressed her Marydale's thigh, touching the thin, rough fabric of her uniform. Beneath it she felt the heat of Marydale's body.

"Listen to me, Marydale. You're getting out. I know you are because I did. I should never have survived. I should be doing meth in some dive bar with my mother and her boyfriend and Sierra, too. I wasn't supposed to go to college. I wasn't supposed to be a lawyer, and I had to fight for every-thing...*everything* I have, and I will not lose now. I will not lose you."

She slipped her hand under Marydale's waistband. A radio buzzed in the hallway, and someone answered with a curt, "What?"

Warnings rang in the back of Kristen's mind, but she had seen the defeat in Marydale's eyes, and she couldn't bear it: beautiful, regal Marydale with her blond curls and her dark tattoos sitting before her with her shoulders stooped. *Sometimes you just lose.* Even in Tristess, when Marydale was just a waitress scraping by on cheap tips, there had been a fierce-ness about her, a cut of blue stone in her eyes, a flame that burned lower and lower every time Kristen visited the penitentiary.

Kristen felt that heat rekindle as she touched Marydale's thigh.

"Oh," Marydale whispered. She closed her eyes. "Oh, Kristen."

Kristen rubbed the tips of two fingers against Marydale's clit, more a symbol than a seduction, a witch's invocation, an ancient liturgy.

"I won't fail now," Kristen said, her voice stern but her

touch gentle. "I won't fail you, if I have to take this to the Supreme Court, if I have to burn this whole fucking town to the ground."

Marydale stood motionless, her legs spread, her muscles tight. Kristen felt her attention perfectly divided between Marydale's body and the sound of voices at the end of the hall. She listened, her fingers moving over Marydale, sliding up and down beside her clit, then dipping into her body, then rubbing quickly and lightly over her whole sex.

"Trust me, Marydale." Kristen could feel Marydale's legs tremble. Kristen didn't dare kiss her, because she couldn't take her attention from the door, the hall, the sounds, the footsteps.

The footsteps! Suddenly they were close.

A guard said, "We'll need the room for Brosch."

He was right outside the door. She could hear his keys. Kristen pulled away. Marydale looked as shaken as Kristen felt.

"They're coming," Kristen hissed.

Marydale rushed for her seat, dropping into it as the guard appeared at the doorway. Kristen thought she could smell Marydale's sex in the air. Her hand was slick with moisture from Marydale's body, her face flushed, her breath ragged. Still, she had not clawed her way into the best law firm in Portland for nothing.

She turned slowly, as she would in court, knowing exactly how to pose.

"Yes?" she asked the guard who had appeared in the doorway. "I'm with my client."

She knew in that instant they had staged the perfect tableau. The inmate slightly flustered, trying to guess the right answer to a question that had no solution. The attorney losing patience, starting to think about her next case, perhaps unnerved by being in a prison, but hiding it well. Their intimate distress translated into the awkward flush of strangers about uncomfortable business. Kristen turned her back to the guard. *We will win*, she mouthed. Marydale nodded, but Kristen couldn't tell if it was desire or defeat that darkened Marydale's eyes like the smoke from wildfires at night.

Kristen drove back to her motel and paced her room for an hour, then walked over to the Heavenly Harvest, where she was to meet Grady. She waited, staring out the window. Main Street looked even grimmer than the day before. *Lifetime supervision*, she thought. *Forever.* She had promised Marydale that they would win, but good attorneys knew never to make promises like that. She remembered her torts professor declaring, *The law is a blunt instrument. If you want justice, look to God. If you want rules, look to the law.*

Grady slid into the booth across from her, interrupting her thoughts.

"City food!" He picked up a menu. "You probably like this stuff. What is *pecorino* anyway?"

"Cheese," Kristen said wearily.

"Ah, it doesn't matter," Grady amended. "What have you got on Marydale's case?"

"I told her we'd win."

"You find something?"

"Nothing."

"Then why'd you tell her…?"

"I can't let her lose again, but with Ronald Holten in charge of parole…" Kristen trailed off.

"This town," Grady said.

A thin, early sun came through the windows, making Kristen's eyes water and casting long shadows across the table.

"How was she?" Grady asked.

Kristen thought of Marydale's hard, desperate kiss and the sadness in her eyes.

"She doesn't think she'll get out, and she probably won't. I lied to her. I couldn't look her in the eyes and tell her to give up hope," Kristen said. "She was seventeen. It's not fair. Now she's stuck. If she gets a traffic ticket or a PO who doesn't like her, it's back to this."

Across the street, Kristen saw Sierra exit one of the motel rooms. Somehow Moss, Frog, and Sierra managed to share a single room in perfect harmony, the men in one bed, Sierra in the other. They'd even decorated with a roll of Scotch tape and whatever maps and leaves and twigs they'd found in Tristess. It looked good in an odd, vegan co-op sort of way.

"How'd you come out the way you did and your sister…?" Grady asked.

Kristen squinted into the sun. Sierra had wrapped a green scarf around her dreadlocks. She had a drum slung over one shoulder and a laptop tucked under her arm. A second later, she burst through the door, waving at the hostess and sliding into the booth next to Kristen. She dropped the drum on floor with a resonant thud and opened her laptop.

"Look at this!" she said.

She whirled the screen around to show Kristen and Grady.

"It's your article about Marydale," Kristen said.

"Look at the header."

"You sent it to the *Oregonian*?" Kristen asked, noting the familiar script at the top of the screen.

"The Associated Press picked it up."

"You're part of the AP?" Kristen asked.

Grady was watching Sierra like one might watch an interesting sea creature.

"It's gone viral." Sierra hit a few keys. "Look at our website. We got more than thirty thousand hits. And look at the comments." She pushed the computer back toward Kristen. "People love her. They get it!"

Kristen scanned the feed. There were a few of the usual Internet rants in all caps, but the majority of the comments were composed in full sentences and complete paragraphs. A man in Austin said his father had been imprisoned for being gay in the 1990s. A fifteen-year-old girl in Baltimore said she'd been sent to a juvenile detention center for six months for skipping school and creating a fake Facebook profile for the vice principal at her school. A woman in Tulsa told Marydale to keep her head up; a rodeo queen can do anything. A judge in Detroit wrote, *It costs fifty thousand dollars to remand a felon to prison, and we're sending people back for minor infractions like failure to report. If our schools could leverage that kind of money for at-risk youth, this would be a different country.*

"Don't you see?" Sierra said. "People are ready for a change! They want to lock up the bad guys, but they don't want to see people like Marydale go to prison for life. They don't want nonviolent offenders sucking up resources. That money could go back to the community. We could build day care facilities and schools and nursing homes where young people take care of the elderly. We could…"

Sierra went on. When she finally left with a breathless, "I've got to go to the prison and tell Marydale," Grady and Kristen both watched her go, the drum bouncing against her hip.

"I've never heard her play it," Kristen said.

"She still thinks she can change the world," Grady said.

For a moment, Sierra's excitement had cheered Kristen. Now, in her absence, the air felt heavier.

"She's young," Kristen said, still staring at the place where Sierra had disappeared into the motel across the street. "She's a kid."

"Out here there are kids running the family ranch at eighteen," Grady said. "There are kids running herd at sixteen. She's old enough."

"To know better," Kristen said sadly.

"No," Grady said. "Just to know."

17

Marydale entered the visiting room Tuesday morning. It was never busy. She'd overheard the guards talking about visiting days on the men's side. Sometimes there were lines around the building, sometimes a one-hour limit per visit. Today, on the women's side, there were only five or six prisoners in the visiting room. Two women were seated at a round table talking to the same well-dressed man. One woman sat in the children's play area while a little girl beat two blocks against each other. The rest were paired up with their visitors in facing plastic chairs.

Marydale looked around for Kristen, then for Aldean, then for Kristen's sister and her friends. She recognized no one. She turned to the guard who had let her in.

"Over there."

The guard pointed to two young women at the far end of the room. They looked about twenty. One sat in a wheelchair, but they both looked athletic and cheerful in pastel sweaters and stocking caps with earflaps and pom-pom tassels. Except for the wheelchair they could have just come in from skiing. The woman in the wheelchair waved.

Marydale approached slowly. "Are you here to see me?"

The girl in the wheelchair held out her hand. She had a firm, warm handshake. "I'm Nyssa," she said. "And this is my friend Brit."

They didn't look like the kind of emissaries Gulu would send from the outside world, but Marydale couldn't be sure.

"We came from Bend," Brit said. "Nyssa wanted to meet you in person."

"We're on the staff of the newspaper at our college. The *Broadside*, at Central Oregon Community College," Nyssa said. "We saw that article your girlfriend's sister wrote. Shit! That was crazy what happened to you. I mean, I studied the criminal justice system in American society, but I hadn't thought about it, not really, not until I read the article."

The girl kept talking, and Marydale sighed inwardly. Some of the women at Holten Penitentiary got visits from strangers—preachers, fetishists, or liberals. The prevailing sentiment was that any visit was better than the routine of prison life, but there was something in the monotony of count and yard and work and dinner that made the hours pass. Standing at the counter folding laundry in the subterranean facility, she lost track of the minutes. If Gulu was out of sight and she felt relatively confident none of the women on her work crew were working for Gulu, she could escape into her thoughts. Visits from the outside world, even Kristen's, made the prison days longer, her cell colder, her fate a fact, not an abstraction.

"As soon as I read about you," Nyssa was saying, "I knew I had to do something. I mean, this is what journalism is all about. And I know our teacher at the *Broadside* says a reporter's job is to accurately report the news, but journalists can do more. I don't care if they say I'm a crazy millennial. I'm going to make a difference."

When Marydale worked the tasting room at Sadfire, she had kept up an ever-flowing conversation with the customers. Were they following the Portland Timbers and did they hear about the emu farm out in North Plains? Was it unseasonably warm in Salem, too? Now she could not think of anything to say.

"What do you want?" Marydale asked.

"I got in an accident," Nyssa said cheerfully, patting the arms of her wheelchair. "When I was little. Dad bicycled a lot. He was really into it. We had a tandem bike. And we got hit." She shrugged. "It happens."

"Are you going to tell her?" Brit asked.

"Do you think we can talk somewhere private?" Nyssa asked.

"I don't think they're going to let us do that," Marydale said. "Unless you were my lawyer."

"Just tell her," Brit urged.

"I'm going to tell her." Nyssa fiddled with the pom-poms hanging from her hat. "Okay. Here goes." She took a deep breath like someone about to jump from a diving board. "I'm Nyssa…Neiben."

It took Marydale a second to understand. "Eric Neiben was my defense attorney."

"He's my dad, and he's, like, my best friend, too. He went with me to get this." She pulled up her sleeve and pointed to a tattoo of a bicycle. "I still ride," she added. "I've got one of those hand-power bikes. People at school couldn't believe that my dad went with me to get a tattoo."

Marydale's heart raced. She hadn't seen Neiben since the day she was escorted from the Tristess courthouse.

"Why are you here?" she asked.

Nyssa sat back. "He took a bribe."

"What?" Marydale leaned in.

"He—" Nyssa rubbed at the tattoo. "He took a bribe to lose your case." It came out all in one word.

The noises of the visiting room faded. Marydale stared at the girl.

"I was little," Nyssa said. "My mom and dad were still together, and my dad and me, we'd just had the accident. Some guy called and said he'd give my dad ten thousand dollars to take this case…and lose. My dad told me years later."

"My case?"

Marydale saw the Tristess courthouse. She remembered her Walmart separates suit drenched in sweat. She felt Neiben hugging her. *I'm sorry. I did everything I could.*

"My family had a ranch," Marydale said. "I lost my house."

"He and my mom fought about it," Nyssa said. "That's why she left him."

Anger surged through Marydale, and she understood the

women who tossed their cells, who ripped the metal shelving from the cement with their bare, bleeding hands.

"I had a life. I could have had a life. Who paid the money?" Marydale sank her head into her hands. "Ronald Holten. It was fucking Ronald Holten!"

She felt Nyssa's hand on her knee.

A guard called out, "No touching."

"I know," Nyssa said. "I know. I read the article about you and everything that happened. My dad doesn't know I'm here."

"You have to tell someone." Marydale looked up. Only the guards' motionless stare kept her from grabbing the girl by the hand or by the neck. "Please. You have to talk to the court. Will you talk to my lawyer?"

"She wanted to meet you," Brit said.

"I wanted to see you," Nyssa said. "My dad could be in a lot of trouble if people find out."

For a moment, they stared at each other, and the space between them expanded. Marydale felt like she was going to throw up. But behind the effort it took to sit still and not cry or scream or throw her chair across the room, she felt hope welling up inside her like oxygenated blood coursing through her arteries.

"You seem like a good person," Nyssa said.

"If I give you my lawyer's number, will you call her?" Marydale asked.

"Yes," Nyssa said. "Today."

18

Kristen gripped the edge of the windowsill in her motel room. On the other end of the phone, Eric Neiben spoke so slowly he could have been forming the words out of clay.

"I know my daughter told you what happened."

"I'd like you to testify," Kristen said.

"It's a crime what I did."

"I know."

"I could get in a lot of trouble."

"I'll do everything I can to make sure that doesn't happen."

"I would like to talk to you in person…if you could come over to Bend."

Kristen wanted to reach through the phone and shake him. *Just talk to me now!*

"We could have this conversation over the phone," she said.

"No." There was a silence on the other end. "No. I've been

thinking about this for a long time. I want to really *talk* to you."

She wanted to scream. "I can leave now," she said.

"How about tomorrow?" he asked. "I need to get a few things in order."

She ended the call and stumbled out of her room and around the motel. She knocked on Sierra's door, but the HumAnarchists were occupied elsewhere, so she knocked on Aldean's.

"The lawyer. He's going to talk to me," she said. "I'm going to go to his house tomorrow."

Aldean opened his arms, and she fell into them. She could feel the hard muscle of his chest against her cheek. In another life, she would have found him handsome. She would have breathed in his cologne and the slight, pleasant gamy smell that clung to him like wood smoke. Now she just drew back and shook her head.

"What if he changes his mind?" she asked. "What if he runs? He could be in Mexico by tomorrow or Canada or anywhere. He took a bribe. It's a fraud against the court. There's no statute of limitations on that, and he knows it. Or he could kill himself. I should call Nyssa. I think she lives with him. She could keep an eye on him. We've come this far. What if I get there and he doesn't want to talk?"

Aldean put his hand on her shoulder. "Come on in."

His motel room was as clean and spare as the HumAnarchists' was cluttered and personal. He opened a dresser drawer and pulled out an unmarked bottle.

"Consummation Rye." He took two glasses off the counter. "Do you have a gun?"

"I don't have a gun!"

"I can get you one. Gold House Pawn should have a few, or we can just drive over to Burnville and get one at the Walmart."

"I don't want a gun. Why would I want a gun?"

"You're right." Aldean sipped his drink. "I'll go with you. Mary would kill me if she knew I let you go visit some guy's house alone. Cheers."

Kristen raised the glass to her lips and then lowered it without tasting. "I can't have a drink. What if I have to drive? I need to see Marydale. God, it's too late. They won't let me in after five."

Aldean set his drink down. "It's going to be okay."

"What if this Gulu women gets to her before I can get her out? What if Ronald Holten does something to her?"

Aldean put his hands on her shoulders. "This is what you've been waiting for. Right now. This is it. You did it. You found the unicorn."

The next day, Kristen met Aldean in his motel room, trying not to notice as he tucked a pistol into a holster beneath his canvas Sadfire jacket.

"Never hurts to be careful," he said, and picked up his keys without asking if Kristen wanted to drive.

Kristen thought she caught a glimpse of Marydale's childhood in the casual way Aldean pushed the HumAnarchists' SUV into gear, saying, "We'll get you there before ten." It was a world of hard work and long shadows, of young mothers and poor fathers. A world where men were men, women were women. At their best, they were noble siblings to each other. A world in which, for a brief moment, Marydale had stood on the edge of that divide, her radiance so blinding the villagers could not burn her at the stake for breaking their sacred codes.

"Thanks for driving," she said.

"Of course," Aldean said.

And then they were silent.

The drive to Bend felt like it took a lifetime, and yet Kristen was surprised when they suddenly found themselves in the squall of urban traffic. Aldean seemed to need no GPS. He glanced at the address Kristen had written down, then drove them past the Mill District, with its decorative chimneys and palatial restaurants, down a long frontage road lined with half-forgotten strip malls, to a neighborhood of tiny bungalows.

Kristen counted the address numbers.

"Here," she said finally.

The curtains were drawn, and walls of blackberry vines separated the yard from its neighbors on both sides.

"Do you want me to come in?" Aldean asked.

"I don't think he'll talk to us both," Kristen said.

She felt Aldean's protective gaze as she knocked on the door. The man who opened the door looked about fifty, with glasses and a few strands of dark hair combed over his head. His slacks and tie suggested he was on his way to work, but his bare feet said otherwise. Behind him the house smelled of TV dinners. A girl in a wheelchair sat at the kitchen table, textbooks and notes spread out around her.

"You must be Kristen Brock," he said. He held out his hand. "Eric Neiben."

The girl spun herself away from the table and wheeled to the door. "I talked to your girlfriend," she said. "She seems nice."

"This is my daughter, Nyssa," Neiben said. "She's supposed to be studying."

"Dad!" The girl held up her book. "I am studying."

"Let's go out back," Neiben said.

"Good luck, Dad," Nyssa said.

Out back, blackberry vines surrounded a small, concrete slab.

"I'm glad you're here." Neiben gestured to Kristen to take a seat on one of the plastic deck chairs, then realized it was wet and wiped it down with his sleeve.

Neiben sat across from her. "Nyssa really liked that story your sister wrote," he said. "You know, I think that's where Nyssa got the idea she wanted to write…from all the press around the Rodeo Queen Killer. She grew up with it."

Kristen felt the damp of the chair settle into the fabric of her pants.

"Grew up with it?" Kristen wanted to tell him *it* wasn't a ghost story or a boy band. It was Marydale's life that he had squandered.

"You don't practice law anymore," Kristen said.

"I do computer security." Neiben laced his fingers and

rested his elbows on his knees, staring at the ground before him. "Do you believe in karma?"

"Maybe, as a kind of metaphor." Kristen waited.

"Nyssa was nine. We could have had a car." He glanced back at the house. "I thought I was doing the right thing, you know? We biked everywhere. We ate organic. I've been taking care of her for years. Of course, she doesn't really need anyone anymore, and she could always go stay with her mom if she did. I like to think she needs me, but she doesn't."

"I don't think you're at risk for a conviction," Kristen said.

"Fraud against the court." He sighed. "I probably wouldn't be charged, but you don't know. After what happened to Marydale, it's hard to trust the system."

Kristen wanted to wring a confession out of him, but there was also something mesmerizing about the small, cold garden space and the pretty girl inside. Kristen could see her through the sliding glass door, tapping her pencil in time to a rhythm only she heard.

"I told Nyssa what happened," Neiben went on. "I tell her a lot these days. Probably too much. But it's just the two of us. She said I had to talk to you. She's very moral. Maybe it's because of the accident. I don't want to think that, but maybe that's part of it. She knows how fragile it all is."

Neiben was circling around the truth, and she wanted to squeeze it out of him with her fists.

"She sounds like a very special girl."

"She is." He paused. "It was a guy on a cell phone who hit us. He was looking down to dial, and he just swerved into the bike lane. We were on a tandem. I didn't even get a bruise. I wish it had been me. She had so many broken bones, a punctured kidney, a collapsed lung. We thought for a while the paralysis would be much worse. My wife quit her job to take care of her. We fought about that a lot." Neiben rubbed a hand across his head. "I told my wife we didn't need a stay-at-home mom. We needed money. The best doctors. The best therapies. She quit anyway. My practice wasn't going well. I was fresh out of law school. In Eugene, with the U of O law school right there, there were plenty of young attorneys. And I'd been losing cases. A couple of clients filed bar complaints. Then the accident."

"And?" Kristen prompted.

"I got a call from this guy," Neiben went on.

A spit of cold rain hit the concrete slab. Neither of them moved.

"What was his name?"

"He wouldn't give it to me at first. He wanted to talk about my practice. I could tell he was one of those guys who hates lawyers, even when he needs one. He asked if I'd done defense work, but I hadn't except for a couple of DUIs. He said he'd take a chance on me."

"And then?"

"We talked a couple more times. He talked a lot about stewardship and knowing what the community needed. Then he told me about the Rodeo Killer. I'd heard about her, but I hadn't really thought about it. Some lesbian teenager accused of killing her lover's boyfriend. It just sounded like the kind of thing reporters love." Neiben ran his hands over his face, pulling his cheeks into a longer, sadder version of his face. "I knew something was wrong. I grew up in a little town east of Wenatchee in Washington. I know how people can be about gays sometimes, especially back then."

Inside, the girl's cell phone rang, and she answered it, then scooted off into another part of the house.

"Do you mind if I record our conversation?" Kristen asked tentatively.

"Are you trying to get her off?"

"It's too late for that," Kristen said, although her heart was racing. *Unless compelling evidence is discovered after the statute of limitations has expired, evidence that could not have reasonably been exposed at the time of the crime.*

"Post-conviction relief?" Neiben suggested.

"Do I have a case?"

Neiben sat absolutely still, staring at the concrete slab in front of him. Kristen didn't dare take out her phone and start recording. *Talk to me*, she pleaded silently.

"The man's name was Ronald Holten," Neiben said finally. "I didn't know who he was. I hadn't been following the story closely enough. He offered me ten thousand dollars to take the case and lose it. I asked him why. I still remember he said, *We got the best DA in the county, and we have a judge who knows right from wrong, but you can't trust juries.* I put my name in to be a public defender in Tristess. No one thought anything of it except that I had to be desperate to work all the way out there. Ronald Holten made sure I was picked for the case. I told myself it was for Nyssa, anything for Nyssa."

"That's tough," Kristen said. She remembered her first

long drive out to Tristess and her frightened, tearful drive back across the sage flats. *The right choice*. She felt a flicker of compassion for Neiben.

"I thought we could get her a new wheelchair, put her in a special school, go to the Mayo Clinic. I don't know what I was thinking." Again he glanced back at the sliding glass door. "You can't do anything with ten thousand dollars. We were so broke, I thought ten thousand meant something." Neiben sat back, staring up at the sky. A drop of rain hit his cheek.

"She seems to be doing really well," Kristen said.

"Marydale Rae didn't do it." Neiben looked certain and frightened, like a man who had seen a ghost. "I mean, she threw that hay bale, but Aaron Holten was coming for her. He was huge. Ronald Holten took me to his house a couple of times and showed me pictures. I think he was worried I'd go back on our deal, so he showed me these photos of Aaron as a boy. I think it was supposed to make me like him, but the kid was giant. And everyone in that town knew the Holten boys were no good. They had all the money and all the trucks and the land and the guns, and they could do whatever they wanted, and they did. I can only guess what he would have done to Marydale if he'd caught her. I'm sure he would have raped her. I think he might have killed her."

"But you blew the case?" Kristen asked.

"I blew the case. At the rate I was going, Ronald didn't even have to pay me, but he did. Marydale reminded me a lot of Nyssa even though Nyssa was still little." He let out a sad laugh. "She had that innocence about her. I let the prosecutor pick the jury. I wouldn't let her bargain down to manslaughter. I told her it was a technique. We never mentioned self-defense, and I didn't let her take the stand because anyone who heard her story..." He shook his head. "She was just a brave kid, and she felt bad about what she'd done. I used that against her. And I spent the money before the trial was even over. My wife left. I guess you can see that."

Watching him, Kristen thought, *This is the most important day of his life.*

"If I can get a post-conviction relief hearing," she said, "will you testify?"

"Nyssa would like that." Neiben nodded slowly. "She believes in doing the right thing."

18

Marydale had not ventured into the yard since her arrival at Holten Penitentiary. Upon hearing of Neiben's confession, she feigned a flu and stayed in her cell, watching the women file past her on their way to meals, watching for the quick flip of Gulu's wrist lest she toss a shiv or some other contraband into Marydale's cell. It had been days since she had eaten a proper meal, but it didn't matter. Her cellmate, Kelso, had not asked any questions and had not offered any confidences, but she had begun sneaking bits of bread in to Marydale, and the woman named Leena had supplied her with packs of ramen, which she ate dry and washed down with tap water.

Then one morning as Kelso left the cell, the guard grabbed the bars before they could swing closed.

"Get up, Rae," the man said. "Infirmary's seen you. They say you're fine."

"Please." Marydale spoke without moving. "I'm sick."

"Lots of people are sick. Come on."

Slowly Marydale lowered herself to the floor. She wished it was the silver-haired guard. She didn't know the man who stood in front of her, his uniform barely disguising his youth.

"Sir," she said very quietly. "I've got a hearing coming up. It's important. I'm scared."

"It's prison. Everyone's scared."

"Please. I'll do my work crew. I just don't want to go out there." She knew better than to mention Gulu's name.

"Get on," the man said, turning his eyes away from her.

Reluctantly Marydale moved toward the door. "Do I have to go in the yard?"

The man latched the bars behind her. "Mr. Holten's orders," he said, his voice taking on a fierceness it had not had before.

Outside, it was still winter. The brown grass was tipped with white, and the air smelled of frost. Marydale gazed up at the low clouds. *Clouds are God's parade floats*, her mother had often said, but these were not the solid, whipped-cream clouds that looked like castles. These clouds were like paint wiped over graffiti, flat and gray. Marydale walked to the outer edge of the yard, where she could lace her fingers through the links of the fence.

Kristen thought they had a case. *Of course, nothing is ever certain*, she had said, but she had leaned forward across the table until the knuckles of their folded hands touched, the first contact since their stolen kiss. *I've got Eric's testimony in writing, and he's agreed to come to the court.*

Marydale took a deep breath. She stared across the brown

landscape, a few ribs of snow still visible on the distant hills. In Portland, the *Tristess* would be bobbing against the pier. The distillery would be filled with the damp peat smell of the fermenting tanks. Portland would be thinking about summer: the Rose Parade, the Big Float, the Naked Bike Race, and a hundred tastes of this neighborhood or that neighborhood, all waiting for a sample of Solstice Vanilla to sweeten the twilight.

"Well, well, well. Who came out of hibernation?" a voice said behind her.

Marydale turned.

Gulu had arrived with an entourage. Four women stood with their arms swinging too casually.

"I heard your fancy girlfriend was 'round." Gulu tucked her hands into the elastic of her sweatpants. "You still think she's going to get you out?"

Marydale scanned the prison deck for the silver-haired guard, but besides the guards in the towers—invisible and armed—the only guard on the yard was a man with a shaved head and tiny, close-set eyes. She'd heard him talking about her behind her back. *I can see why the dykes are out to get her.* She'd wanted to spit back, *I am a dyke*, but she had to walk past him feeling his gaze crawling across her ass.

"Is it true, Scholar? You leaving us?" Gulu asked.

"You told me nobody gets out," Marydale said. "You said we have a *caul* on us."

"You haven't been eating."

"I'm just doing my time."

"See, I don't think you are." Gulu took a step closer, her

voice quiet and her posture loose. "How would that posh Jane of yours like you with a little cocaine up your pussy, or do you city girls do that already?"

Marydale stepped back, but there was only the fence behind her.

Near the prison building, two women were urging the guard over to the exercise equipment, where another woman lay on the ground, holding her leg.

"Really, Gulu?" Marydale said.

Marydale folded her arms and tipped her chin up. As soon as Gulu threw the first punch, the other women would jump in. It was solidarity and it was cover. To the guards it would look like six women breaking up a fight, but when they stepped away, there'd be no one in the middle. She ran her tongue along the bridge that held her fake tooth in place. At the time, she had barely felt it break off. *Who hit you, Rae?* the guard had asked. *I bit my tongue.* Later, in the bathroom, Gulu had held her for a minute, before shoving her away with a quick benediction. *You're tough, Scholar, and you know not to talk. I like that.*

"I looked up to you," Marydale said.

Gulu snorted. "You should."

"And now Ronald fucking Holten. What's he paying you?"

"Who said Ronald Holten is paying me anything? I like you, Scholar. I don't want you to leave."

"Did Holten promise you something if you stuck it to me? Some money on your commissary? A radio?" She looked down at Gulu's sneakers. They were black with white laces like the prison-issue, but there was a little rubber logo stamped on the side. "What are they? Converse? Sketchers? Does it matter? You'd sell me out to Ronald Holten for a pair of sneakers. You're such a badass."

She knew how the first blow would feel. There was a time when she was used to discomfort. Ranching hurt. Prison hurt. Now her body felt like a soft creature that had tip-toed out of its shell. The prison soap stung her skin. Her back ached from the thin mattress. But if she won her case, it wouldn't matter. If she didn't win, what Gulu did to her would matter even less.

"He probably got them donated by some charity, grabbed them on his way in, and you think you're the big man." Marydale went on. "Do you know how fucked that is? You think you're so tough." She didn't want to fight Gulu, but if she couldn't hide from her, it was the only option left. "You can break every rule. Right? You're the one who can get away with anything, but you're going to suck Ronald Holten's dick for a pair of sneakers. And this is what your life has come down to. You think it feels big. You got your vendettas. You think there's something between us. You think this"—she spread her arms wide, inviting the blow—"is something we do."

She remembered Aldean saying, *You and Kristen Brock. It's epic.* It felt epic, as though she and Kristen were part of all the love stories Marydale had read in the grimy volumes in the Holten Penitentiary library. Romeo and Juliet. Tristan and Isolde. Stephen Gordon and Mary Llewellyn. Only maybe, just maybe, there would be a happy ending this time.

"We have nothing, Gulu. I was a kid who got caught up in the system. I was seventeen. I thought you cared about me. I was scared of you."

"You'd better be scared of me."

Gulu balled a fist and rubbed it against her palm and stepped forward. The women behind her didn't move.

"You know what you are outside these walls?" Marydale spoke into Gulu's hot breath. "This is just an ant farm, just a couple little ants running around in a handful of sand. And you think you're something? You were a player back in the day? You weren't even a dyke on the outside. You weren't strong enough to be a dyke. You were just a dumb girl who got caught up with a bad man and did his work for him and now you're doing his time."

"You don't know anything about my time."

"They have programs at this prison. You could be learning something. You could be reading or getting a degree or making this place better for some of the girls."

"Making macramé bracelets with the bugs." Gulu sneered.

"It'd be better than whatever you're doing here."

Gulu's fist shot out, but Marydale dodged faster. Gulu hit the fence. Marydale watched her and watched the women behind her. Their heads were cocked. One woman examined a tear on her cuff. Another leaned to her neighbor and said something Marydale could not hear. They weren't going to fight. As if watching their reflection in Marydale's eyes, Gulu stepped back, and Marydale realized she was winning.

"You little…" Gulu began.

A guard's voice called out over the frozen grass. "Rae! Clarocci! Get over here."

Marydale moved away from Gulu quickly, keeping her distance as they marched to the deck.

A guard approached, his baton in hand, ready to swing.

"Clarocci, that's a shot."

"Sir!" Gulu protested.

The guard turned to Marydale. "Rae, your hearing got moved up. Court transfer will be here in thirty. Transport manager will have your clothing for court."

Marydale froze.

"Well, go!" the guard said. "You have a pass, Rae."

"You'll be back," Gulu whispered. Then, when Marydale was almost to the door, she called out, "Goodbye, Scholar."

19

Marydale was the only prisoner in the transport van. She fingered the cuffs of the suit Kristen had bought her until she felt a button start to loosen. She wished there were someone to distract her. Even an addict coming down in a spray of vomit would have been preferable to the rumble of the engine and the enormity of the thought: she might leave court a free woman, but she might just as easily return to Holten, change back into her prison uniform, and stay. For months...for years, if Gulu had her way.

When they arrived at the courthouse, a van from one of the television stations in Bend had parked outside the courthouse. The guard escorted her in, and Kristen met them in the lobby. She looked beautiful and impeccably coiffed, her soft brown hair swept up into a perfect French twist. She wore a different pair of glasses, their silver frames suggesting a powerful executive more than a sexy librarian. She squeezed Marydale's arm.

Walking into the courtroom, Marydale was hit with a wave of recognition. Here was where it had all happened. She remembered everything: the faux-wood paneling, the wallpaper printed with Grecian columns. It looked like a movie set for a cheap thriller, everything pasted together and painted the color of something it wasn't.

Aldean, Sierra, and her friends sat on one side of the aisle along with Grady, Neiben, and a few other townspeople. On the other side, like parties at a contentious wedding, Ronald Holten and District Attorney Boyd Relington sat in the front row, their backs glowering at her arrival. They had amassed their own small group of locals. One woman sat with her head bowed, one hand raised and the other on a Bible. An old man with a crew cut was furiously writing notes on a legal pad.

"She's here," someone said. There was a murmur of voices. Someone hissed, "Killer. Pervert."

Kristen indicated a seat in the front and positioned herself between Marydale and the aisle. "It'll be okay," she said, but she kept opening and closing the leather portfolio in front of her.

"Who's the judge?" Marydale asked.

Kristen hesitated. "The law is the law."

"But it matters."

Kristen put her hand to her own shoulder, as though to ease some tension that had gathered there. "Kip Spencer."

"Spencer?" Marydale thought she had steeled herself for the possibility of a guilty verdict, but the disappointment she felt at hearing Spencer's name told her nothing could prepare her. "He won't let me out. Kristen, it doesn't matter what the evidence says or the attorney general. You can't hurt a Holten and get away with it."

"But the attorney general isn't going to respond, and that's a good thing." Kristen still looked worried, but there was a note of confidence in her voice. "It's you against the state, and the state is represented by the attorney general. If he doesn't respond, it's like their key witness saying it didn't happen. It means the attorney general doesn't think there's a case against your post-conviction relief. He's basically saying you should never have been convicted, and he won't oppose your release if the judge thinks it's right."

"But Kip Spencer…"

"We have to trust the process. He's sworn to uphold the law."

Eventually the door to the judge's chambers opened. Judge Spencer appeared, older and thinner but with the same white handlebar mustache. He took a seat behind the bench, looking down at the room.

"All rise," the bailiff said, and announced the case.

Judge Spencer motioned for them to be seated. "This is an open hearing on the post-conviction relief plea entered by Ms. Brock on behalf of Ms. Marydale Rae. As you know, a post-conviction relief hearing may reduce the original sentence or revoke it entirely. Given that Ms. Rae has already made parole, Ms. Brock is asking that the court void Ms. Rae's sentence and erase her record. The attorney general has chosen not to respond. Ms. Brock, would you like to proceed?"

Kristen rose.

"Today I will show that Ms. Rae received incompetent council that led to her wrongful conviction for the murder of Aaron Holten. We have records here that indicate the police investigation at the time of Aaron Holten's was…ambiguous. Some notes leading up to the final report suggest that Aaron Holten's death was deemed self-defense." She went on, running through several pages of her report. "Police now say there was no reason to expect that Aaron Holten was at Ms. Rae's house under anything less than free will and that—"

"Get to the point. All this could have been determined at the time of the trial," Judge Spencer cut in, "or at appeal."

"And we have the testimony of Mr. Neiben." Kristen paused.

Relington and Holten eyed Neiben with new interest.

"Today," Kristen continued, "I will prove that defense attorney Eric Neiben failed to participate in voir dire, failed to mount a defense of self-defense, failed to request the charges be reduced to manslaughter, and did not petition to have vital evidence entered into the record. What is more, Mr. Neiben is here to state that he failed in these duties deliberately and at the behest of Ronald Holten, Aaron's uncle, and that Ronald Holten in fact paid him ten thousand dollars to lose this case."

"That's bullshit!" Holten stood up. His ruddy complexion paled. "You know it! Throw this shit out, Kip!"

Spencer adjusted his mustache. "Ronald, this is my courtroom."

"It's lies. Fucking lies! My nephew was a decent man. And she...she lured him into her sick little world and killed him because he wouldn't make a decent woman out of her."

Kristen shook her head, and the anger Marydale saw in every muscle of Kristen's face calmed her racing heart just a bit. At least Kristen knew the truth.

Relington joined in. "I prosecuted that case. I stand by my record. Just because she hired some big-firm lawyer to represent her—we don't do loopholes around here. You know that, Kip!"

Judge Spencer placed both hands on the table. "Boyd."

"Kip, the record stands! This is slander!" Holten said.

"Then let it stand. If it stands, it won't matter what we hear from Mr. Neiben."

"I can't believe you'd listen to this," Holten fumed.

Judge Spencer slowly shuffled his notes into a stack and pushed them aside. He propped his elbows on the table. "Ron, you know Boyd is a damn good attorney. He's served this county for years, and his father did, too, and his grandfather." He looked at Relington. "And we know what the Rae girl did, so let's settle this once and for all, hear them out, and decide."

Marydale wanted to sink her head into her hands.

"Ronald Holten is a good man," Relington said.

"I know. He ran my campaign," Judge Spencer said.

"You don't have to hear this petition. You can throw it out," Relington said.

Spencer ignored him, turning his gaze back on Holten. "I remember, Ron, you said you were glad we elected judges in

the state of Oregon. That was the only way to get a fair hearing. We put your name up on this courthouse, and I stand by
that. But, Ronald, I know your boys get rough from time to
time."

"That's family business," Holten said.

"I agree. But fair is fair. I've kept a lot of stuff out of court
for you. Now the Rae girl wants to be heard. We're going to
hear this petition, and we're going to hear from Mr. Neiben."

"That man is a liar," Holten said, backing away from the
bench and glancing at the exit. "I'm calling my attorney."

Kristen touched Marydale's hand.

"You're making a mistake, Kip," Relington said before following Holten toward the door.

When the door closed behind them, Judge Spencer said,
"Now, Mr. Neiben, if you're ready, come forward."

Neiben walked slowly down the center aisle, his feet
barely lifting off the worn carpet. He took the stand like a
man on the gallows.

"I am." He wiped his forehead, then rubbed his hand on
his pants.

"How are you related to the case?"

"I was Marydale...Ms. Rae's public defender."

"And in that capacity, did you do your due diligence to ef-
fect a positive outcome for Ms. Rae's case?"

Neiben looked around the courtroom. Marydale felt his
gaze dart away from her. Above Judge Spencer's head the
wall clock froze between seconds. Eric Neiben was going to
lie. Marydale's head throbbed. Her ears rang. She wondered
if the adrenaline coursing through her body could actually

poison her. There was no proof. There was no paperwork. No one wrote a receipt for a bribe. Neiben would say no, and the judge would believe him.

Then Kristen would clutch her hand, not knowing when they would touch again, or maybe she would just look down at her papers. Neither of them would cry. It was all too big, too final. Kristen, Portland, the distillery, the *Tristess:* Marydale felt it all slipping away. In their place was a cell and then life in a county where she'd be lucky to find someone willing to rent her a filthy apartment at double the price because no one wanted a felon living around decent, law-abiding citizens.

She hung her head. The second hand strained, then clicked forward. Neiben cleared his throat.

"I took a bribe to lose Marydale Rae's case," he said.

Marydale looked up sharply. She waited for a clue that she had misheard. Kristen mouthed, *Yes*.

"And who offered you that bribe?" Spencer asked.

"Ronald Holten."

"How do you know it was him?"

"I met him. He gave me five thousand dollars in cash before the case went to trial and again after Marydale was convicted. My daughter was... She'd been in an accident. We needed the money."

"Can you describe how you perpetrated this fraud on the court?"

Eric Neiben took an index card out of his shirt pocket and proceeded in a monotone. His explanation took a long time. "Any good defense attorney would have called for a *fo-*

rum non conveniens…have investigated the police department's reports on the case…"

While Marydale did not understand all the terminology, she understood the story.

"Intent was determined based on Ms. Rae's alleged invitation…Her seduction of Aaron Holten was no more than hearsay…If she had taken the stand…"

When Neiben had finished, Spencer asked, "I find it hard to believe that Mr. Holten specifically told you to lose. He's a man of his word and a pillar of this community."

Neiben checked his index card. "He said he wanted the right result. He made it really clear what that was."

"Do you think you achieved the right result?"

Neiben's voice grew rough. "I always thought Marydale was the victim, not Aaron."

"That is also what your written testimony suggests," Spencer said. "Mr. Neiben, you may sit down."

Kristen stood up quickly. "Your Honor, may I question Mr. Neiben?" Kristen asked.

Judge Spencer held up his hand. "I think you've done enough, Ms. Brock."

"Your Honor, I have a right to—"

"Hold your horses, Councilor. Sit down." Judge Spencer took out a laptop from beneath his table and typed something.

"I will file a due-process complaint," Kristen said.

Marydale felt Kristen clutch the back of her chair.

Judge Spencer closed his laptop and propped his elbows on the table in front of him.

"Ms. Rae?" he began, looking directly at her.

"Yes, sir?"

"Stand up when I'm talking to you."

Marydale stood up.

"Aaron Holten was a young man. He wasn't a perfect man, but he was a young man with a future ahead of him, and you took that from him. He never had a chance to raise a family, to carry on his name, to make amends. Do you understand what that means?"

Marydale lifted her chin, feeling her hair drape over her shoulders, unkempt but golden. She could feel Trumpet's saddle beneath her. *If you lose*, she heard her mother whisper, *you ride out tall.* She took a deep breath. She knew what happened in courts, in jails, in prisons, in one parole office after another.

"Yes, sir," she said.

"And your…ways, your life choices, made it very difficult for some people in this town to accept you. You can't burn a flag or spit on a Bible and not expect someone around here to step in and say that's just plain wrong."

"I would never burn our flag," Marydale said. "And I would never defile a Bible."

"Oh, I think a lot of people would say you already have, Ms. Rae…metaphorically speaking."

Judge Spencer paused, looked at his laptop, then hit one more key. "But," he added with a sigh. "The law is the law, and I am sworn to weigh the facts and make just findings given the evidence presented."

He looked past Marydale to the small group of people assembled behind her. "And while I know there isn't one father or uncle out there who wouldn't do what Ronald Holten did to get justice for that boy, I find substantial denial of Ms. Rae's constitutional rights. On account of her attorney's failure to provide effective council and in light of Mr. Neiben's confession of tampering with the court, I hold the original verdict in the *State of Oregon v. Marydale Rae* void. Ms. Rae, your post-conviction relief is granted. You are released from your obligations to the state. I will draft my official statement by the end of the week. You are now free to go." He nodded to the transport guard from the penitentiary. "I have alerted Holten Penitentiary that you will be returning without Ms. Rae."

The guard rose, thanked Judge Spencer, and walked out. The judge gave a curt nod and stood up. A moment later he had disappeared into the judge's chambers. The court was silent.

"Is that it?" Marydale asked. She was waiting for Spencer to reappear, to say that there was an exception, a loophole, a technicality. She was still guilty. Holten Penitentiary owned her, and they were taking her back

"Yes," Kristen said, and hugged her. Marydale could feel her strength and smell the faint hint of sweat. "We did it," Kristen said, her voice warm with tears. She pulled away. "Thank you," she said to Neiben.

He sat facing the bench, his index card clutched in one hand. He glanced over. "I'm sorry." Neiben sank his head in his hands.

"What's going to happen to him?" Marydale asked quietly.

Kristen put her hand on Marydale's back. "Come on," she said. "He did what he had to do."

A moment later, Aldean and Sierra and her friends crowded around them.

"We won!" Kristen said.

Aldean flung his arms around Marydale. "Star of the show," he said. "Just like old times."

Beside them, Sierra hugged Kristen. "I knew you could do it," she exclaimed.

As the group congratulated each other, Marydale slipped out the side door, unconsciously scanning the area for Gulu or Holten or a guard. She knelt down to touch the brown grass that pushed through cracks in the pavement, then pulled a blade and touched it to her lips.

Kristen appeared at her side. "I told them you might need a minute," she said.

Marydale wanted to tell her how grateful she felt and how stunned. She felt like she could breathe in the whole sky, and she felt like she should sit down lest she fly away into the atmosphere. But she didn't have the words, so she flung her arms around Kristen and squeezed her and picked her up for a second.

"I can't believe it," she said.

Half an hour later, Marydale rolled down the window of Kristen's car. There was a spring dampness in the air. In a few weeks the wildflowers would bloom on the Summit, hidden among the rocks where the frost didn't reach them. The birds would migrate through the wetlands on the Harney County line. Then would come calving season, then the rodeo. She could see her mother riding out on Trumpet, his white tail swirling behind him.

They said nothing until they reached the Firesteed Summit and the world stretched out beneath them like a quilt.

"This is where we released my father's ashes." Marydale felt the wind blowing up through the gorge. "He said you can't bury a cowboy in the yard behind the church. And Aldean and I…we threw my mother's ashes here, too."

Tentatively, Kristen slipped her fingers through Marydale's.

"I think Tristess is changing," Kristen said. "No matter what Ronald Holten thinks. I don't think what happened to you would happen again."

"I don't know," Marydale said.

"Do you ever want to move back?" Kristen asked.

"I was seventeen when I was convicted," Marydale said. "I don't even know who I'd be if I was still here."

Kristen squeezed her hand. "I'm so sorry."

"It's life," Marydale said. "'The past is the past,' that's what my mother used to say." She picked through the words carefully, trying to remember the saying her mother had stitched onto a sampler in the living room. "'The present is a gift…'"

When Marydale looked over, Kristen was crying.

"What is it?" she asked.

Kristen dropped her hand. "Don't you see?" Kristen's tears were at odds with the perfect whisper of blush on her cheekbones, her perfect taupe lipstick, her tiny pearl earrings, everything controlled and arranged.

"See what?"

"I should have stayed." When Marydale didn't speak, Kristen said, "If I'd have stayed, maybe you wouldn't have had to go through all this. I should have fought for you then. Maybe we could have done all this five years ago." She took off her glasses and rubbed her eyes, smearing her perfect makeup.

Marydale put her hands on Kristen's arms, holding her and holding her away at the same time. She examined Kristen's face, her thin lips, her restrained beauty, like the tiny wildflowers, at first indiscernible and then breathtaking. Then she pulled Kristen close.

"We don't know what would have happened."

Kristen leaned into Marydale's embrace. "When I first got back to Portland, I had this clock in my mind," she said. "A day. I knew you could forgive me for leaving for a day. Maybe a week? I don't know when it tipped, but one day I was running down by the river. It was rainy. Everyone was out, biking and running with their dogs. And it hit me. I'd waited too long. I can't even remember how long it was. Three months? Six months? I just sat down on a bench and cried. And now you can have any life you want. You can go anywhere you want."

Marydale stroked Kristen's hair, gazing over her shoulder out across the land. "I've been to Nevada. I've never even been to Vancouver, Washington."

"It's not great," Kristen said.

"But you are," Marydale said. "You were meant to be a lawyer and not here in Tristess. We don't know what would have happened if you'd stayed. Maybe we would have been totally dysfunctional. Maybe we'd have adopted a couple of babies and then decided we hated each other. Maybe Eric wouldn't have come forward. Maybe Judge Spencer would have said no. Maybe we wouldn't have won five years ago. We don't know."

"But..." Kristen began.

"You lost your job. You were going to be partner."

"It doesn't matter."

"It does," Marydale said. "You did that for me. You beat the odds...for me." She leaned in and kissed Kristen gently. "You've already put in a day's work. How about we crash at the Almost Home and then head back to Portland tomorrow?"

Kristen hesitated. "Sierra told me something," she said. "We don't have to do this, but the couple who bought your house, they've turned it into a bed-and-breakfast. It just opened, and they've invited us all to stay."

20

Gulch Creek Road had been paved all the way to Marydale's driveway, only it wasn't Marydale's anymore. A sign at the end of the drive read TRISTESS B&B, and someone had planted a profusion of crocuses at its base. Kristen slowed the car and put on her blinker.

"Is this okay?" She tried to read Marydale's face. "You sure you want to do this?"

"I don't know."

Kristen searched her face for a clue. "We could just stay at the Almost Home," she offered. "If it's too…hard. You should never have lost this house."

They were idling in the middle of the road, but no one was coming.

Slowly Marydale shook her head. "I loved this house," she said. "That was my parents' house. I grew up there."

Kristen flicked off the blinker. "We'll go back to town."

"No." Marydale touched her leg. "No, I…I don't know if I'll ever come back here. Let's go. Let's see it."

Kristen pulled to a stop in the freshly graded driveway. The HumAnarchists' SUV was already parked in front of the house. She and Marydale got out of the car, and a woman appeared at the front door, wiping her hands on a faded apron, her long, gray-blond ponytail swinging behind her.

"Marydale Rae," she called out, and her face bore such a look of tenderness, Kristen thought, for a moment, they knew each other. She hung back as Marydale approached the woman.

"I'm Annette," the woman said. She put a hand on Marydale's back, ushering her into the house as though Marydale were an old friend who had been lost in a storm and had now returned. "Please, come in," Annette murmured to Marydale. She nodded to Kristen to follow.

Inside, the interior had been repainted in shades of sky blue with yellow and red accents along the molding and around the windowsills. Annette led Marydale into the kitchen and urged her to sit.

"Your friends are already here," she said.

A tall, skinny man appeared in the doorway. He, too, had a long gray ponytail, although the top of his head was bald.

"This is my husband, Henry," Annette said.

"We heard about what happened today." Henry held out his hand to Marydale. "I'm so glad someone finally came up with the right verdict."

"You heard?" Marydale asked.

"Small town. News travels." He pulled up a chair. "I'm sorry."

Annette placed a pitcher of ice tea on the table. Kristen felt as she sometimes did when interviewing witnesses; she didn't want to breathe lest she disturb the moment unfolding before her.

"I used to teach up at the Correction Center in Gig Harbor," Henry went on. "I know how a lot of those women got there. They weren't all innocent, for sure, but I heard a lot of stories like yours. I realize it's not right, the way we came by this house. You losing it because of that conviction."

Marydale looked around the kitchen. Kristen thought she looked like someone waking from a coma, searching the walls for a clue as to just how much she had lost.

"It was nine hundred dollars," Marydale said quietly.

"Nine hundred dollars?" Annette sat down across from her.

"That's what I owed in taxes. I didn't have the money. Aldean would have given it to me, but I didn't get my mail. I was in jail for hanging out with this woman from Burnville. She wasn't even gay, but my PO thought something was going on between us."

Annette covered Marydale's hand with hers. "I'm sorry."

Marydale pulled her hand away. "Did you know? Did you know what happened? Did you know why the house was for sale?"

Annette and Henry glanced at each other.

"We didn't know," Annette said, "not about you, not about the taxes. But I guess we did know, too. I come from a ranching family out in Avon, Montana. You don't get land without taking it from someone else. You see a ranch for sale, especially a foreclosure or a government sale, and you know. I saw a lot of people lose their dreams that way."

"And if you look back," Henry added, "we all took it from the Indians. But you have a place here if you'll take it. You can come here anytime you like. You and your friends. Free of charge. This is still your house."

"Always," Annette added.

"A bed-and-breakfast," Marydale said. "Who wants to stay in Tristess?"

"Birders. Mountain climbers. We get a few bikers. We want folks from the city to come out here and see how beautiful it is. Maybe we can even bring some new folks into the area, like Sangheeta, who manages the Almost Home. She and her husband came out for a camping trip. They just loved it here, so they stayed."

Kristen heard laughter outside the kitchen window. Sierra, Moss, and Frog were tromping across the yard with bundles of sticks.

"We sent them out to collect some juniper for the fire pit," Annette said. "The Bureau of Land Management did a big juniper cut—it's invasive—and the piles are just there for the taking. We try to recycle as much as we can."

Sierra burst through the door, talking rapidly about a snake they had seen and a wall hanging she was planning on making out of juniper twigs.

Aldean followed a minute later, but his lack of twigs suggested he had not been among their party. And he had someone with him. It took Kristen only a second to place her: Aubrey. She stood a few paces behind Aldean, the baby in one arm, her little boy at her side. Marydale stood up, almost knocking her chair over in the process.

"What are you doing here?" she asked.

"Aldean came by this afternoon," Aubrey said.

The kitchen suddenly felt crowded, and the air tightened around Aubrey and Marydale.

"He said I should look in on you."

Marydale said nothing.

"We're heading to the swap meet." Aubrey took a tentative step forward. "I just thought I'd come by and say I'm glad it all worked out."

"You married Amos Holten," Marydale said.

"He doesn't know I'm here." Her next words came out in a rush. "Aldean said I should have spoken up back then. I know what Aaron said—that he'd kill you—and I should have made someone listen. I went along with it, and that was wrong. I just…I'm sorry."

"You're sorry!"

Kristen thought she had never seen Marydale look so beautiful or so fierce.

"I'm glad you're out," Aubrey wheedled. "I always knew you'd get out of Tristess. It's no excuse, me going out with Aaron and all, but it wasn't that I didn't care about you. I just knew you wouldn't stay. I was always gonna be a Tristess girl, but you weren't. We all knew that."

"I wasn't going to stay? I had to stay. I went to prison!" Marydale wasn't yelling, but her voice was like an earthquake deep beneath the ground. "You could have fought for me. You could have called…someone. You could have helped me."

"I couldn't tell people the truth."

"What truth?"

Aubrey clutched the baby to her chest. The little boy hid behind her knees. Except for Marydale's breath, the room was completely silent.

"That I'd been with you," Aubrey said. "That's why he did it, because he knew I'd never like him as much as I liked you. I couldn't go up in front of a courtroom and say that."

"But everyone knew!"

"It was different back then. Don't you remember? It was okay to be…the way we were…if you didn't throw it in people's faces."

"I went to *prison*!"

"I said I'm sorry. I came here to say I'm sorry."

"You let me go to prison…you married a Holten…because you couldn't tell people you liked a girl? You couldn't stand up for me. You couldn't stand up for yourself for one—"

Kristen thought she saw Marydale open her mouth to say *fucking* then look at the little boy. The word came out in a sharp, silence enunciation.

"—second. You couldn't just say this is who I am, and this is what I want?"

"It was easier for you," Aubrey whispered. Her cheeks had flushed. "We were really young." Aubrey's voice trembled. "You were so strong, I thought…I'm sorry."

"You don't get to—"

The little boy at Aubrey's feet let out an agonized sob. Marydale stopped and dropped to her knees before the boy.

"I'm sorry," she said. "I raised my voice to your mother. I shouldn't have done that."

The boy pressed his check to Aubrey's leg, staring at Marydale with big eyes.

"I won't do that again."

Marydale didn't try to pat the boy or hug him. When she rose, the anger had drained out of her face. She looked older. Kristen remembered seeing her at the Deerfield whiskey tasting and thinking that five years had aged Marydale more than they should have and that she was still beautiful. Perhaps she was more beautiful.

"I'm sorry, Aubrey," Marydale said.

Tentatively, Aubrey said, "I just wanted to see you, to say goodbye. You and your ma were always special. Sun always shone a little brighter on you. Everyone knew it. I just wanted to tell you."

Marydale hesitated for a moment, then said, "Thank you."

Aubrey gave Marydale an awkward one-armed hug, the baby between them. Marydale touched its head gently.

"She's cute," Marydale said.

"Thanks." Aubrey smiled. "Take care of yourself, Marydale."

On their way out, Kristen heard the boy say, "She's scary."

"That's because she's so powerful, like a superhero," Aubrey said. "Do you remember Superwoman? And you know what else? Marydale was the most beautiful rodeo queen in the whole world."

"In the *whole* world?"

"Yep. In the *whole* world."

"Come on," Henry said as their voices faded. "Let's get this fire going so we can grill some burgers." He put his hand on Frog's shoulder. "And veggie burgers."

22

Marydale stood in her mother's kitchen, which was no longer her mother's or hers although the shelves and the baseboards were as familiar as her own skin; a coat of paint couldn't change that. Henry and Annette watched her, looking hopeful.

"You belong here," Annette said.

"It'll be fun," Sierra chimed in. "We're going to cook out, and Henry and Annette have invited some people from Tristess who want to meet you."

"A lot of people are mad at Ronald Holten," Henry added. "This is a win for all of them, for all of Tristess. They want to thank you."

"It'll be potluck," Annette said. "Just a little get-together. People who care 'bout you."

Marydale felt good old-fashioned courtesy pulling on her, like a familiar song she couldn't hear without humming along. She was supposed to say, *Well, gosh, I don't deserve all that, but if everyone's gone to all that trouble, and of course I'd love to see folks again. It's been too long.* Then someone would ask, *How many times did you win that rodeo competition?* She knew the script, and she knew her role, and she said, "No!" The word flew out of her mouth before she realized what she was going to say.

Kristen put a hand on Marydale's shoulder.

Marydale turned to her. "Do you mind if we leave today?" she asked.

Kristen's expression said, *Did I ever want to be here?* To the gathering in the kitchen, she said, "If Marydale and I leave now, we can make it back to Portland by midnight."

Annette and Henry protested, but Kristen held up her hand, polite but final. Marydale hid her smile until they were outside. The sky had cleared, and behind the house, the Firesteed Mountains rose up and up, their outline crisp against the blue. There was a faint hint of green between the last patches of snow. She hadn't seen it from the prison yard. And it felt like a great luxury to leave all that beauty behind.

"Mind if I drive?" Marydale asked.

Kristen beamed. "Go for it."

Marydale pushed Kristen's seat back, adjusted the mirrors, and tuned to the local radio station. On the way out of town they stopped at the Arco for coffee. Kristen poured herself a twenty-ounce cup, tasted it, and said, "Ah! This stuff is awful." Then she wrapped an arm around Marydale's waist and added, "I can't wait to be back in Portland with you."

Marydale leaned down and kissed her with a quick, loud

smack. The woman behind the counter glared. Marydale tossed her hair over her shoulder. She was still wearing the suit Kristen had brought to the prison. Kristen hadn't guessed her size quite right, and the pants hung off her hips, while the cuffs revealed inches of wrist, but it didn't matter. She felt like she was wearing her full rodeo regalia with Trumpet's reins in her hands.

"Did you see that woman in there?" Kristen said as they exited the mini-mart, bags of snacks hanging off their arms and coffees in hand. "She looked like she'd swallowed tack. I mean really...two women. Is it still that shocking?"

Marydale stopped. The attendant was watching them through the window. She caught her eye, then kissed Kristen again, their bags tangling and their coffees sloshing.

"Shocking!" Marydale said.

Then, like a gleeful child, she broke into a run. To her surprise, Kristen followed, her suit jacket flapping.

"Let's get out of here," Kristen said.

Marydale revved the engine of Kristen's Audi the way Aldean had taught her to rev her first Dodge pickup, and they sped out of the parking lot and onto the wide-open highway. The radio blared a triumphant country anthem about a pretty woman and a tailgate party. Marydale sang along, and Kristen laughed.

"I've never heard this song in my life."

"That song *was* my life," Marydale said.

When the radio died away in the high desert between Tristess and Burnville, Marydale and Kristen clasped their hands over the gearshift and talked. Their talk veered from

Ronald Holten to Gulu to Nyssa and Eric Neiben and, in between the serious truths, their laughter came easily, like groundwater running just beneath the surface. Kristen told her about Grady carefully picking the pine nuts off his steak at the Heavenly Harvest. They imagined the HumAnarchists in Tristess, trying to get the old ranchers to draw mandalas. Although the drive was long, Marydale felt as though she would never get tired. And she marked each county line in her heart.

When they finally arrived in Portland, Marydale threw herself on the bed in Kristen's spacious bedroom, letting the city lights wash over her.

"We're home!" she said.

"Does it feel like home?" Kristen asked.

"You feel like home," Marydale said.

Kristen set her glasses on the bedside table and fell into Marydale's open arms. Their first kiss was slow and gentle, as they explored each other's bodies carefully like new lovers.

Kristen lifted Marydale's shirt over her head and unclasped her bra. And Marydale had the feeling that she was something Kristen had worked hard to achieve and was now enjoying fully. She was part of Kristen's life—not a strange exception, not a secret. They were friends and lovers and equals. And she could give herself to Kristen completely because her body was hers to give. Her blood, her bones, her sex, her dreams: they were hers, and she was free.

Then they were casting off blankets and swimming in the sea of pillows. Kristen spoke endearments and compliments, her voice growing rougher as their movements grew more hurried. Marydale gave herself entirely to Kristen's touch. The slight tension that had always stayed in her neck, the sense that she should hold back or finish faster, was gone. She opened her legs for Kristen's fingers. Kristen found the perfect blend of pressure and movement. Then, a moment later, Kristen's lips and tongue were swirling across Marydale's body. Marydale heard herself whispering a joyous litany of cries.

"Yes. Harder. Please."

She closed her eyes. Looking inward, she could see the constellation of nerves in her own body as Kristen filled her with her fingers and swept her tongue back and forth across Marydale's clit, bringing her closer and closer until her body turned to liquid gold, and she was the sunrise spilling over the Firesteed Summit, and she was the spring rains washing the city clean, and she was the first taste of a fine whiskey, and she was loved.

As soon as the last spasm of orgasm flickered out, she touched Kristen's back, urging her to roll over. Marydale guided her to the foot of the bed, so Kristen's knees bent over the edge. Then she knelt in the pile of blankets on the floor.

"I missed you," Marydale whispered as she sank her tongue into the warm salt of Kristen's body.

When Kristen's body was so taut Marydale could not feel her breathing, she took Kristen's hand and guided it to the place where she kissed, running her tongue over Kristen's clit and Kristen's fingers in beautiful collaboration. Kristen cried out when she came, and in her pleasure Marydale heard their whole story. The cautious girl Marydale had kissed on her porch swing. Their first lovemaking. Their loneliness. The snow on the Deerfield Hotel. The distillery. Aldean's quick diagnosis: *You love her in your blood.* Kristen's tears on the Summit and her pride. *We won.*

Epilogue

Kristen could not prove beyond a reasonable doubt that Portland's first annual Rose City Rodeo was the strangest incarnation of the rodeo ever, but a preponderance of the evidence pointed in that direction. She stood in the shade of the Sadfire Distillery, enjoying the summer spectacle.

At Marydale's urging, the rodeo featured only those events that had been certified cruelty-free by all major animal rights organizations and certified *animal fun* by Sierra's spinoff nonprofit the HumAnimal Collective. This, along with the constraints of space—the rodeo was hosted in the small industrial park that housed the distillery—left the rodeo without the traditional calf roping and bronco riding.

The PDX Bike Co-op subbed in with a variety of bike-like contraptions. As Kristen watched, a man in a top hat cycled by on a bicycle ten or twelve feet tall. Pugs in the Park had agreed to host a pug meet-up in lieu of the usual small-livestock competitions. Kristen stood in the fenced-in space, awash with brachycephalic dogs, to which Meatball happily added his number. Some of the dogs were in costume, and the rodeo queen—a very pretty boy named Duchess—was handing out organic dog biscuits and blue ribbons to all the contenders. Across the way, two women had brought alpacas and were doing a weaving demonstration while the source of the wool wandered over to the popcorn stand to graze.

Despite Sierra's avowal that Fishbowl Pocket Moon never played small shows, they were, in fact, a trio of not-so-starving real estate brokers who would play any weekend venue that invited them. They were setting up near the Sadfire tasting booth where Aldean and Marydale were already pouring samples of their latest release, the Rodeo Queen Revival. Behind the tasting booth a twenty-foot banner bore the Sadfire logo, the motto slightly modified. At Marydale's request, she and Aldean had changed the order of the words so it now read *DOLERE. SPERO. AMANT.* Grieve. Hope. Love. Kristen was so entranced by the rodeo and by watching Marydale pouring whiskey that she didn't notice Donna striding over.

"Can you explain any of this to me?" Donna asked, staying safely on the non-puggy side of the plastic fence.

Kristen couldn't stop smiling. "No," she said. "None of it."

Marydale lit a torch, its whiskey-soaked flames flickering in the late-afternoon sunshine. She held it up to the gathered crowd, then lowered it into her mouth until it disappeared.

"Has she thought about my offer?" Donna asked. "We start with Tristess County. Wrongful imprisonment. Nepotism. Then we go after Ronald Holten in civil court. He's broke, but he's got a lot of assets. Where Marydale came from, there are bound to be more lawsuits. It'll open a whole new division for Falcon Law."

Marydale's voice drifted over the crowd. "Now, here you're going to taste some things you don't expect. There is a sweetness to the Rodeo Queen Revival that should come as a surprise and yet *not* a surprise. It's the sun rising over familiar terrain, a girl's first glimpse of her own beauty. It's a woman looking back. It's love, both ethereal and carnal, and yes, you can taste the salt of a woman's body in that sweetness."

"I'll remind her that you asked," Kristen said.

"Convince her!" Donna said. "This is the Powerball jackpot of civil rights lawsuits. Why wouldn't she say yes?"

Kristen watched Marydale raise her glass to the flame. "I think she feels like she's already won."

"And you?" Donna asked. "When are you going to come back to the Falcon Law Group? We're going to sue Tri-State Global for price fixing. It'll be great. You could be front and center on that one. You can't just hide away doing small claims and I don't know…What are you doing?"

Kristen thought of her private practice with the window looking onto the tree-lined street and a bed for Meatball in the corner. Most days, Kristen drove up to Sadfire for lunch. As soon as the weather had cleared, she and Marydale had taken to eating sandwiches on the deck of the *Tristess*. They were always off work by five, and the city spread itself out for them like a banquet of concerts and the food fairs and the strange festivals to which the Rose City Rodeo added its number.

She didn't remind Donna that a quarter of the Falcon Law Group's clients had followed her to her new practice, as was their legal right.

"A lot of small-business stuff," Kristen said casually. "A little defense work. A few parole cases. Tri-State Global says they might be getting sued. We've been talking. I haven't taken a retainer yet. I'm being selective."

"Damn you," Donna said with grudging admiration. "But you should be selective with us."

From behind the bar, Marydale caught sight of Kristen, tipped her white Stetson, then blew her a kiss.

"Thanks," Kristen said. "But I've got everything I want right here."

Please see the next page for an excerpt from
Karelia Stetz-Waters's *Something True*.

Chapter 1

It was late June, the kind of warm summer evening when hopeless romantics make bad choices about beautiful women. The twilight was all watery, yellow-blue brightness, and Portland glowed with the promise of warm pavement and cool moonlight. It was, as it turned out, a dangerous mix for Tate Grafton, who stood at the till of Out in Portland Coffee trying to make out what her boss had done to the change drawer.

"How is it possible," she called without looking up, "that you are eight dollars over, but it's all in nickels?"

Just then, the wind chime on the door tinkled. It was because of that evening light that came from nowhere and everywhere at the same time and filled the city with a sense of possibility that Tate did not say, "Sorry, we're closed."

The woman who had just walked in wore her hair pulled back in a low ponytail and had the kind of sleek magazine blondness that Tate was required, as a feminist, to say she did not like. And she did not like it in magazines. But in real life, and in the dangerous twilight that filtered through the front window, the woman was very pretty. She did not carry anything. No laptop. No purse. Not even a wallet and cell phone clutched in one hand. Nor did she have room in the pockets of her tight jeans for more than a credit card. Tate noticed.

The woman stood in the doorway surveying the coffee shop, from the exposed pipes, to the performance space, to the mural of Gertrude Stein. Right down to the cracked linoleum floor. Then she strode up to the counter and asked for a skinny, tall latte with Sweet'N Low.

"I'll, um…" Tate ran her hand through her hair, as if to push it off her face, although the clippers had already done that for her. "I'll have to warm up the machines. It'll be a minute."

"I'll just take what's in the airpot," the woman said, still surveying the shop.

Tate filled a paper cup and squeezed a biodegradable corn-plastic lid on it. The woman drew a bill from the pocket of her crisp, white shirt. Tate shook her head.

"On the house. It's probably stale."

She was about to go back to counting the till when the woman asked, "How long has this been a coffee shop?"

Tate considered. "It opened as a bookstore in 1979. Then it closed for a few years in the early eighties, opened back up as a coffee shop in 1988, and it's been running since then. I think. I've been here for nine years."

Too long.

"'Out in Portland Coffee.'" The woman read the side of her cup.

"Out Coffee," Tate said. "That's what everyone calls it."

"Any other businesses in the area?"

"There's Ron's Reptiles, the AM/PM, the Oregon Adult Theater."

Across the street, the theater's yellow letter board advertised HD FILM! STRIPPER SPANK-A-THON WEDNESDAYS!

From the back room, Maggie, the boss, called out, "They're all perverts."

The woman nodded and turned as if to leave. Then she seemed to reconsider.

"Are there any women's bars in the area?" She glanced around the shop again, her eyes sliding past Tate's, resting everywhere but in Tate's direction.

"There's the Mirage." Tate gave her directions.

"Is it safe to walk?"

"As safe as anywhere in the city."

As soon as the woman left, twenty-year-old Krystal—Maggie's surrogate daughter or pet project, depending on who you asked—popped out of the back room, where she had ostensibly been studying.

"I heard that," she said. "As safe as anywhere in the city." She hopped up onto the counter next to Tate.

"Get off the counter." Tate ruffled Krystal's short, pink hair.

"Is my butt a health code violation?"

"Yes."

"Well, anyway," Krystal said, swinging her legs and kicking the cupboard behind her, "I heard that. She practically asked you to walk her. *Is it safe?*" Krystal imitated a woman's soprano with an added whine. "*Hold me in your big, strong arms, you sexy butch.*"

"Ugh." Tate rolled her eyes. "Why is she still here?" she called to Maggie in the back room.

"She's part of our family, Tate!"

Kindhearted Maggie; something had happened in utero, and she had been born without the ability to understand sarcasm.

"Some family," Tate said, winking at Krystal and pulling her into a hug.

"Did you like her?" Krystal asked, pulling away from Tate.

"Who?"

"The woman who was just here."

"No." Tate turned back to the cash register and rolled a stack of nickels into a paper sleeve.

"Why didn't you go after her, like in the movies? She probably thought you were cute."

Like in the movies. That was always Krystal's question: Why isn't it like the movies?

"I'm *working*," Tate said with feigned annoyance. "She just wanted a coffee. Anyway, I just got dumped, remember?"

"So?"

In the quiet minutes between customers, Tate had been reading *The Sociology of Lesbian Sexual Experience.* Now Krystal pulled the book from behind the counter and flipped it open.

"'The Alpha Butch,'" she read. "'In this paradigm'"—she pronounced it par-i-di-gum—"'the femme lesbian is looking for a strong, masculine—but not manly—woman who can protect her against the perceived threat of straight society.' That's you!" Krystal sounded like a shopper who had just found the perfect accessory. "I bet that's why she came in here. She saw you through the window and she was like, 'I've got to meet this woman.'" Krystal closed the book and examined the woman on the cover. "You're way cuter than this girl."

It wasn't hard; the woman on the cover looked like a haggard truck driver from 1950.

"Aren't you supposed to be studying for the GED?" Tate asked.

"My dad taught me most of that stuff already, when I was, like, a little kid."

"Then take the test and go to college," Tate said.

"I don't need to, 'cause my dad and I are going to start a club, and I don't need a degree for that."

"Right."

"She was pretty," Krystal said. "Like Hillary Clinton if Hillary Clinton was, like, a million years younger."

Tate took the book from Krystal's hands and pretended to swat her with it.

"I am not 'alpha butch.'"

Nonetheless, Tate did steal a glance at her face in the bathroom mirror before leaving the coffee shop. The woman's perfect good looks made her aware of her own dark eyebrows and her nose, which jutted out and then took a hook-like dive. She looked older than her thirty-five years. She looked tired after the long shift. And she did not feel alpha anything, even with her steel-toed Red Wings and her leather jacket. She did not even feel beta, or whatever letter came next in Krystal's alphabet.

Still, a spring spent rebuilding the network of railroad-tie stair steps in the Mount Tabor Community Garden had defined the muscles beneath her labrys tattoo. She was tanned from the work. Her head was freshly shaved. And it was summer, one of those perfect summer nights that Portlanders live for, so warm, so unambiguously beautiful it made up for ten months of steady rain.

When Tate sidled up to the bar at the Mirage, her friend Vita, the bartender, leaned over.

"She's here," Vita said.

For a second, Tate thought of the woman.

"Who?" she asked.

Vita shot her a look that said, *Don't pretend not to know when you've asked me about her every day for six months.*

Abigail. Tate could see her legs wrapped around the body of the cello, her hips splayed, her black concert skirt riding up, her orange hair falling over the cello's orange wood.

Vita plunked a shot in front of Tate.

"On the house. She's with someone."

Tate knocked the shot back, nearly choking as her brain registered the taste a split second after it hit the back of her throat.

"What the hell was that?" She wiped her mouth.

"Frat Boy's Revenge. Jägermeister and grape vodka. I made one too many for the baby dykes in the corner."

Tate grimaced and cleared her mouth with a swig of beer. Then she noticed something: that indefinable feeling of being watched. She turned. At a table by the door, the woman from Out Coffee sat, one hand resting on the base of a martini glass, as though she feared it might fly away. She caught Tate's eye for a second, smiled, and then looked away with a shake of her head. When she looked up again, Tate raised her beer with a slight smile.

"God, you have it so easy!" Vita said, punching Tate on the arm.

Tate turned back to the bar. "She's not interested in me. Look at her."

"*You* look at her," Vita said, raising both eyebrows.

In the mirror behind the bar, Tate saw the woman picking her way through the tables, hesitating, looking from side to side as though puzzling her way through a maze.

"She's cute. Don't blow it," Vita said in a whisper the whole bar could hear.

"Hello." The woman took the stool next to Tate's. She sat on the very edge, as though ready to flee.

Vita leaned in. She looked predatory. Her hair was teased into a rocker bouffant, and she had on more leopard print than Tate thought was appropriate work attire, even at a bar.

"Will you be buying this lady a drink?" Vita asked Tate.

"I'm fine," the woman said. "I was just leaving."

At that moment, Abigail appeared. Tate took in the sight:

Abigail on the arm of Duke Bryce, drag king extraordinaire. Duke grinned, a big toothy grin, like an Elvis impersonator on steroids. Abigail clung to Duke's arm, a romance heroine hanging off the lesbian Fabio.

"Someone you know?" the woman asked.

"Knew."

A moment later, Abigail released her lover and came over, an apologetic look on her face.

"I'm sorry. I didn't think I'd see you here. I mean, I was going to tell you about me and Duke, you know, earlier."

Tate shrugged. The music had dropped a decibel, and a few of the other patrons turned to listen.

"I mean, I know you're still really upset about the breakup. About us. Really, I wasn't looking for anything. I just saw Duke one day and presto!" Abigail's giggle made it sound like she had suddenly been transported back to seventh grade. "I thought I wanted someone who understood my music."

That had been the explanation when Abigail cheated on Tate with the oboist.

"But then I met Duke, and she's just so…brava."

Duke was an alpha butch, Tate thought. She could take a picture and show Krystal.

"I just know it all happened for a reason, Tate."

Tate was trying to think of a response to this when she was startled by a touch. The woman from the coffee shop had touched the back of her head. She ran her hand across Tate's cropped hair, then slid her fingertips down the back of Tate's neck. Then she withdrew her hand quickly.

"Who is she?" The woman's voice was much softer than it had been in the coffee shop, almost frightened.

Tate was still concentrating on the woman's touch, which seemed to linger on her skin. It had been six months since Abigail officially dumped her, but much longer since she had been touched like that. Abigail had never caressed her. Abigail seduced her cello, everyone in the orchestra agreed, but she had squeezed Tate. Tate had always come away from their lovemaking feeling rather like rising bread dough: kneaded and punched down.

Now Tate stumbled over her words. "This is…this is Abby. She's a cellist."

The woman leaned closer to Tate, and Tate could smell a sweet perfume, like citrus blossoms, rising from her hair.

"What seat?" the woman asked Abigail.

This had been an important distinction that had always been lost on Tate.

"Third," Abigail answered defensively.

"Oh. Only third." The woman turned and, with a gesture even more fleeting than her fingers on Tate's neck, she pressed her lips to Tate's cheek.

Abigail mumbled something Tate did not catch and walked away, disappearing down the hallway that led from the bar to the dance floor. The woman straightened and crossed her legs.

"I'm sorry," the woman said. She took a large sip of her drink. "I don't do things like that. I just don't like all those freckles."

"Freckles?"

Tate had loved the beige-on-white-lace of Abigail's freckles. Plus, one couldn't hold someone's freckles against them. Or maybe, if one looked like this woman, one could.

"She reminds me of my sister." The woman spoke quickly. "The freckles and that whole 'I'm going to be nice to you, but I'm actually sticking the fork in' thing. 'You can't tell me to piss off because that would make you look like a jerk, even though I'm the one who's ruined your life.' I know that routine." The woman finished the rest of her martini in one sip.

Tate was still trying to figure out what to do with the feeling that suffused her body. The woman's touch, offered unexpectedly after months of abstinence and then just as quickly withdrawn, left her dizzy. She felt like she had just swallowed a bowl of warm moonlight. But she recovered her manners and held out her hand.

"My name is..."

The woman cut her off. "I don't want to know."

Tate withdrew her hand, the moonlight cooling. But as soon as she withdrew her hand, the woman grabbed it, holding on as though she were going to shake hands but lingering much longer than any handshake.

"I didn't mean it like that," she said.

She leaned forward, her perfect good looks furrowed by worry.

Behind the woman's head, Vita flicked her tongue between the V of her two raised fingers.

Tate widened her eyes, the only nonverbal cue she could flash Vita. *Embarrass me, and I will strangle you*, her eyes said. But she wasn't sure Vita was listening.

"It's not that I don't want to know you." The woman still held Tate's hand, now stroking the back of Tate's knuckles with her thumb. "It's just…I don't live here. I live a thousand miles away." The woman raised Tate's knuckles to her lips and kissed them. "Right now I don't want to be me."

"You're straight," Tate said.

Behind the woman's head, Vita mouthed, *So?!*

The woman said nothing.

"You've got a husband and two kids at home." Tate extracted her hand. "A husband with a shotgun and two kids who will spend thousands of dollars on therapy when they realize you weren't going to the PTA meetings at all."

The woman bowed her head and laughed. Tate could only see her dimples, suddenly apparent in the smooth face. *All right*, Tate thought. *I'll take it.* It was the first time in months that she had sat at the Mirage and not thought about Abigail. She hadn't even looked up to see if Abigail had come back in the room.

"I don't have any kids," the woman said. "I can promise you that. I was married once, but we divorced years ago, and I'm not straight. I just wanted one night where I'm not what I do or where I work or who I know, but that's silly, isn't it?"

Tate thought about Out Coffee. About Maggie, Krystal, Vita, and the Mount Tabor Community Garden Association. About her studio apartment off northeast Firline and the old Hungarian couple who lived in the unit below hers. She thought about Portland, with its mossy side streets and its glorious summers.

"If you're not who you know, where you work, where you live, who are you?" she asked.

"I'm this," the woman said and took Tate's face in her hands and kissed her.

At first it was just a soft kiss, lip to lip. Then Tate felt the woman's hands tremble against her cheeks. Their lips parted. Her tongue found Tate's. Beneath the bar, their knees touched, and Tate felt the woman's legs shake as though she had run a great distance.

A second later, Tate pulled away, but only because she wanted the woman, and she felt herself going down in the annals of barroom legend. She could already hear Vita's rendition of the story: *Tate just reached over and grabbed the girl, practically swallowed her. It was like she unhinged her jaw, and the girl's head was in her mouth. Bang! Like a boa constrictor.* Friends and customers would listen attentively, waving away Tate's protests. Who wanted a story about a lonely barista longing for summer romance when they could have Vita's tale about Tate Grafton, Python Lover?

"Would you like to play a game of pool?" Tate said, to get out from under Vita's grin and to give herself a moment to think.

She was not the kind of woman who picked up girls at the bar. Vita picked up girls. Vita had picked up so many women she remembered them by taglines like "The Groaner" or "Wooly Bicycle Legs." She often told Tate that Tate could do the same, if she would only "put out some effort." According to Vita, half the girls at the Mirage were in love with Tate.

But Tate did not believe her; nor did she want an assortment of half-remembered encounters.

But she wanted this woman.

They moved toward the side of the bar where two pool tables stood on a raised platform under low-hanging lights.

"Are you any good?" she asked.

"I'm all right," Tate said.

The woman rolled her pool cue on the table to see if it was true.

"None of them are straight," Tate said.

"I suppose not." The woman glanced toward the door. "Not here."

Tate laughed.

"You break, then," the woman said.

Tate cracked the balls apart, sinking two solids and following with a third.

"So, if you won't tell me your name," Tate began. "Or where you live or what you do, what are we going to talk about?"

"We could talk about you."

The woman sank a high ball but missed her next shot. Her hand was unsteady, and she looked around the bar more than she looked at the table. She looked at *Tate* more than she looked around the bar—but only out of the corner of her eye.

"I already know where you work," she said, casting that glance at Tate and then looking down. "And I know that, prior to right now, you've had bad taste in women. So...what's your name? How long have you worked at the coffee shop?"

Tate took another shot and sank a ball.

"No," she said slowly. "I'll tell you what you tell me."

"Okay." The woman leaned over the pool table and her hair draped in a curtain over one side of her face. She took her shot but missed. "I learned to play pool in college with three girls who I thought would be my friends for life. We played at a sports bar called the Gator Club. And I don't know any of them now. They could be dead. They could be professional pool sharks." She leaned against the wall and surveyed the table. "How about you?"

"I learned to play here the summer I turned twenty-one," Tate said. She sank another ball and shot a smile in the woman's direction. "The table is off. It slopes. It's not fair, you being from out of town and all. I should give you a handicap."

"Tell me how it slopes and give me two out of three."

Tate had never been the kind of person who made bets or the kind of person who sidled up to beautiful women, looked down at them lustfully, and said things like, *What will you give me when I win?*

But apparently that was the kind of woman she was. Tonight. In the summer.

"What will you give me if I win?"

The woman did not step away. Or laugh. She rested one hand on Tate's chest, right over Tate's racing heart.

"I'll answer one question," she said. "About anything. I'll tell you one true thing. And if I win—it's that corner, right?—I want you to take me someplace."

"Where?"

"Someplace special. You've been playing pool here since you were twenty-one. You must know someplace no one goes. Someplace I wouldn't see otherwise. Something I'll remember."

"Okay."

They played in silence, standing closer than necessary, touching more than necessary. The woman seemed to relax, and her game got better. Tate won the first game but only just barely. The woman won the second, masterfully compensating for the uneven table. Tate was in line to win the third game but scratched on the eight ball. The woman laughed a sweet, musical laugh tinged with victory.

"Take me somewhere," the woman said.

At the bar, Vita pointed and mouthed, *You rock.* At a table near the door, Abigail leaned against Duke's leather vest and scowled. But Tate did not see them. She slipped her hand through the woman's arm and stepped out into the moonlight.

About the Author

Karelia Stetz-Waters is an English professor by day and a writer by night (and early morning). She has a BA from Smith College in comparative literature and an MA in English from the University of Oregon. Other formative experiences include a childhood spent roaming the Oregon woods and several years spent exploring Portland as a broke twentysomething, which is the only way to experience Oregon's strangest, most beautiful city.

Her other works include *The Admirer*, *The Purveyor*, and *Forgive Me if I've Told You This Before*. She lives with her wife, Fay, her dog, Willa Cather, and her cat, Cyrus the Disemboweler.

Karelia loves to hear from readers. You can find her at KareliaStetzWaters.com.